THE ANIMA CORPS

THEY HAVE ONE MISSION...
TO SLAY THE DEMON.

N.P. CONTI

First published in 2025 by Natalie Psarakos

www.npconti.com

Cover Design: Rena Violet

A Cataloguing-in-Publication entry for this book is available from the National Library of Australia.

ISBN (Paperback) 978-1-7638140-0-4
ISBN (eBook) 978-1-7638140-1-1

We at N.P. Conti acknowledge that the Wurundjeri Woi-wurrung peoples of the Kulin Nation are the Traditional Custodians of the land, waters, and skies in which we live and work. We pay our respects to the Elders past, present, and emerging, and extend that respect to other Aboriginal and Torres Strait Islander peoples.

CHAPTER 1

Every Anima marine strategizes for one outcome: slay the demon.

The sergeant hugged the soiled sleeping bag over his broad shoulders as he peered down the blackness of the tunnel leading deep into the earth. He curved his tall frame in an agonizing hunch as he shuffled into the hollow where he had slept for two years.

Two years since he had gone rogue—since he had become a wanted fugitive.

The Australian winter sun had disappeared hours ago, not that he had seen it that day, nor would it have thawed his freezing body if he had. Head bowed, he felt prickles of heat behind his eyelids as they shut and he slumped uncomfortably against the cold wall of dirt. He clamped the military ID tags that hung to the center of his chest inside his closed fist until he could feel the metal compressing against the bones of his hand. They were the only proof of identity he possessed. The only proof that Ryder Everett was still alive.

Gurgling and heaving sounds echoed from the entrance of the tunnel. Ryder's eyes shot open and he grimaced—it was the fourth demon today. And as crippled with exhaustion as he was, there was nothing coming out of that hellgate that wasn't going to have to go through him first. Not with all the families living on the farms that bordered this forest. He'd studied the patterns of the demons coming out of this tunnel, and they rarely lived to return to whatever hell they'd come from. He made sure of that.

Ryder prepared himself by urging, *willing*, adrenaline to intoxicate his bloodstream. Even with his supernatural speed, agility, strength, and senses, it was getting harder and harder every time. But sure enough, his heartbeat raced like a stallion being flogged into full speed and he sat frozen, awaiting the next warning.

It was coming.

He scrambled out of the hellgate as screeching and crumbling sounded from the depths. With his back against the wide trunk of a mountain ash tree, he pulled a combat knife from his green camouflage pants, which were smeared with mud and stiff in places with dried demon guts. He released the folded blade and watched as black spindled legs clawed the ground like grappling hooks as the demon hoisted itself out of the hole in the forest floor.

The *thing* contorted itself into a standing position of almost double his height, its skin oozing blobs and trickles of black tar-like liquid onto the ground. The nauseating sound of its breath whistled through the hundreds of needle-like teeth, each the length of his forearm, that banded around its tiny shrunken head. It bowed threateningly as it screamed through the forest, the sounds of the nocturnal animals going silent.

There were two things of which Ryder Everett was absolutely certain.

One: if you were a marine who belonged to a species of angelic shapeshifters that could partially take on the form of the animal inside you, you *would* be safe hiding here at the hellgate. Because no one in their right mind would approach this godforsaken place.

And two: he was nothing short of an idiot for stationing himself here alone when there should be a squad of marines at his back.

But here he was—fangs bared, skin glowing, eyes alight like flames of heavenly fire were burning inside them.

The demon's speared feet sank into the earth as it lurched onward, passing the tree he was hiding behind. The whole forest seemed to clench its very essence and retreat. The branches that reached down from the towering eucalyptuses looked lifeless and limp, and the hardy, twisted trees—bare from the icy south-westerly breath of winter— were wiry and mangled, taking on the shapes of people hiding from the horror. The earth whispered through the hissing of the leaves:

It doesn't belong.

Ryder slid out from behind the huge ancient trunk, silent and fluid, bending into a prowl as he approached. He was instantly walloped with unending demented screaming. It was so loud that he fought the urge to groan, to hear some other vibration to break its hold on him. An icy breath of paralysis poured over him, concreting him in malice and deadening every cell in his body. This place was taking its toll. Every fight with another demon was weakening him as punishment for living somewhere as evil as the hellgate.

The demon's head of teeth was dipped. It was sniffing. Ryder slipped back behind the massive trunk, melting his shoulder blades against it.

He unclipped the radio and brought it to his lips with a weak whisper: "Sergeant Ryder Everett. Wolf Anima, of the Sarpedon Rangers. Australian hellgate—black on ammo, fuel, and water." He paused, releasing a jagged breath. "Over."

Ryder let the radio drop to the ground. There was no team. There was no company.

He head checked the demon, who had circled back, almost at his tree. "Day of wrath for every demon in hell," he recited. Clutching the handle of his blade, he stepped out.

The demon was looking directly at him. He locked onto its insect eyes. A foul smell that made bile burn the back of his throat came from the slimy mucus dripping from its teeth.

It let out an ear-splitting screech as Ryder hurled his combat knife by the blade and lodged it into the demon's chest.

The demon curled like an eel and Ryder catapulted himself forward, snatching spears he had scattered about the woodland. He angled two through the demon's spindled feet, drilling them far into the clay beneath and covering his ears at the deafening screams that followed.

He planted his boots onto the demon's thighs to spring upward and used his pocketknives as pickaxes to scale up the slimy, potholed torso. The demon caved in agony as Ryder retracted each knife, black tar dripping from the blades.

"Don't take this the wrong way…"

He stood on the demon's throat, his battered boots digging into its windpipe.

"…but you have really bad breath."

Ryder dodged the demon's enormous, rancid claws as it swiped at him in desperation. He caught hold of its dagger-straight horns and dove. Air whooshed past his cheeks and underneath his khaki T-shirt as he slammed the back of the demon's neck onto the thick girth of a raised tree root. It didn't break on impact, as Ryder had hoped. The demon screeched and squirmed as Ryder yanked his arms downward with all the force he could muster. His biceps bulged as he crunched inward, and just as he heard the crack, one long, shining claw impaled his thigh before the creature's arm went limp.

Ryder's cry fractured as it traveled up to the night sky. With a quivering breath, he inspected the deep puncture, spotting the bright white of bone before it was flooded over with blood. It began spurting rhythmically, soaking his pant leg. He placed a shaky hand over his grievous wound and gritted his teeth, retracting it quickly in shock.

Ryder couldn't feel pain. Not normally. That was one of his special abilities… or curses, depending on how you looked at it. So the fact that he was in immeasurable pain now told him that something was wrong. Fatally wrong.

He unzipped a pocket on his opposite pant leg and pulled out a tourniquet, straining as he lifted the injured leg to wrap it. He pulled the strap tight with one quick yank, fastening it as high on his thigh as he could, his breath hitching at the agony. He raged through his teeth with every twist of the tourniquet, until the bleeding ceased.

Great... He'd gone and punctured an artery. Breathing heavily, he slumped against the tree root and slowly wrapped the rest of the strap around his leg. The trees around him whirled in a haze.

Fading in and out, Ryder didn't know how long he had been sitting there, but when he came to, the demon's body had already atomized and been consumed by the earth. It always knew what to do with demon remains. He looked up at the night sky through the canopy of ancient eucalyptus. His whole body trembled, years of trained emotional reactions defying him. He felt himself erupting from within, so he held his breath and cast a sharp glance to the side. His grief was quickly replaced by chagrin.

He laughed. He laughed so hard that his whole body began to shake, then sighed bitterly.

Animas had accelerated healing abilities, but it would still take him a few days to recover from an injury like this, let alone to be battle-ready for the next demon. And if he left the hellgate unguarded to go to a hospital, demons would continue to escape. Not to mention that a human-looking person with sharp teeth, glowing skin and eyes, and unquantifiable supernatural abilities would look a tad out of place among regular humans. And then there was the giant wolf the size of an SUV that emanated from him during battle... or whenever it felt like it, honestly. One look at his Anima and the general public would run screaming in the opposite direction. He hadn't seen his Anima appear for months, though—also not a good sign. His own *soul* would rather abandon him than spend another second in this place. The only sustenance he received was from a White Wolf Anima that had been soothing him in his dreams since he was a child. He had never met the person that the White Wolf belonged to, but she always appeared as a reminder that he wasn't alone.

He didn't know why the Australian hellgate had been so active over the last two years, and didn't have access to military intelligence to find out. But what choice did he have now? He wasn't going to survive another fight. Not with a punctured artery and zero medical supplies.

Commanding male voices shocked him out of his thoughts. They were shouting a lingo he understood all too well—the language of espionage. Ryder raised his nose into the air and inhaled. They smelled human.

He managed to stand, putting all of his weight on his other leg as he hobbled to the nearest tree and leaned on it for support. Light from several flashlights—at least ten—panned this way and that. He bounced his hand against the trunk as he moved around it, staining it with blood, before he stumbled on the downward-sloping terrain. The only thing saving him from falling the whole drop was the next tree. He caught onto it, hugging it, but their scents and voices were getting closer. His open wound was raw and sticky with blood against the material of his pants. He couldn't run. This was it. Once he was found, he'd never see the light of day again.

The sound of rustling leaves surrounded him in the

pitch-black. Ryder heard quick footsteps before the stock of a rifle smashed him in the back of the head.

Blood debts.

The wagers of silent wars and those who acted out their crimes had their debts paid in blood. How much blood was for *her* to decide… and witnessing her meant that the last thing you saw was red.

She waited in the darkness, her wolf senses picking up every sound as three agents moved through the narrow mineshaft behind the wall of rock and ice. One walked with haste—he had been here before. The second was heavy-footed, and the third's cologne peppered her nose. The men entered the area resembling a large room with another connecting tunnel on the opposite side. They were sure the mine was empty, and she watched them in the dark with hungry animal eyes, waiting for her prey to move into the perfect position for her to strike.

The heavy-footed one with hair slicked into a low bun fiddled with a matchstick between his beefy fingers. When the match failed to spark for the fourth time, the agent with shoulder-length dark curls—the one in charge—snatched it irately.

"Can you do anything right?" He pulled another match from the box.

The flame burst from the red tip for a fraction of a second before she pounced, kicking it out of his hand.

The three men yelped in unison. The one with the

strong cologne slashed at the air blindly with a knife, then stopped. It was so silent that drips of melting ice were audible somewhere in the mine.

She sliced forward with her twin khukuris. They were the length of a second pair of arms, the threatening recurve of the blades were silent as she removed them from the scabbards behind her back. One of the men managed to turn on a flashlight; it flickered to life just in time for him to see his colleague's head hit the ground. The expression on the beheaded man's face was shocked, his mouth ajar as if frozen mid-word.

The heavy-footed one screamed while the one holding the flashlight choked with disgust. Her eyes illuminated in green fire to state her presence. She heard them swallow and stiffen.

"Good. You've heard of me. That saves time." Her voice was crooning, mocking.

The man in charge addressed her. "Hellfire… I'm sure we can work something—AHH!"

Her khukuri sank into his left forearm and silenced him.

"I'll do the talking," she told him, cracking a chemlight that emitted a bright blue glow, illuminating their faces and the square shape of the mine. "This is for you, not me. I can see just fine in the dark." She circled them. "So tell me. You've been in this mine, what, three times now? What element has he got you looking for?"

Their lips tightened in response. Before the men could blink, Hellfire slid the blade out of the leader's arm and plunged it deep into the middle of his stomach. He bent forward in agony; his screams shook the walls of the empty mine.

"You're hemorrhaging from your abdominal aorta. You have a few minutes to live—so talk fast." The heavy-footed man's feet barely lifted off the ground before she warned him, "Don't. I can outrun you." He stood rooted to the spot, and she turned back to the stabbed man.

"I d—I don't know which mineral it is!" he gasped. "Vangelis said it's made of ice, so we've been searching in Alaskan mines for months!"

Hellfire side-kicked the handle of the sword, lodging it further into his abdomen, sending him flying into the icy wall of the mine and pinning him standing up. He slumped, blood pooling everywhere.

"Where is he?" she seethed.

He shook his head, pale and losing consciousness. "I don't…"

The man collapsed, head drooping, before he could finish.

Hellfire snatched the khukuri out of his body, letting him slide to the ground as he released his last breath with his eyes still open.

She rolled her eyes to see the man with the clunking gait fleeing down the dark shaft toward the exit of the mine. In one powerful bound, her teeth bared, she landed on his back and bit down on his neck. She tore through his sweaty flesh and into the juices of his carotid artery and shook him violently, her long blood-red hair veiling him. The mine echoed with gurgling screams until the shaking broke his neck and he dropped lifelessly to the ground.

She felt for the silver chain of the military ID tag around her neck and removed it, glancing at the rectangular clear crystal with a thin gold spiral inside it. She thumbed its rounded edges before drawing a large circle in front of her. It detached from the ether-fabric, creating a vibrant spectrum as a dimension portal vortexed before her and stayed open long enough for her to step through, leaving the mine and her kills behind. Her destination pulled her ahead like a vacuum; when she arrived on the other side, she was facing a waterfall, its narrow chute plummeting off steep columns of rock.

She had traveled back to the location of her tent on a stretch of coast far from her own kind, called Ravenscliff. She wasted no time in taking off her clothes and walking into the waves before diving in fully. The alpine freeze of the silver sea shot currents of ice over her skin as she scrubbed her face and clothes clean of blood.

She tossed her mane carelessly as she dried it in the confines of her small tent, its voluminous ends flicking and unfurling, brushing the top of her hips. She unzipped the tent, buttoning up her khaki utility pants and breathing in the chilled seaside air. She scraped her tongue over her palate, tasting the basalt sand as she gazed over the rugged evergreen cliffs at the end of the beach, west of the water-fall that arched like a stretching feline. Although it was summer on the Island of Kore, a gray veil draped over the sky, dimming the sun. The island would remain sunlit until August, the sun never dipping lower than the horizon. It made sleeping in a tent difficult, and she spent the few hours of rest that she needed covering her head with the one pullover she owned.

A slow-approaching scent told her she wasn't alone. She tilted her head slightly, stealing a glance behind her, then rolled up the sleeves of her navy checked shirt.

This was wolf country.

And somebody was in *her* territory.

The trespasser, concealed by the gray fog behind her tent, shifted in the damp seagrass. Her hand curled around the leather hilt of her dagger—slow, deadly. And the movement stopped. A shock of frightened gulls launched into the air, and Hellfire spun, flipping backward as gigantic wings descended on her from above.

The man landed in front of her, blocking her onslaught, their forearms colliding with her dagger angled toward his throat. Her punches, though fast, weren't quick enough to stop the man from blocking each one. An open-handed slice to her wrist made her drop her dagger into the sand. On the last punch, she shoved him back just as his hand-carved wooden staff sliced through the air in circular motions like a propeller.

The staff clobbered her high kick. She barely had time to cry out through gritted teeth before he struck her again. Lightning fast, with both hands catching the whooshing staff, she catapulted off the ground, turning mid-air and landing, crouched, atop his shoulders. Her brilliant white jaws were ready to tear out his throat. She paused a fraction of an inch away, smelling his cardamom-and-aniseed scent.

"Good morning to you too, Ansel." The tone of her greeting was unwelcoming, albeit a little self-satisfied.

"Don't sound so disappointed, young Wolf," the elder replied. The white of his snowy owl wings gleamed despite the overcast sky; the pattern that covered them made them look like they had been painted by black rain. He folded his nine-foot wings behind him to help her climb down, meeting her eye as he turned to face her.

General Ansel Winters stood a few inches taller than her. His face had deep lines that curved like water canals away from piercing eyes, ice-lake white beneath thick, dark brows. His brown hair, longer than hers, touched his waist, and in certain light you could detect the odd glimmer of silver. Animas lived long lives, some reaching one hundred and fifty years old before reincarnating. Ansel's lifetimes bled into each other; she didn't even know how old he was. Thousands of years. He had to be, if he'd known the Sumerians.

"You have quite the view." Ansel waved a hand toward the ocean before looking back at her with narrowed eyes.

Hellfire trudged to retrieve her dagger. She sheathed it in her belt behind her back. "Why are you here?"

Ansel raised his brows, enlarging those cool eyes—if he was ruffled by her frosty attitude, he concealed it well. He walked closer, dipping his staff in the sand. "It is my duty to make sure you are protected. Aspen…"

Aspen. That sound—that name. No one had spoken it in years. Not since—since…

There weren't many who knew her birth name, but she had known Ansel since before her activation—before she had become Anima, or had even known what that meant. "I'm perfectly safe with the southern wolf pack," she answered with a stern glare. An unspoken dialogue coursed between them. *You have no right to call me by that name.*

His body language—soft yet focused—told her that he'd heard it. His voice was as anchoring as a deep drum. "You have been in contact?"

She nodded. "I hunt the demons in Wolf Country. They allow me safe passage and a place to live here."

He pretended to be impressed. "Quite an understanding."

"I'm their ally. Don't give me that judgy look."

He jerked his right wing. "I am not judging you, daughter—"

Daughter. *Daughter... How dare you.*

"Look around you." He motioned his staff over the landscape. "Is this solitude all that you seek? Don't you see, there is so much more waiting for you—"

"At the Corps?" she interrupted bitterly. At the Corps indeed. She remembered a time in her life when she would have given her right arm to even be considered to become a marine in the Corps. Not just any corps... no. It wasn't a typical *have to be the best in your rank* situation, either. It didn't matter how damn good you were—if you weren't Anima, if your soul's lineage wasn't from one of the sacred Virtues, there was nothing the gods could do to save you from the missions you were destined to endure.

"Yes, at the Corps! You are Anima—we stay together. You are our daughter, our sister."

There were those words again. *Daughter. Sister.*

Her blood could have boiled hell into liquid. She had to school herself through years of training all over again before answering with a dead stare. "Spare me the big happy family talk, Ansel. I don't want anything to do with your army of spirit animals."

She turned her back to him; as far as she was concerned, that was goodbye. She walked to the edge of the dense forest, her bare feet chilled by the dry grass, feeling the pulsing code of Kore's consciousness underneath. Phosphorescent eyes burned through the shadows of the forest as the wolves emerged at a predator's pace, heads bowed low, whining and yipping as if singing a song passed down generations. From the towering spruce trees they revealed themselves, one by one.

Ansel's voice was velvety beside her as he marveled, "It's the whole pack." She couldn't ignore the foreboding undertone in his words.

Aspen had named the alpha wolf of the southern Kore pack Killa Moon. She moved to the front of the pack with her gray tail held high and proud. The four beta wolves, three males and one female, let loose high-pitched whines as Killa Moon fixed Aspen with a regal yet amicable stare. The earth beneath Aspen's feet shifted, pulsing and vibrating like blood passing through veins. The wolves' ears were erect; all stood unmoving—wolves, woman, and elder. This had been happening for the last three months.

"They sense something," Ansel said in a hushed tone.

Aspen gazed into the alpha's wild yellow eyes and whispered, "Just tell me what it is."

The wolves sniffed the ground, trying to pick up a trail. The air was tense. The cautious way they stepped off the rocks concerned her. So tentative—hesitant, even… They moved as if there were pain in their paws and the joints of their legs.

A beta wolf growled into the trees, but the alpha snapped her jaws, silencing him in an instant. All was quiet, even the forest, like they were waiting—the land, and the wolves.

The alpha finally locked her eyes on Aspen, hackles rising aggressively. Killa Moon's voice echoed from the ether:

Another wolf.

CHAPTER 2

Ryder's head was sticky with blood, lolling heavily as he blinked away his hazy vision. The back of his skull throbbed with shooting pains, making him see tiny fireworks. He squeezed his eyes shut. Every slight movement was agony as he knelt on dry dirt, held down by two men built like oxen in the middle of… Virtues-knew-where.

"Call the boss and tell him we have him." An agent wearing a tailored black suit with silk lapels gawked over his shoulder at Ryder, a phone pressed against his ear. He spoke in a low growl, his next words dissipating as sparks flew across the black screen of Ryder's closed eyes, but Ryder could make out an accent. Something European.

The agent slid the phone into his pocket, his footsteps causing clouds of dirt to rise up, making Ryder cough onto his perfectly polished shoes. He was of average height, with slicked-back espresso-brown hair and a smirk that reached his eyes.

"Today will be your reckoning, my fugitive friend."

The agent's fist smashed into Ryder's face, again and again. It wasn't enough for him to taste blood, but it hurt enough to make him wonder what in the hell was happening for him to be grunting over being slapped around by a human. And this bastard was thoroughly enjoying himself. The men holding Ryder down gripped him so tight he could feel their fingertips pushing into his arm bones.

Yeah… something definitely isn't right.

"I bet you don't have the slightest idea who I am…" The agent rolled his neck before punching Ryder in the gut. "I'm Vangelis Katopodis."

Greek, then. "I don't care," Ryder answered, groaning as pain seared through his leg.

"Oh, we'll be getting to know each other quite well; I imagine we will be friends for a very long time." Vangelis's eyes flashed to Ryder's incarcerators, and they pulled him up.

"I sincerely doubt that," Ryder answered.

"I have to commend you on your efforts to evade the US government for this long—what has it been, close to two years now? I have to admit, I'm impressed. Not just any run-of-the-mill marine, are you? Even for an Anima."

Wow… this son of a bitch knows way too much.

"Slaughtering dozens of government officials, bringing down a whole secret government agency and stealing the evidence of its existence…" Vangelis bent close to Ryder's face and laughed ruefully. "They hired me specially to hunt you down, and you have not made it easy for me, Ryder

Everett." There was vengeance on his lips as he said Ryder's name. "Actually, you have made something of a mockery of me—which I don't appreciate."

At a head tilt from Vangelis, the two agents began to drag him.

"You know, I know who your boss is," Ryder stated, his voice more confident than his wobbly steps.

"Do you now?"

"Gregory Finch. There's nothing he can do to me now that he hasn't already done. So go ahead… take me to him, so I can dismantle whatever new criminal organization he's built since I destroyed Mercury Sixteen."

A flashlight beam revealed a gravel track and a black SUV. An agent opened the car door as Vangelis spoke.

"Gregory Finch is the last thing you need to worry about, because where I'm taking you… The things you will be made to do…" He shook his head. "You'll wish it was Finch you were dealing with."

Vangelis's phone rang. He held his hand up to stop the men, who were about to sandwich Ryder between them into the backseat of the car. Ryder figured that his one chance to escape would be now, but he buckled under the drilling fingers of his incarcerators.

Vangelis's voice was gruff. "Make this quick."

Ryder grimaced at the pain in his left leg. The tourniquet was still in place, his entire pant leg drenched in blood. Hopelessness numbed him, something inside him giving up. Whatever spark had been keeping him alive inside the hellgate was smothered at the sight of his limbs—two arms that felt like they had ten drill bits sticking out of them, and one leg that had given up on him.

"*What?* How are they all dead?" Vangelis hissed down the phone. He growled like one of the nocturnal animals that occupied the bushland and made a sudden move, as if to throw the phone. He exhaled slowly instead and placed it back against his ear. "Did they have it?"

A sigh of relief. Ryder figured the answer to that question had been "No."

Vangelis nodded vigorously. "No, I know who it was. Tell the others to lie low, because that little bitch could screw everything." He swore colorfully in his mother tongue as he put the phone back in his pocket.

The man holding Ryder's right side asked, "Everything alright, boss?"

Vangelis exhaled sharply, face tilted upward and eyes closed. "No. We have a serious problem. There's a player in all of this that I did not account for. Get him in the car."

The agents shoved Ryder into the back of the SUV. In the same moment, a monstrous bang dented the roof of the car.

The black interior of the roof almost met Ryder's face. He could vaguely see the alarmed men scrambling in the darkness. They had dropped the flashlight, and it was streaming light from the dirt road into the bushes. A shadow three times the width of the SUV swooped overhead, chasing Vangelis and his agents into the bushland.

Demons.

Ryder didn't want to know which beast that shadow belonged to, and if he ran now, whatever demon had bent the roof of the car would still be there, waiting. He quickly reached over the backseat to close the door and seal himself inside.

The beast jumped from the roof and onto the road, and Ryder could have sworn that the SUV shook as it landed. Its shadow swallowed the light as it stalked around the car at a predatory pace.

Ryder fumbled for his combat knife, silently thanking the Virtues he still had one as his knuckles turned white from his iron grip on the hilt. With all of his Anima powers rendered useless, this could be the weapon that saved him tonight. Back pressed against the door, he sucked in breaths through gritted teeth and a clamoring heartbeat. Sweat dripped down his neck as the figure prowled closer. The light magnified the tines adorning the beast's head like a speared weapon; bars of shadow rhythmically passed over the windows. It was at the door.

A human hand pulled it open on its last hinge.

"Ry? That you?" the man asked breathlessly.

Ryder was so stunned he couldn't believe his eyes. "Holy shit—Thex?"

"You look like a soup sandwich," Thex declared, extending his hand to help Ryder out of the car.

Thomas Thexton looked exactly as he had the last time Ryder had seen him two years ago, until Ryder's focus flicked to the military uniform he was wearing. It was a dark shade of pine green compared to the usual khaki he was used to seeing, and pinned onto the breast of his jacket were more elaborate ribbons and metal decorations than before: some gold, others ethereal blue. Thex was a Deer Anima and bore a crown of majestic antlers atop his head. His facial structure and high cheekbones left you to wonder whether his lineage was aristocratic, until he pulled his full lips into a prankster's grin.

There he is.

Ryder's hand clamped onto Thex's and they tugged each other into a hug. This was the kind of hug that meant you would die for someone if it came to it. They squeezed each other like their lives depended on it; after all, there were demons nearby.

Ryder's grip broke loose first. Something was off, though he couldn't distinguish what… Thex pulled away enough for Ryder to stare into his friend's dark eyes and behold their unearthly glow, like a firestorm had kindled behind them. Thex's black skin had a golden undertone that made everything around him gleam; he was full of vitality, and every graceful shift of his body spoke of precision and power.

Ryder brought his arms to his sides in a stiff soldier's stance. Force of habit.

"They told me you were dead," Thex said.

An awkward pause.

"Come on, you know me better than that."

Those glowing eyes searching, Thex said, "I can't tell you how good it is to see you, brother." Emotion reverberated as he clapped Ryder's back—still ramrod stiff. "You look like you've been in the trenches… Tell me you haven't been here all this time?"

The charade never went on this long. Ryder had watched demons take the form of his mother, sister, and father many times before, only to attack him. Then he would look into their faces and see the betrayal in their eyes before he broke their neck or stabbed them to death, walking away as they bled out.

Ryder could only issue a cold reply, barely more than a murmur.

A powerful screeching call cut through the night air. Their heads shot upward, searching the darkness.

The demon was back.

Its wings were the width of the road, slanting back for the creature to land abruptly before them. Ryder recoiled when he realized it was a man. He pressed his fingers into the corners of his eyes to rub them.

The man was surely wearing a costume, and on that note, a terrible one. Not in the sense that it was poorly made; in fact, the silver embroidery on his linen shirt was intricate and fine. It was more the fact that Ryder couldn't put his finger on who in space and time he was pretending to be, but he had the air of a chief or great leader from some ancient world.

"Ryder Everett." The man said his name with such affection that Ryder was taken aback. Moving closer, he folded his gigantic wings, arching them behind him and placing his engraved wooden staff on the gravel road. "My oldest friend. In this life, my name is Ansel Winters."

"General Ansel Winters," Thex added.

Ryder raised his brows. "What are you talking about?"

Ansel Winters smiled, cheekbones soaring and wrinkles streaming away from his pearly golden eyes. They too were illuminated, and as though inscribed with ancient wisdom, their gaze sank into Ryder, resting in his bones. Ryder had to tear his eyes away. He had met many species of Anima in his twenty-five years, but this winged man didn't seem like an Eagle. Didn't smell like one, either…

Ryder glanced back and forth between the pair suspiciously before he slumped against the back of the SUV, scowling at the illusion of his best friend adjacent to him.

Was he so desperate to see a familiar face that he would imagine this? He braced against the surging disappointment and despair, sealing it inside him with a wicked grin.

"Now that's a step too far—impersonating my brother like that. That's just…" He gritted his teeth to say the word. "Cruel."

The gun clicked as he took off the safety. He had taken it from Vangelis before he'd got into the SUV, and now he was aiming it at the surprised impersonator of his best friend.

"Easy, Ry," Thex coaxed with his hands up.

Ry. Only Thex called him Ry.

He pointed the gun expertly from one man to the other. "I'm giving you five seconds to tell me who you are."

"I'm your friend." Ansel's voice remained steady.

"Yeah, you said that already. Only I never recall meeting you… like, in my whole life. Besides, it's not you that pisses me off. It's you!" He pointed the small barrel at Thex.

"Ry, put the gun down so we can talk. We have a lot to fill you in on."

Ryder shook his head, disappointment and disdain gassing out his true feelings. "I hate that you chose *him* of all people. Just attack already so I can shoot you in the head and be done with this."

"Ry, it's really me—"

"Prove it!" Ryder roared. "Prove to me that you're Thomas Thexton, because you sure as hell have done a good job looking the part."

Thex walked closer to Ryder's outstretched handgun and rested his forehead against the barrel. He locked his glowing dark eyes with Ryder's and spoke slowly. "You've been inside the hellgate for two years. I'm not going to pretend I know what it's like being all alone with no one for backup in the most violent place on the planet."

Ryder pushed the barrel harder onto Thex's forehead.

"But I've got to ask… Does the hellgate have control over you?"

"What? No!" Ryder's gun shook and he angrily wiped away the sweat rolling down the sides of his face. "No, it's not controlling me."

The gun dropped.

"So who are *you*, marine?" Thex barked like a drill sergeant.

Ryder slid down the SUV with a thud, feeling the pain of his injured thigh again. "I'm Sergeant Ryder Everett. Wolf Anima of the Sarpedon Rangers," he reported, like he was communicating to base. To let them know he was alive— that there was still one marine left. Backup had come. For the first time in two years, the backup had come. An icy breath washed through his body and froze him to the spot.

Thex let out a sigh of relief, and Ansel, who had watched in admiration, joined them and closed their circle. As they bent down to Ryder's level, it dawned on him: if this winged man wasn't an Eagle, he had to be…

By the Virtues, he couldn't believe it.

An Owl Anima.

There were only a handful of Owls, and they all worked for…

Ryder's focus flicked from the general to the embroidered shoulder badge on Thex's uniform. There, in ethereal blue stitching against deep forest-green camouflage, was the insignia: two wings outstretched, two more angled up to the heavens, with twin swords crossed downward.

The insignia of the Anima Corps.

Ryder's mouth fell open.

The general's voice gently stirred him from his thousand-yard stare. "Listen to me, son. You're badly hurt, and I can hear Vangelis and his men circling back. We have to leave, but first, drink this."

General Winters held up a vial of something silver-blue. Ryder looked at it questioningly.

"It will help the wound to heal. Quickly, now." The general placed the vial in his hand.

Ryder uncorked it and examined the liquid. From this close it looked like bottled moonlight, with swirling specks of silver dancing in its self-generated current. He took a quick breath before throwing the liquid to the back of his throat.

Everything around him turned white, like he was looking directly into the center of the sun. His chest expanded and opened, and he took in more oxygen than he'd had in years, as if he had been breathing through broken ribs this whole time. His eyes watered, but he was damned if he was going to let it out.

A muffled voice asked him if he was okay, then the faces of the two men faded.

The light was gone.

CHAPTER 3

A vaulted ceiling with open trusses and a light fitting made of shed antlers were the first things Ryder saw as he slowly opened his heavy eyelids. He wasn't sure how long he had been out, but it felt like a whole day, which was more uninterrupted rest than he'd had in years.

His focus flew directly to his left thigh, where he'd been wounded by the demon's claw. His cargo pants were still torn and covered in dried blood. He pulled himself up to a sitting position on the couch he was lying on to inspect the injury in the glow of a nearby light. A sense of pure awe filled him as he rubbed his leg.

The deep puncture wound had completely healed. Vanished. He flexed his leg carefully and didn't feel so much as a pinch of pain.

He rubbed his eyes and glanced around what looked to

be a cabin. The cabinetry was made of the same honey-colored wood as the walls and ceiling. A small window was open just a crack above the sink; a single leafy vine from outside had curled through. He could smell dense forest firs. They were not in Australia anymore.

Ryder spotted Thex making tea in the small kitchen in the furthest corner. "Where are we?" he asked.

Thex stirred the contents of his cup and leaned against the bench, motioning with his eyebrows at the steaming cup resting on the coffee table. "You should drink that. We're in Kore."

Ryder's eyes widened in shock. Kore was a hidden dimension on Earth that you could only get to if you had a key. The only way you could get a key was if you worked for the Anima Corps.

"Yes, I'm serious," Thex answered, reading his body language. Animas could do that; if you were really in sync with someone, you could speak through body language alone. With the number of years he and Thex went back, they could have an entire silent conversation.

Ryder took in the cabin once more. The mantel of the fireplace in front of him was made of old stone; abutting it was a metal holder stacked with firewood. A distressed tribal rug housed an armchair, the chocolate leather couch he was sitting on, and a small rustic coffee table in the center. Behind him was a staircase and an entrance to a corridor.

Ryder's stomach knotted. He wasn't just hiding from the US government... He had gone rogue against his own kind. He had without a doubt been brought here to be court-martialed. Which meant that Thex had had a part in all of this— that turncoat bastard. Not that Ryder was one to talk, but he would never hand-deliver his friend like this, even if his life depended on it.

He was shocked out of his skin when a circle of spectral light swallowed the view of the front door. Everything inside the circle swirled together, warping the fabric of this dimension enough for General Ansel Winters to step through.

Thex's whole frame went ramrod straight as he saluted the general.

"At ease, marine."

"Permission to speak?"

"Granted, child." The general's tone was warm and enveloping.

Thex cleared his throat. "The captain is awake."

"Captain?" Ryder questioned.

The general's piercing gaze rested on him. "So he is. I trust you are feeling better?"

"Yes, sir," Ryder answered as he rose from the couch.

"Come." The general beckoned him to follow as he glided to the small dining table. "There is much to discuss."

He lowered himself into his chair with a grace that defied his age. Ryder stood behind the seat opposite, and Thex resumed leaning against the kitchen bench beside them. Ryder hesitated, pausing with his hands on the back of the wooden chair. A glint in the general's eye encouraged him to sit, so he lowered himself into it, cautiously.

The general's bone-colored staff lay across the small table. The carving of an owl at the top held the glowing blue crystal in place. Owl Anima were exceptionally rare. They were known as lodestars, and only a handful incarnated every generation. It made sense, Ryder thought, that Ansel's own Anima was represented in his power source. His gaze trailed to the carvings below of the heads of the primary Anima species: Deer, Fox, Lynx, Eagle, Bear, and lastly, Wolf.

Ryder ground his fist into the palm of his other hand, anticipation building. Through lowered lids he asked, "Are there any left?"

The general knew exactly what he meant. He shifted, watching Ryder through those molten pearl-and-gold eyes. "One."

Ryder's strength left his body as he slumped in his chair. One. Only one other Wolf had survived the war. He made to ask another question, but barely a sound came out before the general interrupted.

"I will answer your questions about the war in due time, Captain. But we have much more pressing things to discuss. You are here because you are being summoned to serve in the Anima Corps."

His words crashed over Ryder like a bucket of ice water. "What?" he breathed.

"You have a unique skill set as a trained Sarpedon Ranger—"

"Ex–Sarpedon Ranger."

"—not to mention top scores on all offshore specialist training facilities." He counted on his fingers: "Japan, Nepal, Israel… The Virtues-know-where-else."

Ryder balked. "How did you even find me?" He stared at the general as he tried to form an answer. Because both of them knew the truth. Ryder was completely untraceable— an anomaly among the Anima.

"We were tipped off."

Ryder's expression turned incredulous. "By who? Nobody knew my location."

The general raised a warning hand. "Everett, we don't have time for this now."

"I don't have specialist powers. Did you know that?" Ryder fired at him. "I may be highly trained, but basic Wolf Anima powers is all I got." He knew he had some nerve speaking this way to the general of the Corps, but it wasn't *his* general.

General Winters tried but failed to stifle an amused grin.

"What. Is. So. Funny?" Ryder clenched his teeth, showing his fangs.

The general nodded toward his arm. "I gather you still have the markings on your left forearm?"

Ryder rotated the arm in question, revealing the symbols that covered his inner forearm from wrist to elbow. The symbols appeared as if they had been inked into his skin in liquid gold, but he'd had them since birth. He glared at the general with suspicion.

"You will find that life in Kore will nourish your powers. You have spent very little time around wolves and around your own kind. But now I realize that you were protecting the house nearest to the Australian IO."

IO—*inferno ostium*—was another word for hellgate. Ryder guessed that it was the terminology the Corps used.

He leaned back in his chair and crossed his arms. "I wasn't protecting one house. I was protecting many houses. From an IO that's become a hotspot, by the way… in case you and your Corps hadn't noticed." He made no effort to temper his bluntness. He'd learned the hard way that respect was earned, not given.

Lines deepened on the general's forehead. "We had no reason to believe any activity had surfaced in the area. After all, that entrance has been dormant for over six years. It didn't occur to me that you would have traveled from America to Australia."

"More like escaped," Thex corrected. "But this is very far from our home. I had teams checking in and around Boise, Idaho, thinking you would have tried to stay close to your family."

Ryder shook his head. "No. I couldn't risk something happening to my parents or my sister."

"Did you see any of the other houses in the vicinity of the IO, other than the white weatherboard farmhouse?" the general questioned.

Ryder thought for a moment. "Negative."

"And you never went inside? That house is abandoned."

"No, sir."

"Why not?"

Boy, was the general pressing him. "Because I sensed that something bad had happened there. It didn't feel right."

The general nodded slowly, though Ryder gauged that it wasn't because he understood—rather, he was reading something deep in Ryder's being. "Your senses are correct. Something terrible did happen there."

"It was demons?" Ryder assumed.

Thex nodded. "Affirmative. That's where the War on Wolves broke out."

"Many civilians and Anima perished, including the family who owned that house," the general added. "But a few years ago, when the war ended, a strange darkness escaped the IO. We have sent search teams to try to find and disable it, but it is elusive—like nothing we have ever seen before. We believe the demons surfacing at this rapid rate have something to do with this dark presence. And we need you to lead Special Forces to find and stop it before it gets worse than the danger it already is to Earth and its people."

Ryder stared at him with his arms crossed over his chest. First he cracked a grin that he couldn't possibly keep restraining. Then a chuckle turned into a full-bellied laugh.

The elder rolled his eyes and gripped his staff tighter as he realized he was being made fun of.

"Listen, I don't work for anybody," Ryder said. "I'm done."

"Would you prefer to be put on trial?"

Every fiber of his being grew tense. He lost the humor in an instant.

"Because you can spend the rest of your life as a fugitive… but the moment they find you—and they eventually will—a trial is exactly what you will face. If you're lucky."

Ryder's stomach dropped to his ass. Even the Virtues knew the old man was making sense.

General Ansel Winters sighed. "Son, we have a common goal. You believe the demons are cruel and evil and make this world a darker place. So do we. This darkness, Everett… It's already here, and it will destroy everything. This isn't just a war against wolves anymore. It's a war waged against all Anima, all humans, all living things."

Thex leaned in, clamping the side of the table with his hands. "Promise me you're not going to sit back and watch this happen because of old wounds."

Ryder released a deep exhale. "But I'm a danger to everybody. The US government is after me. I've been shutting down their top-secret operations to weaponize demonic beings for years—it's why I left the Sarpedon Rangers in the first place. Even if I did come with you…"

He paused. The general's eyes were a blazing liquid pearl as he waited for Ryder to continue.

"Even if I did—"

"You would live," the general interjected.

Ryder didn't see what other choice he had. If he stayed, Vangelis wouldn't stop hunting him, especially if he was working for Gregory Finch. Ryder was exhausted and depleted, and he wasn't going to keep running. He couldn't if he tried. His only options were to join the Anima Corps, or die here in a hunter's trap.

"And besides," General Winters continued, "what possible danger could you be to a supernatural military corps? Each marine with unquantifiable powers… You haven't even begun to comprehend the abilities that you possess."

Ryder only drew his next breath when the general rose from his chair. Ryder rose with him, and Thex straightened from his bent position over the table.

A self-satisfied smile deepened the general's crow's-feet wrinkles. "In your closet upstairs you will find three uniforms: your field uniform, your winter field uniform, and your dress uniform. I trust you'll find that your cabin is comfortable and fully contained."

Ryder opened his mouth and closed it again. "Did you just say *my* cabin?"

The general continued like he hadn't heard, "And I must warn you to not go wandering about Kore until tomorrow morning, when you'll have your briefing at oh eight hundred hours. You can get started reading the Corps Handbook on the coffee table; inside you'll find your reading list. Most of the books are on your bookshelf on the staircase landing. To get to your briefing, just follow the gravel path—it will lead you straight to the Corps. We will be having our annual solstice celebration tomorrow evening, where you will meet your Special Operations team. Until tomorrow, sleep well, Captain."

Ryder stood frozen until the general had his hand on the front door. He sped over to catch him before he could leave.

"General?"

The elder turned back, waiting with his owl wings arched high.

"Aren't you afraid?"

"Of what, child?"

"Of me stealing intel or sabotaging Corps protocol?"

The general suppressed a laugh and leaned in. "I'm counting on it."

CHAPTER 4

Ryder reveled in the hot water as he showered in the ensuite bathroom of the cabin. His cabin. A couple of hours ago, all he'd had to his name was an old sleeping bag, a knife, and a kerosene lamp.

The bathroom was designed to bring the forest inside. The walls, including the shower, were made of stormy gray stacked stone. A small vanity with a black marble top encased a raised stone sink and was flanked by two black wall lanterns. The bath opposite the vanity sat against a window that overlooked the pine forest. The trees gleamed in the golden morning light.

Ryder dried himself and inspected his reflection in the mirror. He groaned. His long, shaggy beard and lack of hygiene of late had him feeling like somebody he no longer recognized. He bent down to the duffel bag Thex had given him and found a razor—

A numbing feeling spread through his chest. A feeling he dreaded.

Not again.

The razor dropped from his grasp and he gripped the vanity to steady himself. His lungs felt like they were failing, like his body had shot adrenaline through him to keep him alive. It felt like fighting death. His breath dragged and heaved, dragged and heaved, as he fought to regain himself, sliding down the cabinet. The bathroom swirled nauseatingly around him, so he closed his eyes and held his head until it finally passed.

A knock at the door startled him. "Are you okay in there?" Thex's voice sounded.

"Yeah, I'm fine," Ryder replied weakly. Shame grew in his stomach like a dead weight. He knew Thex had just heard him having a panic attack. He didn't need to embarrass himself further by explaining it.

He picked up the razor and hauled himself up. He shaved until his jawline finally appeared, and didn't linger long afterward; he hadn't come to terms with his fatigued and weakening body. Anima or not, insomnia and nutritional deficiencies were taking their toll. The mysterious vial he had drunk that healed his leg wound had also managed to remove the dark circles and some of the shadows that haunted his face, marking the years that he had lived inside the hellgate. But there was no magical vial that could take away the shadows he was left with on the inside.

Ryder padded into the loft bedroom, wearing a towel around his waist. He sensed Thex waiting out of sight at the library wall on the staircase landing before his voice floated up.

"You remember the last time we saw each other after the bust?"

Ryder had already been recalling the memory before Thex had asked the question. He remembered them hiding in the shrubs after they'd burned down Gregory Finch's lab building. The flames rising high into the night sky. The look on Thex's face, making Ryder fight everything inside himself not to lose it.

It had all been planned. It was going to be the last time they would ever see each other. Ryder had made his decision to go against the military company that had trained him into the weapon he was today. Too many Anima Wolves had been lost at war, and he wasn't going to drag Thex down with him. They hadn't even had a chance to say a proper goodbye before they had to escape, going their separate ways before the government agents found out they had been there.

That memory had left a deeper wound than the one the demon had given him the previous night. This one had never healed.

"Yeah, I remember it all too well," Ryder answered as he tugged on the pants of his new field uniform.

"I want you to know that despite the death stares you've given me since I first saw you a few hours ago, I never told them you stole the intel, or helped them find you. Just like I promised I wouldn't." Thex took the steps two at a time and flopped down on the armchair that faced the bed.

Ryder yanked on a dark olive-green T-shirt and sat at the foot of his bed. "So you're not the turncoat bastard

I made you out to be?" His smile was tight-lipped as he pulled his arms into his military blouse.

Thex sighed and shook his head. "The Virtues know it's good to see you, man."

They talked a little while about where they'd grown up in Boise, and about other comrades who had served in the Sarpedon Rangers and where they were now. Thex soon checked his wristwatch, announcing that he was heading to DFAC for breakfast. He asked if Ryder wanted to come with him, but Ryder declined. The last thing he wanted was to socialize with other marines before he'd checked out the Corps floor plan and marked all the exits.

He heard the front door downstairs click shut behind Thex and threw himself backward onto his new bed—another novelty that wasn't going to wear off anytime soon. He picked up the handbook stacked on top of other books on the small chest next to the armchair and began studying the Corps map.

The Corps was broken up into six divisions—one for every Anima: round buildings that surrounded headquarters. Two other buildings shaped like crescents sat in the center. In between were gardens and quiet areas, and outside the main entrance was a large training field.

Ryder was turning the page when he stopped dead. He'd heard something faint in the distance—a cry from the wild. He stopped breathing, trying to hear it again. Seconds passed as hope spread its wings inside him, ready to soar.

A haunting, mournful sound echoed through him, to the depths of his soul.

A wolf.

Not just any wolf…

His Anima.

He sprang off the edge of the bed, stomped into a new pair of military boots he found in the closet, threw open the door from his bedroom to the balcony, and leaped over the side. His boots hit the ground with a thud. There was no stopping him now.

He catapulted himself at full speed into the forest. More howling echoed through the trees like an invitation, beckoning him home. His legs pumped, excitement rising through him. He could go on running like this for days; a Wolf's stamina was unrivaled.

More howling called him closer and he realized there was more than one wolf. A flicker of worry slowed him. It sounded like a whole pack. A deep inhale through his nose confirmed it.

The fact that there was only one other Wolf Anima on the Island of Kore meant that he was dealing with real wolves—the bushy-tailed, fur-coat kind. That wasn't good. Wolves didn't take kindly to lone trespassers. But his Anima was here, and Ryder had to find him.

He slowed to a stop when the pines became sparse. The soil was interwoven with veiny tree roots that originated from a gigantic oak behind him. Tensile hanging vines draped over each enormous branch's girth.

Ryder's gaze followed the oak into the blue sky above. It looked to be about one hundred and thirty feet high, and ancient, like it had been a sapling at the dawn of time. It was drenched in golden sunlight, and as he looked beyond it, he noticed that the light seemed to recede as it reached the edge of a spruce forest. Between the trees, which stretched as far as he could see, the forest was dark and thick with fog, the ground ahead covered in a thin blanket of snow. He idled closer to the forest's edge, the quiet making him skittish.

The flapping of wings made him start as a raven landed, bobbing on a lower branch and peering at him with an amber eye. Ryder cautiously walked beneath it, crossing the threshold of the spruce forest.

His blood ran cold.

An electric-shock feeling in his throat made his breath seize as he realized what he had just walked into.

Wolves. They were everywhere. Snarling, inching closer, surrounding him. They were glorious in their glossy arctic coats of different shades, circling him with tense, powerful bodies, ready to lunge for the kill. The dramatic plumes of their tails were straight and rigid. Their eyes dared him to move just a fraction of an inch, so that they may begin their attack. They were opponents of which he was not worthy— not against this many of them. They were kings here, and he had foolishly trespassed.

Ryder slowly stepped backward. His boot snagged on the labyrinthine tree roots. He fell with a thud, shuffling away until his back was against the tree that the raven still occupied. His next breath felt suffocating as heat emanated off his face.

The wolves closed in.

Their muzzles were stained and dripping with blood, growling and snarling as they communicated to each other in their primal dialogue. Ryder was dipping his head below his balled fists to block his face when the last wolf arrived, bending the ferns until they cracked as it came to a halt. Ryder's fists dropped slightly as he took in the magnificent creature. The alpha.

The whole pack's focus was redirected, waiting. It was the alpha's decision if he lived or died. His Anima was nowhere in sight, and he wouldn't dream of running while having eight wolves chasing him down.

A flurry of fog made Ryder squint into the swirls of silver. A figure tore through the path the wolves had made and threw itself in front of the gray alpha. The fog lessened, curling away, revealing a woman.

Blood fresh from the kill dripped down her arms as they held back the proud chest of the alpha.

Ryder's fists dropped completely. He wasn't sure where the blood finished and where the woman's waist-length red hair began. She appeared to be stunned, her hands moving slowly toward the handles of the weapons she carried on her back.

Sliding up the tree for balance, Ryder stood. A black-furred wolf—the one closest to him—growled and snapped its jaws at his movements. The woman rose from her haunches with cautious slowness. She stood about as tall as his shoulder, glaring at him with burning emerald eyes.

Those eyes…

He now knew the creature that haunted his slivers of sleep—knew it in his being.

A white wolf.

She sniffed the air between them. In an Australian accent, her voice like honey, she muttered, "You're a Wolf."

She was it. The only other surviving Wolf Anima. But she looked surprised, like she hadn't been warned about him. Perhaps it was the way she squared her shoulders, but something in her body language told Ryder that she felt deceived.

It was as if his presence alone were enough to wage a war behind those eyes.

She asked in a deadly low voice, "Who are you?"

Before he could answer, a thunderous boom shocked the forest. The trees wobbled, then became deathly still in the aftershock. Ryder could have sworn his feet lifted off the ground. The wolves scattered, immediately retreating into the mist.

Another boom. It reverberated within the tree trunk Ryder was leaning against and knocked his feet from underneath him.

In the shadows to the west of the forest, a monstrous silhouette idled.

Ryder's stomach knotted. He carried no arsenal; his knife was in the duffel bag he'd left in the cabin. His throat constricted as he swallowed. He had never seen a demon that big.

"Run!" he shouted at the woman, who was frozen in position. She ignored him and unsheathed two long sacrificial khukuris, the blades at least eighteen inches long.

She launched one of the swords into the sky and shot into the trees, heading toward the demon. Her feet sprang off the ground, flying, reuniting her with her blade. She drove the curved iron into the demon's shoulder, severing its arm clean off. It made a hideous slopping sound as it hit the ground, exploding in a mess of black blood.

Ryder gave a low, appreciative whistle, at the woman's efficiency as much as the weapons. "I've got to get me some of those."

The demon, now incensed with rage, charged forward, black liquid spurting from its amputation. It was running straight for *him*. The circumference of its remaining arm was almost larger than that of its torso, with rounds of thin spears made of rough bone. That was why the woman had taken out the arm first, he realized. He searched his surroundings to find something, anything, to use as a weapon.

He was out of time.

The ground shook under the demon's footsteps. It swiped at him as he ran and slid under its legs. Ryder launched himself onto its back, climbing up the quills that covered it, then leaped onto a low branch of the gigantic tree. The woman was beating the demon's head in devastating blows with her fist and the handle of her sword.

Ryder climbed two more branches until he was looking down on them both. He untangled a strong vine from the branch he was standing on and hastily tied a knot. He dropped it down, lassoing the demon's neck, careful not to entangle the woman in the process, and wrapped it twice around the branch—Something shot past his face, the cutting of wind whispering at his cheek.

He glanced at the knife wedged in the tree trunk behind him, then back at the woman.

"Stay out of this!" she shouted over the demon's roar.

"Already involved!" Ryder argued, matching her irritated tone.

The demon jolted the woman from its shoulders and she fell to the ground, scrambling backward to avoid being stomped on by its huge feet. Ryder dove with the thick vine in his hands, praying that he was heavy enough. The rope tightened around the demon's neck as it was lifted off its feet until they were dangling, writhing viciously.

It twitched before going limp. Ryder dropped to the ground, letting go of the rope.

He managed to raise himself on trembling knees. When he was satisfied at the demon's stillness, he looked down at his hands, burned and chafed from the vine.

Something stirred in his periphery.

Before he could look up, the demon shot a long spear, lodging it through his neck.

Ryder collapsed. He could not call out; blood poured from his mouth. All he could taste was metal. He convulsed as his blood hemorrhaged rhythmically; his surroundings fuzzy. He crashed into the soil, his body slumping to the ground.

He could barely move his eyes and realized that this was the last thing he was going to see: the White Wolf, and her Anima, its coat as brilliant as starlight, emanating from her as she dove through the demon.

Its last breath hacked as she crossed her khukuris and sliced downward. Black innards spilled from its torso.

Ryder's eyes were closing as the woman rushed to his side, her red hair falling around him. He felt her hands on his neck.

As he lost consciousness, his last thought was that he didn't even know her name.

CHAPTER 5

Sunlight heated Ryder's eyelids, turning his inner vision red as his body slowly awakened. He could feel grooves digging into his back and an effervescent energy vibrating along his skin. He tried to open his eyes, but every time he did, sharp needles of light pricked them. Wherever he was, everything was *too* bright, so he shuffled until his face was shaded.

The smell hit him then, burning his nostrils: fresh *soil*. His blood roared through his veins, his heart racing, his palms clammy. No. He couldn't be back—back in that god-forsaken place. Had he dreamed it all? Thex, the elder, the woman with hair like blood?

His breath seized as an excitable female voice, also with an Australian accent, made him snap to attention.

"He's stirring… I wonder if he'll remember what happened to him?"

An accompanying male voice with a Scottish accent answered. "We'll find out soon enough, lass. He's been down there a couple of hours now. Did you let Gunner know we found him? Is he on his way?"

"Yes, I called him ten minutes ago—what's taking him so long? You'd think 'lost Anima' would be top of his list."

"He's probably already at solstice."

"No, word was that this marine was meant to have a briefing with him before he disappeared."

Ryder's eyes flickered open. He saw only darkness, then a canopy of spruce trees reaching for the sleepy blue sky above. He recalled the briefing he was meant to have—not a dream, then.

Two shadowy silhouettes peeked over the opening of the den he lay in. The female voice was soothing: "It's going to be alright, brother, you're safe. Just take your time."

"Aye, don't rush yourself," said the taller silhouette.

Ryder rolled onto his knees and knelt at the entrance of the den. A cherubic round face with pearly skin and soft, full lips came into his focus, looking down at him. Ryder took the woman's outstretched hand and climbed out, confusion flooding him.

Two powerful beings stared back at him, their auras surrounding them in silver flames. The woman was pretty; her cotton-candy-pink curls fell loose to her mid-back, and she wore a long silk slip dress—the most luxurious white silk Ryder had ever seen, with whispers of blue, gold, and silver.

The woman's hand slid out of his, her lavender eyes widening as she whispered, "Oh my—you're a Wolf Anima…"

The man next to her gave her a quick nudge. The woman blinked rapidly before her eyes darted away, then back. Ryder looked from one to the other, panic rattling his bones. *What are they staring at? What's wrong with me?*

As if she sensed his rising terror, the woman whispered, "It's going to be alright."

Ryder's hands flew to his ears. In the distance he could hear music, and people—lots of people.

The woman introduced herself as Vox Bellerose, and the man as Declan McAndor. Declan had fashionably messy brown hair, and a sharp jaw and nose. He was taller and leaner than Ryder, wearing a relaxed white linen shirt that unbuttoned to the middle of his chest, and matching pants—*must shop at the same store as General Winters*—and sophisticated black frames that failed to hide his glowing pale blue eyes.

"It's a pleasure to meet you," Declan said with a tight-lipped smile. There was a pause before Ryder realized they were waiting for him to tell them his name.

"Uhh… Ryder Everett."

"You should see your eyes right now!" Vox beamed. "They're a magnificent glacier blue, and gold around the—"

A deafening sound filled Ryder's ears, an explosive sensation rupturing in his chest.

He bolted, unsure what he was running from. Was it land mines? Bombs? He couldn't see straight to tell. All he knew was that the noise was too much to bear. He'd lost sight of the two Anima. His legs pumped, the forest blurring around him. The ear-shattering noise happened again, filling the sky with pink and green blooms above the canopy.

"Ryder, stop!" Declan shouted.

Not knowing where the voice had come from, Ryder did a head check behind him—nothing.

Declan landed before him, appearing like a ghost in the woods, blocking his path with two enormous dark brown wings with downy gray bands lining the inside. The wings of a golden eagle.

Ryder skidded to a halt, unable to hide his shock, flicking leaves and dirt all over him.

"Thanks for that," Declan remarked, unimpressed.

Ryder's attention snapped behind him as the thicket was disturbed. A large fox ran through, slow and deliberate. Ryder's lungs emptied as he stood rooted to the spot between the two magnificent creatures. The fox had cross-colored fur—her legs, chest, and delicate muzzle were night black; her cheeks, ears, and underbelly as orange as wildfire.

Vox's human form followed behind her Anima, stopping in front of him. "Ryder, they're just fireworks for our summer solstice celebration. I know this is confusing and probably overwhelming your senses right now, but we're here to help you."

Declan nodded. "We're like your welcoming committee."

Ryder's whole body snapped around as he heard someone approaching from four o'clock.

Thex jumped off of a huge fallen log with a sardonic eye roll, walking with a brown-haired man who looked to be in his mid-forties.

"It was one simple instruction, Ry—just follow the path to the Corps. But you just had to detour, didn't you?" Thex punched him lightly on the shoulder. Ryder eyed his friend's attire in commiseration. *Again with the linen suits?*

"We thought we'd lost you, Captain." The other man stopped dead for a fraction of a second. That look… It told him that the man knew he was a Wolf Anima. If he was proceeding with caution, he didn't show it; the man extended his hand and looked mildly irritated when Ryder didn't take it. "I'm Major Michael Gunner."

Ryder failed to stifle a chuckle, and the major's demeanor became more impatient. "Oh, you're serious," Ryder realized. In the Marine Corps they had called the gunnery sergeants 'Gunner'—he hadn't known it was a *real* last name.

As he waited in the awkward silence for somebody, anybody, to say something, he noticed the silver scar that started on the major's forehead, slashing over one moody green eye and traveling down almost to his jawline. Without the scar, the man looked like an older version of Ryder himself, with a square jaw and rugged features. He had the same stardust glow that Declan and Vox shared, but he was a Lynx Anima. Ryder could sense it, having worked with some Lynx marines when he was a ranger.

The major's hands straightened at his sides with a stiffness Ryder knew could only come from years of training. "I'm afraid so," he finally replied. "Most marines just call me Gunner. I'm the one in charge of all you rabid animals. Welcome to Anima Corps… or rather, the forest outside Anima Corps."

Ryder abruptly became faint. He hadn't eaten a proper meal in days. Vox guided him to sit on a boulder nearby and Declan handed him an oat-and-raisin cookie. The first bite made him sigh. Virtues, it was good. He wolfed it down in three more bites.

"Want another one?" Thex offered his stash.

"Yeah, it didn't even touch the sides."

A mechanical voice began speaking, giving Ryder a start. A small machine no bigger than the size of his palm floated up between himself and Vox, initializing a scan.

Vox read out its data from a tablet in her hand. "Your heart rate is one hundred and ninety-eight, normal, and your energy is sitting at one hundred percent... Though it's coming up that your stress is high, sitting at eighty percent."

"Okay..." Ryder stood, awkwardly tapping a closed fist on the side of his leg. Being a marine, he was used to having his vitals checked regularly, but he didn't appreciate an audience.

To his relief, the major changed the subject. "Can you tell us what happened before you passed out?"

"Yeah—but I have to find the woman."

"What woman?" asked Gunner.

"Redhead, about yea high." His hand leveled at his shoulder. "Gorgeous. Carries more iron on her than her own body weight."

Declan's enormous eagle wings arched back and vanished, making him appear *somewhat* human again. "You'd be looking for Hellfire."

"What?"

"Hellfire. We only know her by her codename. But she's a rare sight around these parts."

"And if you're smart, you won't go looking for her," Thex added.

"Why wouldn't I? She saved my life," Ryder explained, brows knitted.

Gunner laughed, his raised brow suggesting Ryder had lost his mind. "Is that what you think she was doing?"

Ryder felt suddenly doubtful. Had his memory lapsed before he blacked out?

"We were fighting this huge demon, biggest one I've ever seen, and I got speared through my neck. She healed me, somehow…"

Gunner stepped forward, an expression of pity upon his rugged features. Ryder swallowed.

"She shoved you into a shallow hole, marine. She left you to be eaten by the wolves. You're lucky Vox found you not long after." The major slapped him on the back. Ryder pretended not to notice the troubled glance he exchanged with Vox before he began walking back in the direction he'd arrived from. "I'm heading to solstice," he declared. "There's a meeting for the Special Operatives being held during the celebration tonight. It'll be great for you to meet the rest of your team—and who knows?" The major's arms splayed out. "Maybe she'll show."

"And look, you've met three of us already!" Vox exclaimed. "I'm an analyst and a scientist. I provide you with all your data for the missions. Declan is—you guessed it—aerial defense, and Thex—"

"I provide all communications between Special Ops and base," Thex finished.

"Why am I not surprised? I can never get you to shut up," Ryder teased. Thex elbowed him in the ribs, hard. A grin cracked across Ryder's face, because he couldn't feel a damn thing.

"Come on, celebration is this way." Declan beckoned him toward the trail.

Ryder followed them through the forest. The fog had dissipated, and the thicket thinned until it was nothing but sparse trees to weave between. He schooled himself into composure as the sudden sounds ahead of them shocked and rattled him. He hadn't been around this many people in years. It was going to take a bit of getting used to. He fixated his attention on Vox's even heartbeat as she walked beside him, relying on it to keep his own internal pace calm.

Kore smelled amazing: the decomposing earth; the minty, woody scent of the spruce; Vox's balsamic-and-floral scent… and people, even though they were still at least two miles ahead. And food! Glorious, slow-cooked food. Wild salmon, rosemary potatoes, and roasted meats. He had to swallow to keep from salivating; he could feel it dripping from his fangs.

Ryder was happy to learn that Vox was chatty. He didn't interrupt her much as she began telling him everything she thought he should know. She explained that there was no going around a large introduction like this one, so this was as good as any.

She held his arm back, letting the others walk ahead. To human ears, her whispers would have been completely inaudible, though she seemed to know how far ahead the others needed to be before she said, "If what you're saying is true… that you saw Hellfire, and you're two Wolf Animas in the same territory… that's ammunition for a fight."

He met her lavender eyes and flashed her a half-smile. "Do I look scared to you?"

Dimples appeared as a flush of rose hit her cheeks. "No, but have you seen how wolves claim territory?"

He paused.

"Exactly," she answered, reading his expression as a muscle clenched in his jaw.

"She'll fight to the death?" he asked.

"She doesn't fight any other way." Another pause lingered between them before Vox ushered him onward. "Come on. The sooner we find General Winters, the sooner we'll know what's going on."

They crossed the threshold of the forest into a large clearing of lush grass filled with feathery white blooms bending in the gentle breeze. A turquoise alpine river gushed to a constant relaxed rhythm. Beyond it was another dense forest below tall, mossy cliffs that bore a narrow waterfall. The air was fresh, warmed by the sun, and Ryder couldn't remember ever experiencing beauty quite like this. Even his home state paled in comparison.

"Wow, this is…" He took a steadying breath, at a loss for words.

Vox smiled, enjoying his wonder. "Kore is something else."

"Where are we, geographically?"

"Still on Earth," Vox assured him. "It's through a portal, deep beneath the Earth's crust—that's why we have a sky and an atmosphere. It's a hallowed place for our kind, completely untouched by humans."

Ryder clasped his wrists, rubbing them. "But there are demons here."

Vox nodded. "But not everywhere. You'll be fully briefed by General Winters when we meet soon. He'll explain everything about the demons." She grinned as a shudder escaped her body. "Gruesome work that you're into, Captain. But something tells me you're fit for the task."

He loosed a breathy laugh. "Don't tell me you're not up for the action?"

"Ha! No… I'm happy in my lab, thank you."

They both grinned as they approached the large gathering. Ryder thought it resembled a festival. People were dancing, soaking up the midnight sun. Laughter and chatter filled the air, and somewhere past the river's bend, he could hear music.

"Now, don't make any sudden movements as we walk through," Vox instructed. "Most of us haven't seen a Wolf in years."

"Right."

Like magnets, the Animas moved fluidly in motion with him. Some were drawn nearer, angling their faces toward him, and some moved further away. Some smiled in delight, shoulders rolled back; some gave him a nod. The gold or silver undertones of their skin were radiant in the light peeking over the horizon.

Ryder inspected his own hands and arms in wonder. It was still his usual sun-kissed skin tone, but with a shimmering golden glow that covered every cell of his body like it was a liquid he had bathed in. It was back to its former glory, like he'd embodied the sun itself, an aura of golden flames.

The ocean of people parted for them. In the vibrant and otherworldly glow of their irises was an embedded message, their voices like whispering echoes swirling around him.

"Welcome, brother. It is good to see you again."

"He's a Wolf."

"A Wolf. I've never seen…"

"I hear his howl."

"I smell a Wolf."

Two women leaned in so close he had to go around them to get past.

"Oh, don't be alarmed." Vox grabbed his elbow to keep him from getting caught up with them. "They're just getting your scent." Ryder curved a brow upward in displeasure, making her chuckle. "Yes, I hear you—it's ridiculous."

"Not to mention a lack of personal space. I forgot what it's like being around so many people."

Vox sighed through her nose. "Soon enough it will feel normal."

They caught up to the others, where Vox gave Declan a peck on his cheek. Giving the couple their space, Thex asked Ryder, "So, what do you think?"

He sighed, taking in the view again. "It's a lot, I'll admit. But we have to find out what's making the IOs so active."

Thex stretched his long, muscular arms out behind him. "Can we just enjoy the celebration without you… Rydering?"

Ryder raised a brow. "Rydering?"

Thex nodded. "Do you see any other marine going through battle strategies tonight? No, you don't. You know why that is?"

Ryder sighed. *Not even half an hour and he's already starting.*

"Because they know how to get their heads out of the mission and have some fun."

Ryder rolled his eyes. "I know how to have fun."

"Off-mission?"

Asshole had a point. "You know what?" He slapped a hand on Thex's shoulder. "I'm really happy for you that you get to switch off at the end of the day—"

"There you go, being a dick."

"—but I don't have that luxury," Ryder finished.

Thex winced. "Don't. Don't do that."

They talked over the top of each other, shaking their heads, each claiming that the other was in the wrong. This went on for half a minute before they both cracked Cheshire Cat smiles and laughed like idiots.

"Well, you'll be pleased to know that the general likes to go into the old stories when we have meetings," Thex explained. "You'll hear about the demons then."

In his periphery, Ryder noticed a woman prowling within their vicinity. They made eye contact as she walked up the sloping land toward him. He could sense, even from a distance, that she was a Fox Anima. Her shoulder-length chocolate-brown locks bobbed as she walked, and she swept aside the strands that had fallen across her face to reveal bright cognac-colored eyes—eyes that suggested she wanted to take him somewhere private. She wore an ethereal silk dress like Vox's, only hers plunged into a low neckline, revealing tanned, gleaming skin.

"Oh, Ryder," Vox began enthusiastically, "I'd like to introduce you to—"

"So you must be the missing link." The woman cut her off in a raspy voice, her smile now in sync with the message of her bedroom eyes. Her scent hit him then—red wine and chocolate.

"Mackenzie Bale," Vox finished, rolling her eyes.

Mackenzie took a sip from one of two hand-carved fox-shaped wooden tumblers and passed Ryder the other.

"Thanks." He tipped the tumbler toward her.

Mackenzie didn't seem to take notice of Vox or Declan at all. She motioned to the cup. "I'd give you a wolf-shaped one, but we don't have any."

"I suppose the cups didn't survive the war, either," Thex

said in a clear attempt to sever the growing claustrophobia, despite them being outdoors, in the wilderness.

Mackenzie gave him a contemplative smile before turning back to Ryder. "So, how are you settling into the Corps, Captain…?"

"Ryder," he filled in.

"You must admit, the divisions, the barracks, the training field… It's all very impressive."

"Uh, I only got here earlier today, so I haven't seen much."

Both manicured brows raised, the corners of her lips upturned, she said, "Well, if you ever need to explore whatever it is that you can do, just—"

"He doesn't know what he can do other than the standard Wolf powers yet, Mackenzie," Vox interrupted in annoyance. "Like he said, he got here just this morning."

For the first time, Mackenzie addressed Vox, looking over her with a bored expression. "Yes, well, you would know all about missing standard powers, being so guile-deprived and all. You're a travesty to vixens everywhere."

"But she's smarter than all o' ye put together." Declan shot Mackenzie a stern glare.

"Pity that such brilliance is packaged in such bizarre ensembles."

"I'm not bizarre!" Vox exclaimed. Little dimples appeared on her forehead as she scowled. "I'm just… quirky."

"Whatever. I'm sure the captain wants to see the rest of the party, not stay chained to the slope with you lot."

Vox scowled and left Declan's side in a huff, tugging at Ryder's arm. "Come on."

Mackenzie followed them as they neared the source of the music: four musicians situated at the forest's edge, which was lined with hanging lanterns. All four were slowly writhing as if the music came from their bones as well as their instruments. The man playing the flute paused, releasing his mouth from the top of his instrument to tip his head back, his bright needle-like fangs catching the light. Next to him, a woman with night-black hair beat the tambourine where the split of her silk gown revealed her bare leg, her eagle wings open to the dancing crowd, hiding the other two musicians from Ryder's view. The music was tribal and raw, the deep drums causing a full-body vibration that tingled the skin. Hips were jolting and lunging; bodies unfurling in proud, slow movements; feet stamping and swiping at the earth—worshiping the ground, Ryder realized.

They walked the circumference of the dancing crowd, passing fire pits encircled with comrades and lovers, some watching Ryder with curiosity and nudging each other.

"I'll show you the other half of the party. It's kind of a tradition here in Kore." Vox led them to where the crowd was becoming sparse. A swarm of people was gathering where the river curved. The shallow waters of the bank gushed over smooth rocks before becoming a turbulent flow toward the river's center, racing away from the alpine peaks that loomed in the distance, still and ancient.

The Animas here were dressed in Corps greens. Their grunts and battle cries competed with the sound of the river as they hurled themselves at each other, every inch of them caked in mud.

Fighting. A demonstration that could only be delivered by people made by the stars. Their flamed auras shone through their earth-smeared bodies; the whooshing sound of claws, like daggers, slashed the air, bodies pouncing and leaping to heights unimaginable compared to human strength. And their Animas—divine creatures with fur that gleamed like the brilliant constellations of the Milky Way, their animal eyes calculated and reflective as they lunged at their opponents.

Ryder turned to Thex. "Are they really hurting each other?"

"Do you want to go and find out what that feels like?" Thex pointed at a luminous Bear, growling gutturally and boxing the air with its huge paws.

"Those claws—they look like karambit knives," Ryder marveled as he watched the sheer force of the raven-haired man the Bear belonged to. He'd removed the top half of his uniform, sporting only his military pants. The mud smeared over his torso did nothing to conceal the deeply defined lines of his muscles beneath his russet complexion. He crowed victoriously as his opponent fell to the ground and con-ceded. The man held out his hand to help his opponent to his feet before turning their way.

Thex chuckled ruefully at the battle happening before them, or for the man's victory, or maybe both. "That's River Borealis," he explained. "He's on the team too."

A burst of excitement coursed through Ryder, energy rising until he couldn't take standing there any longer. He clapped his hands together. "What's the objective here, exactly?"

Declan's wings jolted, half unfolding at the sudden clap. "We're warriors first, Captain. This is our life force. We can clearly express ourselves this way."

Ryder glanced sidelong at him. He hadn't meant to shock Declan; he knew that feeling well. Something told him that an apology would make a bigger deal of it than Declan would appreciate, so instead he asked, "Through fighting?"

"Through movement," Vox clarified. "And I don't know about you, but dancing does it for me."

"And all my life I thought I was just a troublemaker," Ryder said.

"They didn't do this in the Sarpedon Rangers?" Declan asked.

Ryder shook his head. At a final tug from Vox, Declan went with her to join the dancing crowd.

Thex shouldered Ryder. "Yeah, but you're still a troublemaker."

Ryder rolled his eyes, yet couldn't argue the fact.

"Oh my Virtue," Mackenzie puffed hoarsely, like she'd just completed a cross-country sprint.

Ryder and Thex cast their eyes in the direction she was staring. In the shallow waters of the riverbank, a Deer Anima dropped to his knees with a cracking sound. Both the emanation of the Deer's proud body and his crown of carbon spears dissipated, leaving a man with an abnormally bent neck lying limp in the water.

The attacker left the man to drown in the shallows, but two onlookers raced to collect him as the attacker entered the circle of fighters. A Lynx Anima deemed himself the next contestant, striding forward and throwing the first punch at the challenger.

It was *her*.

She was a cocktail of the deadliest martial arts. Ryder observed her every move, noting where and when she shifted her weight, like a predator about to ambush its prey. He waited for her to reveal her weak spot. She stood stark against the other marines, the only one not wearing the Corps uniform and the only one clean of mud. She fought in a black tank top and a pair of black utility pants that clung to her strong legs as close as silk.

The beginning of the fight displayed flawless technique from both fighters, until her opponent got under her skin. Literally. The Lynx marked three gashes on her right arm, and she rolled her shoulder inward and inspected the wound, blood dripping down to her elbow.

She snarled, her fangs bared at the Lynx, then attacked close contact. And there it was… The weak spot. Ryder sealed the information away for later, feeling a charge in the center of his chest that reached the tip of his fingers before settling as a giddy sensation in his stomach.

Her opponent changed, and with that so did her fighting methods. From where they stood, it was becoming a swarm of twelve against one.

Ryder took a step toward the fight, but Thex's hand pushed him back. "Let them work it out."

"The Deer Anima—is he okay?"

Thex nodded. "He's not dead, just unconscious. A broken neck never killed an Anima."

Ryder looked over at the man, who had been relocated next to a fire pit. It looked like he was coming to. Someone had called a medic, who lifted the man's eyelids and passed a flashlight over his pupils.

Ryder had forgotten Mackenzie was still there. He and Thex turned to her as she said, "I'm guessing you've never heard of Hellfire and Hurricane?" Her mouth gaped in surprise when Ryder gave her a blank look. "The infamous husband-and-wife serial killer duo?"

"War criminals," Thex corrected.

"What's the difference? They're murderers. Known for the worst crimes in Anima history."

"Are they both Wolves?" Ryder asked.

"No. Hurricane was an Eagle."

"So if they're so bad… why aren't they locked up?"

"Hellfire was brought here about eighteen months ago. She had to be heavily restrained and put in isolation, then they gave her an ultimatum—join Anima Corps or be banished. I'd only *heard* of her arrival… I've never actually seen her in the flesh until now. And nobody has seen or heard of Hurricane since she got here… Word is, she doesn't speak of him."

"Well, maybe she got tired of banishment and wants to use her powers for good." Thex shrugged.

Mackenzie huffed. "Thex, I used to work in intel. I've been involved in missions where she's savagely killed her own kind. Believe me, nothing about that woman is redeemable."

The Wolf woman's last opponent fell to the ground. Hellfire stepped over the unconscious bodies left in her wake, walking in the direction of the forest like she'd tasted the blood of her next prey.

"So, how do you feel about *her* being on the team?" Thex asked Ryder with a challenging grin.

He folded his arms and eyed the trees where Hellfire had just disappeared. "Like I got a harpoon to the chest."

Vox and Declan rejoined them, and when Ryder was convinced the group was busy in conversation, he told Thex he was getting another drink. He made his way through other groups before slipping unnoticed into the dewy ferns.

A sparse section of forest followed the river to his left; the right side was dense and shrouded in darkness. He ran at a brisk pace through the darker region until he could sense that he had caught up with her.

It still amazed him how evocative the air element could be. He pulled back into a slow prowl before pausing, feeling the air fluctuate against the tiny fibers of his skin. He could sense where it was warmer, where it was disturbed, where it was welcoming—until he was suddenly engulfed by a scent so mesmerizing that his lungs felt unable to drink enough of it in.

The slightest sound of material dragging against bark made him freeze. A high kick rounded from behind him, the woman's military boot stopping but a hair's breadth away from his face as he blocked it just in time. With one hand catching Hellfire's boot and the other gripping her thigh, Ryder launched her high into the air in a hammer throw. She cut through the air like a rag doll, a blur. She managed to regain control, landing with her arms out to balance herself. She looked over the whole length of him, her green eyes dazed.

"We've got to stop meeting like this," Ryder declared. Assuming a fighting stance, he held up his fists in a welcoming manner.

Hellfire bit down on a snarl and catapulted into a powerful leap. Flying toward him, she crashed against him, wrapping her legs around his ribs, twisting him to the ground. She punched into his blocked arms before he threw her off. Ryder's reflexes were quick enough to evade her low kicks, but he took a blow to the jaw when she went roundhouse, spinning into a tree trunk.

He pushed off the bark and rubbed his jaw. "I came to thank you for saving me."

"I don't save anybody, Wolf," Hellfire growled.

Ryder grinned deviously. "Liar."

They circled each other, fangs bared, ready for the next attack. He caught her punch, using it as leverage. She thrust her boot into his chest, sending him stumbling backward. Ryder shook with silent laughter.

"You think fighting is funny?" she asked.

It spurred another burst of amusement, and Ryder held onto a tree trunk, regaining control of himself. Fighting for air, he finally said, "This isn't fighting. This is playing."

Hellfire's eyes narrowed, her stance stiffening. She didn't like that at all, Ryder realized. She sprang against the tree trunk closest to her, pushing off and tackling him to the ground, landing on top of him. He wasn't quick enough to stop her teeth from sinking deep into his hand. She ripped off a chunk of his flesh between his thumb and index finger. He watched the light of victory in her eyes dim as he glared at her, unimpressed.

"You didn't feel that?" she asked, panting.

"Not a thing."

Ryder punched her with the same bloodied hand, and she fell to his side, rolling away from his grasp before she sprang to her feet.

"Who could be so stupid as to follow a serial killer into a secluded forest?" Hellfire sneered as she ducked his next swing.

Ryder ignored the question that aimed to throw him off. The thrill of trying to pin her was too great to back down now. "How did you survive the War on Wolves?" he asked. "Tell me what happened to the others."

Her pressure against him yielded for a moment and his grip on her arms loosened, though he didn't let go. Hellfire took a long look straight into his eyes before they were ripped apart as Vox forced herself between them.

"You'll have to excuse my friend. She's rather uncivilized." Vox glared at Hellfire, who was still staring steadily at Ryder.

River Borealis, the Bear Anima, slowed to a jog as he reached Hellfire's side and muttered close to her ear, "Is everything alright?"

Hellfire's only answer was her jaw tightening like an iron clamp as she looked over the length of Ryder, her sensuous lips slightly parted, revealing her cuspid teeth.

To break the awkward silence, Vox explained to River that Ryder was their new captain. The Bear Anima shook his hand and welcomed him as a brother, but Ryder noted suspicion in those mahogany eyes.

"Do you two know each other?" River asked, looking back and forth between Ryder and Hellfire.

Before Ryder could answer, General Ansel Winters appeared, climbing over a fallen log with Major Michael Gunner and an elder Ryder had never met. Beneath the elder's large antlers, hair of moss swept over the rounded features of her face and trailed downward, fashioning itself into a gown that glided over the forest floor as she walked.

"I see it didn't take long for you two to find each other," Ansel said.

Hellfire turned to face him with a fierce glare. "You lied to me," she seethed.

"My daughter, there was no way of knowing he was alive."

Her whole body was stony and rigid as Ansel put himself between her and Ryder.

"Ryder Everett, meet Aspen Lovetta."

CHAPTER 6

Defiant and aloof, Aspen Lovetta crossed her arms over her chest, peering at the Wolf who was to be her new captain.

"Wait…" the captain said. "Aspen Lovetta? As in the Lovettas from Livinia's Orchard in Australia?"

Aspen could hardly believe the words that had just come out of his mouth. She gasped as if she had been struck in the chest. He'd said her mother's name, the name of their family business. Which could only mean one thing.

No… No, this isn't happening. Can't be—

Reading her panic, the captain explained, "Your initials are carved into the tree of the farmhouse near the Australian IO."

The tree… The chestnut tree? A million years ago. Another life. Another girl.

She turned to Ansel in outrage. "That's where you found him? At my house? You had me believing for seven years that I was the only Wolf left. You said there would *never* be another one in this generation."

A familiar voice spoke, one she hadn't heard in years. "Look, if it's any consolation, we only got intel on him when all the other IOs were active besides Australia—we knew someone had to be there guarding it."

Aspen turned, loosening every taut muscle as she faced him. She took slow steps, letting the fall of her hair waft just enough of her scent to make him stiffen as she approached. She stopped directly in front of him. He smelled like the fir forests of Kore in the winter: clean, fresh, and strong.

"Well, well…" she crooned, tipping her head upward so their gazes met. "If it isn't the do-gooder, Michael Gunner. It's been a while… What do they call you now? Major?"

Flustered, Michael issued a warning glare down at her. "This isn't the time."

Aspen smirked, throwing her arms up. "Let me know when you can fit me into that full schedule of yours."

The major's lips were tight. "You better watch it, marine."

She bit her lip with a coy smile as she backed away, creating distance between them. She took every bit of pleasure in getting under his skin. "Uh-uh," she taunted. "We're off-duty. And I don't take orders from you."

The elder, who stood as rooted as one of the trees off to the side, spoke for the first time, looking at Aspen and the new captain. "Right now, taking orders has never been so important. We need your combined strength to fight what is coming. I am Justice Asintmah Eubank." She turned to the captain. "But I assume you don't know what a justice is yet. We are the members of the Anima Chamber."

Aspen watched tension zap like an electric current over the captain's broad shoulders and through the golden flames of his aura. "The governing body?"

"Yes," the elder replied. "And it is my greatest honor to finally meet you, Captain."

He gave her a tight-lipped smile, which seemed to dissipate the tension. Asintmah turned to face Aspen then, her gown dragging over the tree roots as she walked over. The captain was also watching her. Aspen folded her arms over her chest, ignoring the elder completely.

"If it were up to me, I would say that you are not ready to be here." Asintmah's eyes, fern green with golden flecks, were filled with an emotion that Aspen didn't care to read. Asintmah took this as an invitation to walk closer and place her hand gently on Aspen's arm. "But desperate times have called you here. The general and I are risking lives having you among us. Do not make us regret this."

Aspen shrugged her off with a loathing glare. She took enough steps back to create distance between herself and the rest of them. "I don't want to be here. And I don't know what sick game you're all playing—"

"It's not a game," Vox interrupted, shaking her head.

"You're here because we need you." River stated what they must all have known to be the truth, for no one corrected him.

Ansel smiled; it seemed to have a restorative effect on everybody except her. "And with both Wolves as partners, the whole team is reunited."

"Wait... partners?" River questioned.

"You want me to be partners with Captain Beefcake?" Aspen nodded toward the new captain, who folded his arms over his chest and threw her a sidelong glance, then fixed his focus upon Ansel.

"I've never heard of military personnel having partners, sir."

The general replied in earnest, "*We* do. I told you that things work differently here."

The captain gave a nod like the good marine that he was. Eyes of ultramarine fire focused on her. Feeling that flame ignite all over her body, Aspen squared her shoulders—a warning, telling him he was making a mistake. The captain had no trouble reading the unspoken message, and his response came in clear as he moved his feet shoulder-width apart. Resolute and stubborn, this bastard wasn't going to budge. She had saved him within inches of his life, and for what? For Ansel to throw him back into the hell he looked like he'd just crawled out of?

"Is this a joke?" Aspen asked. Silence followed, and Ansel's expression was unwavering. "Are you out of your mind?" she erupted at the general. "How could you, above anybody, not understand how dangerous this is?"

"Do you honestly believe in your heart that *we* would ever put you in danger?" Asintmah answered in a breathy whisper.

"What I can't believe is what's coming out of your mouth," Aspen muttered darkly. The air shifted instantly, like Kore could sense the bloodthirst behind her words.

The captain met her with a challenging glare. "I don't think I have much to prove by way of looking after myself. I'm sure I can handle it."

Aspen opened her mouth, but Ansel cut in quickly with a cheerful smile. "It's settled, then. Let us begin the preparations for our meeting, or by the time we begin, it will be morning. I don't know about you, but I wouldn't like to wait until next year's summer solstice to greet the Virtues."

Partners indeed. The captain didn't buckle under the glare she gave him as they exchanged a vow within a dangerous silence that belonged only to them. It lasted until Ansel prompted them, "Come along!"

Aspen lagged behind with Vox as Ansel led them to the narrowest part of the river, easy enough to jump across. Vox and River had been the first Anima Aspen had met after that fateful day of her activation. The way *her* activation had happened? She wouldn't wish it on her worst enemy—not even the lowest of the malignant scum that had made it onto her list over the years. Death would have been easier. But the Corps had ensured that she'd suffer fates worse than death—and now everybody had to pay.

The truth was, nobody knew what Vox knew. Or River, for that matter… River had been the one, at the ripe age of eighteen, to scoop her up out of that cellar, every inch of it, and her, dripping with blood. He'd taken her to the carrier, and they'd left for Fort Gippsland—an Anima military base hidden at the easternmost point of Victoria, Australia.

Aspen could see Vox biting down on her thousands of questions as they leaped to the other side of the river, landing on the threshold of sacred ground. But she knew very well that they weren't out of earshot to sensitive ears.

Justice Asintmah handed bags made of scrap fabric to Aspen, River, Thomas Thexton, and the captain. "Put these on," she instructed. "No weapons or uniforms on sacred soil. You must wash thoroughly in the river and leave everything here." She placed a duffel bag bearing the Corps insignia at the base of a pine tree.

Aspen watched as the men pulled out their pure linen clothes. She clenched her teeth as she reached into the bag and pulled out a bundle of silk, letting the length of it tumble to the ground. She had been warned by River about the silk robes and had left her khukuris in her tent; there was no way she was leaving them here for any of these marines to find.

As the men dropped their blades into the duffel bag, Vox pulled Aspen further downstream, out of sight of the others. "Did you know he was another Wolf Anima when you saved him today?" she asked Aspen as she scrubbed her skin in the freezing water.

No, she had most certainly not known. "Don't make me regret it, Vox," Aspen huffed.

Vox grinned as she twisted her torso left and right, her pink curls swishing around her. "I'm not going to tell anyone. I don't think he will either."

Aspen dried herself and slipped the dress over her head. "Why does yours get to be shorter? I can't fight in this," she complained, looking up at Vox, whose violet eyes lit up as Aspen beheld her. The gown hugged every dip and curve of her body and opened to reveal the full length of her back. Her supple skin belied her years on the battlefields—not a scar in sight, thanks to her healing powers.

Vox said nothing as she walked over, put her delicate hands in Aspen's bundled hair, and took it down, letting it fall around her, curving and voluminous. Vox's soft hands sent a pang through Aspen's stomach as she remembered the first time Vox had touched her hair. The memory was too painful to recall now; she violently shoved it away. She hadn't meant to, but she physically flinched, leaving Vox shocked into stillness, looking at her wordlessly.

"Sorry," Aspen muttered.

Vox pursed her lips, sadness filling her eyes. Before turning away, she said, "That's the point, by the way. To not fight…"

Aspen stole a glance at the sky, annoyed at herself. All she wanted to do was reach out and tell her friend how much she really meant the apology, but years of unspoken pain had wedged a wall between them—a barrier that was there more for Vox's benefit than her own, she told herself. Vox knew too much about secret information *and* Aspen's motives during the silent wars, the kind of worthwhile information that any war criminal would torture her for. It had happened once, but Aspen would be damned if she'd let anything happen to Vox again because of her.

She trailed behind Vox, lost in her thoughts. The silk moved like water, hugging her close as she walked to meet the others. It was the oddest sight: marines dressed in sacred robes, standing stiff as boards. Five pairs of eyes darted over each other in awkward silence as they waited for Asintmah to return. She felt Thomas Thexton sidling closer to her; there were only a few reasons an Anima did that. He was either gauging her size, looking for weaknesses he could use to his advantage in a fight, or the most common option… trying to get her scent without being too conspicuous. Aspen bristled. If the icy glare she shot at him wasn't enough, the flash of her cuspid teeth made the Deer Anima step back.

Asintmah called to them from the threshold of the sacred ground. They walked through a small section of pine forest to reach her before she turned and guided them onward. The edge of the forest opened up to a clearing blanketed in blooms with silver petals and deep purple centers. Aspen heard Thex tell Vox they were frost poppies.

The marines—mainly Vox—sighed in awe and made excited sounds as they approached the towering statues. In a perfect circle, the six Anima Virtues were depicted in poses frozen mid-action, like moments from the first war in history had been captured when the Eagle was swooping or the Fox leaping. Aspen's legs turned lead on the perimeter of the circle. They were godlike, with dying sunlight saturating their crystal forms, exploding in color as if the northern lights were trapped inside the stone. Their bodies were gilded with ancient golden symbols, and every Virtue had four wings: two spread wide, two angled up to the heavens, like that of the Corps insignia. The Eagle Virtue was even more formidable with its six gigantic wings.

Aspen's eyes were torn away when Ansel beckoned her to enter the circle after the others had already walked onward. She looked down at her bare toes peeking out from under the silk dress. She took a step.

She wasn't sure whether she was meant to feel different on sacred ground, or whether the Virtues would come alive, open up the ground she stood on, and damn her to hell for all she'd done.

She walked past the captain, who was admiring the statues as River stopped and explained, "This was the first Anima team to exist thousands of years ago."

"But they're in animal form?" the captain questioned.

River nodded. "They were Absolute—in the highest form of power that we can ever evolve to."

"Must have been tough times."

Aspen could feel the heat of following eyes. Her attention snapped to the statue beside her. Lykaion.

Something about the Wolf Virtue made prickling pain jolt through her thighs, begging her to run out of the circle. She found it peculiar that the statue of Lykaion was that of a Wolf standing, head pointed north. Not howling, nor in a threatening stance ready for battle… but as if the statue had been erected in remembrance of a magnanimous leader. She felt a twinge of sadness that she couldn't quite place and turned her back to her deity.

In the center of the circle lay fallen tree trunks arranged in a U-shape, surrounding a bonfire. The flames reached taller than her, casting a warm orange glow on all of their faces. Three other marines were already waiting there. Vox skipped toward the tall, handsome airman wearing glasses; Aspen figured that was her boyfriend, Declan, and watched as Vox interlocked her fingers with his and sat beside him. Declan paled at the sight of Aspen. She wasn't sure why he appeared so shocked, as if not even the rumors that she was on the team had prepared him for the moment of their meeting. Deciding she wasn't ready, Aspen evaded his eyes until he turned his attention elsewhere.

General Ansel Winters and Justice Asintmah Eubank had been joined by three other members of the Chamber: Justices Calais Joffrin, Chaska Bravebird, and Silla Borealis—River's father.

Aspen balanced across a log to perch at the furthest distance from the majority, except for River, who sat beneath her as she dangled her legs on either side of him. Vox slid over next to River, and Declan tentatively followed suit. Aspen knew her presence had been mostly mythical to the other marines in the Corps until this point, and she felt stolen glances from all of them now. The captain appeared to be on high alert, subtly clenching his fists at the smallest of movements made by the team as they each took their seats—he was sandwiched between Sergeant Thomas Thexton and Sergeant Mackenzie Bale. He peered behind him to the pine forest, then over to the lake beyond the sacred ground.

Aspen darted her eyes away when that ultramarine gaze rested on her. She knew *that* feeling all too well… Suspicion that someone was going to close in when she least expected it. As an Anima marine, letting down your guard could be fatal. The marines who had seen the worst of the wars didn't know how to switch it off… The constant overthinking, the lack of sleep, being easily startled— in one glance, the captain told her he experienced all of that. Aspen dared to steal another look at him. Mackenzie was whispering into his ear, but his eyes, all the while, remained directly on *her*. There was something about his body language that told her he *knew* she'd suffered the same price of war.

"Welcome, my sons and daughters," General Winters began, his arms outstretched as if to embrace them all. "Your service records, your powers, and your skills exceed the norm, and that is why you have been hand-selected for this Special Operations task force. It is by some miracle of the Virtues that we have been reunited with our brother— your captain—who we had previously believed was lost in the War on Wolves. Please sit and enjoy as we begin our traditions of storytelling before we later discuss… Well, the doom and gloom."

Some of the group chuckled on cue. Aspen just rolled her eyes. *Fools.*

Justice Asintmah's verdure gown had sprouted tiny forget-me-nots that had not been there before. Aspen saw the team's spines straighten as Asintmah introduced the six Virtues that surrounded the sacred birthplace of the original Anima team. Mackenzie was stuck so close to the captain's side that their shoulders were touching, though he was doing a good job of pretending not to notice.

"Please stand to honor your Virtue when I call their name," Asintmah instructed with a smile.

The team seemed giddy, shuffling in their places, awaiting their turn.

"Aquila—the Virtue of vision, speed, and victory." Asintmah's hand opened in the direction of the six-winged eagle, poised to snatch prey with its talons. Declan stood quickly, his wings shooting from his back, causing a burst of air to blow the team up from their seats.

"S-Sorry," he stammered, embarrassment flushing his cheeks as he sat back down.

"Orion—Virtue of grace, vigilance, and determination." Asintmah smiled as she motioned to the charging stag with magnificent antlers—a crown for the king of the forest. Thomas Thexton took his turn to stand, flashing a joker's grin.

"Ursa—Virtue of strength, power, and benevolence." Asintmah pointed to the Bear Virtue and River stood briefly, a frost poppy clamped between his hands in prayer position over his heart.

"Lyncis—the Virtue of truth, stealth, and solitude." The team looked to the Lynx and Major Michael Gunner stood with a nod at his Virtue, followed by a marine Aspen had just fought at the solstice celebration.

His name was Sergeant Levi Zalman; she'd known of him prior to arriving in Kore. He had made quite a name for himself in his birth country, Israel, as one of the best Krav Maga fighters. All she'd done when she had trained there was try to beat his technical stats, but six months of training had nothing on his lifetime's worth. In fact, the only reason she'd taken part in that fun little battle earlier had been to fight *him*. His dark brown hair was beautifully coiffed and his amber eyes were distinctly lynx-like. His distinguished features bore a no-nonsense expression, and he was overly formal and indifferent as he glanced at his Virtue.

"Vulpes—the Virtue of ingenuity, agility, and adaptability." Asintmah pointed toward the Fox. Vox jumped up excitedly with a swish of her cotton-candy tresses. Mackenzie brushed the captain's side as she stretched up into a standing position, touching her shoulder in a sensuous manner.

"Lykaion—the Virtue of loyalty, guardianship, and spirit."

When nobody stood, Thomas Thexton nudged the captain.

"That's you, dear," Asintmah said.

He stood briefly, and the others smiled at him.

"Psst." River tapped Aspen on the knee. Everybody was now staring at her.

"Will you not honor your Virtue, Sergeant?" Ansel asked.

Her focus was directed solely at the general, her voice tight. "No thanks."

"We must have confused her with all the loyalty, guardianship, and spirit talk," Levi jeered.

Aspen chuckled, flashing her top fangs at him. Vox sensed the attack before it manifested, pleading with her violet eyes for Aspen to stop.

Aspen's conniving grin disappeared. She rolled her eyes and stood stubbornly before sitting back on the log. It was plain on the justices' faces that they were furious about her threatening another marine on sacred ground, and there was a long pause as Justice Asintmah waited for the attention of the team to return to her.

"I'd like to take a moment to honor your general, and a dear friend of mine, who founded the Anima Corps and brought us together from our separate species. General Winters, you are our symbol of unity and peace. We could not have anyone more worthy to lead us."

The team and the justices clapped enthusiastically, and River crowed so loud that it echoed across the plains over the lake. Ansel showed his gratitude with a thin-lipped smile.

"Thank you, thank you." He waved down their cheering. "But no greater deed have I done than the deeds of our Virtues. Tonight, as we commemorate the summer months in our homeland of Kore, I will share with you their mysteries. For the stars have stories, and your Anima has memories... and it is only when we are together in this way that they will collide."

Every marine and justice was silent, gazing at him, transfixed.

"Tonight will be a story I have never shared. The story of Lykaion."

Mackenzie gasped as if he had spoken of some controversial gossip. Vox made a silent clapping movement.

River seemed perplexed as he said, "General, I have never come across any texts of Lykaion. Why is that?"

The general looked into the blazes of the bonfire, as if the answers lay within it. "The answer to that is quite simple—of all the Anima, Lykaion is the most misunderstood, and responsible for some of the greatest invisible acts of power in our history." As he took in their sunken expressions, he added, "While the other Virtues all did great things in their own right, Lykaion led them to victory and was the first to become Absolute. After their victory against the primeval demons, Lykaion's Absolution became so powerful it broke the fabric of its soul."

Vox crossed her arms in front of her and replied, "Are you saying Lykaion died?"

"Lykaion experienced a death of sorts, yes…" Ansel raised his staff and angled it toward the bonfire. At the top of the flames, he demonstrated the story. For the first time, Aspen straightened.

Ansel created a perfectly circular fireball and the team watched it, mesmerized. "But only to be reborn into a new form."

They watched as the fireball split into two separate entities. Sergeant Thexton blurted out, "I don't get it… Now it's balls?"

Declan made an explosive sound as he choked back a

laugh. The two fireballs morphed into running wolves and an eerie howl escaped the flames.

"Two wolves, Sergeant Thexton," Ansel answered.

Thex leaned back on the log, stretching his legs out and crossing them over his ankles. "Well, that makes more sense…"

"So you're saying that Lykaion is two Virtues?" Vox clarified in amazement.

Ansel nodded as the flames spat.

Aspen ignored the captain's brief glance and crossed her arms over her chest, neither surprised nor fascinated. She remained mute when Vox leaned in to ask her if she'd known about the mystery, keeping her unyielding focus upon Ansel.

"How did this happen, exactly?" River asked.

"Around ten thousand BC, there was a war we refer to as the War of—"

"Primes," River finished.

Ansel nodded. "Archdemons had completely taken over. They ravaged the Earth, killing innocent civilians, impregnating women, abducting children. It almost destroyed humanity. The Virtues were the only force powerful enough to guard and defend. It is considered the greatest war in Anima history, and its catastrophic effects carried on long after it was over. Lykaion generated a power so unfathomable that it changed Earth's biology."

They were all leaning in now, hanging on Ansel's every word.

"Two things happened that day… Lykaion's metamorphosis, and the passageways into the Earth from the lesser planes—which we know as IOs—redirecting to come through Kore, and only Kore."

"Wait, so you're saying Lykaion turned Kore—our sacred land, literally heaven on Earth—into a hellgate?" Mackenzie asked.

"That is correct." Justice Calais stood swiftly, his tawny barn owl wings folded behind him in the shape of a heart. His pointed features were more severe in the bonfire's glow as he looked around the circle with deep brown eyes. "Before the War of Primes, Kore was pristine and untouched by darkness. Lykaion's sacrifices changed the dynamic of the planet, saving humanity… but in the process, made Kore a permanent surrogate so that Earth would be rid of the demons."

The marines processed this until Justice Silla Borealis broke the silence. He had River's raven-colored hair, but it was cropped at his shoulders, and although his skin was weatherbeaten, Aspen knew he'd been even more handsome in his prime days of war. "The need to call upon Special Forces has never been so vital as the times we find ourselves in now. The legend of Lykaion was retold tonight because, on that fateful day, Lykaion battled against an unknown entity. Something so ominous it came from the belly of hell itself."

Justice Silla delivered the latter part of his warning while looking directly at his son, as if the responsibility rested upon River alone.

"Worse than an archdemon?" Declan asked.

Justice Silla nodded gravely. "Much, much worse."

Vox reached down and placed a hand on River's

shoulder protectively—or as a silent plea toward his father, perhaps. She asked in a small voice, "What was it?"

General Winters looked over them all as a concerned father would. "We do not know what it was. We have reincarnated many times after that era and we have no record, no memory. We know the stories of victory because they are preserved in the underground caves of Kore. All that is shown of this entity is a being, painted in black. But the interesting thing is that it was as if someone tried to erase the image of the entity after it was drawn. We have had teams analyze the ancient caves, but unfortunately, we aren't able to make it out."

Vox shivered. "Ugh… It just gives me chills."

"For now, you must begin your training assessments. We will inform you when we have more intel," advised Justice Calais.

Justice Chaska straightened her round orange glasses upon her narrow face. Her hair, white as first snowfall, draped over both shoulders as she dug into her silken robes and pulled out a Phaedra—the key to the Anima Corps— and called the captain to accept it as a symbol of unity.

As the captain stood, Aspen used this as her cue to leave. She swung her legs over the log, feeling River's quick tap goodbye on her bare foot before she began walking in the opposite direction of the solstice celebration and the statues of the Virtues. She ignored Asintmah softly calling her name, but halted with her back to the elder when a curling velvety fern hugged around her upper arm.

"You have suffered great loss, my daughter. I hope you will someday forgive me that I was not present to hold you in your time of grief. But I have never been happier to see you rejoin your people, to fight on the same side."

Aspen turned, a snarl upon her lips. She ripped her arm from Asintmah's ferny embrace, snapping the tendrils, which dropped lifelessly to the ground. "The only reason I'm here is to kill whatever escaped the IO. You asking for forgiveness only shows me how weak you've become. And don't talk to me about old sentiments, because I feel nothing!"

"I will never believe that, child." Asintmah's voice was thick with sadness.

In the melodic, foreboding voice she reserved for the moment before a kill, Aspen crooned, "The only reason they're dead is because of you. We will never be on the same side."

Asintmah blinked, tears splashing onto her bronze cheeks.

"Aspen, what are you doing?"

River approached her with a wince, waiting for her to answer. She noticed now that the team had been watching the entire time.

She sheathed her fangs beneath her lips and looked upon Asintmah's face once more in disgust. Her hair caught the breeze as she spun, nothing but a silken stream of death as she bounded into the dark forest.

Ryder was sure that the distance he'd created between himself, the Anima Special Operatives, and the Justices was enough to sneak away unnoticed. Major Michael Gunner explained that he would escort Ryder to his cabin, but he had to stay hidden.

The hair on his arms stood on end, a rupture of ice from deep within flooding his whole body. He shot over the river, barely skimming the rocks he'd leveraged for higher leaps, until he reached the seclusion of the other side. The forest was darker here, midnight-looking. The trees stood dense and close, and although he could hear birds, they were miles away.

He didn't venture further; he just needed somewhere to hide until he could stop shaking. He trembled violently against a pine tree, his teeth chattering as he hugged his arms. He turned his head toward the river to see if Thex had wandered back to look for him, and to his relief, he hadn't. Ryder watched the orange glaze over the river, cast by the summer sun that wouldn't set until fall… at least, that was what Vox had told him earlier.

With shaking fingers, Ryder inspected his new ID tag that Justice Chaska had called a Phaedra, squinting to refocus his long-distance sight. He swiped a thumb over the glass-like tag with a golden spiral set in the center. His name was engraved on the edges with a new military number, his birthdate, and at the end—*Wolf.*

He lingered on the word, chills still prickling him like he'd jumped into an ice bath. He looked down at his hands to make sure they had ceased shaking before heading back over the river. He was one of the only Wolves left in a world where they were misunderstood. He'd seen Aspen Lovetta's Anima when she'd saved him that morning. That White Wolf had been a constant in his life, forever living in his dreams and leading him out of the darkness of the hellgate. But today she was real. Not a figment of his imagination or some coping mechanism—*real.*

Ryder wasn't going to sit around waiting for the Corps to give him the intel. He suspected a certain redhead knew more than she was letting on with her *I've been estranged from the Corps* routine.

And he had a plan to test whether he was right.

CHAPTER 7

At just past oh nine hundred hours, the Corps was bustling. Aspen's Phaedra opened the double glass doors from the training field into DFAC. She walked briskly, ignoring the marines she passed who recognized her—she could hear them whispering *"Hellfire"* under their breath. She had a private mission to fulfil, and only a small window of time to pull it off.

DFAC had high ceilings and a buffet-style arrangement with a line as long as any tourist attraction. The food smelled sensational, and Aspen's stomach growled as she scanned the room, spotting Vox sitting down with her tray alongside River, who was already halfway through his loaded breakfast plate. Aspen slid onto the naturally shaped wooden bench that matched the tables, leaning on her forearms, using her hair as a veil to conceal her face.

"You know it doesn't work, you hiding like that—they can *smell* that it's you." River's voice was muffled by a mouthful of bacon.

"If she wasn't such a mystery and actually showed up to her drills and ate with all the rest of us, it wouldn't be 'the Hellfire show' on the odd occasion that she does appear," Vox said as she took a bite of the egg that sat atop her two fluffy pancakes. River's mouth went slack as he hovered across Vox's plate, asking where she'd gotten the pancakes.

Aspen shrugged. "I don't jump hoops and do circus tricks." She stole River's toast from his plate the moment he was preoccupied. River rolled his eyes but allowed it.

Aspen couldn't place the last time they'd all sat at breakfast like this... It had to have been years ago, as cadets. She forced the memory down with each scratchy piece of toast lathered with butter. *Cadets...*

All that had transpired during the fall of Fort Gippsland, where they had attended their last year of cadets, had been a catalyst for who she was today—why she was known by the masses as the woman akin to the fire of hell... The only ones who knew the truth sat at this very table.

"Is something wrong?"

River's question snapped her out of her daze. "What?"

He gave her a probing look, but she was saved by Vox directing their attention to a door to their left. "Look, it's Captain Everett! You know, I went through basic drills with him and Gunner this morning... His strength exceeded the Wolf records—like, it was Bear-category power. And his tracing ability? I've never seen anybody trace as fast as him."

Aspen saw River bite the inside of his cheek, studying

Vox, then her, as the captain strode in with a growing entourage. They watched as he sat at a far table with Mackenzie, a friend of Mackenzie's whose name Aspen didn't know, and Thex. The captain was mostly concealed from view by the people stopping to speak to him.

"Well, well, look who decided to mingle with the rabble."

Aspen looked up at the marine who had her knee propped up on the bench, blocking Aspen's view of the captain. Her blonde hair was shaved on both sides with sweeping bangs that framed her white-spotted gray irises.

Aspen grinned back at her. "Ten."

Lance Corporal Tenille Edwards sat down beside Aspen. Lance Corporal Nia Colson joined them, too, sliding off her military blouse as she sat on River's other side. She greeted everyone before tilting her head at Aspen in a tentative way. That look, combined with the tight smile she flashed, intended to hide the tension between Nia and Aspen that had accumulated over many years. Nia worked in Fox Division as the editor-in-chief of the *Anima Corps Observer*. She had been the columnist who'd written the very pieces that made Hellfire infamous. The stories, truth or fiction, all came from Nia.

She slapped a folded newspaper onto the middle of the table and beamed at them all. "I was up all night writing the last piece about the captain's arrival before it hit the printers this morning."

Ten glanced about. "So, who are we scouting?"

"The illuminating arrival of the new captain," River groaned, looking at the newspaper with a sulky expression.

Ten flashed a taunting smile. "What's wrong, River,

baby? You already comparing the circumference of your biceps?"

He raspberried his lips in response.

Nia watched the captain with admiration. "The guy has serious Hercules vibes."

"What do *you* think, Hell?" Ten asked.

"Hmm?"

"C'mon, you have to admit…" Nia ran a hand over the coarse curls that formed a perfect ball atop her head as they all glanced over at Ryder. "To say he's easy on the eyes is the understatement of the century."

Aspen looked back into the glass of orange juice she had taken from Vox and mumbled, "Please. He's overconfident, intrusive, and… too tall."

"Height and surety? They're the best insults Hellfire can come up with?" River scowled, making Ten smirk.

"And that dark blond hair… like butterscotch." Vox smacked her lips together.

Ten chuckled before leaning a little closer to Aspen, muttering through her hair, "I mean, a new Wolf in the territory, a new captain to take orders from… You don't have an opinion on any of this?"

"This isn't my territory, and I don't take orders from anybody," Aspen replied bluntly. Ten threw her hands up in defeat.

Aspen had met Lance Corporal Tenille Edwards at Fort Gippsland in her first year of cadet training. At the time, Ten had been in a relationship with another young Fox like herself—Tlalli. Aspen had had to carry Tlalli's dead body a three-hour distance back to base after a Volucer demon—a winged demon—dropped her from the night sky. Ten hadn't quite been the same ever since; it was as if the Anima glow inside of her had burned out. She was better at hiding it in larger groups.

"There's my wee lass." Declan approached, surprising Vox by putting his arms around her. She kissed his cheek in response. River and Vox shifted for him to sit between them. Declan looked awkwardly at Aspen. "Top of the morning, Hell—I mean, Aspen."

Aspen had used her access to the labs to hack into the Corps records in the early weeks after her arrival in Kore to make sure she knew everything there was to know about Airman Declan McAndor. He'd been born to an Irish mother and a Scottish father, the last child of three. His mother, who, as a child, had lost both her sister and father in the civil war in Northern Ireland, had fled to Scotland. Declan had grown up in Scotland until he came of age to join the Corps, where he'd excelled in all his air force training.

Aspen had made sure she was in the labs a few times to observe him from the windows that looked out onto the field when he trained, and man, was he *fast*. He could hit speeds of twelve hundred miles per hour *with* his pretty face still intact. And the glasses? The only reason he wore the damned things was because he had a three-hundred-and-forty-degree visual field—he could see you coming, no matter what direction you came from. Wearing the glasses meant he could talk to you without his eyes swiveling to the back of his head during conversation. What Aspen hadn't found was his blind spot, and the only way to do that was to get into combat with him.

Before last night, Declan had been unaware that she and Vox were friends, and Aspen sensed that they'd since had the mortifying conversation about his girlfriend being best friends with a serial killer. That thought, and the giddy feeling of finding his blind spot now, made her smile slyly.

She watched him grow nervous as she greeted him in a low tone. "Always a pleasure to meet Vox's friends."

"Oh, he just looked over here," Nia said, attempting ventriloquy.

Vox turned. "Who? Ryder?"

"Don't look!" Nia hissed.

River shook his head. "It's like I'm reliving high school."

"He's coming over here!" Ten rasped.

Aspen faced the opposite direction, checking the clock that hung high on the wall. She had to leave, now.

She stood to make a quick exit and found herself in front of the captain.

"Leaving so soon?" he asked smoothly.

"No, she's staying a while," Vox blurted out. "Please, take a seat, Captain."

Agitated, Aspen lowered herself and the captain slid in beside her. Vox shot her a warning look: *Don't attack him.*

"So, Captain, how are you liking it here at Anima Corps so far?" River asked.

"It's incredible," he replied, making Vox and Nia smile gleefully. "And please, just call me Ryder."

Aspen straightened her already rigid spine. She schooled her features into neutrality, hiding her alarm. His spellbinding scent enveloped her so completely, it had the power to hook her chin with invisible hands and guide her into the crook of his muscled neck. If she did, she knew she'd experience the full sensation, and by the Virtues, she wanted to… and hated herself for it.

She inhaled again, amber and cedar hitting her like a cold spray against her lungs, a kindling in her abdomen she hadn't known she could feel again. A sigh escaped her lips, the kind of euphoric relief that came from the doors to heaven opening on somebody who had perpetually been locked out.

Slowly and discreetly, she shifted her gaze, looking at him sidelong as he answered questions about his time at the Australian hellgate. He'd angled himself in just the right position to be nearer to her scent, so close that their knees almost touched under the table. If he so much as caught a whiff of *her* scent from this short distance... things would get out of control. She placed a trembling hand over the dagger behind her back, waiting, watching every movement he made.

"Isn't that where you grew up, Hell?" Ten asked.

Aspen did her best to ignore that as Nia continued the constant stream of questioning, now asking where the captain had grown up.

"So what's with you? You don't call, you don't write," Ten muttered close to Aspen's ear. She had clearly hoped she'd ask unnoticed, but the whole table went quiet, the focus now on them.

"I've never called or written to you," Aspen muttered back, incensed that Ten had drawn attention to them.

"Not me, Hell... Her." Ten pointed at Vox.

Vox met her eye awkwardly for a brief moment before Aspen looked down at the glass of orange juice.

"Is that what she's been telling you?" She took a sip, feeling the captain's eyes boring into her on her other side.

River shifted uncomfortably in his seat. "Nice to know I've been a topic of conversation between you."

Vox glared at Ten. "Did you have to open your big mouth?"

"What? I was just voicing what everybody was thinking," Ten argued. "They expect more of you, Hell."

Aspen's lips drew back into a smile that revealed her cuspid teeth, sending Ten shooting up from the bench they shared. Ten clearly expected her to attack, but Aspen turned her back, signifying that the moment was over, so long as Ten stayed the hell away.

Ten's lips formed a thin line, disappointment shining in her gray eyes. "I'll catch you guys later." One last look at Aspen and she took off through the archway leading into the corridor of Deer Division.

River cast Aspen a disapproving look. "Way to kill the mood."

"Maybe you should watch who you trust," Aspen fired back at him and Vox.

"Well, at least I'm trusting somebody." Vox's voice shook as she clutched the edge of the table.

"Alright, both of you, stop it," River interjected.

Declan hid his face with his hand. The captain remained in watchful silence, shooting an empathetic glance at Vox, whose eyes were now glassy.

Aspen clenched her jaw. "I don't have time for this."

She stepped out from the bench and weaved through the long tables to the exit without saying goodbye. She had only a small window to execute her plan. Vox and River may have known about the past, but they understood nothing about the future. Better to keep them disappointed in her than let them in and risk their ranks, or worse, their lives. She would have to deal with them later.

The circular corridors of the Corps were wide and made of natural wood. Aspen avoided eye contact with other marines, especially those of superior rank. There was no time to be saluting; she needed to get to the speed portal as fast as possible.

She stepped into the sphere of spectral light and was transported to Corps headquarters at rocketing speed. She stepped out of the portal and into the glass hallway, certain that even though it was busy, nobody had noticed her.

She stopped directly in front of General Ansel Winters's office. It was unlocked. It had taken her a full week to get into Corps security on the ground floor of headquarters just to make sure this door would be open when she needed it. Aware that she wasn't the most silent of the Anima, she padded across the floor as quietly as she could, careful not to alarm neighboring offices. Another problem was that if someone caught her scent, the game was over.

Ansel's office layout was more like an apartment's. It was spacious and circular, much like the rest of the Corps' design, with a three-hundred-and-sixty-degree view of the Corps. She had to stay in the middle of the room to avoid being spotted by any passers-by who happened to look up while walking the hallways on lower floors of the other divisions.

The glass roofs of the six circular buildings shone like crystal in the morning light. There was a secluded wing to the left where Ansel slept, and along that wall was a small sitting area with cushions embroidered with the Corps insignia. Aspen looked to her right and breathed a sigh of relief. She had found what she was looking for—a tree with delicately twisted branches scaling the wall, Ansel's staff displayed lengthways in the center.

A creaking sound from the door made her start. She whipped around at super-speed, her eyes darting over the room. No other movement and no scent.

When she was confident it was just a breeze from the hallway outside, she walked closer to the pale blue crystal fastened at the top of the staff and caressed it with her fingertips.

"Now, what are you, exactly?" she whispered. The crystal gleamed as she inspected it more closely, touching her nose to it to inhale its chemical composition. She turned away sharply, pinching her nose at the pungent odor. "Ammonia and methane?"

She was zeroed in, focusing on its characteristics, when a tinge of another scent descended upon her. She spun with lightning speed, unsheathing both khukuris from behind her back.

The captain caught her left forearm and right wrist.

"What are you doing?" she whispered.

He let go of her arms. "I was going to ask you the same thing."

She pointed at his chest and sighed in frustration. "You attached your scent to mine when you sat next to me so I wouldn't sense you coming. I'll admit, that's sneaky." She glanced into his blue-fire eyes and hastily looked away. "So you caught me. Go on, Mr. Universe, arrest me for breaking and entering."

"The door was unlocked, so I doubt that it counts as forced entry," he whispered.

She stood back and studied him for a moment.

He nodded to the staff. "What do you want with that thing?"

"I don't know what movies you've been watching, but the villains in real life don't monologue how they fabricated their plans."

"You're not a villain," he stated with surety.

She stared straight into those eyes—*damn him, where did she know them from?*—that told her he believed his words, and scowled. "Don't underestimate me, Captain. All you'll do is offend me."

"I'm not underestimating you, but I do think everybody else is. A villain doesn't acquire not one, but two khukuris handcrafted by the blacksmith who forged the swords for the first King of Nepal without earning his respect." He turned her wrist so that the sword gleamed in the light streaming through the glass walls. His warm hand left a fizzy feeling against her skin. "And that's the largest bend I've ever seen in one of these swords—that's a sign of honor."

Aspen's stomach plummeted. She shook her head at him, speechless for a moment... until she heard her heartbeat growing loud in her chest. She was sure he could hear it too.

"You're wrong," she breathed, taking a step back, realizing their proximity was close enough to be unsafe.

"Am I?"

"Don't come any closer," she warned.

The captain raised both hands in compliance. "Do you think I'm going to hurt you?"

Aspen answered by angling her body lower, closer to a

fighting stance. "How could you possibly know all of this?" One of her khukuris was now pointed at him.

He didn't answer right away. He seemed to be more interested in her left wrist, which was bent back, holding the other khukuri behind her.

"Being observant isn't exactly a superpower, but I'm very good at it... I know that you've trained in Japan, Nepal, and Israel—I'm a trinity marine too."

"Wow, we should start a club."

He flashed a smug grin as he assumed his stance. "I'm going to take that sword out of your hand now."

She chuckled darkly. "You can try."

"Let the games begin."

Aspen attacked first. His hand caught her wrist and he angled the khukuri away from them, kneeing her in the stomach twice. She crouched over from the blows.

"When I said I wasn't going to hurt you, I meant—"

She dug her boot into his shin before planting the handle of the blade into the bottom of his sternum, sending him stumbling back.

"You know what I meant," he wheezed.

"I forgot about your maximum pain threshold thing. I wonder how deep I have to dig to find where it hurts?" Aspen challenged, finding the prospect delicious.

He blocked her punches, his movements as fluid as water. "You know, I never did thank you properly for healing me."

"Never mention it again."

"Shouldn't people know that they've got you all wrong?"

"Ha! They wouldn't believe it anyway."

He dodged her roundhouse kick. "River and Vox do."

"They're different."

They maneuvered quickly around each other, the captain blocking the downward slices of her twin blades until he spun out to create the space he needed to lift himself into the air and fly kick one sword out of her hand. The khukuri cut the air and lodged into Ansel's desk. The captain gritted his teeth as the desk caved into itself from the damage.

"Oops." He grinned, striking the fist that held the other khukuri in an effort to get her to drop the final blade. When it didn't work, Aspen shot him a pitiful expression.

"You surprise me, Captain. You're kind of a rebel."

"You have no idea. I'm more interested to know how you're married. What are you, like, twenty?" He arrested both her arms and squeezed her hand until the other khukuri clattered to the floor, leaving them in a tense entanglement.

"I'm twenty-three, and I haven't seen my husband in over two years." She struggled against his iron grip.

"What's wrong, lovers' quarrel?"

"No. He's dead."

Aspen shoved him off, and they both stood there, panting, as she wiped blood from her lip.

"I'm sorry," the captain said in realization.

"Don't be. He had it coming."

"How do you mean?"

Her arms went slack at her sides. The captain wasn't easy to fight. They were matched in skill, and he had at least sixty pounds of muscle on her. In a fight like this one, she would usually take him out limb by limb, but that proved difficult when your opponent couldn't feel a thing.

"He got tangled up with the underworld. And he died because of it."

"So your whole family dies in the war… and then your husband dies?" The captain furrowed his brow. "Asintmah wasn't kidding when she said you've endured great suffering."

"Look, I don't need your pity." She walked closer to him, tipping her head so they were inches away. "I'm not what they say I am—"

"I know," he breathed.

"No, you don't. I'm worse." She trembled, squaring her shoulders to stop it. "I've done… unspeakable things. In the east, they call me Red Demon, and in the west, they call me Hellfire. You have no idea what I'm capable of."

He didn't flinch. Not one bit. He just watched her in that unyielding way of his.

A creaking sound had both their noses sniffing an approaching scent.

The captain cast his attention to the door. "It's Gunner."

Aspen narrowed her eyes at him suspiciously. "You decoyed."

He shook his head as Gunner walked in with a folder tucked under his arm. The major stopped when he saw them, glancing over at the broken desk, then back.

"What's going on in here?"

"Sir, there's been a development since last night's meeting," the captain began.

"What is it?" Gunner asked, joining them in the center of the office.

"The intel suggests that the demonic entity that escaped piggybacked through the portal during the war, then suddenly went AWOL. All this time you've been searching for a demon… but what if it doesn't have a body?"

Aspen was pulling the sword out of the desk when the whole thing crumpled further inward. Her blood froze.

"We don't have any records anywhere in history of a demon not having a body," Gunner replied, sounding concerned.

Aspen sheathed both blades behind her back. "And as I was just telling the captain, I don't debate war strategies… so just debrief me when there's an arse to kick."

She felt the men watch her until the door clicked shut behind her. She proceeded down the corridor, only relaxing as she stepped into the speed portal, taking a direct route out of the Corps.

All the parts that didn't make sense were like puzzle pieces from different boxes, jumbled up together in a pile of nonsense. What perplexed her most was the mystery of Ansel's staff. She had only ever seen him use it for useful everyday things, like opening dimension portals and simple energy or light manipulations. But what better way to keep something valuable safe than to have it on your person almost every minute of the day? Something in her gut told her there was more to it.

She walked into the forest until the Corps was no longer visible, until she was alone and safe. She didn't want to be here, let alone a part of Special Forces. Now she supposed there wasn't much of a choice—she had to do what she could to take Ansel's staff and pass the captain's upcoming assessment in order to find her answers.

A wave of heat rushed over her skin, making the hair at the base of her neck stand up and goose bumps form on her arms. She tried to push the thought away, placing her hands against her forehead as she looked back in the direction of the Corps. Why did the captain's scent make her feel so nervous?

Vox, Gunner, and the captain were all hovering over Gunner's tablet when Aspen crossed the field, the wet grass brushing against her boots. The Special Operations team had formed a semicircle, awaiting their orders. She placed herself at the end, next to River, brushing his shoulder with hers to bid him good morning.

"It's about time you showed up, Sergeant," Gunner called out, his voice gruffer than usual. "Is there somewhere more important you had to be?"

The captain didn't so much as look in her direction. He took the tablet from Gunner's hands and continued to study it.

Mackenzie crossed her arms over her chest, shifting her weight onto one hip. "She'd much rather spend time with the wolf pack. Don't you think it's suspicious that she can't live in a shared cabin with the rest of us?"

The major tutted. "Speaking without permission, Sergeant Bale."

"I'm the last person you'd want around when you close your eyes to go to sleep." Aspen's venomous sneer was enough to make Mackenzie swallow visibly.

Gunner glowered at her. "That's enough."

The captain handed the tablet to Vox, who started

walking to the opposite side of the field. "Welcome to your first assessment in Special Forces," he said. "We'll be evaluating your combat, tactical skills, ability to complete tasks within timeframe, and strategy. On each of these armbands is a concealed number; remember your own number, then fight your comrades to acquire all five of the others. You do not need to worry about which order the numbers go in—just retrieve them. The assessment is specifically designed so that you combat all of your comrades at least once. Whoever accumulates all the numbers will use them to disarm the bomb in the middle."

"Permission to speak, Major?" Levi asked in his gravelly voice.

"Granted."

"Is this some kind of joke?"

"That's not a real bomb, is it?" Declan's finger was shaking as he pointed at the case on the grass before them, his face pale.

"Captain, this is insane!" Mackenzie argued.

"Oh, come on! It'll be fun!" River swung a playful punch into the air.

"No weapons, just your powers," Captain Everett stated, ignoring their banter.

"Guess you better sit this one out, Lovetta," jeered Levi.

Aspen dropped her scabbard onto the grass. "I don't need these to declaw you… cat."

"I can't take on all five of them at once," Declan confessed.

"T-minus ten minutes and counting until that bomb goes off! What are you all waiting for? Go!" the captain ordered, his arms spread wide.

Hesitantly, the team spread out on the field. "What part of 'start with a drill' didn't you understand?" Aspen heard Gunner mutter to the captain, who grinned in response.

Aspen watched as each marine put as much distance between themselves and the bomb as possible. All she heard was the sound of Declan's wings beating and the air rushing upward as he left the ground. The captain observed their movements and the alliances they formed to get ahead. As Levi and Mackenzie took on Declan and River, deep tremors in the ground from Mackenzie's leaps sent Aspen stumbling. The slashing sounds of Levi's claws made her hyperaware, like they were coming from right beside her.

Thex's dark stare found her first. The magnificent crown of antlers atop his head was ready to charge at her as he assumed a sprinter's stance. He produced tree roots that curled up out of the ground; she flipped over them as they swiped at her legs. They came faster and faster, like gigantic whips, until Thex predicted where she'd move next. She jumped straight into the swinging root. He imprisoned her, enclosing more branches around her to form a cage as he raised her higher above the ground, making her stomach lurch.

She ground her jagged teeth against the smaller vines and plummeted down, landing on her feet. The second Thex had enough distance, he charged at her with his saber-sharp antlers. They collided viciously in front of the captain, who stood watching them with his arms folded. Aspen wrestled Thex by his antlers, shock clear on his face as he staggered before she pinned him to the ground. She ripped off the cover of his armband—*2*.

Levi's claws, fully extended, were ten knives slashing

at her. He grew more frustrated every time he missed her—amber eyes burning; the lines on his forehead standing out under his coiffed hair, which now had tiny pieces falling out of place. She continued to dodge him until they moved within earshot of the major and the captain's conversation.

"Some things you need to understand about *her*," Gunner was saying. "Don't be blindsided by the pretty face—she is *always* waging a war, and one day it could be against you. She doesn't care about anybody except herself."

"You giving me a safety brief, Major?" The captain's upper lip curled in amusement.

"All I'm saying is, the war ruined her, now her judgment's fried. You're both Wolves… At some point, you'll have to initiate some dominance, make her conform that way."

Aspen fly kicked Levi, her boot connecting with the side of his head. He fell to the ground, unconscious—*8.*

Aspen surveyed the rest of the marines. Declan had puncture wounds on his arms and chest from River's claws. Mackenzie shook the ground as she landed from one of her leaps just before Thex could roll out of the way. Declan hovered, his wings creating a large shadow overhead, brewing a hellacious storm. Aspen and the others had to shield themselves from the force. It was obvious how Eagles could win a battle with little effort. Declan had clear passage to reach any of the marines quickly, and the force of his wings immobilized them.

Aspen saw Vox gasp in horror at the same moment she sensed the whizzing of a blade through the air. She released a steadying breath and twisted her body high off the ground, her legs expertly spiraling as she kicked the flying combat knife, changing its direction and aiming the shot to trim

Thex's cheek instead. It flew past him, leaving a small cut close to his ear. Aspen's boots slammed into the field and she shot a deadly glare at the thrower—the captain. He'd been testing her. She trusted her answering message had been clear: *Come for my friend and I'll come for yours.*

"Now you've pissed her off," Gunner told the captain.

The challenge in the captain's shadow of a grin made her smell blood, taste blood. She whirled around. Declan and River were taking down a now conscious Levi, but Declan changed his focus, torpedoing into Thex. He bowled Thex over, then flapped his gigantic wings to climb above them all.

"Aspen, no!" Vox yelled hoarsely.

She sprinted. Her boots dug into River's shoulders, using his body to catapult herself through the air, her arms stretching out and catching Declan's foot. He tried to shake her off, but she climbed to the center of his back between his wings faster than Declan could bend down to detach her. Everybody below stopped fighting and watched as Declan bucked his wings and tried to reach behind him, but Aspen was quick to evade him.

"Aspen, that's too far! Please stop!" Declan pleaded before he flew up into the clouds.

She laughed as the team became nothing but specks on the ground.

Ryder tried to catch sight of them weaving between the clouds above. "She'll fall."

"Is that what you're worried about?" Gunner protested.

"There they are!" River pointed.

Declan was struggling miles above them—dipping, flailing, and turning in the air with Aspen attached to his back. His scream pierced the sky.

"Is somebody going to stop her?" Mackenzie demanded.

Vox looked dismayed as she announced, "She's going to make him HALO."

"He's done for," declared Levi, rubbing his face.

"Send some other Eagles up there," Ryder urged Gunner, who was scowling up at Aspen with his arms folded.

"I'm not sacrificing more marines," he answered sternly.

Ryder shielded his eyes from the sun as he looked up. Aspen pulled Declan's wings back, hard, plunging him into a free fall.

Vox hid her face. "I can't watch."

"Five thousand feet," Ryder heard a marine behind him say. He realized a crowd had formed around them.

"Two thousand," said another.

Declan drew close enough to the ground for Ryder to see that his skin was pale and his eyes were closed; he was unconscious. Seconds before impact, Aspen pulled back his monstrous wings and they sailed to the ground, tumbling in a heap of sprawled limbs and feathers.

Aspen somersaulted and stood in one swift movement, her expression proud, challenging. "What?" She motioned at Ryder. "He said no weapons."

Vox's cheeks were wet with tears. She balled her fists as a horrifying raspy scream blasted through the field, ripping through the folds of the ether and into their plane of existence. The sound of a screaming Fox—her aggrieved

Anima—shook Ryder through to his bones, as if he'd awoken in fright from a terrible nightmare.

He tore his focus away from Vox just in time to see Aspen's arrogant grin fall from her features. With River in tow, Vox turned and ran to Declan in despair, sobbing as she turned him over, other medics now rushing through the field to his side. By the time Gunner ordered Aspen to his office in a deadly tone, she was watching from afar as her friends, with their backs turned to her, tended to Declan's corpse-like body.

Aspen turned to follow Gunner back to his office. Ryder folded his arms and glared at her, but she shouldered him hard as she walked past, wearing a mocking smile reserved only for him.

CHAPTER 8

"Mandofun—do you even remember what that is since you took up residence on the Australian IO?" Thex asked Ryder as they walked through the hollowed tree trunk hallways of the Corps.

"Where do you have your mandofun if there are no towns to visit?"

"We got the bars built in, brother."

"Seriously?" Ryder asked. They had just finished eating baked salmon with summer green vegetables in DFAC and were walking the longer route through Bear Division to their destination.

"No, but some of the marines make booze," Thex disclosed.

"Like that stuff I drank on solstice?" Ryder recalled the honey-pine taste.

"Ha! That's what we drink when Gunner's watching. Speaking of—what happened to Hellfire? Did she get kicked off the team?"

"I don't know. I haven't heard anything since the incident with Dec," Ryder replied. It had been four days since the assessment and he had continued other drills with the team, but Aspen hadn't turned up to any of them.

"It would be the right thing to do, you know."

"Hmm?"

"To let her go," Thex clarified. "They practically brought her here in a straitjacket. The woman's a psychopath."

"Aspen Lovetta is a lot of things, but a psychopath isn't one of them," Ryder assured him.

Thex gaped at his friend in disbelief. "You're on a first-name basis with the serial killer?"

"Well, technically, she's never called me by my name… but I just know that she isn't."

"Right. So if you know her so well, what *is* she like?"

"I didn't say I know her well, but to describe her… Diabolical. And she's smart; she executes her own missions, and I've heard her use anatomical terms like she's studied med or something."

"Great, so we've got the real-life Dexter on our hands. That's a whole new level of ruthlessness." Thex shivered. "Gunner warned us that the war made her reckless."

Ryder raised his brows. "Yeah, she comes with a lot of warnings, but when I threw that knife at Vox the other day… Did you see how she stopped it? That move she did? The skill and precision that takes…" He gave a low whistle. "Sensei Kaito taught me that move in my last days in Japan."

"It's a healthy kind of relationship when you're throwing knives in her direction," Thex replied.

"Yeah, but that's my point… How can she be careless when she stopped fighting in an environment where a bomb was about to go off to protect her friend? Nah, she did that out of loyalty."

Thex's mouth dropped open. "Do you hear yourself?" he groaned. "Ry… tell me you're not doing what I think you're doing."

"That all depends on what you think I'm doing…"

"You haven't got a thing for her, have you?" Thex stared at him, motionless.

"No…"

"Because she's married," he went on.

"She's widowed," Ryder clarified.

"What? Where did you hear that?"

"She told me."

"She told you?"

Ryder nodded, leaning against the wall next to the door they were about to walk through.

"How did he die? Or a better question—who killed him?"

"You think she took him out?" Ryder mused.

"Her infamous murderer of a husband just turns up dead because of 'the underworld'. Said from the mouth of the underworld itself?"

Ryder thought for a moment.

"Yeah… That's some messed-up black widow shit," Thex went on. "And Ry… executing her own missions? If she's on the team, she needs to be executing *your* missions, listening to *you*. She needs to be looking out for a brother or a sister, and honestly… I don't think she's capable of that. I'm starting to wonder why Ansel put her on the team in the first place."

Thex pushed the door open to the crowded common room. It was designed like a large winter cabin with round tables where marines were sitting, many playing card games. There was a buzz of chatter over the beat of modern music. The volume was on the brink of being uncomfortable, and Ryder had to cover his ears a moment to adjust.

Mackenzie spotted them instantly and led them to a table where drinks were being mixed. Ryder tried the first thing they put in front of him in a shot glass. It was rather bitter, and he was impressed with the strength.

Mackenzie passed him a glazed cherry, giggling at his sour expression. "You're meant to have these straight after."

"It's called Devil's Fireballs," Thex said, putting two cherries in his own mouth. Mackenzie offered Ryder another, but he declined.

The circle grew tighter as more of Mackenzie's friends gathered. The smell of alcohol and marines, each scent different, swirled together, making Ryder lightheaded. He noticed Levi sitting one seat down, but Levi ignored him, flaunting an unimpressed disposition.

Another marine sat between them and introduced himself as Levi's partner, Zuri Balogun, a Deer Anima who was graceful and open as he tamed the awkwardness between Ryder and Levi. Zuri was from Nigeria and had moved to Kore when he'd changed his military operations specialty from frontline to intel.

Ryder moved to let Thex stand up to speak with other

Deer Anima. Mackenzie took Thex's seat and leaned in close.

"Pretty thrilling assessment, Ryder. Are you always such a risk-taker?"

"I just do what I have to do to prepare the team." He leaned back slightly, noticing that she didn't care.

"Hmm, I bet." Mackenzie's back curved as she inched closer so that her scent was overpowering him.

Ryder cleared his throat. "You deactivated that bomb in record time. I didn't even see you accumulate the whole password."

"Oh, I didn't. I tipped the gears and did it manually." She smiled coyly.

"That's pretty impressive," Ryder admitted.

"But wait… there's more."

They both laughed light-heartedly. "Is that right, ma'am?" he answered, glancing casually about the common room.

"Am I not able to keep your undivided attention, Captain?"

"I didn't say that," he replied nonchalantly.

He saw Vox enter the busy common room, twisting her fingers self-consciously. Two marines stumbled past her and she had to jump out of the way to avoid being bowled over.

Ryder pretended he couldn't hear Mackenzie call after him when she asked where he was going. Vox looked relieved when she saw him.

"Oh, good, you're here."

"You look lovely," he commented. She was wearing a white floral dress and sandals and she gave him a grateful smile. "How's Dec today?" he asked.

"He's much better, but he can't have anyone accidentally knocking his wings, and this is too crowded."

Ryder nodded sympathetically. "Did you get any more intel from the analysts tracking the threat?"

Vox sighed. "We've got nothing. It's like it's hiding, or waiting. It's making my stomach churn. I mean, we don't even know what it wants. As soon as demons arrive here, they start trouble straight away. This one is just... ghosting."

Ryder was thoughtful for a moment before Vox caught on.

"What?"

"Ghosting. Something that was living, that previously had a demonic body but doesn't anymore."

Vox nodded. "Gunner mentioned your hypothesis of the threat being an Obscuritas demon."

Ryder had already read the *Basic Handbook of Kore Demonology* by Cathan O'Sullivan cover to cover, the first on his long reading list. His first experience with the demons in Kore had sparked a hunger to delve straight into battle strategy. He already had formulas for supremacy for just over half of the demons outlined in the book, and all were compellingly different to the Corps' current strategies—Vox was in for a treat.

"No, something completely different. Think about it. We haven't been catching it on heat signatures... Intel is looking for species we know of, but what if we haven't dealt with whatever this is before?"

Vox's violet eyes widened. "So if it was previously living, then where?"

They brainstormed possibilities, but it proved to be a dead-end question.

Ryder broke their pensive silence. "Have you seen her?"

"No." Vox exhaled, knowing exactly who he was asking about. "You'd think she'd come and apologize. You know— 'Sorry, Vox, I had one of my berserk tunnel-vision killer moments and hurt your boyfriend. And while I'm on an apology streak, sorry for completely forgetting about you for almost two years.'"

Ryder remained quiet as Vox found her composure and sighed heavily.

"You know, the last time I saw her, she had just come back from Nepal. She hadn't seen Maxen in months."

"Who's Maxen?"

"AKA Hurricane, her husband. Believe me, that piece of work is another story altogether." She huffed. "Anyway, she turns up at Fort Gippsland just before we got stationed here in Kore and tells me she did what she'd set out to do and wanted to do fieldwork." Vox's lips twitched. "And River and I waited at the carrier. We held them up as long as we could, but she never showed."

Ryder tried to remain casual. "What happened after that?"

"She disappeared for a few months, and then she was everywhere... Ansel spent so much time on damage control: covering up media coverage of her kills, deploying troops to try to catch her, and having to tell their families they were dead when she killed them. It went on like that for months, and then..."

"And then they caught her?"

"Caught? I think she turned herself in. I think whatever happened with Maxen was the end of whatever mission she was on."

Ryder watched Vox sigh again, his spine straightening in realization. "Until she realized it wasn't the end."

Vox studied him. "How do you mean?"

"Do you know why she would want to steal Ansel's staff?"

Vox thought for a moment. "You caught her doing this?"

Ryder nodded. "What's that thing on the end of the staff, that blue frozen liquid crystal?"

Vox's posture straightened too. "I have no idea."

They stood frozen for a moment before Vox slapped her knee.

"Aspen has a locked file drawer in my lab."

"What for?"

"She undertook various studies over the years dating back to cadet training, and Ansel never took away her basic access to Anima Corps, so she had access to education even when she went AWOL. She's studied many science disciplines, from anatomy to astronomy—she even finished medical training."

"Which has to do with her healing powers."

Vox almost said something, then apparently changed her mind. She raised a finger at him. "If she asks, you worked that out on your own. I absolutely didn't tell you about those powers."

He shrugged. "She already knows that I know."

"Well, Aspen may be what she is, but she isn't mindless. Recently she's been training herself to identify rare elements, and she's had a particular interest in elements that don't exist on Earth."

"How would she know what they are if they don't exist on this planet?" Ryder asked, confused.

Vox sighed heavily. "I don't know."

"Can't you just read her research?"

"She's written it all in a different language, and I don't know or trust anyone enough to show them something like this."

"Which language?"

"Japanese—what are you smiling at?" Vox asked when Ryder grinned.

"You trust me, don't you?"

"You can read Japanese?" she asked, shocked.

Ryder shrugged. "Read it, speak it, write it—just tell me what you need me to do."

Vox clapped her hands together. "Fantastic! But they've closed access to the labs for tonight—not fantastic."

"And they have us doing the other team assessment tomorrow morning, and FYI, it's happening at zero stupid thirty," Ryder added.

"I'm sure it will be as good as melted chocolate in a warm croissant." Vox's smile reached her eyes, and Ryder couldn't help but smile too.

"How about tomorrow afternoon?" he offered as he stood up.

Vox stood too. "Meet you there."

"I'm racking out. I'll see you bright and early."

He left the common room before anybody could object and walked straight from Bear Division to the lake, skirting the banks back to his cabin. He was pensive as the golden rays of midnight sun doused the turquoise waters. The light over Kore was dim, making him sleepy, but he couldn't help indulging the notion that there was more to Aspen's story. It was clear that Ansel knew something about her that the others didn't. And if this was all a well-kept secret, how was Gunner involved? Ryder was going to get to the bottom of it.

A formula was being uncovered in his mind as he reached his cabin and unlaced his boots on the porch steps. He held his hand over the lock on his front door and it opened, reading his prints and power signature. Ryder predicted a recon mission looming, and everything was banking on this assessment going right—and on *her* showing up.

CHAPTER 9

The next morning Ryder woke at oh three hundred hours, dressed in his greens, and ran at the fastest speed he could muster to the Corps entry. He smiled at his wristwatch, which read one hundred and eighty miles per hour. He took a speed portal to the Special Ops debriefing room located in Lynx Division. He had reached the panel on the computer and was buzzing every member of the team just as Major Michael Gunner arrived.

"I trust you have something a little more suitable for an assessment this time, Captain, not another excuse for daredevilry."

"Well, Major, it all depends on what you consider daredevilry."

"Good grief."

They looked up as Declan and Thex arrived together.

"Are you sure you should be here, Airman?" Ryder asked as Declan stood at attention before him.

"I'm sick of lying down in the hospital wing, Captain."

Ryder looked him over before conceding. "If you insist."

Vox entered with her tablet. She'd had time to braid a headband into her hair and tie it back into a high ponytail. "I've been up for hours. I barely slept." She yawned, taking her place next to Declan.

Levi and Mackenzie dashed in simultaneously in a flurry of colorful glow.

"Really? Zero stupid thirty… for an assessment?" Levi complained as Mackenzie began stretching beside him.

Everyone sensed her moments before she arrived. Aspen walked in slow, silent strides, looking mildly aggravated at all the eyes upon her. Declan grimaced and shifted nervously. They waited in awkward silence until River arrived at last.

"Great, Sleeping Beauty's here," Ryder announced. "We can start the debrief—Major?"

Major Gunner stood on the raised floor and began pacing. "Today will be your final assessment demonstrating specialist skills and tactical field knowledge before we proceed for future deployment of missions. Whatever Captain Everett has planned, I'm sure you're in for a treat." Gunner nodded for Ryder to continue.

Ryder stood with his arms folded over his chest, his glare making it obvious that he was unimpressed. "The wounded airman arrived first, so the rest of you must have your OPTEMPO set to pathetically slow. I saw most of you moving faster in the common room last night… Well, now that you're here, the map on the screen has the location of the assessment."

"I know where that is. That's on the border of Lynx territory." River pointed to the borderline on the map.

"No, it isn't," Levi spat. "It's *before* the Selendont Ranges."

Declan gave them both a quizzical look. "Naw, see the curve in the river? That's right next to those yellow fields *behind* the ranges."

Mackenzie rolled her eyes. "I've never heard of yellow fields in Kore."

Sensing the air becoming zappy, the group turned their attention back to Ryder.

"You finished?" He glanced from one marine to the other. They remained silent. "No, really, I don't want to interrupt whatever this is…"

"Geez, touchy this morning," Levi muttered.

"Your mission is to work together as a team to get from here"—Ryder pointed at the starting point closest to base—"to here." He drew a line with his finger to the endpoint on the border of Lynx territory. River made a fist in celebration and Levi scoffed.

Thex broke his dutiful silence. "But Ry, that's almost twenty miles of treacherous terrain."

"You'd better be fast," Ryder replied.

"And that pocket is… crawling with demons." Mackenzie sounded short of breath.

Levi squinted at her questioningly, then turned to Ryder. "There's usually a battalion stationed there, not just six marines."

"Lucky you're not just any old marines."

"Why do we need to do this assessment while you get to be captain just like that?"

"You want me to hold your hand, Sergeant?" Ryder replied.

Levi's lips formed a tight line in response.

Ryder leaned in, staring directly into his defiant amber eyes. "I can't hear you."

There was a pause before he replied, "Negative, Captain."

"Move out!" Ryder ordered. He glimpsed Aspen's smirk as he passed her on his way out the door.

They geared up in Eagle Division as one of the load-masters in the hangar assured Gunner they were ready for deployment. Airman McAndor was captain of the flight and was debriefed along with an Eagle co-pilot, Airman Arianne Garner, on the weight distribution and flight path. The team boarded the transport glider for the hour-long flight as Gunner moved to the back of the hangar—he was to meet them at the second checkpoint.

The team was quiet for most of the journey. River looked like he'd been hit with a tranquilizer gun, sleeping with his mouth open. Aspen sat directly across from Ryder. A staring contest was taking place, a wager of who would yield first. Her dangerous smile left a smoldering impression along his spine. He bit the inside of his cheek and she looked away when he showed no sign of discomfort.

Thex nudged River awake as the back door of the aircraft started to open. Before Ryder could say anything, Aspen dove gracefully off the edge.

"Show-off," Mackenzie mumbled.

"After Crazy." Thex ushered River forward.

The co-pilot flew the glider back and the team

marveled in quiet appreciation at Declan's lack of need for a parachute.

His landing had Mackenzie charmed. "Next time, I'm falling with you." She flicked her hair, walking onward after the team.

Vox growled, balling her fists at her sides. "I'm going to shove her straight into a—"

"C'mon, lass, that spot's reserved and she knows it." Declan wrapped his wing around her until Ryder couldn't see her anymore.

"Wow, I don't think I've ever been here," Mackenzie marveled, staring at the beautiful sight ahead.

The sunlight was soft across the vast openness of Kore, although it was biting cold. The forest soared before them with narrow white trunks full of brown swirling knots like eyes on their smooth bark. The canopy was bushy with round, bright yellow leaves.

Mackenzie placed her hand on one of the first trunks they passed. "What are these—birch?"

"Nope, quaking aspen." River glanced over as he tied back his long raven hair and leaned in to whisper in Aspen's ear. "Something I'd personally love to see."

She shoved him, but he barely moved. River laughed deviously.

The ground covering was mainly yellow-green grass, but young trees forced them to stick to a winding trail. Ryder trailed behind; the team was waiting for him to officially begin the assessment. None of them were aware that it had already begun.

Aspen signaled for them to stop.

"What is it?" Mackenzie asked.

Aspen spun with her finger to her lips.

Mackenzie threw her hands up in indignation. The others watched as Aspen swept her feet out, bending the grasses in stealth as she proceeded. The team followed suit. Ryder put his arm out to stop Vox from following.

"Don't go in there," he whispered.

She looked back at him, then at the squad, freezing instantly. "Now what?" She gripped her tablet tightly to her chest.

"Now we wait for one of them to notice."

He watched Thex and Levi freeze, then Aspen, then the rest. Thex looked back at Ryder in realization.

"Don't anybody move," he called. Their energy shifted; they were stuck, paralyzed in their balancing positions.

Mackenzie's voice quavered as she said, "The ground is hollow."

A giant mass moved beneath where they stood. Vox gasped and jumped behind Ryder.

"Octopedes," Aspen breathed.

"What? What are those?" Levi asked, panicked.

"Don't ask," River groaned.

"If you'd stopped to get to know the terrain, you'd know exactly what they are," Ryder called, arms folded.

"We're standing on top of an ambush," Aspen told them. She tried to move off her crevice, but the ground moved with her and she froze again.

Declan's wings spanned out and he rose off the ground, sailing to a further point adjacent to the squad. He landed as lightly as he could.

"Wishing I had a pair of wings about now," Thex muttered.

The ground imploded as monstrous legs shot out from the trap beneath them, ensnaring Declan, crushing his wings and pulling him under the surface. He screamed before he disappeared.

The team called out to him and Vox screamed, running closer to see if she could still see him.

"Ryder, do something," Levi pleaded.

"Don't look at me—I'm not your captain. Get your head together, marine, and save your brother."

"Shit."

Aspen tied a rope to a khukuri and threw it up to a branch. It swung around the high perch. She pulled to check its tensile strength and climbed up, reaching the branch and hoisting herself up.

"Great, now help me up," Mackenzie called to her.

Aspen looked down at her. "Nah… I like this way better."

"Damn it, Aspen."

The ground moved fast underneath them, as though the squad stood upon waves of rock.

"Mackenzie, you could leap off here," River offered.

She shook her head. "I won't make it. It's too far."

Thex grew some branches horizontally out of the nearby trees. He climbed on and kept them growing until he reached the other side. Levi sped light-footed over the crevices to join Thex, and they moved toward where Declan had disappeared.

A trap door shot open behind Mackenzie. Long, bristling legs trapped her against the belly of the creature. River caught her hands just before she was pulled underground.

"I'm not going to let go," he told her hoarsely.

She began crying in terror as the demon hissed. It attacked with another spidery leg, hitting River away and sucking Mackenzie below ground.

CHAPTER 10

"Are you going to help?" River shouted up at Aspen.

She hung upside-down on the rope and reached for his hand. "I'll swing you."

They gripped each other's hands. River lifted his feet off the ground as another trap door flew open. As the demon charged straight for her, Aspen swung River out of the way and sliced off one of its legs with her sword. It hissed and squealed as more bristly legs surfaced. Soon almost its entire grotesque body was outside of the trap. Aspen tried climbing back up, but its legs were reaching for her, touching her. She slashed at them, cutting the tips clean off as she clawed at her branch for safety.

"The Octopedes are changing their tactics under there—you better be ready!" Ryder shouted.

River punched into his palm. "Alright, are we ready for a game of Whac-a-Mole?"

Aspen jumped down beside him, both khukuris poised at the ready.

"Let's do this," he crowed.

They ploughed through the prehensile legs as they leapt over the crevices. River broke straight into a trap door, crashing his hulking body through it. Mauling and hissing sounds escaped and the ground jostled beneath her feet.

River emerged moments later, covered in a sticky gray substance, carrying Mackenzie in his arms. She was conscious but shaking, her head lolling with every step River took. Aspen turned just in time to see a demon chasing after River.

"Hey!" she screamed after it. It turned, black dots sliding around inside its many gray eyes, making its way to her.

In a matter of moments, she became a focal point, surrounded by spidery demons stamping about her. Their venomous legs struck at her and she flipped again and again, feet barely touching the ground before she hurled herself into even more airborne somersaults. She leaped and jumped, weaving through the lashing legs, her body becoming one with the flow until one leg struck her arm, leaving a deep, bleeding gash. She shrieked as she was thrown into the body of another demon. Legs closed around her, prickling and crushing her at the same time.

Aspen's instincts took hold. "This is not how I go out." She gritted her teeth, pushing against the sea of legs. She squeezed her eyes shut. "C'mon… C'mon… I need you…"

An emerald glow burst from her body, and her breath relaxed until it was nothing but pure stillness. The White

Wolf emerged, lunging at the demons, jaws open. She spun, her twin swords slashing in a circle around her as she jumped through the gap her Anima had cleared for her. The demons fell around her until the blue sky above the canopy was visible once more and light pulsated through her veins.

She looked around to see that all the Animas had been unleashed from their sources—prowling and attacking what was left of the demons. Levi had Declan slumped over his back and was clawing at the Octopede clinging to his leg from beneath the forest floor. Thex was making the earth rise with his hands to hoist Levi out of the crevice, while their Animas, the Deer and the Lynx, chased away another demon. The Octopede hanging onto Levi finally fell into the crevice, calling out in one final hiss. Levi slid Declan off of his back into the ferns nearby, where he lay trembling, covered in gray slime, wings folded protectively around himself. Vox ran to his side, trying to ease them open.

The team was panting and filthy as they looked back at the captain. The overwhelming sense of defeat showed in their posture as all but Declan and Vox stood awaiting his orders, silent and shaking.

"If you're waiting for me to tell you where you went wrong, then you can get the hell off my team." A pause. "Go on... because now's your chance. Don't wait. Next time, you might be dead—or worse, your stupid actions might get your comrades killed."

They all glanced sidelong at each other, then away in the awkward silence that followed. Aspen clutched her upper arm, where the poisonous sting from the demon dripped blood onto her uniform. She concealed the wound as much as she could, but the captain had already noticed. To her relief, he pretended that he'd seen nothing.

He stepped toward them onto the hollow ground that was now motionless, empty, and stained with black blood. His next words rippled like thunder through them all. "Something has escaped the IO. It's something we've never seen before. We don't even know what we're up against… and YOU'RE NOT READY!"

"We're sorry." Mackenzie's voice was raspy.

"Sorry's not going to help you when you're dead," was the captain's sharp reply.

He trudged past them. The team followed, heads bowed in disappointment. A feeling of numbness hung in the air. They came to the entrance of a lush green valley flanked by hills and were approaching the second checkpoint when a wolf howled in the distance.

"We've reached Wolf Country," Thex announced.

"Thanks for that, genius," Levi scoffed from behind him, their prior sense of teamwork spoiled by the result of the assessment.

The captain looked down the line at Aspen as she scanned the western hills, alarmed. There was a graveness in his expression when she looked back at him, one that confirmed her instincts—something was here. Something was coming.

A red fox scampered from the forest at the top of the hill, through the grass, right up to Mackenzie's legs. Mackenzie dropped her gear onto the ground and lowered herself to her knees. She cradled the fox's slim snout and looked deep into its autumnal eyes.

"Ryder…" She turned, her eyes wide. "There's trouble."

"What kind of trouble?" River asked from over her shoulder.

"I don't know," she said in a hushed tone.

They listened for any signs of movement as they scanned their surroundings.

"Is this part of the assessment?" Thex asked.

The captain shook his head. It sent a nervous wave of energy through the team.

The phosphorescent eyes of the wolves lurked in the darkness where the forest met the top of the hill. There was a message in their distant growls. The team watched, hypervigilant, as Aspen took careful steps toward where the land began to incline, anticipating her translation. Her rigid posture faltered as she received the message.

She turned to face the others. "Intruders."

Thex's antlers protruded from his head, ready for defense. Ryder told the team to stay close as they trekked on, following the fast alpine stream that cut through the valley to where Major Michael Gunner was waiting. When they reached him, his expression was more disturbed than usual, his hooded eyes made more prominent with a furrowed brow. "I've called General Winters," he informed them. "Something's not right, and it's got all the animals scared."

"The wolves said it's intruders," Ryder told him.

"That's impossible," Gunner muttered, rubbing his jaw. But Ryder sensed the note of worry in his voice as he gathered the team in close. "Stay alert," he ordered. "We're on the perfect ground for an ambush."

"Our base isn't under threat, is it?" asked Levi.

"Sergeant, the fact that anybody's even here is near impossible; base is too far for them to know where it is, and besides, we have extra measures to conceal it."

"How could anybody get in?" Vox pondered, her eyes searching the edges of the rocky flanks of the valley, where lush grass met the now overcast sky.

"Dec," Ryder said.

"Captain?"

"How're your wings?"

"Good form, sir."

"Good. Fly up and give us an aerial, stat."

"You got it." Declan's wings beat off the ground, raising him higher until he was gliding the length of the ravine.

"Zalman and Lovetta, take the highest point. Report any high-value threat activity." Ryder pointed to a bulge near the top of the cliff.

Aspen and Levi shared an awkward glance before sprinting to the foot of the ravine. They exchanged words; Ryder assumed it had to do with Aspen not being able to climb up, because Levi took her hand in his with a grip so tight he could see their knuckles turned white, and climbed the rock face in three jumps. Ryder waited until both marines were completely camouflaged.

"You're with me." Gunner wrapped an arm around Vox's shoulder and began steering her to the west to conceal them in the trees. "We're going to wait on the general."

"Bale, take the midpoint with Borealis—over there, in

those bushes." Ryder pointed to a spot halfway up the face of the ravine.

"Let's go, prima donna," River teased. Mackenzie gave him an eye roll and they departed in a flurry of red energy.

"Thex."

"In the trenches, like old times?"

"Where else?" Ryder shrugged as they took a point further north.

The ravine was now dead quiet as they hid behind the shrubs and waited.

Ryder put the radio to his lips. "Raptor, this is Blood Howler."

Within seconds, Declan's voice crackled through. "This is Raptor."

"What's your twenty?" Ryder asked.

"I'm just past the ravine." Some crackling ensued. "I've got a visual on portal ripples, I repeat, portal ripples."

Ryder pulled out the digital map and swiped it upward so that it became a screen around them, revealing Declan's location. The ripples had become a full vortex, and the area was colorful with heat signatures.

"The hell is that—an army?" Thex asked, aghast.

"Raptor, send us cam footage," Ryder ordered down the radio.

A screen popped up moments later. Ryder watched, wide-eyed, his fist digging into his mouth, as people walked through the portal into Kore. He saw someone he recognized and swore under his breath.

"Vangelis," Thex confirmed, swearing as well. "How did he follow us here?"

"Who is he working for, is the better question." Ryder

dragged the footage into the corner of the screen and passed it to Thex. "Send this to intel. I want facial recognition on every single one of 'em."

Declan's voice came through the radio. "Raptor to Blood Howler: targets are taking to the forests. Wildlife is under threat—they're hunting them! Over!"

"Roger that." Ryder peered through the bushes to the location of his operatives, all still concealed. "Vixen and Switch-Hitter, take the south-east of the forest—"

"Break, break!" Declan exclaimed. "Threat is heading toward the ravine! I repeat, the threat is approaching your position!"

Ryder had eyes on the group of men walking through the ravine toward them. They were still at least fifteen hundred feet away, but Declan's cam gave them a clear visual on their faces. The group was led by a man who looked to be in his mid-fifties, wearing a black suit. He was of medium build and his hair was graying from its former dull brown.

Gunner's voice was grave over the radio. "Blood Howler, this is Slasher."

"This is Blood Howler."

"The mission is to capture the target. Stand by for confirmation on which target."

Thex turned the tablet toward Ryder, revealing a photo of the leader of the group. "This just came in from intel."

"Target confirmed," Ryder announced into the radio.

It crackled and Gunner said, "This is a DEFCON 1–level threat, I repeat—"

The hair on Ryder's neck, arms, and thighs stood up. Gunner's voice faded, and all Ryder could feel on his face was heat. DEFCON 1 was an immediate response. A fatal response. There were eight marines in this ravine…

He was responsible for all of them coming out of this alive.

"Blood Howler, do you copy?"

Ryder felt Thex watching him sidelong with concern as he breathed his request into the radio. "Repeat that, sir."

Gunner enunciated every letter he spoke. "Terminate all threats except the target. That's an order. Do you copy?"

The radio began to shake in his hand. He released a sharp exhale. "Copy that." He announced to the team's internal radio, "Raptor and Silver Lynx, take the southwest forest; drive all threats toward the battalion stationed in the Selendont Ranges. Everybody else, in the center of the ravine with me. Operation is a go. Let's move."

Ryder, Gunner, Thex, Vox, and Aspen shot like cannonballs across the ravine. They shook the ground as they landed, a gust of earth and light settling as they appeared before the intruders.

Aspen wore a shocked expression, as if she had seen a ghost. Ryder had to hold her back from attacking before his word. He realized Vangelis was shaking his head in warning at her. Aspen stopped, despite the foreboding promise in her lit-up eyes.

"This is your first and only warning to return to where you came from," Ryder announced to the leader, who nonchalantly straightened his suit jacket.

"Ryder Everett, I presume?" His voice was husky and confident. "So you're the man who single-handedly shut down my initiative."

Ryder swallowed. "Gregory Finch." Every cell inside

him was fortified with wrath, his lips pulling back just enough to show his fangs. "To what do I owe the pleasure?"

Gregory held his gaze thoughtfully at first, then laughed darkly. "I'm going to make this very simple." He cocked his head to the side as his covetous black eyes looked over Aspen. "Leave your team. Come with me willingly. Nobody has to get hurt. We'll set up our base here…" He sensed their forthcoming rebuttal. "We *won't* cause the Corps any trouble."

"That's not going to happen," Thex seethed.

A pang of doubt shot through Ryder's stomach. If all Gregory wanted was him, the rest of them could be kept out of the equation. He turned to his team with pleading eyes as River, Mackenzie, Levi, and Declan rejoined them.

"You'll have to go through us first," River threatened. The team's determined faces told Gregory that River had spoken for them all.

Gregory chuckled; a vibration inside him rang out at the same time. A sound that wilted trees and caused the ground beneath them to buckle. Doubt crashed like a wave over the team's challenging stances.

Gregory's probing focus circled back to Aspen, who stood at Ryder's side, hands on the hilts of her khukuris. He approached her in a leisurely manner. "I have to admit, it is enchanting to meet the people they call Anima. Such… stamina and vitality that you radiate. It really is pure… *life*. What is your name?"

Aspen's expression was analytical, her lips upturned. "You don't know who I am?"

Gregory gave a coy smile that made Ryder's fists clench. "I would surely remember meeting you." He glanced questioningly back at Vangelis, whose gaze was also fixated on Aspen.

"What kind of sick game are you playing?" she fired at him.

Gregory's eyes flashed.

Vangelis stepped forward. "Sir…"

Gregory tilted his head to catch his words more clearly.

"I believe we're after Ryder Everett only. Disgruntling the team may cause unnecessary problems."

Gregory smiled at them all. "That doesn't mean I don't want to get to know them. I am genuinely intrigued by their existence."

"If you want to evade our supremacy, leave now," Ryder warned. "Your men are no match for our numbers."

Gregory peeled his gaze away from Aspen and stared Ryder down, long enough for Ryder to see something in his eyes shift.

Ryder's veins became iron cords as he clenched his fists. He decided, then: fuck his orders. Something had *moved* inside those dark eyes. And he was going to hunt it down.

Ansel and Asintmah arrived in a gust of wind. They flanked the team on either side.

"We understand you have found yourselves here, travelers, but it is now time for you to leave," Ansel announced, folding his angelic, patterned wings back and planting his staff on the ground.

"Once I have what I came for, I will be on my way," Gregory said.

"And what is it that you want, exactly?" Asintmah asked.

"I've already discussed it with your team. One man for the sake of all… One life. It's a fair deal."

"He wants us to give him Ryder, and to set up a base here," Thex clarified.

Ansel was the epitome of calm as he faced Gregory. "I'm afraid that's rather impossible. You see, only Anima can reside on this land."

A slow, menacing smile crossed Gregory's rugged face. "I think you and I both know, Ansel, that this was not always the truth."

Ansel's eyes narrowed.

Gregory returned his attention to Aspen. "A destroyer to the core. Forgive me, I am intrigued… What are you doing among all these heroes? You know you don't belong here."

Aspen snarled, revealing her fangs. "You will never comprehend the monster you've created. And today…" She freed her khukuris from their scabbards, crossing them in front of her. "I'm going to show you why they call me Hellfire."

Gregory laughed excitedly.

Ryder leaned in and asked her, "How do you know him?"

Her eyes never wavered from her target. "This is the man who sanctioned the death of my family."

Ryder glanced at Gregory Finch and Vangelis. Softly, he whispered a code in Aspen's ear that only she would under-stand.

"How much iron does your khukuri have?"—*He is yours.*

Aspen's eyes blazed with an emerald glow as she answered. "All of it."—*My pleasure.*

Gregory clicked his fingers at his agents and pointed at Ryder. "Change of plans. Instead of taking Ryder Everett, kill him and take the she-wolf."

At Ryder's orders, the team was alight, radiating a glow that soared in flashes and waves inside the ravine, their powers blinding their targets as Declan descended from above. The storm created by his wings separated the agents. River mauled one until he was bloody and limp, and Levi slashed at two on the outside of the tight circle surrounding Gregory Finch. Mackenzie descended from above in a ground-shaking leap that crushed one man's lungs with her boots. Aspen ploughed her way through to the middle of the invader's group, but Vangelis jumped in the way of Gregory Finch, blocking her.

"Don't do it, Aspen."

"Don't think I'm not coming for you too." She threw him out of the way, creating access to Finch, who beckoned her closer.

Ryder bent the agent he was fighting backward and bit into his neck to rip out his windpipe. He bit the shoulder of another agent, who began convulsing in the electric-blue shocks Ryder's powers imparted to him. When the agent went limp, Ryder dropped him to the ground. He was running his thumbs over his fangs — the source of the power — when Gunner arrived at his side.

"That was new."

Ryder's smile was wide. "Tell me about it."

With that, they both shot forward, colliding with the two agents running at them. As they combatted their next opponents back to back, Ryder told him about Gregory's plans. "He mentioned 'one life' more than once. He wants someone dead today, and he prefers for it to be me. Let's keep it that way, Major."

He and Gunner threw two agents into each other and

they were knocked unconscious. "Looked into it already while you were stalling him," Gunner said. "If he's made a deal with a demon and it's inside him, calling the shots, he's going to need an Anima's soul to strengthen him, to keep him harbored in that body."

Ryder plunged his knee into another agent's abdomen and Gunner punched his own opponent in the face at the same time. Both went down.

"So I'm preferable because we have history, but he doesn't necessarily need *me*." The breath caught in Ryder's throat before he said his next words, and Gunner shot him a grave look. "He could take anyone's life today… He doesn't care who."

Ryder looked around the battle in a panic to find Aspen. Her swords were nowhere to be seen, and she was scrambling backward, away from Gregory, who was coming after her. Aspen managed to get up, but Gregory trapped her in a lock around her arms. More agents flocked to her to hold her there.

Ryder bolted, leaving Gunner combatting two agents, ignoring him when he called him back. He bowled over three agents in his way, lifting them off the ground as he bulleted toward her. He could barely see Aspen, sur-rounded by a cage of bodies. Gregory had a key, a Phaedra, to open up portals at will. They were going to get away, taking her with them, if he didn't do something.

A charge ignited from deep within, from a place that felt like the velvet expanses of the universe, from a night-dark void he never knew existed. It fired in the center of his chest, down his arms and into his hands, and shot out in a stream of light—one aimed at Gregory Finch and the other at the flocking agents. They were thrown violently away from Aspen, and she stared back at him, shocked.

Ryder looked into the palms of his hands at the blue waves of energy. The blast had killed the agents, but Gregory Finch lay motionless for a moment before he stirred. They watched in horror as Vangelis helped him back to his feet.

"He's not human," Ryder stated as Aspen came to his side.

"He overmatched me." She shook with anger, picking up her swords.

River, who was behind Gregory, bounded to him in heavy strides before Aspen could get there first.

"River, no!" she screamed.

Gregory held River down with a dark pleasure-filled grin across his face, his clawed hand poised high, ready to strike.

Asintmah was an evergreen blur appearing in front of them. "Let him go!" she bellowed. Her vines lashed out like whips, cracking and snapping at Gregory, holding back his powerful arm. River struggled beneath him.

"I told you, somebody needs to die!" Gregory's hand veered closer to River's head. Snapping Asintmah's vines one by one, descending closer and closer to the kill.

Ryder sensed her before she moved. Aspen rocketed from the ground, turning as she leapt over Asintmah, the iron elbow of her sword hooking around Asintmah's neck.

She slashed viciously.

A red spray of blood splashed across the team and Ansel.

Asintmah's severed head and body fell to the ground with a heavy thud.

It happened so fast that Ryder's vision became hazy for a moment. There was no sound. The faces around him contorted and bulged and hid, horrified, behind their hands.

He sobered when he heard Mackenzie screaming uncontrollably. He looked down at the blood on his uniform, at Thex dropping to his knees near the fallen justice.

"There's your death. Now get out," Aspen demanded.

Gregory gave her a long, appreciative stare before letting out a confused laugh. He turned toward the vortex that he'd drawn open with a Phaedra. Vangelis's brow furrowed into a hard glare, and it appeared that he was about to say something before he hesitated and disappeared, too, into the portal.

River came scrambling from his captive position and crumpled to the ground near Justice Asintmah's remains. "What did you do?"

Ryder glanced at Ansel, who was clutching his chest in terror. Declan stumbled to a boulder and began retching over it.

Gunner walked behind Aspen and pushed her shoulders down so that she was kneeling. She complied as he bound her wrists. When he was done, he forced her to spin to face him. She didn't meet his eyes; her expression was blank, staring down at the ground. Gunner pushed her forward, and Ryder watched as they began the long walk out of the ravine.

CHAPTER 11

Ryder barged through headquarters toward the heavy iron doors of the guardhouse, where two officers were posted. They saluted him and stood at attention as he approached.

"Good morning, Captain."

Ryder nodded. "At ease." When they didn't allow him to pass, he cleared his throat. "I need to see her."

"Major gave us orders for no visitors, sir. Sergeant River Borealis was here earlier and we had to turn him away too."

"Only Justice Silla Borealis was permitted to enter, a half hour ago," said the other officer.

Ryder huffed, disgruntled.

Gunner rounded the corner. "You can let the captain say his goodbye," he told the officers, before casting Ryder a solemn glance. "You've got ten minutes."

Aspen was sitting on the ledge when the door to her cell opened. She didn't look up; she had smelled his scent down the corridor and heard the smooth bass of his voice outside. She continued staring at the dirty floor as he entered through the first door, listening to the creaking of the second barred door. He stood there for a while after the guard left them. Aspen didn't dare look at him. She sat just on the cusp of where the light was shining on the bench next to her from the horizontal barred window above. He found a seat there, mirroring her, their legs apart, forearms resting across their knees. He looked sideways at her and she tilted her head away from him.

The captain sighed. They sat in silence for what felt like forever. Aspen knew how the conversation was going to go. He would tell her exactly what she was, as if she didn't already know it. A demon, a monster… a murderess. Then he'd ask why she did it and if she felt remorse, just like Ansel, Gunner, and the justices had done.

He finally spoke. "Are you scared?"

The question caught her off-guard. She glanced at his blue-fire eyes that never failed to arrest her.

"No."

"You don't have to pretend with me."

"I'm not pretending." She glowered at him. "I'm not scared… I've been through worse."

"Worse than being banished to the Tundra? Aspen, nobody makes it through Deathly Pass—"

"You're not meant to be dragged to hell and make it through that either."

"I'm glad you've still got your sense of humor."

She crossed her arms over her chest. "What are you doing here, Captain?"

"I want to know why. And don't tell me that bullshit you told the justices about how you were plotting revenge against them."

She shrugged. "It's the truth."

He let out an irritable groan. "Don't patronize me."

Aspen found herself unable to lie. She was going to die anyway; even if she wanted to leave the Tundra, nothing survived there and she knew it.

"Only Justice Silla knows the truth…" Her voice shook. "I traded her for River, okay? Gregory wanted a dead body, and so I gave him one before he could take River's life."

The captain straightened, a quick exhale escaping his lips, his eyes darting over the floor in thought. "What did Justice Silla say?"

She looked up at him and paused. He shot her a warning glare; he must have seen her forming an answer other than the truth. She gave a quiet sigh through her nose. "He thanked me for saving his son."

The captain's eyes widened. "Why didn't you explain that to the rest of them? Surely Justice Silla has some influence over your sentence…"

"What does it matter? They were going to send me to the Tundra anyway."

He shook his head at her. "You don't know that."

She moved closer to him. "Let me fill you in… Ansel and the Corps gave up on me a long time ago. It's time for you to do the same." She watched a disturbed look flicker across his rugged features and said in a low tone, "I know you wanted this to turn out differently."

"How would you know what I want?" he snarled.

"You wanted to find the good. You wanted to be the one who got the serial killer to conform… To make a hero out of me. I heard you talking to Michael at the first assessment. Trust me, I know you heroic types… It's nothing Gunner hasn't already tried—or River, for that matter."

"Vigilante," he said.

"What?"

"Everybody's got their chosen noun for you, and that's mine."

She glared at him incredulously. "I didn't stop killing after I found the people responsible for murdering my family."

He folded his arms over his chest and flashed a glance toward the door. "To be discussed…"

"We seem to be out of time," she pointed out as the door opened and one of the guards entered to see him out.

The captain rose from his seat. "I'm not finished."

"But—"

"Get out!" His voice boomed through the cell.

The door swung shut behind the guard. Aspen stood to face the captain.

"Listen, we don't have time for this—Gregory Finch isn't who he says he is," she declared.

"No kidding. I don't recall government agents being indestructible."

"Not to mention he died years ago."

"How do you know that?" he asked.

"Because I killed him."

"Well, you obviously didn't do a good job."

"Captain, I'm about to be sent to my death. Don't make the miserable mistake of insulting me."

"I concur. Why go down without a good fight?" He grinned, an invitation—she accepted, chuckling at their usual repartee until it faded into silence.

"Goodbye, Captain." She held out her hand for him to shake.

His smile dimmed before vanishing entirely. He looked down and placed his hand over hers, but didn't shake. She looked at him questioningly before he tugged her into him.

She collided with his firm chest and felt all her muscles relax in his warm embrace. With his fingertips in her hair, he bent toward her neck, where she could feel his warm breath tingling against her skin. He hovered there, like he was asking for permission. She blinked rapidly in anticipation.

A muffled gasp escaped her when she felt his lips upon her neck, soft and warm. He tasted her signature and drew it in with his breath, encoding it to his memory. Her embrace around him tightened as she felt him begin the sequence, butterflies fluttering chaotically in her stomach as she awaited the bite that was coming—

In one swift movement, he let go of her. The iron door opened, revealing Major Michael Gunner. Michael's expression was shrewd as he paused, stunned, considering their closeness and Aspen's breathlessness. She had only ever experienced tracing once, but this time had made her dizzy and weak, like she'd sprinted from one side of Kore to the other. She shuddered as the intensity faded and she remembered what was about to happen.

The captain tried to halt the major within his first few steps toward them. "No, wait, Major—before the sentence, you have to listen to me."

Gunner didn't look at him, or her. He walked briskly between them and cuffed Aspen before removing her from the cell.

"Aren't you listening to me? It was because of River," the captain explained.

"Don't make this harder," Gunner warned as he tugged on the cuffs, despair painted in his hooded eyes, his shoulders weighed down by the world. He walked her out the door with one hand on the cuffs and the other pushing against her shoulder.

Outside the cell, four rods were attached to her cuffs while another four guards surrounded her, leaving the captain helplessly holding on to the door frame. Aspen looked at him one last time before she was shoved forward, forced to walk down the hall.

They escorted her out into a full field of marines who were policed by a barricade of commissioned officers. The marines pushed against the officers and were blasted back by a translucent wall that shocked a silvery tech grid when it came in contact with a body.

They screamed that she was getting what she deserved.

That she didn't belong here.

That she was a murderer.

She said nothing as she was brought to the lake, where a rowboat waited on the narrow gray shore. She was placed in front of the justices; she didn't so much as wince at the cold expressions of Calais and Chaska. There was a gap between them and where General Ansel Winters stood off to the side, glancing at her in despair and then away. Aspen sensed he was sick to his stomach; it was evident on his face.

There was a closer barricade, which the Special Operatives stood behind. In the front, black streaks running down her face, was Vox, demanding the officer let her through.

Justice Calais stepped forward, his indifference toward her as plain as the creases around his mouth. "Aspen Lovetta, today we discharge you with dishonorable conduct. You are henceforth no longer a marine and no longer belong to the Anima Corps. The justices have found you guilty for the unspeakable crime of murdering a beloved elder. Do you pledge your remorse for the crimes you have committed?"

Aspen smiled, noticing that he'd said *crimes*, plural. She forced a harsh, quick laugh. "No."

A loud shock startled them all as River collided with the gridded wall. It took the captain, Thex, and Levi to hold him back as he shouted at Justice Calais, "She did it for me! Can't you see that? You're making a mistake! It was for me!"

The men were pulling him away when Gunner ran to him with a medic at his side. With one injection in his arm, River was sedated. His body became dead weight and the men helped him to the ground.

Justice Silla Borealis's hand grasped the fabric of Calais's heavily decorated military blouse. "She saved my son, Calais… Is there no pardon or leniency for that?"

Calais's eyes bulged at him. "Get back in line, Silla, before you, too, find yourself under the scrutiny of the chamber." Calais looked back at Aspen like he was restraining himself from spitting at her. "You murdered an elder. There is no limit to your destruction. And so, you are sentenced to a lifetime of banishment to the Tundra. Do you have any last words?"

She sealed her lips and threw him a stubborn glare.

The four officers who had walked her there approached to guide her into the boat and help her get in. With her cuffs still on, Aspen headbutted one officer, who dropped to the ground, unconscious, and she shoved the others off of her. She stepped into the tiny boat by herself and sat down.

As the rowboat was pushed into the lake, she saw Vox kneeling against the transparent wall, crying. "Goodbye, old friend," she whispered, knowing Vox could read her lips. There wasn't any life she would put before Vox's or River's. She would have done it again. And if this was how she'd meet her end because of her sacrifice, then so be it.

She could no longer see River. Her focus rested on the captain, who watched her, arms folded in silent determination, as she floated into the whiteout that flurried on the surface of the lake. It swallowed them all, erasing them from view. Aspen disappeared into the white, looking behind her, where the opening of Deathly Pass waited.

CHAPTER 12

The team was given two days' bereavement leave after the passing of Justice Asintmah. Thex had accrued leave and took this time to go home for a little over a week to see his wife Julia and his two young girls, and Ryder had managed to evade everybody else by seldom entering the Corps. The funeral was carried out in the traditional way: they placed Asintmah's body on a boat covered in flowers sacred to Kore and sent her into the ocean. The marines watched from the shore in silence. About half the Corps attended, arriving by way of multiple portal openings drawn by senior officers. General Winters told Ryder that the ocean currents surrounding Kore knew how to guide Asintmah's boat into the burial cave where she'd rest—for her sake, he hoped that was true.

Afterward, Ryder ran the length of the Deer

Country headland and didn't stop until he'd reached the south of Wolf Country, where he took his time discovering the forest. While skirting Ravenscliff, he was hit with a familiar scent—*her* scent.

He followed it, jumping off the cliffs and landing in a spray of basalt sand, where the scent became more potent. He scanned the shore and found her camp. When he reached it, he realized it was abandoned—she had not returned. He took the tent down and wedged it under his arm, taking it with him on the three-day trek back to his cabin.

On the journey, Ryder replayed the moments of being close to her in his mind. The scent of jasmine in her hair, the way she angled her neck to allow him to taste her skin, her breathlessness… Ryder's hand clasped the back of his neck as he rolled his eyes. What did it mean in the end, for it all to be ripped away from him?

The wolf pack were making themselves scarce, and when he finally found them in the forest well past the border of Wolf Country, they howled in an orchestra so painful he found himself shaken, needing to leave.

When he reached his cabin on the east side of the lake, Ryder collapsed onto the couch. Despite the trek and the comfort of a new bed, he didn't sleep well. He spent most nights overthinking and checking through the windows, even though Thex had told him that there was a protective shield over the grounds of the Corps… That no demons could get in.

From the side pocket of his camos, Ryder pulled out Aspen's Phaedra. He had taken it from Gunner's office after he'd walked in on the major drinking bourbon at his desk.

Gunner's tone had been gruff when Ryder left the training reports on his desk—it seemed like he had been sitting there with his bottle a while.

Aspen had somehow known that Gregory Finch wasn't who he said he was. As for why the imposter wanted a sacrifice, and not just any body, but an Anima body… That sparked Ryder's curiosity. He sprang up, swinging his military blouse over his shoulder and heading toward the Corps. Perhaps whatever Aspen had been researching held pivotal information as to what could have happened to the real Gregory Finch.

Ryder took the speed portal from Deer Division to Wolf Division and briskly walked to the labs, using Aspen's Phaedra to open the door. It granted him access, the electronic voice repeating her name as he walked in. The labs were quiet and Vox's office was vacant. He walked into NEON-12's main control room and sat in the wheeled chair, rolling it forward. NEON was a deep learning intelligence system, programed to process data via multilayered neural networks. It functioned much like the human brain but with added robotic engineering to help with medical data, voice recognition, computer vision, language processing, and anything else it was programed to do. He inserted the flat edge of the Phaedra into a slot on the side of the keyboard.

"*Aspen Lovetta—initiating retinal scan.*"

"Oh no," he groaned.

"*Access denied.*"

In the corner of the holographic screen, an option read: *Use alternative login methods.*

Ryder touched it with his fingertip and another screen

appeared. He assessed the options. Fingerprints, voice recognition, access codes—all required Aspen's presence. Ryder sighed in frustration and scowled at the screen. He stood from the chair and bent over the computer, trying her military number first, then her birthday: *2708.*

"*Denied.*"

He gave the confounding holographic screen a lightning-fast strike with his hands. The screen shuddered for a moment—and then, to Ryder's utter surprise, an electronic voice announced, "*Access granted.*"

He stared, awestruck, as the computer showed him the last file that had been opened. "That was weird," he said to himself as he sat down again. "Okay, Lovetta, show me what you've got."

In the corner of the screen, real-time surveillance footage was rolling from a place in the Corps he had never been to. He considered the tall shelving set in a labyrinth of rows; it appeared to be a library. What puzzled him was that he had seen the Corps library, and this did not look like the same room.

Ryder pressed on an open tab and brought it forward, zooming in on the notes, all handwritten in Japanese. He read Aspen's last addition:

Sample from the staff's power source shows no match based on the periodic table and chemical composition has not been previously identified. Tests so far indicate that the matter in question is a refractory substance, but was once volatile. My

Ryder thrummed his fingers on the desk, staring at the symbols as he let the information sink in. *Yes, but tell me what cryolava is and why Finch wants it…*

His fingertip was almost touching another open tab when he sensed someone approaching. He shot from the chair to the door and leaned his weight against it—if he wiped the screen, he may never get it back. The access on the other side was granted and he recognized the scent as Vox's. She pushed the door, then realized it was jammed. He heard her inhale.

"Ryder? Is that you in there?"

He opened the door a crack. When he saw she was alone, he pulled her in.

Vox launched into spewing facts; he didn't know it was possible for anybody to speak so fast. "I've been looking for you everywhere! I ran tests on your powers that developed during the battle in the ravine, and I still have so much more work to do, but I found what it is, Ryder… You're not going to believe it. The power from your bite and the blasts from your hands were gamma rays mixed with ultra-violet light."

Ryder took a step back. A mixture of amazement and shock overwhelmed him; the room felt like it was closing in. What did that even mean?

Vox read his body language and her tone became gentle. "Don't worry, I'll keep looking into it. This is a good thing. Anyway… where have you been? I haven't seen you since—"

Vox's mouth gaped open as she walked slowly toward the screen.

"How did you get in?"

"I have no idea. I tried to break it and it just gave me access."

"Fair dinkum?" she gasped.

"Fair what?"

"Never mind. What did you find?" she asked, staring in awe at the symbols still on the screen.

Ryder translated the passage he had just read. "Yeah, that's what I thought," he said in answer to her puzzled expression. "Do you know where this is… or *what* it is?" He pulled up the surveillance of the unknown library room.

Vox peered closer. "I've never been in *there* before. It must be above our clearance level… and she's hacked the camera somehow."

"We need to know what's kept in there. There's got to be a reason she was watching this."

"Ryder…"

"Maybe there's information held in there about the power source on Ansel's staff… This cryolava. If we can get a hold of it, we'd have a better understanding of why the Finch imposter wants it."

"Ryder."

"I need you to pull up surveillance on the closest camera to this one—"

"Ryder!"

"What?"

Vox looked at him sympathetically. "I miss her too."

He swallowed and looked away. "I barely knew her."

"But you still managed to not buy into the Hellfire story—you gave her a chance." Her round cheeks dimpled as she smiled. "You know, I just keep telling myself she's out on a mission somewhere… and that any minute she's going to come back." Vox's eyes welled with tears. "But this time she's really not coming back."

She covered her face as she wept. Ryder stood awkwardly for a moment before putting his hand on her shoulder. Vox hugged him, then pulled herself together, straightening her shoulders. She glanced at the screen and then stared at it, awestruck.

"What is that?"

Ryder turned around. The surveillance screen had popped forward. Ansel had entered the unknown library and was pushing books in and sliding others out from one of the rows.

"What is he doing?" Vox asked.

The sequence unlocked a secret door in the round center where all of the rows met. A staircase appeared and Ansel began descending it. The surveillance followed him.

"I thought this cam was wall-mounted?" Ryder questioned.

"No—she's built a nano-drone and programed it to follow any heat signatures," Vox replied, sounding impressed.

"Brilliant." Ryder shook his head, the corner of his mouth upturned.

They watched as Ansel lit a lantern on the wall and a glow lit up the small concrete room. There was a bookshelf set against the wall, and the drone landed in the opposite corner, giving them a view of it.

"I'd give anything to know what's in those volumes," Vox said.

Ansel moved the books aside to reveal a safe inside the wall. He entered a code and the safe opened. With gloved hands, he pulled out what looked to be a dark book in the black-and-white footage. A padlock crossed over its cover.

Ansel suddenly dropped it, crying out in ear-splitting pain. He took a few moments to regain himself and looked down at the book, now on the concrete floor, a hand against the wall to stabilize himself.

"What the hell is on the cover of that book?" Ryder pondered.

Vox's eyes were wide. "I don't know, but whatever it is… it's totally dangerous."

"Can you zoom in to get the title?" Ryder suggested.

Vox asked through NEON-12's audio service and it magnified the book. She groaned. "I can't make it out, it's too blurry."

She zoomed back out as Ansel was traveling back up the stairs, the drone following him. He closed the secret door and the drone returned to its hiding place.

Vox sighed. "Whatever that book is, he can't even open it. Did you see how much pain it caused him? Like it was attacking him somehow. I've never seen anything like this. Somebody would have to open that book and heal themselves at the same time to be able to read it."

Ryder grinned. "And we have a friend who can do exactly that."

"But she's gone," Vox replied weakly.

Ryder gave her a steady glare. "We're going to get her back."

CHAPTER 13

Ryder rubbed his forehead in annoyance as River, Declan, and Vox debated the plan to find Aspen in the Tundra. River slouched on the chair he was sitting backward on, evidently hungover; he yawned, piping up every once in a while as Vox explained to Declan for the umpteenth time that they were counting on Aspen's previous field missions to put together the clues.

"Lass, that's what we have reconnaissance and intel for. We just execute the missions; we don't have to work them out. I understand you provide us with our data, but if Hellfire was so detrimental to the team's success, they wouldn't have given her the boot… And another thing—she wouldn't be going around with her personal vendettas, trying to kill us off one at a time."

Vox shook her head. "That's not what she was doing, Declan."

"Yes, you've already told me that River would have died instead. But in a situation where nobody knew what to do, she made the fatal call before the captain could even give us orders." Declan crossed his arms. "I'm sorry—I know you both think she cares about you, but I'm not helping you with this."

"Dec, we just need you to fly us in and back out again," Ryder clarified.

Declan glared at them all. "Do you have any idea how difficult it's going to be to get an aircraft on the runway and into Kore's airspace without being detected?"

"You know everything there is to know about how Eagle Division operates," River insisted.

"And you're the best pilot in the whole Corps," Vox added.

"No! Don't you all get it? I'm not doing this!" Declan threw his hands up in the air and briskly walked off, leaving Vox and River looking on with helpless expressions.

Ryder caught up to him before he could leave the labs, stopping him in his tracks. "Just hear me out."

"You know, out of everybody, I'm most stunned at you, Captain. I thought you were responsible and did the right thing, made the right decisions for the team. If this is Special Ops, I want no part in it."

"I never came here wanting to be your captain!" Ryder barked.

Declan recoiled in astonishment, but waited for Ryder to continue.

"Let me tell you something about me. I am never 'by

the book'. I make up my own tactical plans to sneak us through the window of opportunity we have to destroy the opposition. So when you think about it, I'm no different to Aspen Lovetta. Forget the conventional roadmap to victory, Declan… because I don't follow directions. But you'll be damn sure I'll take you through the secret passageway, and you will always make it out before I do."

Declan stared at him in silent awe.

"So what do we have?" Ryder continued. "One banished team member with a bad reputation who knows more about what's threatening the world than we or the Corps do. One unexplainably back-from-the-dead government official who appears to be bulletproof and can get to and from Kore. And one captain, seeing exactly one way out."

Declan hunched a little and looked away as Ryder awaited his response. "I'll admit it: I get the appeal. She's as beautiful and as war-driven as the goddess Freya, and her scent is… Well, purifying, to say the least…"

Ryder waited intently as Declan kicked the ground.

"When she hijacked me on the first assessment, she knew I was afraid of HALOs… like she could sense it. I saw the way she was watching me after I accidentally bumped into her before the test started, like she had decided she was coming for me. I gave her the benefit of the doubt. I thought, *What kind of friend does that to her friend's boyfriend?*" Declan was becoming sweaty as he recounted the memory. "And when she jumped onto my back and got hold of my wings? I couldn't shake her off, no matter how hard I tried. She knew exactly what she was doing. She began cutting into my back, she grabbed hold of the muscles that control my flight…" Declan's eyes were wild with fear as he urged him to understand. "My *flight*, Captain. She told me that although she didn't think I was giving Vox the runaround, that coming close to her was a big mistake, especially when we aren't in combat."

Ryder's brow knitted together. "What else did she say?"

Declan huffed. "That she was going to give me a choice. Promise to never do it again and she'll land me in a way that I'll eventually regain consciousness…"

"Or?" Ryder prodded.

Declan's Adam's apple bobbed. "That she would make other arrangements."

They exchanged a look within the pause that followed showing just how much this had rattled him to his core.

"She completely humiliated me, in front of the whole Corps. She would never do it for me. Why should I do this for her?" Declan finished shakily.

Ryder sighed bitterly. "I understand, and I'm not saying what she did was right. But if Vox got herself banished to the Tundra and the chance of Earth surviving something catastrophic from the underworld depended on her… Would you trust that Aspen was capable enough to get her back?"

Declan thought for a long moment. Then he answered in a small voice, "Yes."

Ryder put his hand on Declan's shoulder. "That is exactly how Vox is feeling right now… Why she's asking you to do this. Don't do it for Aspen; do it for Vox."

Declan's expression turned to one of acceptance. "Okay."

Ryder followed him back into the office, where Vox and River were waiting.

"Rebellious *and* persuasive," River commented to Ryder.

Vox threw her arms around Declan. "Thank you."

"So while you were out there, Vox and I discovered a problem," River announced.

"What problem?" Declan asked, relaxing his embrace on Vox and turning to face him.

"Nobody has a trace on Aspen. That's how she keeps herself imperceptible. When she leaves, she's practically invisible—believe me, Vox and I have been through this many times in the past."

"She's quite the… absconder." Vox fluttered her lashes.

"Aye, that is a problem," Declan agreed. "Not to mention, the Tundra is covered in a thick white cloud; you can't see your hand in front of your face. Flying is going to be a hard task. Landing without crashing is going to be near impossible."

River grimaced. "And it's all glacial terrain. The crevices have drops over three hundred feet… You could practically nosedive into Earth's center."

"And there would be undiscovered species of demons," Vox added.

River stood, folding his arms. "So what's the plan, Captain?"

Ryder straightened. "Declan and Vox, you'll pick out the best aircraft to take us through the Tundra; I'll make sure the runway is clear for take-off. And River, you're the decoy—I need you to cause a distraction in the Eagle control tower and then make it back for lift-off. You'll have to be fast."

"And what do you propose I do as a distraction?" River asked, baffled.

"I'm sure you can think of something," Ryder replied.

"Doesn't Airman Naida Camwell work in air force traffic control?" Declan reminded him.

"That she does, Dec. That she does…" River responded, sounding pleased.

"And on finding Aspen?" Vox said.

"Don't worry about tracing. I have that covered," Ryder assured her. "Okay, let's move." He headed toward the door.

"What do you mean 'you have it covered'?" River called.

Ryder turned back. The three of them hadn't moved and were staring at him in anticipation.

Ryder faltered a moment. "I mean I've already looked into reconnaissance history, geographical characteristics, and the conditions of the Tundra, and I have some coordinates for where I think she could have gone."

"Oh," Vox murmured.

River's eyes narrowed. "That still doesn't explain how we're going to find her with no scent tracing in snow-covered barren terrain."

Ryder answered River's suspicion with a glare, and the air around them suddenly fizzled.

River's mouth dropped open. He skipped over and swatted a massive hand at Ryder. "Oh-ho, shit… You two traced each other?"

"Wow, I really didn't see that coming," Declan said. "When were you going to tell us that this mission was entirely personal?"

"It was a last resort before they took her away, and it's none of your business," Ryder warned.

"Ryder, no matter how it happened or however dire the circumstances, this is a really big deal," Vox explained.

"She's never let either of us trace her, and that's including during wartime."

River shrugged his broad shoulders. "Nobody except Hurricane…"

There was an eerie pause after his name, a shift mainly from Vox that Ryder couldn't quite put his finger on. "Exactly, and they were husband and wife. Ryder, it's a very intimate thing that you can't reverse," Vox stated.

"So how has she not been able to find her way back to you?" Declan asked.

"Because we only had time for the tracing to go one way," Ryder divulged.

"How did she let you, is more the question." River raised his brows, grinning wide. "And where? Were you alone? How long did it last?"

Fucking hell. "It's not like we planned it—it just happened."

"It doesn't *just* happen!" River exclaimed.

"Every minute we waste turning over the details gives us less of a chance to find her," Ryder told them firmly.

River rolled his eyes and groaned, "You're no fun," before sauntering out of the lab.

Vox exhaled loudly and gave Ryder a grateful smile. "Let's go."

A howling gale blasted ferociously over the Tundra as Aspen placed one unsteady foot in front of the other, the wind almost picking her up. She was enveloped in an unending white cloud. It had swallowed her cries for help in the days she had walked. After a three-day journey, she had found a small hook in the snow where she hid so she could sleep. It took her what felt like another full day to work up the courage to travel further. There seemed to be nothing but this. The wind never slowed, and the obscure cloud never lifted, and neither the sky nor the sun ever showed.

A sound broke through the deafening wind. It was a guttural moan at first, before it became louder: thunderous, growling, and angry. It shuddered her bones more than the white wind, troubling her more than the absent sky. She stopped dead in her tracks when the sound ceased.

Moments went by as she looked blindly around the swirling abyss. Had she imagined it?

She was about to take another step when, out of the clouds, a heavy, dark mass attacked her, throwing her onto the icy ground. A grizzly bear stood on its hind legs, as enormous and powerful as the Virtue Ursa herself.

It came after her as she ran, sinking into unstable ice pockets. It swiped at her, shredding down her side as she fell to the ground. The wind caught her scream and carried it far away, silencing it. Blood poured from the deep gashes, and as she continued to run, it dawned on her... She wasn't healing. She had been fighting the conditions of the Tundra for too long, and it had robbed her of her powers. Every step stretched and tugged at her wounds, slowing her down.

She realized this was the beginning of the end. There was nowhere she could hide from the bear, who was as hungry and lost as she was.

Aspen hobbled on, just missing the swipe of the bear's

paddled paw before a wrong step. In seconds, the icy ground opened like a black hole, caving in on itself. She felt an upward pull, like her Anima was being ripped from her body, as the Tundra swallowed her whole.

CHAPTER 14

Ryder buckled his seatbelt at Declan's command as they lifted off from the tarmac in a steady climb toward the ranges ahead. River crowed in celebration as air force workers chased the aircraft down the runway and skidded to a halt, becoming smaller as the plane ascended. The exhilaration of their witty plan showed in all of their faces as they laughed at their success. But the celebration was brief as they turned their attention to the plan ahead, Ryder enduring River's Cheshire Cat smile and suggestive eyebrow waggling all the while. He shook his head. *This motherfucker.*

River just gave him another shit-eating grin.

Vox pulled the cord she had been fiddling with to cut the radio transmission back to base so their location couldn't be traced. Declan maintained a high altitude two-thirds of the way along the summit, giving them a remarkable view.

He turned the plane east, and Ryder asked over the motor's noise, "Why did we turn off?"

Declan answered without looking back at him. "I can't fly through Deathly Pass."

Vox placed her hand on Declan's arm. "But it could have clues as to which path she took."

River rolled his eyes. "It's the Tundra. There are no paths."

"You don't have to be so brash, River," Vox scolded.

River's playfulness died away as they approached the danger zone. "We're going into the Tundra and you're acting like we're following Little Red Riding Hood to Grandma's house. You realize finding her could be a one-way mission? And I might as well die out there, because if I don't, my dad's going to fucking kill me anyway."

"I don't recall Aspen second-guessing herself when she saved *your* life!" Vox exclaimed.

"Stop it, both of you. I can't concentrate." Declan looked down at the planned path on the navigation screen.

Vox unbuckled herself from the cockpit and walked to the back, standing over River as he slumped in his seat. "Pull it together!"

River scoffed. "Pull it together? Dove-cake… we're minutes away from flying into *Deathly Pass*."

Ryder raised a brow. "Dove-cake?"

"Yeah, look at her… She's pure as a dove and sweet as a cake."

"Oh."

"Angel-cake is also appropriate."

Vox exhaled through her nose, clearly drawing on the

last of her patience. "And if *he*"—she pointed a finger at Ryder—"didn't trace her, we wouldn't be able to find her. This *will* work."

River huffed in exasperation.

"It has to work," Vox said, more to herself than either of them.

Ryder unbuckled himself and walked into the cockpit, hovering near Declan's shoulder. "We can't go around it; we have to go through it. The terrain is unpredictable at best and there might be areas she wouldn't pass through on foot."

Declan sighed. "Ryder, the plane is too wide. We'll collide with the ranges." He shook his head. "I'll take us over Mount Ira, where the whiteout starts a little further back… It's safer."

Ryder leaned in, clutching the back of the cockpit seat. "McAndor…"

Declan's hands shook as he clamped the steering wheel and looked at Ryder, adjusting his glasses on his nose.

"There's nothing about what we're doing that's safe. If we don't go through Deathly Pass, we might as well go home."

Declan glanced at Vox. Her expression was grave.

He pulled the steering wheel and the plane began its circle back.

Ryder slapped his shoulder. "Thanks."

"Awa' an bile yer heid," Declan replied, accentuating his Scottish accent so that his words were almost indistinguishable.

Ryder chuckled and sat back down, mouthing to Vox, *What?*

She leaned in, covering her smile with her hand. "He means 'get lost'."

Aspen woke, eyelids drooping, in the ice bath she'd landed in. It had already been working to freeze her to death where she sat. She couldn't feel her arms, hands, or legs; the only part of her body she could move was her head. She wasn't shivering—a bad sign—and it took her a full minute to lift her head to see how far she'd fallen. She saw the white cloud reaching into the crevasse and figured it must have been at least a fifty-foot drop. The water she was dying in was crystalline blue. She would have smiled, but her mouth wouldn't move. She felt no pain, not in any part of her body… not anymore.

She noticed a mass in her periphery. More of it was revealed as she craned her stiff neck toward the edge of the water.

Aspen saw her legs first, shimmering white and slender in the snow, then her proud chest and muscular body, her delicate muzzle, and her fierce emerald stare. The White Wolf.

At first, only indecipherable sounds escaped Aspen's unmoving lips, her breath barely producing a wisp of vapor. But she tried harder. She had to tell her Anima this one last message. Her voice was so unlike her own, so soft and weak, that she didn't recognize it.

"You were… n-n-never there. For me."

The White Wolf's wild eyes narrowed in answer. Aspen's body began to feel warm and fuzzy, like she had been cocooned in a thick, downy blanket. Her eyes were unable to stay open any longer as the hypothermia's caressing embrace brought her closer to her death. Her last words were carried on the final icy breath curling into the air from her lips.

"Just leave me here."

Declan told everybody to buckle their seatbelts again as they entered the pass. It was a dark corridor with both mountainsides flanking the plane. The temperature on the dash dropped below ten and the dial continued to descend into the blue. The creek below them before the pass had been turquoise blue, like the lake. It was now the color of anthracite and still as it wound the contours between the mountains.

Declan exhaled slowly and kept the steering wheel as steady as possible as River pointed out the fast-approaching narrow gap between the snow-covered slopes.

Vox was panicking. "We're not going to make it!"

"Can't say he didn't warn you," River fired at Ryder.

A faint swing of fabric behind him made Ryder turn around.

Mackenzie stood there, looking at them all in satisfaction. "Nothing a little math can't get us out of."

"How did you…?" River started.

"Your stealth is terrible. Mine, however…"

"How did we not smell you?" Vox asked, sounding annoyed.

Mackenzie shot her a coy smile.

"She attached her scent to us at breakfast, then mixed it with the plane's air," Ryder surmised.

River squinted suspiciously at Mackenzie. "That's sneaky." He turned to Ryder. "How do you know that?"

"*A World of Scent*—chapter eight."

River grimaced. "Please, don't school me. I can smell blood from miles away."

"You'd think you'd use that excellent sense of smell to know when you need a shower," Mackenzie mocked, referring to his scent being mixed with that of a certain marine from Eagle Division.

River smirked. "I don't wash it all off straight away."

Mackenzie chuckled and Vox gagged.

"HOLD ON!" Declan shouted.

The plane tilted sideways, and Ryder, River, and Mackenzie fell against the cabin wall as Declan passed through a narrow gap. Ryder almost landed on top of Mackenzie, his hands braced either side of the wall, saving them from colliding.

"Your restraint is almost offensive," she remarked as he reversed his body weight, pushing himself away from her.

"Um, guys…" Vox said. They looked to the side of the plane.

Climbing fast over the mountainsides, matching the speed of the plane, were hundreds of small, skeletal demons. Thin, transparent skin covered their bones; their eyes were hollow, and they had long, whip-like tails and beak-shaped mouths.

"It's okay, they can't reach us from over there," Declan reassured them.

They all shrieked as a loud bang shook the plane. Declan pulled forcefully on the wheel to straighten the aircraft.

"But they can glide over here!" Mackenzie clarified.

Ryder saw another demon push off the mountainside toward them, its empty eyes enlarged, its arms reaching forward, extending its gliding wings of skin. Another loud bang swerved the plane and almost sent them into the side of the mountain.

The scream of metal made them all clench their teeth as the demons began cutting into the aircraft, the plane now sloping downward from the weight of them clinging to the outside.

"Tell me there's a protocol for this?" River pleaded.

"Well, taking a plane through forbidden land isn't exactly protocol to begin with," Vox squeaked.

"We have another problem," Declan called.

"We're growing those by the second," Mackenzie replied as the team followed her to the cockpit.

The towering rocky wall was nearing.

"Ryder! I can't turn the plane around!" Declan shrieked.

"So go over it!"

"There's not enough time to pull a plane this size up that fast—it's too heavy." Declan's hands were shaking as he clenched the wheel.

Mackenzie leaned over the back of Declan's seat. "He's right—a patrol plane can't make that kind of trajectory that quickly."

Vox brought up a hologram from her tablet. "It isn't a wall. There's a narrow opening in the center, like a ridge, before it blocks up completely… After that, the only way is up through this tunnel." She traced her finger along the cavity.

Another jolt shuddered the plane. The demons were breaking off its tail.

Ryder thought for a moment.

"We're doomed," River muttered as he clung to the frame of the cockpit.

There was an all-consuming silence before Ryder announced he had an idea.

"Mackenzie—work out the equations to get this plane through that ridge and direct Declan from the hologram. Vox—keep us on the planned path and keep watch for any more environmental threats. River… cover me."

"Cover you from what?"

Ryder grabbed a rope with a hook and attached it to a loop in the dented ceiling of the aircraft.

"From the demons I'm about to let in."

"What! Are you crazy?"

Ryder's jaw tightened. "Somebody's gotta get them off the plane before they break their way in."

River exhaled. "Are you sure this is going to work?"

Ryder grasped the handle and looked down at River before opening the hatch. "We'll have a better chance if you hold on tight to this." He threw River a few feet of rope.

River grinned like the devil. "I'll tell you who you wish was holding it."

Ryder kicked the hatch open and swung himself through, shouting, "Shut up, asshole."

River's chuckles faded as Ryder balanced on the curved roof of the plane. One demon tumbled straight into his trap; he could hear rasping screams and scuffling as River mauled it. Ryder killed another by grinding it through the propeller.

Another demon crashed into the side of the plane and the whole aircraft swayed. Ryder slipped on the smooth surface. With nothing to grasp but the end of the rope, he blew around like a rag doll in the rough winds before crashing sideways into the tail with a thud. He shot a gamma blast at the two demons weighing down the right side and they atomized, their fragments scattering into the wind.

Demons were still chasing the plane from the sides of the mountains. Ryder blasted another three mid-flight and realized their remains were falling backward, not down. He knelt and looked down at the stream below. Black water plunged past the plane as though they were flying down a waterfall.

They were flying inside an optical illusion.

He had to warn the others. Ryder scrambled to the body of the plane, ultramarine gamma rays shooting four of the five remaining demons still clinging on. The last one dove for him and they both slid, falling off the side.

Ryder hung there with the demon scratching and crawling onto him from the bottom of the rope. They swung as the plane tilted to evade the protruding mountain. He timed it well and swung the demon into the piercing rocks, its screams fading in the distance.

Ryder clambered back to the hatch and shouted, "VOX!"

She met him at the bottom, looking up at him. "Thank heavens, you're alright!"

"Vox, we're flying down!"

"What? Down?"

"Affirmative. The surroundings look like we're flying straight, but we're really flying down."

He was met with a flabbergasted expression. "How can this be?" Vox asked. "It doesn't geologically make sense."

Ryder jumped back down into the plane to follow her.

"So why can't we feel the gravity pulling forward inside the plane?" Mackenzie asked, hearing their discussion.

Declan sank a little. "I turned on a gravity stabilizer through NEON so our weight wasn't being thrown around. There was too much turbulence with the demons on the outside."

"They've stopped chasing us," River reported, looking out the window. "Why doesn't that feel like a positive thing?"

Vox walked to NEON's controls and zoomed out of the hologram, holding a hand over her open mouth in horror. They all saw it. The first time Declan had flown sideways, the mountains dipped downward, just like they had come off a cliff. The mountains were now protruding outward from the waterfall and the overcast sky was just endless, gaseous Tundra.

"We've been in the Tundra this whole time!" River exclaimed, holding the sides of his head in terror.

Mackenzie's breath caught in her throat as she gasped, her eyes filled with trepidation.

The ridge beneath was fast approaching.

"We have to get out of this nosedive," Ryder told Declan. "Pull up into the fog."

"The air pressure is too dense! We're just falling… I can't pull the wheel up!"

"Everybody brace yourselves. I'm about to screw up the gravity," Ryder announced.

Everybody took hold of the handles. Ryder held on to Declan's seat and kicked out the windscreen. The whole glass piece blew off. The team fell forward as the gravity corrector disarmed. Declan pulled the steering up as tightly as he could without breaking it off.

The plane pulled out of its vertical position and Declan started the engine again. The motor faltered.

Mackenzie had a sick look upon her face. "We're going to die."

Ryder ignored her. "We need to buy a few seconds."

"What do you want me to do?" River asked quickly.

"Not you. Vox? I need you to jump out of the plane."

"Say what now?" River answered on her behalf. Vox's expression was terrified.

"Jump out and leap from the ridge back up. When you do, push the plane upward. I'll pull you back in."

"Ryder, I…"

"We don't have time for fear. Go!"

Vox moved toward the cockpit window and clung on, trembling. The aircraft began spiraling, making them dizzy.

"Go!" Ryder shouted into the wind.

Vox jumped, screaming, into the fog below.

Seconds later, she was racing toward them at high speed, pushing up the plane as Ryder jet-streamed his powers against the ridge, soaring them high into the swirling cloud. Declan fired the engine. Ryder clasped Vox's hand as she lost power from the jump. Relief washed through her violet eyes.

She was hauled straight into River's arms. "Are you alright?" he asked. "I'm so proud of you."

Vox nodded, panting from the adrenaline. "That was wild! I almost see the frontline appeal. No…" She shook her head vigorously, tossing her pink curls. "I can't believe I just said that. Where's my tablet?"

Declan activated cruise control and rushed to Vox, hugging her tightly. Then they all turned to look at Ryder. He was leaning against the side of the plane with his arms folded, settling his adrenaline.

"You've got some nerve, Captain," Declan said.

Mackenzie glanced at his hands. "You've got some serious powers, too."

"We could have been killed," Declan continued.

River shrugged. "I got my fill of demon guts—but I don't like what you did with Vox."

"He saved us." Vox approached Ryder slowly. "You believed I could do things I didn't even know I was capable of."

Ryder just leaned against the cabin wall in quiet reception.

"Thank you." Vox broke his crossed arms and hugged him.

CHAPTER 15

This is what death feels like, Aspen thought, as her sight sharpened with every groggy blink. When one had been a demon slayer from a young age, death was something to be vividly imagined, or at the very least, considered. That was how she had rationalized how frequently she'd pictured her own death—and it had looked nothing like this…

She was wedged, or cradled, in a large mound of dark blue fur that she brushed between her fingers as she tried to feel them again. Above the furry hills was the long gash of the crevasse opening, flanked by rocky black walls, the white mist dancing through. She was sweltering. Sweat ran down her arms, or was it melted ice water? Her bones groaned as she tried shifting her body.

Jolt.

Aspen's eyes grew wide. The muscles in her legs fired like they were getting ready to run for her life.

She wasn't dead. Couldn't be… Fear didn't exist in the afterlife.

Shift. Jolt.

What the hell was that? Aspen put her palms flat onto the dark blue fur.

Oh, the Virtues have mercy on her soul, it had a *heartbeat.* If she scrambled off, she'd surely wake the beast… Demon… Whatever it was.

Slowly, heavily, she rolled over, her bones and muscles resisting, having only been half thawed. She tried to break her fall with her arms as she hit the dirt with a thud on the edge of the pool of ice water she had almost frozen in earlier.

The enormous mountain of fur uncurled in the dim light, its four legs bulging the soil as it towered over her. She lay face down on the ground beneath it, her limbs juddering. The beast's wet snout and hot breath pressed against the back of her head. Aspen could only whimper as white teeth the size of swords clamped down on her flannel jacket and dragged her. She hung from the beast's mouth, her boots scraping against the frigid soil until she was dropped.

Aspen pushed against the ground and thudded onto her back to see the beast. Her lips quivered and her voice cracked as she said, "Midnight Wolf."

The Midnight Wolf, with eyes of ethereal blue, looked into her being. It could see past her physical form, past all of her dimensional realities, its gaze resting on her inner child. She could feel the child she'd once been tugging at her clothes, eyes full of wonder as she looked upon her greatest protector, and at the same time, the woman she was now, with a heart smashed to pieces, that had healed, mangled

Aspen gritted her teeth as she propped herself up on her forearm. She reached for the wolf's paw. The tips of her fingers stopped short a few inches from it. Midnight Wolf didn't move closer. Pangs of guilt surged deep in her stomach. She averted her eyes from the wolf. Now she'd even lost the respect of the Anima that had protected her for her whole life. She supposed she deserved it, after all she'd done.

Midnight Wolf lay down, flurrying particles of dirt all over her as he curled up close, his plumed tail—almost as long as her whole body—pressed against the back of her legs and her spine. She rested her head on one of his folded furry legs and stared deep into his eyes.

"This is the second time you've saved my life."

Midnight Wolf puffed hot air from his nose in answer. She was becoming warm again, the heat emanating from the wolf's body thawing her.

Aspen was hit by a wave of emotion. She strained through clouded vision, clearing her throat before she asked, "Now, you're not going to want me to waste it, are you?"

The bear had waited, cold and hungry, ready to devour Aspen when she climbed out of the crevasse. She was chased like prey until she arrived at a place where the fog diminished.

She had made it to the sea at the northernmost coast of Kore, where she slayed the bear. Every muscle in her body shook as she plunged her khukuri through its temple.

A cry escaped her lips as she slumped next to its lifeless body. Her Anima was weeping; she could feel it as she placed her hands on the bear's warm fur. To kill any animal that belonged to a Virtue wasn't just unholy… It was unforgivable. She panted as she buried her forehead into its fur and closed her eyes. This had unlocked a new dungeon in the pits of hell, the only place for a depraved soul such as hers.

She rose to her feet, all the color and life draining from her face as she angled her sword and hacked underneath the bear's fur. Blood spilled as she tore pelt away from muscle. *No mercy,* she thought. There would be no mercy for her in the afterlife for wearing its skin. None.

She surveyed her surroundings. The thick layer of ice over the ocean was either fractured or beginning to separate, revealing dark waters beneath. It was somber yet beautiful here.

She traveled the coastline until she found a cave. She made a fire and sat there for hours, feeling warm for the first time since being cradled in Midnight Wolf's fur. She lay the bear's skin out to dry at the entrance of the cave, which helped to block the glacial wind.

It had taken her almost an entire day to heal from two broken legs and hoist herself out of the crevasse. Since then, she had healed from frostbite three times and the onset of hypothermia twice after she'd almost died the first time. She was out of energy. Again. All there was to feed herself with now was the carcass of the bear. She hadn't eaten regular meat in years, let alone bear meat, and it was near impossible to keep down. She kept dry retching every time she took a bite, and decided that when she regained her energy she would start looking for fish.

She spent some time mapping the coastline, running the perimeter to determine its shape, trying to recall the lines in the maps from the Corps. Either way, this was nobody's country, yet it felt like one of Kore's best-kept secrets.

Aspen spent the whole day on the sound. She found dry, hardy bushes that she cut with her machete for firewood. Even the sun made a fleeting appearance, and she sat on the rocks and watched until it disappeared beyond the wall of fog. She had caught two fish on her travels and began making her way back to the cave in the hopes that the bear's hide had dried.

She had traveled halfway back when she heard something that made her freeze. She stilled her breath and blocked out the billowing sea breeze.

A mournful cry echoed from the direction of the cave. Aspen bolted, jumping over the rock and pristine waters. She reached the cave in minutes and idled silently behind it, their scents filling her nose.

"She's gone. The fire is cold," Vox cried through hyperventilated breathing.

River walked out of the cave and over to where Aspen had first set out on her journey that morning, screaming her name down the length of the sound.

"We waited too long," came the captain's voice, laced with regret.

"Maybe she just moved on, lass," Declan soothed Vox. "We don't know she's dead."

"Leaving her khukuris?" Mackenzie's voice and scent caught her by surprise.

She moved closer to see Vox walking out toward the ocean, looking down the coast. Aspen walked out past the cave; Declan and Mackenzie were inside its shadows. River was now walking back from the sound. He saw her first.

Relief flooded his worried expression as he began running back. Vox, who had her back turned, whipped around in a flash when she heard Aspen's voice.

"Am I a secret squirrel?"

"Aspen!" Vox ran to her, reaching her at the same time as River.

Aspen threw down her bundle of twigs before they trapped her in their embrace. She closed her eyes, reveling in the warmth of their entwined arms, hearing their steady heartbeats, smelling the lavender scent of Vox's hair and the musk of River's skin.

"I never thought I'd see you again." Her soft voice surprised even her. She stayed buried in them a little longer before they broke away.

The captain was leaning against the entrance of the cave, a reserved sense of pleasure contained in his slight smile. Mackenzie and Declan were also watching from inside the cave, both seeming meek.

Declan nodded toward her. "Secret squirrel… So covert not even the Corps knows about it."

"To what do I owe the pleasure of being in the presence of Special Forces?" Aspen walked by them and into the cave, throwing her twigs into the fire bed.

River came to sit beside her, lighting the pit with a match. She watched his beautiful features glow in the dim light of the growing fire.

Aspen looked down at her hands before looking back at him. "I'm sorry about the bear." She knew he had seen it as they walked in, and when his rich brown eyes settled on her, she cut him off. "It was her or me."

Her nerves frayed in the long pause before he huffed, "I know it was."

The others were gathering around the fire. Aspen narrowed her eyes at Mackenzie.

"They didn't kidnap me, if that's what you're thinking," Mackenzie stated, smoothing down her hair.

"You're not first on my campfire circle list," Aspen admitted with a tight-lipped smile.

Mackenzie chuckled softly at first, but scoffed when she read Aspen's unyielding stare. "You're serious?"

The captain, who was leaning against the cave wall, rolled his eyes. "She stays. We need everybody on board for this."

"Where's Venison and Kitty Cat?" Aspen asked in a sour tone.

"Thex has taken leave, and Levi isn't aware we've left… although I'm sure he's worked it out by now," Declan answered.

Aspen was arrested by the captain's gaze. He was behind this whole rescue mission and she longed to know why.

She snapped to attention as River cleared his throat. "We need to know which room at the Corps your surveillance was filming."

Aspen chuckled, revealing her brilliant teeth, before casting Vox a knowing glance.

"Don't look at me... He found it." Vox pointed to the captain.

Aspen ran her tongue over her cuspid teeth. "Which means you have my Phaedra."

The captain's only reply was a half-smile that she could have sworn caused her cheeks to flush. She broke eye contact.

"And you're not getting it back unless you help us," River explained with a glare.

Aspen scoffed. "*You* came to find *me*—which means..." She crossed her boots and folded her hands behind her head. "The force is at an all-time low, needing a serial killer's help for a mission."

Vox exhaled. "Well, you're not wrong. Your information on the mission is more than even the Corps knows... We saw Ansel open a secret room inside the library you were filming."

Aspen jolted upright at the news, waiting for Vox to continue.

"And when he went down there, he tried to open this locked book—"

Aspen's trembling hands covered her face; she cursed the Virtues. "He didn't open it, did he?"

"He... he was crying in pain, as if the book was somehow hurting him," Vox replied, the rosiness draining from her cheeks.

"But the book is closed?" Aspen repeated.

"What's in the book?" River asked.

Aspen took one look at their distressed faces and jumped up. She began pacing the front area of the cave, her hands pressed firmly against the sides of her head.

"What's wrong?" Declan asked in a shaky voice.

Everything felt like it was slowing and blurring. She

was either fainting or operating at superspeed; she couldn't tell which. Her legs felt weak, and the light outside was suddenly too bright—the darkness of the cave seemed to be growing.

It all stopped when the captain's hands touched her forearms, anchoring her. A little zap snapped her back to the present. They both looked down at their hands as the electric current faded.

"You can't let him open that book," she murmured.

"Why not? What does it do?"

She glanced back at the others, who were intent on her next words. "I… I can't tell you," she stammered.

"Aspen, we need to know," River insisted.

Mackenzie crossed her arms and sneered. "I bet it's wrapped up in a 'Hellfire falling from grace' story… Please, don't leave us hanging."

The captain's incredulous glare made Mackenzie shrink back.

Aspen looked down at her hands. "The book is called the *Ars Daemonium*, and it's one of the profane texts of the underworld."

River scoffed. "Hell has a library?"

"The darkness Ansel was telling us about at the solstice… It came from that book," Vox realized, snapping her fingers. "That's why he's trying to open it."

Aspen nodded. "It mostly has incantations that act as keys to the underworld portals."

"Which ones?" the captain asked.

Aspen swallowed. "As far as I know… all of them."

Declan sighed and ran his fingers through his hair,

causing it to stand on end. "So who let it out in the first place?"

"A few years ago, I set out to recover sections of the *Ars Daemonium*. Its pages were spread out all over the world, hidden for Earth's safety. It's considered to be so dangerous that its contents could destroy the entire Milky Way…"

"Why would you go and put something like that back together, Aspen?" River demanded.

Mackenzie backed him up. "Everything with you leads to destruction."

"I was trying to get there before Gregory Finch," Aspen replied sternly. "He was after them already. If he had gotten his hands on them, we wouldn't be here having this conversation."

"So you put it together, and then what?" Declan pressed.

Her hands tremored. Knowing the captain had seen it, she hid them behind her back. "I found the last piece of the text in Israel. It was the most dangerous piece of the whole book. I killed Gregory before he could take it and I went into hiding for months. Maxen kept telling me that we should keep it as insurance against the Corps—"

"Who's Maxen?" Declan asked.

"Hurricane—pay attention." Mackenzie rolled her eyes.

"Where is it now?" Vox pressed.

"I wanted to give it to Ansel. The text had this kind of… energy field around it. You could hear it haunting you day and night. It would whisper things, and sometimes I found myself doing things and didn't remember getting there—like I'd woken up sleepwalking. By the time Ansel could get to us, it was too late… Maxen had been opening it. Reading it." Aspen released a heavy exhale and watched the team's mood shift. "There was nothing I could do." She blinked back tears before they could form. "It's like he was just… gone."

Tears fell against Vox's pearly cheeks. "And that's how he died?"

Aspen nodded.

"Why didn't you tell anyone?" Vox breathed.

"Ansel said if I handed it over once I got to Kore, my sentence would be reduced, so I did. I just wanted to move on… You understand that, right?" she asked Vox and River, who answered her with hesitant expressions.

"Why weren't we sent on a mission like that?" Declan questioned. "I mean, why send you by yourself?"

Aspen's voice was grave. "Because the only one who can touch the cover of the book is me."

"Come again?" River asked, confused.

"The cover is made of sinew and skin. The book is a living organism of the underworld. When you touch it, it shows you more darkness than any one person can consume all at once."

Vox covered her mouth. "How dreadful!"

"You still didn't explain what happened to Maxen," Mackenzie pressed.

Aspen stood still a moment, feeling the captain's searching eyes upon her. "I killed him."

Mackenzie slowly sank onto the rock.

"Because you had no choice." Vox's even tone aimed to reassure her.

"He came under possession," River agreed.

Aspen shook her head and threw her hands up in the

air. She stormed out of the cave and didn't stop until she reached the murky ocean edge.

Vox called after her, cotton-candy curls blowing in the wind. "You did what you had to do… What did I say that was so wrong?"

"*Stop* making excuses for me, Vox. I *killed* my husband. And all you can say is *You had no choice; you did what you had to do.*"

"Well, if you had told me about your covert operations against the Corps—"

"You. Would. Have. Stopped. Me!" Aspen shouted.

Vox was shocked into silence. A pained expression flickered across her face, unbearable for Aspen to watch.

"I would have been with you," Vox finally managed to reply.

Aspen cast her focus to the ground before grasping both Vox's hands in hers. "When people follow me, they wind up dead. You made a mistake… You should never have come here."

Aspen released her hold and took off toward the sound, leaving Vox hugging her arms.

In a blur, the captain appeared in front of her, blocking her path.

"What do you want?" she complained.

"I came to give you this." He dangled her Phaedra before her.

"I'm not coming back."

"Maybe not. But it will get you off the Tundra." The crystal tag caught the light as he placed it in her hands.

She stared at it hard before looking back at him. "Why did you come back for me? After everything I've done…"

"It belongs to you, doesn't it?"

Aspen scoffed and turned her head toward the ocean. "I don't belong there."

He was pensive as he watched her. She found herself folding her arms in front of her, mirroring his body language.

"The only insider we have is Vangelis. Something tells me you know his location…"

Aspen raised her brows. "Nothing gets past you."

"I'm coming with you," he affirmed.

She laughed, but when she saw he wasn't joking, she reviewed his stance. His balance was even… Steadfast.

"What's your game?"

"Don't have one."

"Why would you risk coming with me?"

The captain shrugged. "Let's put it down to me wanting to listen to your pretty little accent."

She tilted her head in scrutiny. "I don't believe you."

He chuckled incredulously. "What part's throwing you off?"

"How do I know they haven't ordered a hit on me?"

The captain stepped closer, giving her a searching look. "You think I'm here to kill you?"

His words made her shuffle in discomfort. Her voice was tight as she replied, "To make sure I'm dead… It wouldn't be the first time."

She felt his gentle breath and her shoulders dropped. He pushed back the strands of hair falling over her face in the wind.

"Why are you really here?" she asked.

"Aspen… I—"

A step closer and her hands were pushing back against his chest.

"I can't do that," she breathed, shaking her head. He had a way of penetrating straight through her soul. "We can't bring that up, not ever... Understand?"

The captain took a step back and her hands fell to her sides. "If you didn't want me to trace you, I think you and I both know you never would have let it happen." A shaky breath escaped her lips as he tossed his head back toward the cave. "Get back there, because you're letting the entire team down." He began walking.

"What team? I don't belong on your team. An eternity of exile—remember?"

He turned. "She needs you... We all do."

She knew very well he was talking about Vox. "They'll die because of me!"

"We're all going to die anyway!"

Aspen dropped her shoulders, his reply sending a ripple of shock through her. He walked back to her.

"Look, I have a team to take to war, and it's now up to us to protect the world from a galactically huge book explosion—"

"That's not exactly—"

He held up a hand to silence her. "The way I see it, you have two choices. You're either going to die protecting your friends... or die alone. Or everybody you've ever killed to protect the people you love died for nothing."

Aspen felt as if he'd shot her.

"Asintmah died for nothing... Maxen died—"

Anger surged through her blood. "OKAY! ALRIGHT!

Geez." She could sense his smug smile as she stormed off toward the team waiting on the shore.

"What do we do now, Ryder?" Mackenzie asked as they rejoined the group.

The captain sighed. "I have a plan."

"Aw, pray to Odin. Is it as crazy as the one that got us here?" Declan complained with his hands on his hips.

The captain's gaze was focused. "This will work if you do exactly what I'm about to tell you. Here's what's going to happen… Aspen and I are going to track down Vangelis to uncover who we're dealing with here. The rest of you are going to go back to base and take the *Ars Daemonium* without anybody knowing."

"You want us to steal from the Corps?" Declan exclaimed. "We could be dishonorably discharged for pulling a stunt like that!"

River rubbed his hands together. "This is so cool."

"Debrief Levi. You'll need his inaudibility to pull this off without being detected. Aspen will give us all the passwords to her data so you can follow the map that's in there. Mackenzie, you'll work on putting Corps surveillance on a temporary loop."

"What do we say to Ansel and Gunner about you being gone?" Mackenzie asked.

"Tell them I left to spend time with Thex's family. Ansel will believe you."

"Ryder, I don't like this… She shouldn't be going with you," Mackenzie warned. "We don't know her motives. She could screw up this entire operation."

"I love it when people talk about me like I'm not here," Aspen said.

"It's true," Declan agreed. "It happens all the time at the Corps."

"You want out, marine?" the captain challenged Mackenzie.

Looking taken aback, she answered, "Negative, Captain."

"Good. Move out."

With the captain standing next to her, Aspen drew a circle with her Phaedra that opened up a swirling spectral portal. "You'll have to take my hand, or the force of the vortex will pull us apart."

His fingers found hers. An electric current danced subtly in the spaces between their touch. Her stomach somersaulted and she looked away from him.

"Who's to say you're not going to let go when we jump in?" He raised a dark gold brow at her.

"Well, I guess you'll have to find out."

CHAPTER 16

T he sound of birds calling welcomed them as they stepped out of the swirling portal that devoured any remnant of the Tundra and the team they'd left behind.

No crevasses. No hungry bears. No whiteout—thank the Virtues.

There was a moment of sereneness as they took in the town, hearts stilled and eyes full of wonderment. Jet-black shards of mountainous rock were dusted with pristine snow. The sun that skimmed the horizon made the canal's Baltic-blue waters seem metallic and acted as a fractured mirror to the stage of earth giants that stole their attention at every turn. The gentle current wrinkled the surface of the harbor, where white boats slept in their bays. They heard drifting music and the sound of clanking dishes and beer glasses from locals reveling in the extra hours of sunlight.

Aspen realized she was still holding the captain's hand. She broke his firm, warm hold, parting with an awkward glance. She read his stance in that moment. So fleetingly that an onlooker would have missed it, it told her that she alone had chosen to let go, to break their contact. His focus lingered on her a moment longer and she blinked rapidly.

Somebody say something!

Like he'd heard her, he asked, "Where are we?"

She exhaled, relieved at the break in tension. "Valdez, Alaska. We should move if Vangelis is here—"

"He's not going anywhere," the captain interjected.

"How do you know that?" *Good. Missions. Let's talk missions…* Missions were safer.

"Because I have enough of his scent to track a general location, and he's here," he answered, casting a glare over the town like he was waiting for a camouflaged animal to reveal itself in the wild.

"Sneaky," Aspen admitted.

"He hasn't left this place since he arrived a week ago."

She squinted. "You can tell all that?"

The captain read her grimace. "If it makes you feel any better, you're a couple of miles faster than me."

Aspen's mouth pulled into a smile without her consent, revealing the points of her fangs, a breath of a laugh escaping. "That does make me feel better."

The captain was smiling too now, like he was aware of the rarity of such an unbridled reaction. The moment slowed as she watched him, unaware of the words he spoke, her consciousness stretching out in relaxation over the baseline of his sound, his smooth vibration of voice.

Aspen released a sigh. "So what do you make of him staying put for the last week?"

"I haven't worked that next part out yet. I'm hoping he'll reveal all over a cold beer."

She threw him a puzzled look.

"I'm going to kill him," he disclosed.

"But he was my kill."

"They can't all be yours."

They began walking. Aspen stretched her arms out as she yawned. The only thing she could think of hunting down was a bed to sleep in. The captain was still dressed in his uniform, and they were going to have to find a base somewhere so he could change into something less conspicuous.

They traveled down the blocks of red weatherboard buildings, past civilians and store owners locking up their shops.

"Wait. That can't be right." The captain halted, taking a deep sniff in through his nose. She watched as he analyzed every molecule, his eyes searching, alarmed.

"What is it?" Aspen's voice was barely a murmur as a loudly talking couple passed them.

He looked around carefully. "A demon. Coming our way."

"Direction?" She too began scanning their surroundings, palming the hilt of the dagger hidden at her waist.

"Twenty feet, west." He breathed a slow steadying breath, and she knew he was blocking out every irrelevant noise. They looked behind at the path they'd come from.

"A demon... just roaming around the town?" she

whispered through gritted teeth. "Do you think it followed us through the portal?"

The captain's chest rose as he sniffed again, calculating. "Ten feet."

Aspen slid the dagger out of her waistband. "Where the hell is it?"

"Nine, eight, seven—"

"Ryder?" She spun in all directions, ready to attack.

"Four, three, two—"

Ryder was bent over, holding himself up on the electricity pole, shaking as he laughed into his belly.

Realizing it was a hoax, she punched him in the sweet spot where his deltoid met his bicep. It should have hurt like hell, but all Ryder did was laugh harder.

"A practical joker… Great! I'm already regretting taking you with me."

He straightened, still chuckling. "What's the point of being partners if we can't have a little fun along the way? You have to admit, I got you good."

She fought back a smile, walking off to hide it. He caught up to her, walking by her side with a wide grin.

"What?" she asked, annoyed.

"You called me Ryder."

"That is your name, isn't it?"

"I'm just saying, we haven't gotten past Captain since we met."

She held her breath for a moment. "It was you who came up with the mission to come and get me, wasn't it?"

"Would it make a difference?" He shrugged, deflecting the point of what it meant. What it meant to *her*.

She stopped walking. "Why?"

Ryder sucked in a breath. "You had too much information on this mission to not have you involved. You have a vendetta against the threat already, which makes the enemy of my enemy my friend. And… your sentence didn't make any sense to me." He knocked his closed fist against his leg as he watched her, quiet in thought, then looked down the next street. "Come on, I see a motel."

They made their way across the wide, open street. Ryder entered the red-and-gray weatherboard motel to check in while Aspen waited outside. He returned holding a room key, and she followed him through the parking lot toward a row of individual suites nestled closely together. When they found their suite, she idled in the doorway as Ryder entered and threw the keys on the kitchenette bench beside the door. Beyond was an intimate living room setting; beyond that, a double bed.

"It's not ideal, but we'll crash here for the night," Ryder stated.

Aspen shrugged, thumbing the door frame. "Are you kidding? I've been sleeping on the ground for months—this is paradise… But then, I suppose nothing compares to the views in Kore."

"Amen to that," Ryder replied, walking into the bedroom. It was a timber-paneled room with a honey glow cast from the tiny lampshade wall sconces fixed on either side of the bed. It was deliberate, the way he closed the double sliding doors, the wood knocking together, sealing the bed and any prospect of intimacy inside with it.

"Okay. Housekeeping," Aspen announced.

Ryder turned around, the corner of his mouth upturned. "You're going to wanna close the door first."

She swung it closed with a quaking hand, eyes never leaving his. She cocked her head to the side. "Touch the khukuri and I'll kill you."

"Oh, come on!" He threw his arms up. "But—"

She held her finger up and he closed his mouth in a huff, rolling his eyes.

"Anything else?" he added, disappointment lacing his tone as he sat on the edge of the faded couch.

Aspen's boots were heavy on the vinyl floor as she walked past the small kitchenette, glaring at him all the while. She set her khukuris down on the dark wood dining table, its varnish long worn off. "Yeah…" She edged closer to where he sat, her voice sounding more like that of a timid child. "What do you… want?"

"I don't follow," he replied with a little sarcasm.

Aspen twitched where she stood. "What—why are you here? With me? You're risking your rank."

"I don't give a damn about rank… If the Corps wants us to stop Gregory Finch, or whoever it is, we're doing what needs to be done. They sought me out. I do it my way."

He spoke with such resoluteness that she found herself getting lost in admiration. Realizing that a softness had snuck through her defenses, she snapped herself out of it. With no energy left, she collapsed onto the couch and lay looking up at the ceiling.

He broke the silence. "How do you know Vangelis?"

Aspen turned her head at the sound of him shifting as he took off his military blouse. She looked back up at the ceiling, pretending to ignore his scent and the way his arms tensed and flexed as he laid the blouse over the couch. When Ryder spoke, he was both self-assured and a gentleman, though in his body language there was much more to uncover. He never hid his robustness or solidity, even when he was silent… He owned the space he occupied and moved with military prowess. The man was all Wolf.

Her reply was soft. "It's kind of a long story."

"I'm not going anywhere." The intensity of his eyes enveloped her as he waited for her to begin.

Aspen turned to face him, laying with her head propped up on her elbow. "I met Vangelis when he was scouting for Wolf Anima during the war."

Ryder glanced down at his hands before looking back at her. "How old were you?"

"I was sixteen… He came to my family home with Gregory Finch. They tried to invite themselves in, saying they were government officials wanting to question my father about the murders going on at the time. But they were there for me."

"What happened then? Were you activated?"

"No, I was still living a human life. Shortly after that I met Ansel, and then everything changed." Her lips pressed together as she tried to hide the old wound becoming raw again—a burn on top of a burn. She tried to pass off her sorrow as tiredness.

Ryder leaned forward. "How did they…"

"Die?" Aspen finished, her tone blunt.

"Yeah." Regret flickered across his features.

"I came home after I'd found the first piece of the *Ars Daemonium*… It was a close battle—Finch almost got his hands on it. Then I realized they'd led me out purposely. It had all been timed and planned. While I was out trying to stop Finch, they came after my family. And when I got back, they were dead."

Ryder was unwavering, compassion pouring from him—a response she somehow couldn't receive. Aspen glanced down at the fibers of the rug, her voice laced with vengeance.

"There was nothing left of them. There was blood covering every inch of the house. There were pieces… of their remains." Her breath hitched; every muscle inside her clenched. "I looked for my brother everywhere… hoping that they hadn't found him too. But when I looked in the underground cellar outside… It had been broken into, and it looked the same way as the house did. Red. He was only eight.

"I couldn't remember if I'd passed out or if I was knocked out, but Maxen activated me. He said he'd take away the pain. And when I woke up, I was different. I was… I was Hellfire."

When she looked up at him, Ryder had his fists covering his mouth. He moved them down, holding her gaze. She chuckled; the sound rose from her like it was bubbling up from somewhere dark within—from wherever she'd drowned her innocence. For she had died too, that day she'd lost it all—that day of becoming…

"I don't know why I'm telling you this." She walked around the couch and leaned on the door frame of the bedroom. She sensed him standing, but somehow didn't hear his footsteps until she felt his warm hand touch her shoulder.

"What happened to you wasn't fair." His voice was smooth, the vibration humming along her nerves.

She looked at him over her shoulder, her reply as barren as the Tundra. "I don't want you to feel sorry for me."

"No. You're telling me because deep down you want me to understand."

She winced, his words dousing her wounds in liquor. He had some nerve, showing up and rescuing her from exile. After all, no one had ever cared... No one had rescued her the day her family was slaughtered, or any other time she'd been forced to carry out missions alone. Kindness always had a price. Maxen had *taken away the pain* only to force her into activation before she was ready— before he'd become the cause of even more pain.

She wanted to shake this man who stood before her, and at the same time, thank him. Thank him for saving her from the Tundra, for trying to stop them from exiling her, for closing the damned bedroom door...

Aspen turned to him fully, standing only inches away from him. "How do you know what I want?"

Ryder was clearly choosing his next words carefully. She watched him grow pensive, and only when something shifted in him, making his stance more open, did she realize that he'd made a decision. He stepped forward. Their eyes locked, but this time was different... This time he was giving her something, his eyes asking her to receive it.

"When I was young, about fourteen... I was kidnapped walking home from school." He paused, watching her expression become grave. "They were looking for Anima—I didn't know that at the time. I thought they were just a bunch of corrupt scientists illegally experimenting on kids."

"You were a stolen kid?" Aspen breathed.

His lips made a tight line as he nodded. "They did all kinds of things to us... They'd blindfold us and tell us they'd run us over with a car. I still remember the car's engine revving and the screeching of the tires. That was the easiest way to break our bones. But that wasn't the worst part… The worst part was when they stood on our broken limbs."

Aspen realized that she had stopped breathing at some point while he'd been talking. Her eyes darted away, then back to him, until she composed herself in a rigid stance. "How did you get out?"

"After about three weeks, I escaped. It killed me to leave without the others." Ryder took a step back. Aspen felt the anger fizzle off him as he leaned against the back of the couch, arms crossed. "And then when I was eighteen, I signed up to become a marine. I trained hard, applied myself—and then I used intel to track them all down. It took me almost a year to find them all and kill them. Then I couldn't stop. I kept finding more organizations to take down. At that point, Thex started helping me. Then the time came to take down the ringleader, and it was none other than—"

"Finch," she finished, darkness lacing her tone.

Ryder nodded. "It took months to train for the mission. I made sure not to leave anyone alive—not even me. But Finch, he… he got away."

"You faked your own death?"

"My family thinks I've been dead for over two years."

They were both plunged into silence, left to stir in the somberness of their vulnerability, until Ryder's voice cut through it, the usual spunk returning to his tone. "So, as it turns out, Sergeant Lovetta, we have more in common than you think."

She held his gaze for a long moment. He scratched the back of his neck, breaking their eye contact.

"I'm going to take a shower."

Aspen watched him open the door to the bedroom and enter the ensuite bathroom. She heard the door click shut and the water turn on as she walked back to the couch, lying down in a huff.

If Ryder Everett was a stolen child, he too had suffered in the War on Wolves, just as she had... Not to mention at the hands of Gregory Finch. A common goal gave warriors a purpose to fight... but being his comrade was going to come with major ramifications. She could feel those ramifications stirring inside her, taking form, threatening to knock down the wall she'd built to keep others out.

After all, everybody who dared to get close to her ended up dead.

CHAPTER 17

Aspen woke beneath the comfort of a warm blanket in the peaceful darkened suite. Her boots were beside the couch, though she couldn't recall kicking them off. Come to think of it… she didn't recall getting herself a blanket, either.

She rubbed her eyes and assessed the room. The heavy blackout curtains were drawn. The duffel bag full of civilian clothing that Vox had thrown through a portal sagged on top of the dining chair. She could hear the splashing of salmon coming from Port Valdez.

Her focus returned at the whisper of Ryder's breath. He slept in an unnerving stillness on the couch adjacent to her, one powerful arm bent behind his head, the other resting along his side. She watched as his chest rose and fell, the soft gleam of his golden aura serving as the only light in the suite, aside from her own. His face was so serene, and yet every visible muscle, including the ones that stood out beneath his black T-shirt, promised skill, force, and power. He was built like a god, with not so much as one strand of dark gold hair out of place.

Aspen hadn't been tucked into bed since her parents were alive. She told herself that it meant nothing—him taking off her boots and covering her while she slept. Ryder was a do-gooder. He would have done it for anybody.

She rose as silently as she could. It wasn't going to be easy, leaving without waking him. But she had to try.

She padded to the table and changed into a gray hoodie, black biker pants that molded to her legs like a second skin, and a matching biker jacket. She fixed the straps of her khukuri scabbard, her eyes on the sleeping captain, and held her boots in her hand as she closed the door to the suite.

In a blaze of moonbeam light, she sped out of the motel complex and stopped at the edge of the highway. The road and shrubs had been soaked by the passing rain, accentuating every scent surrounding her, and long clouds that resembled stretched cotton hung low in its aftermath. She'd had two hours sleep, only half of an Anima's ideal amount, but she had to make sure the captain was out cold.

Arm's length, Aspen, she reminded herself as she gazed down at her wristwatch to observe the tracking of Vangelis's phone that she'd synced with Ryder's tracker. The coordinates indicated that it was half a mile down the highway, heading out of town. She was doubtful that Vangelis had possession of his phone—he was much too clever for that.

Aspen walked at a civilian pace past the rugged green slumbering mountains, glancing down at her wristwatch every so often. She came to a fork in her path; one followed the highway and the other led down a quiet trail. She leaned toward the direction of the trail, sucking the air into her lungs. The wind carried three scents—Vangelis's agents, no doubt.

She followed the scents until she spotted them further up on the path. Three men dressed in outdoor gear, like they were locals out for a stroll, veered off the trail and into the bushes. Prowling low to the ground, Aspen started to follow them off the trail when she heard footsteps coming from behind her.

Three more of Vangelis's men closed her in.

She shot through the trees and made a loop until she reached a yard full of blue tin sheds, hiding behind the rows of tires. Seven agents broke through the shrubs and paused on the asphalt, its potholes full of water. Their eyes scanned the area; they had foolishly lost sight of her and began scattering in different directions.

An eighth agent entered from the deserted garages and growled, "You lost her?"

The agents searched around the parked trucks and boats and behind large pieces of scrap metal. Aspen waited for her moment.

As one agent came close, she attacked his neck. He twitched and shook as blood poured over the asphalt. He dropped to the ground, and when another agent noticed, he ran to attack her. He was met with a flying khukuri that sliced through his middle; he too fell to the ground.

"I take it Vangelis wants me alive, seeing as none of you have pulled out your guns. I have to say… I'm kind of flattered."

She twisted one agent until his neck was compressed in her iron chokehold and put her hand out to stop another from approaching. There was a pleasant warmth in her stomach, something that felt like… No, it couldn't be.

The feeling expanded, engulfing her entire body and radiating out of her. A powerful force shot from her hand in sparkling crimson light, throwing the agent thirty feet down the road.

"Did I just do that?" she asked the other agent standing dumbfounded beside her. He nodded in awe.

Aspen dropped the unconscious man in the chokehold and punched the other, knocking him out.

"I'm also kind of annoyed," she announced to the three agents still standing. "Vangelis didn't come to get me himself. We're old pals, after all. I mean, what else could he possibly have to say to me after all these years anyway? Why not just kill me now? No? Nobody has answers? That's a Hellfire cue for death… although—"

She threw her other khukuri, decapitating another agent. The remaining two were now shaking.

"Do you know anything about relationships? I have this friend who's kinda having guy trouble." She approached the agents, who moved hesitantly backward. "So this girl has these powers that nobody knows about because they're embarrassing, but she meets this guy, and he follows her through a portal even though he knows she's a serial killer… Now, my thought is that he's caught up in the spell of the stupid useless powers that the girl has… Are you—what are you doing? Are you paying attention?"

One agent looked behind him and made a run for it. He tripped over his feet and shuffled back from her.

"Please, just let me go."

"You haven't heard the rest of the story yet." She issued a loud exhale before continuing. "So now the girl is left somewhat clueless as to whether the guy likes her for who she really is, which would be seriously messed up…" She read the agents' expressions, both mystified and queasy. "Because she's a serial killer."

That expanded feeling pulled at her being, like there was a light inside that was bigger than her body, more than she could wield. She could do nothing but stare as the power lit up her hands. The men started running away, so she sent the pooling energy toward them, like a red aurora, levitating them high into the air before smashing them into some rusted tow wagons.

She walked to them as one rubbed his head and the other clutched his side. Her voice was somber as she stood before them. "Or… maybe he'll never really know how he truly feels, because her pheromone powers blind that."

Something entwined in that sentence drained all the fight out of her. Her chest caved, the structures she'd built collapsing underneath her, opening up to a void she only knew how to close with revenge.

Who is he to you?

"What did you say?" she asked one of the agents.

The man looked at her pleadingly. "I didn't say anything."

The voice came through louder. *Who is he to you?*

Aspen's hand covered her gaping mouth as the realization washed over her—a truth she wouldn't allow herself to believe, and yet something she had known all this time.

"I know him," she whispered.

"What are you guys talking about?"

She spun at the sound of his voice. Ryder stood there, wearing charcoal cargos and a navy parka, the black T-shirt he'd slept in, and his military boots. Suspicion coated his features. "I see you've been busy, and… making a mess." He glanced at the dead agents on the road.

"They were just telling me where Vangelis is… Weren't you?" Aspen hit one agent in the gut.

Ryder placed his hands out in front of him and they charged with deep purple rays. "Don't be rude. Answer her!" he ordered.

Aspen stared at the violet firestorm emanating from his hands, then looked down at her own hands. The power had gone. But it had been like *his*. Her powers looked like *his*.

The agent on the right held the side of his head as he answered, "We just report heat waves back to the boss—he doesn't tell us anything. To meet, we have to have found something valuable enough for him to make an appearance."

Aspen and Ryder exchanged a smile.

"Tell your boss you caught Hellfire and you want to meet him at the port in half an hour," Ryder demanded.

The agent was slow to react.

"Well, come on! Don't keep the captain waiting," Aspen snapped.

The agent hesitantly puffed into his phone, "Boss, we've got Hellfire."

There was a pause on the open line. Vangelis was silent; all they heard was breathing. Finally, he muttered, "Good. Where are you?"

"I'm almost a mile out from the port… She's h-h-hard to hold down. You're going to need to come to me."

"Was she with the other Wolf?" Vangelis asked.

Ryder shook his head at the agent.

"Negative, boss."

"Send me your coordinates. I'll be there as soon as I can… No, change of plans," growled Vangelis. "I'll send you coordinates to a bar." He hung up.

Aspen snapped the man's neck. He fell limp to the ground as she stabbed the other man through the heart.

She turned to face Ryder's unimpressed glare. "What?" she asked him carelessly, taking the agent's phone from the asphalt.

"You left to find Vangelis by yourself," he answered.

Aspen went about retrieving her khukuris. "Is that jealousy I sense? Sad you missed all the action?"

Ryder rolled his eyes as they began walking in the direction of the port. "We get nowhere playing lone wolf."

Aspen scoffed. "Are you saying I can't handle myself? Because I've done it all my life."

"This isn't about capability, Aspen, this is about nobody being here to watch your six."

"So now you're criticizing my strategy, or lack thereof? Need I remind you that you can't lose me, because you traced me."

"Well, now that you've brought it up—I traced you because we're partners, whether you like it or not, and when you're done being reckless in the face of unimaginable danger, we can get on with the mission."

"Oh, please. Nothing happened, and besides, it's not like you're going to go back to Kore and they'll interrogate you about my death… Stop pretending like—"

"Like I care what happens to you?" he fired, fixing her with that intense glare.

She went silent; he'd caught her off-guard. He stopped walking and it made her halt too.

"Are you honestly telling me you don't feel this?" Ryder clasped his hand over her jacket above her wrist. Their touch ignited a swirling deep purple storm of light.

They held each other's gaze for a long moment before Aspen abruptly let go. She wasn't ready to show him what was hidden underneath his grip.

"It could mean anything. Maybe it's just your powers—"

"This doesn't happen with anybody else."

Her eyes darted around, not knowing where to look. She ran her fingers through her garnet locks as she began walking off. "So?"

He followed at her heels. "So you don't think it's strange that I somehow accessed your computer locked with *your* frequency code with *these* powers, or that it somehow activates when we touch? And we haven't even started on scent…"

"Don't go there," she warned, stealing a glance at him.

The corner of his mouth turned upward. "Nice to know I'm not the only one."

She scoffed. "Can we just… get on with it?"

"Be my guest. Carry on being the fortress that is you."

They super-sped the rest of the way, nothing but two streams of light as they ran to the port. They stopped at a railing at the water's edge.

"The bar is on the waterfront, just over there." Aspen tilted her head toward a lodge, a weatherboard building much like the rest of the town, painted in fawn brown with blonde timber creating a new texture every few feet.

They walked the length of the building, past the boardwalk that led down to the boats and the newspaper vending machines, to the entrance of the bar.

Ryder released a sharp exhale. "When we go in, you wait alone at one of the more private booths for him to arrive. Think you can do that?"

"Affirmative."

Ryder waited, one arm holding the door open. She wanted to blurt out that he didn't have to do that, but there was something about the way he pressed his lips together in a smile that told her he already knew that. So she walked through, catching his amber-and-cedarwood scent as a draft danced around them.

Their steps were muffled against the coffee-brown carpet in the small lobby. They turned the corner and walked through wide double doors that opened to rows of seating set before a bar that stretched the length of the room. The heat of the stone fireplace welcomed locals to stop and chat, so Aspen sat at a booth in the furthest corner, doused in the light of a large window that looked onto the port. She waited there, watching Ryder take a seat on a nearby barstool, leaning his elbows on top of the bench.

His hand signal was a mere flash. *Five, four.* Aspen's focus pinned to her nine o'clock—the door.

Ryder slid off the barstool. Her stomach flipped as Vangelis walked through the double doors. Ryder appeared behind him with a flare building in his hand, pointed into Vangelis's back. Aspen smiled, sweet yet devious, as Vangelis realized the predicament he had walked into.

He scowled at them both. "Bloody hell…"

Ryder waited until Vangelis had slid into the booth

opposite Aspen, blocking him in. Vangelis's eyes darted around self-consciously, his jaw clenched.

"You've both got some nerve showing up here."

Aspen's smile was dangerous. "Hello, Vangelis."

He nervously eyed the power accumulating in Ryder's hand, pointing at him from beneath the table. "Just my luck that you two have become pals—you have no idea how much danger you're in."

Aspen chuckled. "You're caught between two Wolves... I'd say that's checkmate."

Vangelis looked her over. "I haven't seen you in years, and when I saw you in Kore... I barely recognized you."

She made sure that her eyes flashed a dangerous warning before she snapped, "Let's skip the 'little town girl's all grown up' part and fast-forward to where you tell us who's impersonating Gregory Finch."

Vangelis exhaled through his nose. "Listen to me, Aspen. Play this smart and call Hurricane, because this mess... There's no stopping Ignatius."

"Who's Ignatius?" Ryder demanded.

"Your worst bloody nightmare, that's who... I'm not joking. Get Hurricane!"

Aspen's quick glance at Ryder was a wordless message of alarm. She had never seen more austerity in Vangelis's demeanor than in this moment. "Hurricane can't help us, on account of the fact that he's dead. So how about you start by explaining why this Ignatius guy needed a dead body?"

She watched the blood drain from Vangelis's face, his mouth pulling downward at the news. He paused before continuing, his tone quieter this time, "Ignatius needed someone to die so he could feed off them to regenerate his human form."

"Attractive," Aspen remarked.

"So he's some kind of demon?" Ryder asked.

"Not a demon… He is something far more powerful. Ignatius is what they call a Primordial being. A force so ancient it predates life on Earth. He's been sourcing nutrients to appear in full bodily form so that he can carry out his plans."

"Don't leave me hanging," Aspen warned.

Vangelis glared incredulously back at her. "Do you think we braid each other's pigtails and he tells me his master plan?"

"So this Ignatius comes to Kore to find an Anima sacrifice as a power source, and to take our general's staff?" Ryder clarified.

"That's not the only reason."

"He wants the *Ars Daemonium*," Aspen realized.

"Exactly." Vangelis nodded. "But the problem with Primordials is that only something as old as he is can destroy him."

"How do we find him?" Aspen demanded.

Vangelis looked incredulous. "Did you not hear what I just said? Even an Anima can't stop him!"

Before Vangelis had blinked, Aspen plunged her dagger through the middle of his hand resting on the table. She skewered it there, splitting the wood underneath. Vangelis's mouth opened into a silent scream and a burning red covered his skin as he held in the explosion of pain. He struggled to breathe, his arm going limp.

"We're going to ask you again," Ryder began. "Tell us

where he's hiding, who's working for him, details about his armory—"

"EVERYONE! Everyone is working for him! He has people everywhere! Just get this knife out of me!"

"Not until I have everything I need." Aspen's voice was smooth and deadly.

Vangelis labored through heavy breaths. "He doesn't have everything he needs yet. He's still looking for this… I don't know… This thing called Enceladus."

Aspen felt Ryder's eyes on her. She threw him a worried look, feeling the blood drain from her face. She pulled the dagger from Vangelis's hand; he retracted it with a whimper.

Ryder slouched against the booth and sighed through his nose. "We can't kill him… We need him for more intel."

He'd seen it—the moment when everything deadened inside of her. Sometimes, in that state, she couldn't even hear her own heart beating. Ryder waited, with the kind of calm reserved only for somebody as highly trained as he. Aspen held out the dagger for him to take. His hand covered hers for a moment, before a faint ticking sound painted fear on both their faces.

As if in slow motion, everything lifted from the ground.

The napkins on the table. The benches. The barstools. The bottles behind the bar. Ryder dove on top of her. People were tossed like rag dolls in the antigravity.

The explosion blasted the walls open.

CHAPTER 18

Aspen had her hands clamped over her ears against the excruciating, high-pitched ringing. She opened her eyes to see Ryder half on top of her. His eyes were closed, his body dead weight. The bar had been obliterated; there was nothing left but splinters of furniture and large holes in the plaster. The bar bench had caved in on itself, leading to a cascade of debris in its center.

Most of the people who had been seated nearest the bar were now on the floor against the back wall, thrown by the blast, dead. As the ringing in Aspen's ears began to subside, it was replaced with the sounds of people sobbing and groaning. She touched Ryder's shoulder as he came to, and they both sat up. He asked if she was okay, but she ignored his question and instead inspected him all over, starting with his head and working her way down. The question was not if *she* was okay, but if *he* was. For if Ryder had been hurt, there was no way of him knowing… Not with his pain threshold.

Aspen went about her quick checks, avoiding the gratitude in his eyes. She nodded when she was done, then looked over at Vangelis, who was just lifting his head, his eyelids half open in a daze.

In the middle of the bar, the silhouette of a man became clearer through the settling dust. He looked to be in his late twenties, wearing an expensive gray suit and an unbuttoned white shirt. He stepped over the crumbling debris, walking past a man propping himself up on a broken chair with his phone to his ear, reporting the blast.

The man in the suit winced in irritation at the patron's terrified voice. With a subtle flick of his hand, the phone exploded. Blood spurted from the other man's amputated finger and poured from his ruptured ear. He produced a gurgling scream.

Aspen helped Ryder up. The heels of black dress shoes crushed the rubble as the man approached them. He lit a cigarette and studied them with a toss of his shoulder-length brown hair. There were no whites to his eyes; they were dark as night with inferno-red irises, and when he spoke, his voice sent an ominous ripple through the bar, making everybody curl uncomfortably.

"You're seriously the best the Anima Corps has to offer?"

"I take it you're Ignatius." Ryder's hands began to glow.

Ignatius took the cigarette to sneering lips. "I see my reputation precedes me—I am somewhat flattered that my whereabouts has been of high importance to such a sacred existence as the Anima Corps."

He stopped directly in front of Aspen, searching her over as if he could see through her skin with his blood-red eyes. His voice enveloped her in what felt like the deepest, darkest void in the universe. "I knew you would come looking for me. I could feel your desperation for the hunt the moment you laid eyes on Gregory Finch's face." Ignatius smirked, sending a fast spidery crawl up Aspen's spine. "And the bombshell of me—being him—pretending not to recognize you…"

He laughed darkly, his eyes flashing at Ryder.

"I knew the only way to get her to come to me was to spark her curiosity and dangle the burning desire of a new hunt before her."

Ignatius stepped a little closer, and Aspen exhaled a shaky breath.

"You don't know how much it excites me that, since then, you have lived vowing to find me."

His hand rose to touch her jaw, and she felt its malevolent vibration. She met his wrist instantly with the gleaming edge of a khukuri.

Ignatius let out a low, bitter laugh. "Always difficult to catch, pretty Wolf. You need not be coy—must we pretend we haven't been fully acquainted?"

Ryder's stance was defensive beside her, his voice nothing more than a murmur. "What is he talking about?"

"I have no idea," Aspen answered truthfully. Her eyes were wide in anticipation.

This seemed to please the Primordial being. "You offend me, Hellfire. I thought Anima could sense the ether-fields, and I half expected you to recognize mine… After all, we did live together, even if it was only for only a short time. However, I will indulge your game.”

Aspen gasped. Ignatius caught the moment of her recollection.

“So you do remember. I must say, inhabiting your husband's body, even if it was only for a mere week, was an experience I will never forget. Having wings and flying was… Well, euphoric, to say the least, but tying you up and watching you scream for hours and hours… *That* was the closest to heavenly fire I've ever been.”

Aspen doubled back, every inch of her skin covered in sickly heat.

The Primordial licked his lips. “I wreaked havoc for days, making you believe that there was nothing left of Hurricane that was worth saving. Driving you to kill him wasn't easy, even after he… or I… bound and beat you.” A breathy laugh escaped his sculpted lips. “Apparently an act not typical of Hurricane, although I'm surprised… Such a violent fellow, was he not? And even then you tried preserving his life.”

Aspen was panting, as if she had been treading water too long. Her arms felt heavy and her legs like jelly. She looked at Ryder, who appeared as dumbfounded as she did.

Her words stuttered, but the promise was sincere. “There's not enough blood in you to repay your debt, but I'm going to make sure that when I kill you, you'll experience the pain of a thousand deaths.”

Ignatius closed the gap between them faster than Aspen could swing her khukuri, clasping the frame of her jaw in his iron grip. A light blinded her as Ryder's powers shot at Ignatius. He blocked the blast with an arm made of tar; it lashed out like a weapon from his back, protecting Ignatius, but was shattered clean off with the impact. It didn't seem to hurt, because all he did was tut back at Ryder in warning.

Ignatius returned his focus to Aspen. She could do nothing but gaze into his soulless eyes.

"I so very much look forward to it." He tilted his head and ran his tongue along his teeth. "Don't think I don't appreciate your existence… Between the way you fight, the way you slay, and the way you make love—you would make the most astounding Persephone."

Ryder waited for Ignatius to release his hold on Aspen. Only then did she take a rapid, jagged breath, like she'd had to delve somewhere deep to find oxygen.

Ignatius threw the smoking cigarette to the ground. "You have entrapped me for too long… and now you will finally—"

The ground quaked as an ultraviolet beam surged through Ryder's hands into Ignatius's chest. The Primordial strained, his teeth gritted as he slid backward out of the bar and onto the boardwalk.

"You talk wayyy too much," Ryder said. "You're going to bore me to death before you even get to the point." He dug deeper into the wrath he felt inside, sending a beam of power that sent Ignatius tumbling onto the port.

Ignatius laughed as he stumbled to stand, straightening

his suit jacket. Limbs of onyx tar spread from his body. Ryder dodged and leaped around the venomous arms as his Anima was liberated from inside him, illuminating the harbor as it snapped its jaws at Ignatius. Ryder's gamma blasts and his lunging Anima had Ignatius edging back ever further to the side of the pier. It had been months since Ryder had seen his Anima, and something inside him felt whole as they stood together.

Ignatius jumped onto a boat and exploded the timber pole it was tied to with a wave of his hand. Ryder swore as he darted into the enclosed helm and disappeared from view. The boat's engine thrummed.

Ryder was mid-jump when Aspen dashed past him, pushing him aside and landing on the boat just as it began to drift from the port.

Having fallen on his back, Ryder kicked himself up, rolling his spine against the ground and landing on his feet. He called out to Aspen just as she went out of sight with a flick of red hair in the wind.

Ryder catapulted off the pier as the boat detonated, the blast throwing him into the icy water of the harbor. He surfaced to a thick, monstrous ash cloud and realized he'd landed uninjured on the other side of the pier. He swam hastily underneath the pier to the wreckage, seeing a shadow in the deep waters ahead, swimming away. He sur-faced again, taking a breath and shouting her name. Doubt flooded him. What was the possibility of her surviving an explosion like that?

He searched below the water again, seeing debris sinking into the depths of the harbor. He swam around it, dragging metal pieces out of his way. He surfaced again and spotted Aspen face-down in the water. He propelled himself through the wreckage and turned her body over, moving what was left of her hair from her face. His breath was rapid as he looked upon the severe burns that covered her face and chest. He treaded water, floating her body to the side of the pier.

Ryder repeated her name over and over, distracting himself from the fact that he couldn't hear her heart beating. He hoisted her out of the water and laid her down on the boardwalk. He parted her lips and inflated her chest with as much air as he could muster. Aspen was unresponsive, but her raw flesh began renewing. He filled her lungs again and she sputtered, turning to her side, water dripping from her mouth. Her emerald eyes were aglow when they opened; Ryder watched the last of her skin repair itself with her healing powers.

He exhaled in relief. "Are you crazy?" He kept her sitting up, his arms wrapped around her. She was panting, the rouge color returning to her lips. "Did you know you were going to survive that?"

Aspen shook her head and motioned to stand. He rose and pulled her up by her forearm. She wobbled before falling into his chest.

"He got away." Her voice was but a whisper, but the rage it held was palpable. There was no end to the damage a demon could do once it got through and roamed the world. Animas were sentient. They relied on each other, needed each other to survive; when one hurt, they all hurt. Aspen had been hurt too many times for Ryder to turn his back now. He couldn't stomach what Ignatius had done to her.

If Ignatius had already sanctioned war upon the world, he'd made the deadly mistake of making it personal.

Aspen seemed too drenched, cold, and defeated to push herself off of him. He matched her tone when he answered, "I know."

She shivered, trying to steady herself against him, but when her arm shifted, something caught Ryder's eye. He took her wrist and stretched her arm out.

"What?" she asked.

Ryder nodded to her forearm, where symbols of silver ink trailed up to her elbow.

"I've always had it," she explained.

He couldn't bring himself to speak. Aspen watched him questioningly as he rolled up his sleeve, her eyes growing wide as he revealed almost identical symbols inked in gold on his own skin. On her wrist was the other half of the compass that was marked on his own.

Slowly, her fingers laced with his, bringing their wrists together, the two halves of the compass connecting, joining the full band of symbols. The Earth could have cracked at its center and bathed the whole surface in fire and they wouldn't have noticed. The world went on without them as they braced against each other, wrists locked together, eyes searching. Asking…

Ryder broke the silence. "What does it mean?"

They inspected the moving glow that traveled the delicate lines of the symbols. Aspen shook her head. "I don't know."

They lingered a moment longer before Aspen ripped her hand away, her focus darting over the ground.

"It's probably nothing."

Ryder couldn't help a sarcastic response. "You're right, it's probably nothing that our arms are glowing and there's an almost identical marking on both our forearms."

Before she could respond, his wristwatch began ringing. He looked at the screen to see it was Vox.

His glance at Aspen told her they weren't finished, but he reluctantly answered, "Tell me you've got something we can work with."

"We have it—the *Ars Daemonium*," Vox replied. "But it wasn't easy."

Ryder exhaled heavily in relief. "We found out who Gregory Finch is… I'll explain everything when we get back."

Aspen's stance was rigid as he hung up. She shot him a cold glare that he returned with suspicion. *What was that look for?*

She didn't appear to be regaining her strength; her usual spark had been extinguished. She remained silent the rest of the way back to the motel. He almost asked her what was wrong many times, but figured she felt humiliated. Come to think of it, Ryder realized she looked weakened, pale with exhaustion. His brows knitted together in worry as he opened the door to the suite. Aspen fled to the bathroom and locked herself in without a word.

Ryder waited on the edge of the bed, turning the small television on with low volume. He rubbed his eyes as he recalled pieces of the disjointed story.

A Primordial demon needed the *Ars Daemonium* and a rare element called Enceladus. So rare that it couldn't be found anywhere in the world other than on Ansel's staff. But why did he want them? Ryder made a promise to himself that whatever Ignatius was planning, he wasn't going to let it unfold.

The Primordial's words repeated in his mind. *You have entrapped me for too long…*

He cast his eyes toward the bathroom door, and it dawned on him that the shower had never turned on. He walked to the door and leaned against it. "Aspen?"

No answer.

"Aspen?"

He rapped against the door. Still no answer. Ryder looked at his watch. "Aspen, you've been in there for a long time. Is everything alright?"

No answer.

He rolled his eyes. "Aspen, open the door!" But what had started as annoyance quickly became alarm. "If you don't answer me right now, I'm coming in…"

He paused and waited for sound. It didn't come.

One kick and the door crashed clean off its hinges. Ryder swore as he looked over the room. Aspen was lying face down on the floor. Blood stained the sink and the towels, and there were handprints on the wall and the benchtop, but there was no evidence of a wound. Her eyes were closed.

He bent over her, trying to wake her. Her eyes flickered open groggily.

"What happened?" he rasped.

Aspen's lips parted, but no sound came out. As he tried to lift her, she slumped backward. He quickly caught her before her head hit the bathtub.

"Why is there so much blood? Where's it coming from?" Ryder tried to straighten her lolling head.

Drunkenly, she pointed to her shoulder. He twisted her slightly to see. There were lumps underneath her skin.

He looked back into her sleepy eyes. "It keeps healing over itself, doesn't it? Did *he* do this to you?"

She nodded slowly.

"Shit. I have to get these out."

Aspen slumped forward again and he caught her, maneuvering her to sit with her back to his chest and placing his legs on either side of her to stabilize her. He pushed her hair over her opposite shoulder and assessed the lumps. Thin black veins spread from them before her body healed itself again. Despite her healing powers, her skin was gray and pasty with sweat.

With a weak hand, Aspen passed him a small blade she'd taken from a razor. He took it, looking over the area he was about to cut into with a sigh.

"I don't know what I'm doing… If you'd called me in earlier, maybe you could have given me surgery one-oh-one."

Ryder cut into the largest lump. Blood trickled down her back as something that looked like jagged tourmaline stuck out of her flesh. He pinched it and tried pulling it out. It wouldn't budge.

"It must be fragments from Ignatius's demonic… thing." Ryder kept trying to remove it, but the substance was somehow fused to her bones. "Come on!" He clamped over it again and yanked, but Aspen had lost consciousness. "Don't you dare die on me again, Lovetta."

He yanked one more time, to no avail. Until he was struck with an idea.

"I'm sorry. This is gonna hurt."

He clamped over the hard piece and let out a high-voltage blast from his fingers. The piece fell away as the blast jolted her, and she screamed, feeling the aftermath of pain before her skin healed over the wound.

"Okay, this looks like it's working. Get ready to go again."

Ryder repeated the cutting, pinching, and gamma-wave blasts, pushing past Aspen's cries of agony. With each extraction, she regained more consciousness and movement, and soon she was able to speak to him.

"There's two left. Are you ready?"

She nodded, clutching his knees in anticipation. He cut into her back and she gritted her teeth as she watched, looking over her shoulder.

"This is for blowing yourself up and making me think you were dead." He extracted the piece with a *crack* and she jolted, groaning. The fewer pieces there were, the more the process seemed to be easing.

"Can't say I don't deserve the punishment," she agreed.

Ryder cut into the last one, smaller than the rest, and placed a hand on her upper arm gently. "Do you honestly believe that?"

The last piece crumbled and her skin was restored to its luminous moonlight glow. The look she gave him as she peered over her shoulder made everything slow. The strap of her crop top had dropped down her arm. Ryder's heartbeat grew loud, and there was a humming of vibration where he held her arms.

His hand slowly moved to the nape of her neck, his focus on the bow and curves of her lips. Her scent swirled around him, filling his lungs. Unable to drink enough in, he leaned closer—and in a flash she was out of his arms, one hand clamped on the edge of the sink, the other pulling up her fallen strap.

"I'm sorry," she breathed. "Sometimes it just… happens."

"What does?" he asked, confused.

Aspen's brows knitted together in suspicion as he rose, careful, controlled, and studied her body language. She trembled beneath his gaze. The mixed signals confused him further.

As if she couldn't take it any longer, she brushed by him. He followed her to the living area, where she whirled around. "Everything you think you feel about me is a lie."

"Okay…" he said, sounding more dismissive than he'd planned. "That all depends on what you think I feel."

They stood in awkward silence, the couch between them.

She blinked rapidly, then huffed in agitation. "You're telling me that you don't sense it?"

He squinted at her. "Sense what?"

Before she could answer, a portal opened near the door. They watched as Major Michael Gunner stepped out of the ripples.

Ryder's chest deflated. It was over. "Major."

Gunner ignored him, his attention fixed upon Aspen. He strode over to her with feline grace, and halted. His eyes were pleading. She crossed her arms tight at her chest, a sign that she was closing herself off—that he'd *hurt* her. Ryder didn't miss the way her eyes became doe-like when she looked at the major, who stood behind the invisible wall she'd built.

An understanding sank deep into Ryder's bones. She had a loyalty bond with him.

Her walls came crashing down at the major's swift

step into her field. His arms wrapped around her, and her arms slackened at her sides before he crushed her tighter into him.

Gunner's eyes closed. He shuddered as he released a breath into her shoulder. Ryder stifled a smile.

"Go on, say it," Aspen muttered, tight-jawed as she broke away from the embrace, her anger returning with a vengeance.

Gunner shook his head.

"You didn't have a choice… Say that you didn't have a choice."

Gunner deflated. "Aspen… I—"

"Cut him some slack, Lovetta," Ryder insisted, walking between them. "It wasn't his fault."

Gunner sighed. "I came to tell you both that the justices are getting suspicious. Thex came back, and when they questioned him about where you were, naturally he didn't know. I tracked your signal from your wristwatch. I'll tell you this, Everett… you've got a pair."

"You're not mad?" Ryder asked in surprise.

Gunner shook his head. "You did what I couldn't, Captain. You went after her. I'm just glad you're both alive."

"I'm not coming back with you," Aspen announced.

Gunner opened his mouth like he was about to say something, then closed it again. Ryder's throat constricted; he bit the inside of his cheek in frustration.

Aspen sighed. "I'll find Ignatius and take him down before he works out how to get back to Kore."

"Yeah, great plan, considering he just almost annihilated us both," Ryder snapped.

Gunner glanced from him to Aspen, a knowing look on his face. "I'll wait outside."

Aspen's gaze burned into Ryder until the door to the suite clicked shut, leaving them alone again. She rounded the couch. "This is for the best."

"The best for who?" he scoffed.

"You, Ryder! You have a team to lead. And I'm… I'm holding you back. They need you, and I'm sabotaging that."

Ryder raised his voice. "You don't get to take responsibility for where I'm not showing up, Aspen."

She huffed, crossing her arms. "You don't understand—"

"Understand what? That you have powers you hide?" Ryder fired back.

That struck a nerve; it rendered her speechless. There was a long pause before she stammered, "H-How do you know that?"

Ryder raised both hands in defeat, then dropped them to his sides. "I only had to see how everybody reacts around you when you're near—they're drawn to you. And yet you flinch when people get close to you… That's if they even get the chance to get close." He pointed to the door. "Did you see him trying to contain himself when he hugged you just then?"

Aspen turned away in shock, then looked back at him. "So… you only know this because you can see others sensing it? You're right. Observation is a superpower."

Ryder stepped closer. "A minute ago you were upset that I *could* sense it. Whatever *it* is."

"You don't understand," she protested.

"Then. Make. Me. Understand." His gaze probed

deeper into her green eyes. Aspen swallowed and compressed her lips. Ryder released a sharp sigh. "Look, I don't give a damn about your powers. It's not going to change anything. But if you wanna hide because you're scared, don't blame me when I don't understand."

When Aspen remained silent, a heaviness fell over him like a blanket. It really was over. This whole mission. The mission that had gotten them closer to all the answers they needed for what he had to do next… but had also opened up a world of questions about *her* that burned inside him. Why did they both have those markings? Why was leaving her so damn hard?

He shut down inside. The next words he spoke sounded dark, laced with pain. "If you'll excuse me, I have to go back and open the *Ars Daemonium*, and providing I live through that… then I'll probably have a mission to deploy."

"You'll die," she warned as he walked to the door.

Ryder shrugged, pausing with his hand on the door handle. "Life was never a guarantee with our job… And I can't bring myself to say goodbye to you."

Ryder let Gunner back into the suite, where the major drew the portal with his Phaedra before traveling through first. Ryder stood a step away from the portal and looked back at Aspen, ignoring every cell imploring him not to leave her side, before he stepped into the dimensional tide that pulled them apart.

CHAPTER 19

Ryder's cabin materialized around him, the portal lingering in his wake before shrinking to nothing. He'd half expected to find himself at headquarters, holding his breath and waiting for all hell to break loose in front of the justices, or at the least enduring an earful from Gunner. But Gunner must have sent him here instead.

He showered with his fists pressed against the charcoal tiles, too infuriated to enjoy the hot water pouring down his back. He dressed in civvies: a pair of jeans, a black hoodie, and a parka. Even Anima thermal resistance wasn't enough against today's chill. He closed the door to the cabin and ran down the porch steps.

There, blocking his path, was a wolf.

Killa Moon's gray coat gleamed against the foliage

that lined the path. Her steadfast amber eyes demanded an audience.

Ryder could only manage a gruff response. "She's not here."

A low growl rippled from Killa Moon's muzzle.

"Yeah, you and me both…" He walked close to her and squatted down to her level, but he knew better than to extend his hand. "Things are about to get real tense around here."

She was silent, jutting out her proud chest.

Ryder sighed. "Any advice from an alpha?"

He didn't expect an answer, but was shocked when he heard a clear voice. It was strange; he knew it was Killa Moon's, even though she didn't produce a sound. It was like the voice rose up from all around him, hitting him like the first light of dawn across an indigo sky.

"Amaranthine."

It was the first time he'd heard the word, and yet, in the wisdom of the wolf's amber eyes, he knew what it meant. She came forward and placed her paw on his forearm. Beneath the sleeve of his jacket, he felt heat, so he pulled back the material to reveal the golden symbols. He held Killa Moon's stare.

"Amaranthine," the alpha repeated.

At the sound of approaching boots thudding on the forest floor, Killa Moon bolted into the forest, disappearing in a sea of green. Ryder uncurled from his crouched position just as Thex rounded the corner.

"Oh, hi! How are you? Are you *insane?*" Thex exploded.

Ryder sighed. *Here we go.*

"I had to lie to the general's face! And there I was,

stumbling over the details of a completely fabricated story that YOU made up!"

"Look, I'm sorry—" Ryder began.

"No, you're not. Don't bullshit me, Ry. You went behind the Corps' backs to execute that mission to get her back—what the hell were you thinking?"

Thex's hard stare could have lasered through his bones, but Ryder groaned, pressing two fingers against his forehead. "She's the only one who had leads to find Ignatius, and she's the only one who can open the *Ars Daemonium*. Ansel is still keeping all of this information above our access level, Thex. We don't have time…"

Thex threw his hands in the air. "We make the mission happen under the orders of the Corps. You're not in charge! You put all of our jobs in jeopardy, and some of us have food to put on tables and a family to protect!"

Ryder sighed deeply. Thex went quiet, dropping his hands to his sides. Ryder sensed the fear within his argument. He rubbed his forehead. "Thex, we have an opponent who can't be killed unless it's by something as old as he is."

"This Ignatius guy?"

Ryder nodded. "We have to get to the labs. I promise I'll explain everything."

Thex gave a disgruntled sigh as they walked side by side toward the Corps. Ryder asked how Julia and the kids were, and Thex showed him some Polaroid photos taken during his time off. It made Ryder nostalgic.

The Corps was loud and bustling as usual as they detoured through a speed portal to the entrance of the labs. Thex's power signature opened the door; Vox must have temporarily programed it that way, considering Thex had no authority to be in the labs. The whole team stood in a huddle, wearing eager expressions; they'd heard Thex and Ryder coming.

Vox looked up from her tablet with a bright smile. "I told everyone that I needed to use some toxic substances for an experiment, so we have the lab to ourselves."

"Judging by the lack of red hair, I'm presuming she ditched you?" Levi mocked.

"Please. This is the captain we're talking about—he's not interested in anything that compromises the mission," Mackenzie answered on Ryder's behalf.

Ryder stopped beside River, who clapped him on the back. "At least you tried…"

Ryder's mouth set in a grim line in answer. River mirrored his expression. Ryder was thankful to have someone understand how badly today would go without her.

Declan's voice pulled him out of his thoughts. "But doesn't she need to be here to open the blasted book?"

The team waited for Ryder's response. He bit the inside of his cheek.

"What are we dealing with, Ry?" Thex probed.

Ryder removed his fist from in front of his lips. "What we're up against is like nothing I've ever fought before." He watched the flicker of disturbance change the demeanor of every marine. "He goes by the name Ignatius, and he's a Primordial demon. One of the earliest dark forces ever known. All of the information we need to know about him is in the *Ars Daemonium*."

Mackenzie stepped forward. "Did you find out what he wants? And why he's here?"

Ryder sucked in a breath. "Well, for one thing, he wants that back." He motioned toward the locked chest that held the *Ars Daemonium*. "He's gathering what he needs to overmatch us."

"The Corps?" Levi asked.

"No… Earth." His words sent a wave of shock through the team. "And that's just the beginning."

"Hands up who prefers Lovetta?" Declan raised his hand.

River stated matter-of-factly, "So we find this *Ignatius* and stop him before he gets to everything he needs."

Ryder appreciated the optimism and enthusiasm River always showed in the face of danger. He regretted being the voice of caution in this moment. "He can only be killed by somebody as old as he is. Sergeant Lovetta tested the theory."

Vox walked closer. "What do you mean?"

Ryder folded his arms to keep the anger that kindled inside him at bay. "Aspen tried to kill him by blowing him up."

"You met this Primo douche bag?" River piped up.

"Primordial," Mackenzie corrected with an eye roll.

"And then what happened?" Vox pressed, ignoring them.

Ryder tensed his jaw, that flame of anger sparking at the first taste of oxygen. He aimed to keep his tone indifferent, but what came out sounded more like a lament. "And then crash, boom, bang, he escaped."

"Ryder?"

"She didn't come back," he snapped.

Vox froze, the rest of the team standing stock-still. Ryder felt them staring after him as he stormed into the privacy of Vox's office and shut the door. He was pacing with his hands locked at the back of his head when Vox entered almost immediately after.

"Ryder, I have to tell you something."

He glanced over at her, only half interested; he was busy nursing the burning sensation of guilt in his stomach. "Sorry I blew up at you like that."

Vox picked up her tablet from the round table in the middle of the room. With a swipe of her finger, a hologram illuminated. "Never mind that now… I've been studying your powers, and I've pinpointed the source. Most of our powers come from Earth, especially the powers specific to each of the Anima species."

"Like how you and Mackenzie can do the super-jump thing?"

"Yes… but our individual powers have a different source. I've been replaying back the footage of the battle in the valley…" She paused and tapped the screen.

"And?" Ryder prodded.

"So we know your powers are gamma rays, but what's baffling me is the frequency. When I put the sound through the reader, it's incomplete… like part of it is missing. Remember when you miraculously passed Aspen's frequency security?"

"Yeah?" Ryder's curiosity was building, his full attention focused on her now. A simulation appeared before them as Vox changed the display to a re-enactment of him shooting at the screen before they left for Tundra.

"It wasn't a mistake. The frequency of your powers and the frequency of Aspen's are exactly the same signature. Which means… Aspen has another power, other than her pheromone powers." Vox played with the daisy-chain choker around her neck. "It can't be the signature of her healing powers. It has to be…"

Her voice trailed off, and Ryder watched her searching for answers for a moment before he was struck by a thought. "Aspen had some developing powers during our recon mission to locate Vangelis. We didn't have time to look into it, but she seemed surprised, so I doubt she knew about it before then."

"What did she do?"

"She lifted Vangelis's men into the air. She could bring them toward her or away from her."

Vox's lips twisted. "Hmm… that isn't consistent with your powers."

"Maybe it isn't meant to be." Ryder shrugged.

Vox studied him, and he did his best to appear apathetic. "She's different with you."

Ryder replied with a quizzical look before picking up the tablet and lowering himself into her desk chair. "I don't know what you mean."

Vox moved into his line of vision again, leaning against her desk. "You seem to understand the world she comes from, whereas River and I, as much as we try…" She shrugged. "I think I've tried to rationalize the way she thinks, and River, well… River thinks he can make her life decisions for her, and that's the core of their arguments. But you don't do any of that. You let her be whatever she needs to be, or become…"

Unable to avoid her watchful gaze any longer, he looked back into her violet eyes. She dropped her shoulders and a warm smile lit up her face.

"And I know she appreciates that. Even if she never admits it."

Ryder couldn't hold back a tight-lipped smile that threatened to reveal the giddy feeling rising inside him. He bounced up from his seat and swung open the door to the office, pausing in the doorway.

"Where are you going?"

"Are we opening this book or what?"

"Wait, Ryder!" Vox called after him as he entered the lab to find his team strewn throughout the room. River was eating potato chips, swiveling in a chair; Thex had his feet up on a desk, throwing a ball into the air; Levi was leaning against a benchtop, boring a hole into the polished concrete floor with his ponderous stare; and Mackenzie was yawning as she read one of the books from the lab's collection, titled *Numerology*.

Ryder stopped before the locked wooden chest. Just as Mackenzie asked what he was doing, he zapped it. The wood exploded into a thousand pieces like confetti, some landing in River's bag of chips.

"Look, Captain, I know you and I don't see eye to eye, but please think about what you're doing," Levi advised, standing beside him.

"We have no other choice," Ryder answered, assessing the thickness of the volume in front of him.

Thex grimaced at the pungent stench of rotting flesh emanating from the book. "That thing is nasty."

"Is that... human flesh?" Mackenzie asked, moving hesitantly nearer.

"Ugh, now everything smells like old blood," River moaned, putting down the chips.

Declan's wings were poised to fan outward as he approached, terror plain on the sharp features of his face. "Even if you survived opening it, what do you suppose would come out?"

Ryder glanced at Vox beside him as he heard her heartbeat quicken. "Ryder," she said, "I'm unsure of the mortality rate—"

"Welcome to the Corps," he interrupted. "What's inside… is war."

The team fell silent, their full attention on him now.

"Our lives are never guaranteed. When we open this book, there'll be one of two outcomes. What we find will prepare us for the greater war that's coming. Or we'll die trying."

River's heavy footsteps clunked over. "I'm in."

Thex stood beside him. "Always, brother."

Vox stepped up beside them too.

"On your orders, Captain," Declan announced.

Mackenzie stood on his other side. "If this is what it takes."

Levi filled the gap between Mackenzie and Declan and rolled his eyes. "You're all reckless, and you're all idiots. Somebody's gotta make sure you don't die. Suppose that could be me."

Ryder tensed his core, instinctively resuming a fighting stance as he steadied himself for the first touch of the volume's pulsating, bloodied, sinewed cover. His Anima, the Midnight Wolf, prowled the room, growling. Before long, every marine's Anima lit the room with its glow.

The team braced themselves as Ryder flicked back the

cover in a swift movement. It flew open before an unknown force slammed it shut.

One glance at the others readied them for the second attempt. Ryder swiftly flipped the cover again before it inevitably sealed shut. The team looked at him, fear-stricken.

Vox's voice quaked as she said, "Ryder, I don't think it will open unless your hands are on it."

There was an all-consuming silence as his hand hovered over the *Ars Daemonium*. He lowered it onto the slithering sinew. His hand touched it lightly, and revulsion filled his stomach. He was suddenly flooded with hopelessness; all of his cells felt as if they had been submerged in doom.

He opened the cover.

"Ansel was doubled over in pain by now, touching it like that," River recalled as he watched.

Vox exhaled heavily, like she'd been holding her breath. "Ryder, it must be your pain resistance… You're able to open it without your pain receptors being triggered."

He looked down at the first page. It was blank. He flipped to the next page. Also blank. He flipped to the next, and the next, and the next.

"The whole damned thing is blank?" Levi exclaimed.

Ryder straightened, confused. Mackenzie gasped as blood saturated the pages, forming a sentence.

I will only speak when both hands are placed upon the book.

Ryder hesitated before resting his other palm against the page. The pages seemed to cave inward, sucking his hands down and entrapping them.

And then he felt it.

It was like boiling liquid iron, seeping into his bone marrow. He was being cooked from the inside. He sputtered and breathed out hot infernal ash. He screamed from deep in his belly. The pain was excruciating, blinding and deafening him as it spread throughout his whole body. He tried yanking his arms out of the iron grasp, but it sucked him down further still, until he was elbow-deep into its pages.

He felt himself slipping away. Blackness surrounded him, and he felt utterly lost, falling in only one direction. Down.

Piece by piece, Ryder's body was being torn away, separating his physical being from his Anima with long-clawed fingers of darkness that penetrated so deep there was no escaping them. This was what he had always feared, and it was coming true. This *was* the end.

His last thought before the darkness closed over him was that he'd always known it was going to end this way… It was always going to be him getting lost in the dark, losing his balance over an edge that he so recklessly danced upon every day.

He felt the moment it happened: the moment he left the world—that transition as the void flooded over his face like water, and he was ripped away from life.

CHAPTER 20

A spark of light burst through the darkness. The beam was like a lighthouse shining through the black void. Ryder stirred, noticing that it resembled moonlight. The pain began subsiding, the grasp on his arms weakening; he could hear wolves crying out to the light… to the way out.

When he was able to open his eyes, he realized the team was still surrounding him. The lights were out and there were demons everywhere, fighting what the book had expelled from its pages. Ryder looked down at his arms and the rest of his body. He was fused with moonlight etherglow. The source came from behind him.

He turned to see Aspen streaming her healing powers into him, reinforcing and fortifying him. She tossed her mane of hair and Ryder could only smile.

Her emerald eyes were alight, a mocking smile upon her rouge-red lips as she taunted, "Why am I always the babysitter?"

"Aspen!" Vox exclaimed.

"What made you come back?" River asked.

"The captain is something of a motivational speaker." She and Ryder exchanged a meaningful glance.

"Let's do this," Vox announced. "Aspen, you can act as Ryder's anchor with your healing powers. The rest of us will combat anything demonic that escapes the pages until we get all our answers."

Ryder had so much he wanted to say to Aspen, but with little time to waste, he turned to face the *Ars Daemonium*, placing his hands once again on the text. An invigorating stream of light filled him like cold, purifying spring water washing over him. The pages filled with blood again, but this time, he was able to read them. The list of demonic beings stretched over many pages; he flipped past half the text. Aspen stood beside him and they looked over the words.

"What language is this?" Ryder asked.

"Aramaic," Aspen answered. "Here." She pointed midway down the left page.

A demented groaning filled the air as demons sprang from the shadows, flashes of power zipping through the room. It was getting so loud that Ryder wondered how they hadn't been found out.

Aspen paused, her finger hovering over a section. She looked awe-stricken as she translated, "Enceladus is cryolava."

"What is that?" Ryder asked.

"Magma from an ice volcano. Ignatius needs it so he can open a forbidden dimension portal larger than the size of the Earth. To complete the ritual, he needs to cleanse the Earth's surface and return it to its former state."

Declan's wing extended out like a wall to protect Vox from a demon he was wrestling with. Vox moved closer to Ryder, giving the *Ars Daemonium* a scrutinizing glare. "Does it say anything about how old Ignatius is? It could give us a clue as to when he existed here."

"Guys, the longer you keep that thing open, the more demons get released," Mackenzie shouted mid-fight, a Volucer demon hovering over her.

"It's becoming a warzone over here!" River shouted.

Ryder turned a few pages, but Aspen placed her hand over his. "A Primordial is considered demonic royalty. They built legions of demonic armies on forming planets, but once the planets began cooling, they had to move on as life began to form and Earth forced them out."

"Of course!" Vox exclaimed. "When Earth was forming, the elements spent years fusing, turning from cosmic gases into a solidified planet. The process took many years, but Earth was essentially a boiling planet. Ignatius must have resided here while it was volatile."

"So now he's trying to bring it back to a volatile point so that he can live here again?" Mackenzie called, wrestling with a Shadow Hound. Levi helped her destroy it with his extended claws.

"This isn't a fight against humans. They just happen to be in the way," Ryder realized.

"This is a fight of planetary proportions," Vox added. "The fight is with Earth herself."

"Anyone feeling insignificant right about now?" Thex said.

"Wait, that means Ignatius predates Earth…" Declan's tone was grave. "So if he's older than Earth, what in blazes can destroy him?"

The blood appeared and disappeared from the pages, and returned in a single sentence.

We shall not speak of our greatest enemies.

"That's all it's going to tell us. We can close the book," Aspen told Ryder.

He snapped it shut. Levi slashed the last living demon, and the team was left panting and composing themselves.

"The Primordials' greatest enemies are us," Levi said with pride.

"No," River rebutted. "Their greatest enemy at the time was the Virtues."

"So only a Virtue can destroy them," Mackenzie replied.

"Great. We go out to the field and throw our statues at him. War won. Anima, one; Ignatius, nil." Thex leaned on the table, dripping with sweat.

"We're screwed," Declan complained, shaking demon guts from the feathers on his wings. "The Virtues are long dead and practically as mythological as Thor."

"What do we do now, Ryder?" Vox asked.

Ryder's reply was sharp and resolute, his mind made up. "Suit up for Operation Enceladus."

The team jumped as the door to the lab flew off its hinges. Major Michael Gunner stepped over it, claws extended and green eyes seething.

"We're dead," Thex groaned.

"Everett, Lovetta—with me."

With that, the major trudged back over the door and out into the corridor, leaving no option but to follow him.

Major Gunner tapped the wooden surface of his desk with one finger as he eyed both of them. Ryder stood stock-still with his arms crossed over his chest, while Aspen slinked the length of the office, picking up Gunner's belongings and inspecting them with a bored expression.

"Honestly, I don't know where to begin." Gunner pointed at Ryder. "Executing your own missions with Corps resources without my permission *and* taking the rest of the team with you? On the verge of a global catastrophic war that is about to be unleashed!"

"Don't forget bringing back the exiled," Aspen chortled. She went silent when they both stared at her, putting a snow globe of Sweden back onto the floating shelf.

Gunner rounded his desk and unapologetically embraced her. Her arms remained stiff at her sides. "I'm not going to pretend that I'm not happy to see you alive, Lovetta."

He pulled back at Aspen's slight laugh, breathy and dangerous. "My strong, dashing protector… What would I ever do without you, Michael?"

Ryder's eyes narrowed in suspicion at her evocative tone. He watched Gunner swallow hard. There was something he didn't know about these two. Something they were hiding…

"What's that supposed to mean?" he questioned,

looking from Gunner back to Aspen. "Nobody calls him *Michael*."

"Let's just say me and the major go way back." Aspen's eyes glittered like they did when she had found prey.

"I'm done with your taunting, Aspen. Please—I don't want to keep fighting you over something that happened a long time ago. Is it not enough that you remained safe?" Gunner gritted his teeth and shook his head. His feline eyes were glossy with sincerity. "And I'd do it again. I'll take you being angry at me over you being *dead* any day."

Aspen took a slight step back so that she was facing him. "Let the captain deploy Operation Enceladus. We've accumulated all of the recon and the analytics to pull this off, possibly even before Ignatius gets there first."

It occurred to Ryder that she knew exactly how to play it. She hadn't disregarded what he'd said, not entirely… The glint in her eye proved that she'd skipped straight to her plans and used Gunner's guilt to fuel his decision, whether he'd realized it or not.

Gunner loosed a sharp exhale. "But General Winters—"

"Ansel doesn't have to know," Ryder interjected.

Gunner's tall frame sagged as he looked at them both and sighed, rubbing his forehead. "It seems like I don't have any other choice. Are you sure the team is ready for this?"

"We're only ready if we go in together. Sergeant Lovetta included, sir." It came out more like a plea than Ryder had hoped. He awaited a reply, watching Gunner internally fighting with himself.

"We won't let you down." Aspen's gaze met Ryder's in allegiance.

Gunner rolled his eyes in defeat. "I'll make sure you can deploy and get back without anybody seeing you."

"Secret squirrel," Aspen mused.

Ryder cracked a smile. "So covert not even the Corps knows about it."

A small smile lingered on her lips after the inside joke. Gunner frowned.

"I'll meet you for briefing," Aspen said.

"Meet me in the common room," Ryder replied. She nodded from the doorway—she knew which one he was talking about without having to ask—and closed Gunner's office door with a click.

Ryder turned his attention back to the major. There was a quiet moment before Gunner spoke.

"You two seem to be getting on amicably?" When Ryder didn't answer, he sighed. "I'm putting a lot of trust in you, Captain. I'm counting on you to deliver. When I'm not out there, I need you to watch her, do you hear me?"

Ryder glanced up at the ceiling and exhaled through his nose. "And I'm counting on the truth."

Gunner gave him a searching look. "The truth about what?"

Ryder strode forward until he was a foot away from the major. "I'm going to go out on a limb here and say that you're the one who betrayed *her*, and you're the reason she fled Fort Gippsland all those years ago. So please, tell me: what did you do to make her give up the only people she considered her family, and all of this…" Ryder rotated his finger at the ceiling. "And run off with Hurricane?"

Light spilling in from the large window shifted across the major's green eyes. Beneath them lay a story—one that clearly haunted him. His expression was forlorn. "You would never understand."

"Try me."

Gunner expelled a sharp breath, seeming to realize that Ryder wasn't going to let up.

"The first time I met Aspen, she was sixteen and still inactivated. Initially, the plan was that we would protect her until we'd won the War on Wolves. I was posted as one of the guards at Livinia's Orchard." A shadow of a smile made the corner of his mouth twitch. "She was unlike any other teenager I'd known… She was already slaying demons. She used to come out after her family had finished dinner every night and throw me a cold beer from her old man's fridge. She'd ask me questions for hours… about what the Corps was like, about training, about Anima powers, about the other Wolves… I didn't have the heart to tell her there were almost none left."

Gunner pulled at the collar of his uniform, his voice growing hoarse as he came to the crux of what haunted him.

"She looked up to me, and I just couldn't…"

He paused. Shook his head. Ryder realized that he was reliving the deaths of Aspen's parents, so he didn't press; he waited.

"And then, disaster… The Lovetta family were meant to move into military housing in Alaska; they were preparing for the move. But Aspen snuck out of the house one night and we were given orders to find her. By the time we'd found her, her parents were dead, and Hurricane had activated her. That was the first time I let her down."

Gunner's tears spilled onto his uniform. He paused for another moment.

"All of the young survivors of the War on Wolves were carried out and sent to Fort Gippsland to complete cadet training, Aspen included, Vox as well. River was almost ready to enlist in the Corps by then and was carrying out more duties. I didn't see her much at that time—I was overwhelmed by guilt. I started drinking. I'd met my wife, Sophia, by then, and we were engaged.

"Shortly after that, a silent war broke out with all the corrupt government organizations being taken down—which you know all about. Aspen got her sights set on Hurricane, who was rebelling in the area at the time and trying to get her to join his crew. She was full of rage and wanted revenge for her family, and Hurricane promised it to her. This led to the location of the cadets' base being discovered.

"Ansel and Justice Bastian Fallow—the only other Wolf left at the time—had organized troops from the Corps to be sent down. There were rumors that a piece of the *Ars Daemonium* was hidden close by. I knew Aspen was likely to be the first person to go looking for it, because it was the reason she snuck out of her house the night her parents were slaughtered." He gave Ryder a pointed look. "Nobody else knows that—they think she went to warn her friends about government officials scouting the area."

"Secret's safe with me," Ryder answered.

Gunner released a sharp sigh. "I lured her to a safe house nearby, told her I knew about her plans and wanted to talk some sense into her. She trusted me… so she followed me." His mouth formed a grim line. "I locked her in the safe house, threw a veil of protection over it, and moved it."

Ryder baulked. "Moved… the safe house?"

"Yes. I moved the house to another dimension with her inside. A dimension within another dimension… so that no one could find her, and so that she couldn't get out until I came back."

"She could have portaled out of there—"

"She didn't have a Phaedra. She was still a cadet."

"Huh…" Ryder murmured in understanding.

"After she told me her plan—or what I could squeeze out of her—I locked her in and planned to retrieve the piece myself… for her. But Bastian…" Gunner looked down at his hands, then rubbed his sternum, as if his chest were growing tight. "Bastian convinced me that his senses could find the piece, and that I should stay and help airlift all the other cadets out before the fort was attacked. I listened. He was my superior. I followed his orders."

They exchanged a knowing look, one that carried the grief of following orders against your own better judgment. Ryder knew that feeling too well.

"Bastian died trying to retrieve that piece. It confirmed that the Corps had been corrupted… because nobody knew about Aspen's plans except Bastian and me. It would have been Aspen… dead." Gunner's shoulders curled over, like he'd been impaled by the mere thought. "She'll never forgive me. And I don't care. I'd rather her scowl at me for the rest of my life than see her dead."

Ryder pressed his lips together into a smile. "If it had been you who tried to retrieve the piece, she would have stayed locked in that dimension within a dimension."

Gunner's arms went slack at his sides. "I never thought about it that way."

"Do you know how Bastian died?"

"Poison."

Ryder crossed his arms over his chest, his brow furrowed. "Poison?"

Gunner's focus cut to the door, making sure nobody was passing by or lurking. "A rare poison made from demon blood. It was in his system before he left the fort."

Ryder's mouth dropped open. "Fucking hell."

Gunner leaned in. "And guess who signed off his death certificate…"

It was Ryder's turn to glance at the door this time—all clear. "Who?"

Gunner raised his brows. "Let's just say Aspen took care of it."

Ryder froze, his voice a mere whisper. "Asintmah. Asintmah knew he'd been poisoned and signed it off…"

It made sense, how unsurprised Gunner had been when Aspen had severed the justice's head on the battlefield. He'd just spun her around, locked her wrists in his grip, and escorted her back to base. Businesslike. As if he'd seen it coming.

Aspen had claimed that murder was to save River… It wasn't a lie. But why not take full advantage of the situation and make Asintmah pay her blood debt to Bastian Fallow as well?

Ryder's eyes widened. Terror lanced through him, activating the muscles in his thighs, his core… He clenched his fists. Gunner was the only one he could trust.

"Give the word for this mission and I will not let you down," he ground out.

Gunner gave a nod of confirmation and Ryder's hand sliced over his brow in a stiff salute.

"May the Virtues protect you all," Gunner said as Ryder bounded for the door.

The hallways in Wolf Division were almost always empty. Ryder sighed, savoring the silence. When he walked into the common room, Aspen was sitting on her haunches, arranging logs in the growing fire. Ryder noted the expectancy in her eyes as they shot over to him at the door. She stood, and they met in the middle of the room.

"He's going to tell Ansel, isn't he?"

Ryder admired her deep red locks in the amber glow of the flames. "Negative. Gunner's on our side. He's the only one we can trust right now."

Her brows rose. "What did he tell you?"

"Everything."

Her expression became grave and she paced a short distance away, pensive.

"He can't send you away," Ryder assured her.

Aspen tapped her fist against the side of her leg. "They'll send me back to the Tundra and—"

"They won't." He'd aimed to sound reassuring, but his voice was sterner than he'd planned.

"How can you be so sure?" Aspen replied, twisting her fingers uneasily.

He cocked his head to the side. "Do you trust me?"

She froze at his question. "I…"

Ryder walked closer to her, closer than he'd ever been outside of combat or survival… Close enough that he was inside the invisible aura that surrounded her, and her scent overcame him. She was silent as she witnessed him enduring her powers. Electricity zapped and coursed through the small gaps between them.

"I think I've made my point," he muttered.

"Lucidly, Captain," she murmured.

Ryder took another spellbinding breath into his lungs before sitting at the small table in the corner. Aspen stared back at him from her frozen position.

He leaned his elbows on the table. "Aren't you going to join me?"

Aspen seemed trancelike as she answered. "What are we doing?"

"We have an operation to discuss."

She snapped back to attention and took the seat opposite him.

"The squad needs to be split into teams, and since you have medical experience, I need your skills to advise me on which marines complement each other best. I already have Vox's reports on the assessments that show me where they are tactically."

"What do you have so far?"

"She's matched Mackenzie with Levi, River with you, Dec—"

She stopped him. "No… no, don't put River with me."

"Why not?"

"River makes stupid decisions when I'm around him. He tries to jump in front of an attack, he does things for me so I'm not involved at all… He's so busy trying to make sure I don't make a mistake—that I don't kill anybody— that he ends up taking on more danger than he can handle."

"Okay," Ryder agreed. "What do you propose?"

Aspen gazed at him with a blank expression, as if she were gauging whether he was serious. She leaned forward, more engaged than before. "Put River with Mackenzie, and let Zalman snipe alone. He works best by himself. When he's not sniping, add him to River's team—they don't argue."

Ryder tried to subdue a knowing smile.

"What?" She shot him a quizzical look.

"Nothing." He shook his head, still smiling. As he wrote the names down, he remembered something that made his forehead crease with worry.

"What now?"

He shook his head slowly. "I can't have Thex as my partner."

Aspen's hair fell over her shoulder as she tilted her head.

Ryder rustled the paper in his hand. "I do some really dangerous shit on the field… We all do, but…"

"But what?" she urged.

"When I'm in the thick of it, he starts to pull back, questions things, tries to work out if there's another way, and there's just no time. My worst nightmare is telling Julia he's dead because I made him follow me into something dangerous and he hesitated. He needs to be more protected than that."

There was a shadow of a smile on Aspen's lips. "Put Thex with Declan."

Ryder hesitated. "Declan?"

"Don't underestimate him because of what I did at the assessment. He's the fastest out of all of us, he can airlift Thex out of any location, and his wings are bulletproof. I

rectified his fear of falling when I forced him to HALO—
he'll protect Thex."

Ryder's brows rose. "Not the most graceful way to help."

They both grinned. Ryder took the pen out of his
mouth and wrote Thex and Declan's names together.

"That leaves you and me." Ryder bit his bottom lip.

"I let you execute your crazy plans…" Aspen began.

"And I let you destroy what needs to be deconstructed."

"You don't leap in front to save me." She leaned her
elbows on the table, and so did he.

"And when I give the order… *only* when I give the
order, you kill."

She grinned diabolically. "Deal."

They lingered there for a moment, until Ryder felt
the legs of the table quiver under the weight of his elbows.
Aspen's gaze shifted from his eyes to his hands. Her smile
faded. Ryder slid his chair back against the wood floor. *Not
here. Not now, damn it to hell!*

The look on her face was knowing. He walked away
as far as the fireplace before he felt it, like a blanket of ice
covering his whole body. As he began to quake and shiver,
he heard her chair move back as she pursued him across the
room, stopping behind him. Toxic shame filled his stomach and his teeth began to chatter as he lowered himself,
hugging his legs, onto the rug in front of the fire.

Ryder stared into the crackling flames. He wanted to
say something… Wanted to brush it all off and tell her she
probably didn't want a partner who was suffering from
PTSD. But she kneeled behind him, and he felt her hands
grasp his shoulders and pull him in. She embraced him,

one arm tightly bracing his chest and the other cradling his head, her palm over his forehead.

Ryder seldom felt safe, but her warmth surrounding him felt like refuge. He pressed himself into her and closed his eyes, chills running his blood cold. She endured all the jolting and spasming, hugging him tighter each time. He concentrated on the touch of her lips and the softness of her breath on his temple.

He stayed wrapped up in her until all the wood was burned and the flames were low. His voice was soft when he finally told her, "Sometimes, I don't know if I'm living, or if I'm in *there*… with *them*."

Her slender arms tensed as she hugged him tighter. He knew she understood that he meant the Hellgate and the demons.

"I know what it's like," she answered. "And I'm not going to leave you alone."

CHAPTER 21

When the team had boarded the carrier plane, Thex brought up their destination on a tablet. Mackenzie was peeking over his shoulder and whipped around to inform them when the map had finished loading. "It turns out that between the data collected for this mission and all the possible locations, it was a question of variability. I found the equation, and judging by the calculations, the operation will take place in an ice cave deep enough to conceal the other Enceladus."

Ryder sat opposite them in the red seating of the plane's dark metal interior. "Good work, Sergeant Bale. Borealis, what's the brief regarding terrain?"

River was a couple of seats down from Ryder, holding his own tablet. "This particular ice cave doesn't require boat access, but judging by how long Enceladus has been in there, we could potentially be dealing with extraction from ancient ice that hasn't melted in hundreds of thousands of years…" His thick, dark brows knitted together. "It's going to be difficult to keep all the structures in place so that we don't get caved in on."

"And we have all the drilling equipment on board for extraction," Mackenzie added.

Ryder nodded. "Thexton, comms?"

"I'll be providing comms back to Major Gunner in case we run into trouble," Thex announced. "We've set up a private system in his office."

"Good." Ryder nodded at Declan. "No aerial brief at this time, but can we get an ETA?"

Declan nodded back. "Approximately forty minutes to the coastline of Bear Country from our location, Captain."

Ryder swiped the air in front of him with both hands. "Everybody understands what they have to do?"

All members of the team nodded. "Affirmative."

"Then let's fly, Dec."

"Buckle up for take-off." Declan donned his headset and disappeared into the cockpit to speak to the control tower. All organized by Gunner, no doubt.

The plane reversed, then turned to face the runway before it blasted forward. The force of its engines drowned out all other sounds. Once it was in the air, Ryder looked over the three-dimensional hologram of the cave they were about to explore.

Thex unbuckled his seatbelt and plonked himself in the seat next to Ryder with a wide smile, showing his straight white teeth. "This is the stuff we love, right?" He clapped a hand over Ryder's shoulder. "What I don't understand is why we aren't doing it together."

"Ah, Thex, don't be like that about it," Ryder replied casually.

Thex brought his voice down low. "We've been comrades for over seven years, and now I find out you're partnered with Sergeant Boomerang? I get that she's a hell of a lot prettier than me…"

Ryder threw him a look as if to ask if he was serious, shaking his head.

"…but that's no reason to be changing how the job gets done."

Ryder looked up from the tablet and glanced over at Aspen. She was sitting close to River, who was whispering to her under his breath. Feeling her holding him last night was the safest he'd felt in… He couldn't remember how long. After they'd parted and he'd returned to his cabin, he'd imagined how it might have gone differently. All it would have taken was him tilting his head just that little bit more to kiss her.

Ryder realized Thex was still glaring at him, waiting for an answer. He cocked his head to the side so the others couldn't read his lips. "I have to have my eyes on her."

It wasn't the truth, but it was a way to get Thex off his back and avoid explaining that it was safer for him if they weren't paired. Thex glanced at Aspen, barely able to conceal his annoyance. Ryder stole a second look at her, but she had passed them and disappeared behind the chair of the cockpit.

Declan's voice came over the speaker and announced that their altitude was forty-five thousand feet. Ryder unbuckled, walking with Thex in tow to the back of the plane and behind a thick khaki curtain designed to block out sounds that could be picked up by the most sensitive of ears.

Thex folded his arms as Ryder watched the tablet, replaying the simulation River had made about the best ways to extract Enceladus with the drilling equipment. Thex cleared his throat. "What do you see in her? Why are you risking the safety of this team by having *her* so close to the decisions and operations?"

Ryder paused the video and exhaled. His irritation at being interrupted was building, but not hurting Thex was going to require his full attention. He looked directly into Thex's eyes. "I know you're uncomfortable with her—"

"Who isn't?" Thex interrupted.

Ryder spread his hands in front of him. "Hear me out."

Thex closed his mouth and straightened his spine.

"She's starting to trust me… and that's big for her."

"You're doing this as a challenge to see if you can win her over," Thex declared. "To see if you can get in first."

Ryder's mouth was agape before he growled, "It's not like that! Did I judge you like this when you were dating Julia?"

Thex shook his head. "That's because you love Julia, and you know how good of a woman she is."

"I don't deny that, but listen—I've seen goodness in Aspen that I can't unsee. When we're together, she's different. She's shown me that there's more to her than her bad reputation—she has a gentle side. And every time I feel like my life is in danger…" He stopped, his hands at his chest. "She's got it… She's got me. I have a tether to this world like I didn't have before."

Thex's eyebrows knitted together, his lips compressing

the way they did when he was hurt. "Are you saying I don't have your back?"

"No… no," Ryder stammered, part of him unable to believe he was being this honest, this vulnerable. "That is *not* what I'm saying. She's helping me survive this, and when she's next to me… I don't need to fight so hard. And right now, that means everything to me."

Thex didn't know how long he had been dealing with the panic attacks, or that his reality felt scattered even on a good day. Ryder had hoped that, being a marine, Thex would understand the grueling and exhausting need to be constantly vigilant, but his explanation seemed to have made things worse.

Thex straightened, eyes darting around the small space. "Well, I'd better get back to the crew area and let you do your work."

"Thex…" Ryder called, but the curtain swished behind him as he departed.

Ryder rubbed his forehead and exhaled deeply. He was alone for all but a few moments before Mackenzie slipped through the curtain. Ryder winced as he pushed the sinking feeling in his chest away.

"Sergeant Bale? Is there a problem?"

"Yes, Captain, there is."

Had they already run into a fault in the plan? Ryder refrained from groaning and urged her to explain.

"You see, everybody is talking… There are rumors within the team about how close you and Sergeant Lovetta are becoming. It's causing everybody unease that you're encouraging a kinship with a serial killer."

Ryder raised his brow. "Who exactly is saying this?"

There was a glimmer in her cognac-brown eyes. "I'm just saying, we wouldn't want to tarnish such a flawless reputation with a scandal. We could put your wolfish needs to better use."

Ryder's tongue grazed against his sharp teeth. "Everyone is worried about how close I am to Aspen? Or is it *you* who's worried?"

Her eyes grew wide. "I like you, and I don't want you to get killed because of her."

Ryder watched as her fingertips rested on his upper arm. He froze before breathing a laugh. "The only one who can get me killed is me. You have nothing to worry about."

Mackenzie took a step closer, her eyes on his lips. Her red wine-and-chocolate scent swirled around him as she cornered him against the large metal storage boxes. Her fingers traced his jaw.

He swiftly turned his head, catching her hand before she could go any further. "Mackenzie—"

The curtain opened.

Aspen.

She looked from Mackenzie's coy smile to Ryder's mortified expression.

"Aspen…"

Ryder let go of his grasp on Mackenzie's wrist and followed Aspen out to the cabin area of the plane. Levi was swift to wedge himself between them. Aspen had made it to the seating against the wall of the plane. She dropped down, crossing her legs and her arms and turning the other way with her head against the wall of the plane. River lowered himself beside her and looked back at Ryder with suspicious eyes.

Levi looked at his hands before glancing back up at him.

"Captain, I wanted to say, well… how sorry I am for under-mining you at first. The position you gave me in the team is exactly what I was hoping for, and I'm so glad that you see my strengths."

Ryder, uninterested at first, looked upon his comrade and placed a hand on his shoulder. "Of course. I wouldn't have it any other way… but it was Aspen's idea."

Levi smiled and moved along to speak to Thex.

Ryder gauged whether he should approach Aspen while she was near River, who wore a scowl as she spoke inaudibly to him. *Screw it.* It hadn't been what it looked like, and he wasn't going to let her believe what she thought she saw.

As he approached, River laughed at something Aspen said. They both looked up at him in awkward silence.

"Can I help you, Captain?" River's voice was even.

"A word with Lovetta?" Ryder's tone made it clear that the matter didn't concern him.

Aspen paused a moment before following him to the back of the plane. She'd left the curtain open a fraction. "What?" Her arms were still defiantly folded.

Ryder looked around at the others before he began. "What you saw—"

"Is none of my business," she interrupted.

"I know what you're thinking, and it's not what it looks like," he pressed.

"So it's not that you just told Thex you're only my part-ner because you need to have your eyes on me?" Her voice was low, wounded. "After all we've been through…"

Ryder didn't need her to remind him about their time alone in the common room the night before. Every muscle in his body became taut. He reached a hand out to her. "That's not what I meant."

Before he could touch her arm, she moved away. "Look, let's not put expectations on each other, especially ones that we both know I can't deliver."

"I don't have any expectations of you."

Aspen raised a brow. "It's clear how low you set your standards for me, Captain."

Ryder gritted his teeth in frustration. "We are way past 'Captain' and you know it. And what exactly can't you deliver?"

She stepped threateningly closer. "You have me all wrong."

"Do I?" He stepped closer too, so they were breathing in each other's intensity. Lightning flashed between the mysterious markings along their arms.

"You seem like you're a stickler for choice." Aspen glanced at Mackenzie, who was watching their every move. "Just know that I have no interest in competing for your attention. You feel how you're supposed to feel, affected by pheromone power. None of this is real. I'm completely immune to feeling anything for you. So go ahead… I'm not stopping you."

Ryder nodded slowly, completely incensed. "So that's how it is?"

"That's how it is."

"Good."

"Great."

Ryder folded his arms. "All clear."

Like a magnet repelling away from him, Aspen had moved to the opposite end of the plane before he could even register what she'd said:

"I wish I'd never met you."

Ryder opened his mouth. He wasn't sure if he had done so to say something back to her, but a small noise came out instead. Like he'd been shot in the chest, he stood there, unable to take in those words and accept that they'd been spoken.

I wish I'd never met you.

A nervous laugh escaped him. He wanted to hit something. Anything.

I wish I'd never met you.

How dare she? After how vulnerable he'd been last night? How *could* she?

Rage burned through his arms as he kept them solid at his sides. Aspen sat by River again, Vox occupying her other side quickly; Ryder heard her asking, "What was that about?"

Aspen didn't reply.

Declan announced that it was time to prepare themselves for landing. They buckled up, Ryder taking the spare seat beside Levi. The others were discussing the operation and undergoing their various routines as the plane touched down. Ryder watched Aspen mulishly as she sat clasping the edge of the seat, waiting for the plane to stop moving. Her emerald eyes peeked at him for a moment, then stared aloofly out of the window of the cockpit.

"What's going on with you two?" Thex muttered to him.

Ryder brushed him off. "Nothing."

River opened the door and they jumped out onto fresh powdered snow to the sound of slowing engine turbines. In front of them was a small burrow in the ground: the entrance to the ice cave.

"It's too small for a bear to fit through, so the tunnels

won't be occupied," River confirmed, looking through the gap.

"This is a tight squeeze," Levi pondered.

"Aspen could fit through there easily… Could you break up this ice without caving yourself in?" Vox asked her.

Aspen slid on her back into the snow-covered entrance and disappeared. From inside, they heard her voice.

"The outskirts are solid and this passage is too narrow to fit through."

"What if I melted it?" Ryder suggested.

She answered by kicking down the soft snow, revealing more of herself. Ryder approached and carefully radiated his gamma rays, just enough to melt the edges. Aspen shaped the entry by kicking the larger pieces off with her boots, revealing the passageway behind her.

"We're going to have to do that the whole way through," Ryder stated.

She responded with only an insolent glare.

CHAPTER 22

"After you," Ryder taunted.

The team followed Aspen's lead as Ryder continued to melt the solid tunnel while Aspen chiseled it back with the dagger usually kept in her drop-leg holster. Ryder was standing so close behind her that at times her back was pressed against his chest. In some sections of the tunnel, it was so narrow that they had to crouch.

The last beam of light from the entrance went from shining like a burning star to burning out; now they were moving in total darkness, instructed by Vox not to use flashlights in case there were demons in the ancient cave.

"Uh, River, can you move any slower?" The rocky tunnel walls made Declan's voice echo.

"Ow, Levi, that was my calf," Mackenzie growled.

"Well, if you didn't stop unexpectedly every few steps, it wouldn't happen," Levi snapped.

"It's hard to walk properly with Vox's ponytail stuck in my face," Mackenzie grumbled back.

Declan's voice boomed. "River! Did you just crack one off, because I swear—"

Vox's giggle echoed down the tunnel.

Aspen rolled her eyes. "It's the ammonia from Enceladus."

"So we're basically conga-lining into a massive Dutch oven," Thex remarked from behind Ryder.

"How much further, Captain? I don't know how much more of this I can take," Declan complained from the back of the line.

"It's hard to say." Ryder's eyes were reflective as he gazed down the tunnel, whose end they could not see. He softened the next piece of ice. Aspen elbowed him in the stomach as she plunged her dagger into the ice, which fell in a soft blob onto the ground. "You did that on purpose," he muttered. His breath against her ear gave her goose bumps.

"Don't be ridiculous. Besides, even if I did, you wouldn't feel it anyway." Aspen stabbed another piece of ice and stepped over it. She stood rigid as the team pushed everybody forward, pressing her legs against the next protrusions of ice. She whipped Ryder in the face with her hair, then felt his hand push it back over her shoulder, sending a prickling voltage along her neck.

"My ability to feel is completely intact—unlike some."

She groaned as she stabbed more ice. "Don't patronize me."

"Virtues, you two bicker like an old married couple," Thex groaned from behind them.

"I can literally hear you rolling your eyes," Ryder told him.

"I see something," Aspen announced. A bright turquoise light was shining ahead.

The tunnel became wide enough that they could walk through without needing to chisel the sides. They reached the light, realizing it was a monstrous frozen wall that had access to sunlight from above. Aspen's eyes adjusted; the light was enough that she was no longer using night vision. It moved mysteriously as they followed the path into a cave. The ceiling looked like a frozen ocean wave as it dipped and bulged, and a small alpine trickle gushed over the rocks at their feet, turning into an underground waterfall below.

"I wonder what's down there?" Mackenzie wondered aloud.

"Would you like to find out?" Aspen put a hand against Mackenzie's arm, threatening to push her down into the darkness. Mackenzie's scream caused a dark chuckle to rise within her.

"Play nice, you two," Ryder warned.

Mackenzie shot Aspen an infuriated glare.

"After you, princess," Aspen taunted.

With a huff, Mackenzie stood beside Ryder, not taking her eyes off of Aspen.

River and Vox were inspecting the walls. "Some areas are hollow," Vox announced. "That's why there's more light shining through here."

"The color of this ice is inconsistent with the Enceladus on the end of Ansel's staff," Thex pondered.

"I think I found something," River called.

They hopped over the wet rocks to where he was pointing at the large, cavernous wall. Beyond it was a crystal lake—on the opposite side was a luminous, diamond-shaped rock.

"Enceladus," Ryder murmured.

"Wow," Mackenzie breathed.

"It's so beautiful." Vox walked to the edge of the lake's rippling dark waters.

"Let's move fast," Ryder announced.

Levi dropped his backpack on the ground. "I can swim over there, but I'll need help weeding that thing out."

Ryder gave him a firm nod. "Lovetta, go with him. If any surprises jump out, I'm counting on you to heal the damage."

Levi rolled his eyes. "Great. I'm done for."

Aspen shot him a derisive grin as she pulled off her boots. "Quit your whining, kitty cat."

She stepped into the lake first. It was so cold it felt like someone was stabbing her toes. Levi stepped in beside her and swore under his breath. Aspen eyed the hook attached to his belt and gripped it tight. His reflective feline gaze was tentative. She nodded for him to proceed and together they submerged their bodies into the ink-black water before Levi propelled them forward.

The freezing water soaked their uniforms and they were trembling by the time Levi pulled himself onto the bank. His skin was turning a deep shade of blue, his teeth chattering as he breathed out an icy cloud.

"Are you alright?" Ryder called from behind them.

Aspen felt her healing wash through her body. She

placed a hand on Levi's leg and watched his blue lips return to their usual color.

"Affirmative," Levi answered, smiling at her. "I have to admit, Lovetta, that's pretty awesome."

The chill of the water lingered as they stood, their uniforms dripping. They approached the ancient wall of turquoise ice carefully, Levi checking their footing with the soft padding of his feet. What once had been a moving body of water was now frozen mid-stream with bubbles and currents still visible on the inside.

"That's it." Aspen pointed to a slight change in the color of the ice. To Levi it must have just looked like light coming from the surface.

"How do you know?" he asked.

She reached for the dagger in her holster. "Because I can smell it."

Thick claws lengthened from Levi's fingertips, and together with Aspen and her dagger, he tried chipping away at the ice. After about ten minutes, they realized that only a few small chunks sat at their feet.

Levi sighed and wiped his brow. "This isn't working. But if we use the drilling equipment, this whole structure could crumble on top of us all."

"You think?" Aspen holstered her dagger and placed both her hands on the frozen wall.

"What are you doing?"

"Shhh."

"That's not how we're going t—"

His words fell away as the diamond-shaped outline in the ice moved a fraction closer from inside the frozen lake.

Too much power and the wall would melt. Just enough and the mineral could float straight to her.

Careful to not extend her new powers in Levi's direction, Aspen pulled all the control she could from her center, drawing it out of herself and pulling Enceladus closer with her focus. She heard the team murmuring from across the lake as the mineral inched closer from behind the wall. Sprays of water pushed through tiny cracks in the ice as it partially melted. Levi put his hand in front to block the water gushing onto her chest, ready to collect the mineral as the last remnants of ice melted away from it.

Enceladus was the length of both Levi's hands. They stared at it, admiring its ether-glow in awe.

Levi cleared his throat. "Lovetta, I…"

"Yes?"

He opened his mouth and then closed it again. Finally, he rubbed the back of his neck and said, "I lost my brothers in the war too. They were twins, only five years old."

Aspen realized he was panting, his eyes darting over the ground. Seeing how hard this was for him, she went still, never taking her eyes off of him, just waiting.

His lips formed a thin line and he nodded in understanding. "Not everybody gets it… The rage. But I do."

Aspen hadn't realized she'd been holding her breath, but when she took that cleansing air into her lungs, she felt lighter. She hadn't known it until now, but she had needed him to say that. Something inside hurt; Levi knew the same kind of pain. Pain like hers. Unimaginable loss.

At the same time, they braced each other's forearms, and she said, in a voice so unlike Hellfire's, "I'm sorry."

He looked her over, biting the inside of his cheek.

"Your job looks impossible at times, but you manage to pull it off every time. I don't know if I've misjudged you… It's too early to tell that yet. But I passed judgment on you before I got to know you—a bad habit of mine." He sighed. "Just do what you gotta do, Lovetta, and don't worry about the rest of us."

She had never had a long enough conversation with Levi to know how intense an experience it was. He hadn't broken eye contact; in fact, he had barely blinked since he'd begun speaking. It was a sign that he'd spent less time with humans recently. She wasn't sure who he was close with other than his partner, Zuri—she made a mental note to find out.

Her head dipped as she answered, "I can't do that."

His thick brows knitted questioningly.

"I've made a promise."

"To who?" His feline eyes widened as he answered his own question. "To Ryder."

There was something in his smile that she could read as clearly as if he'd said the words. Levi knew her reputation as well as anyone who read the *Anima Corps Observer*, but his smile reached his eyes, because he knew all too well what it meant. It was the smile that said, *I'm under Hellfire's protection.*

Aspen nodded, a shadow of a smile appearing on her own lips as they both began to shiver again. Levi cleared his throat to break the awkwardness building between them before they turned back toward the lake. The team was still waiting on the edge.

Aspen put the heavy mineral in the backpack and handed it to Levi as they entered the water up to their knees.

"It won't be safe swimming with such a heavy object," Declan called. "You should throw Enceladus over."

Levi tightened his grip on the strap of the backpack. "That's a terrible idea. What if it breaks?"

"There's a current in that lake going down there."

Declan pointed to the right. All Aspen could see was a dark opening and the crashing water of an underground waterfall. It might have led to Kore's stomach for all she knew.

"That thing is going to drag you down, and we are wasting valuable time."

Declan was right; their limbs were freezing by the second.

River matched his urgency. "Levi, throw it over and we'll catch it."

Aspen unzipped the backpack, pulled out the heavy diamond-shaped rock, and handed it to Levi, who threw it over the water, aiming at Ryder with a powerful overarm. Declan dove in front of Ryder, clutching Enceladus to his stomach and falling to the ground.

"What are you doing?" Mackenzie shouted. "You could have lost it in the water!"

"Are you ready to cross?" Levi asked Aspen.

She gripped his arm. "Wait…"

Levi looked ahead and saw what she had just seen.

The shifting beneath Declan's eyes was so quick that they could have missed it—until the whites of his eyes began seeping an inky liquid.

"DEMON!" Levi shouted.

Ryder launched into an attack. The fiend inside Declan lunged, contorting his body in ways that were unnatural. Thex attacked from behind, trying to subdue him in a headlock while Ryder tried prying Enceladus from his elongating arms. Vox was screaming "No" over and over again, like the word could banish the demon from her lover's body.

Levi launched them into the water. Aspen watched in horror as what was left of Declan's insides began dissipating, the demon completely overtaking him. It was half Declan's body and half of its true form as it sank its monstrous jaws into Thex's forearm. Thex's screams echoed through the cave as blood pooled on the rocky floor. He staggered back against the cavern wall, taking harsh, jagged breaths as he clenched his forearm to try to stop the bleeding.

Declan lashed at Ryder with long, slick claws. A second demon appeared from the tunnel, and Enceladus went flying from Declan's hands straight into its sinewy arms before it escaped back down the tunnel. Ryder pinned Declan onto the rocks with one hand, his other poised with gamma power building around him in a violet storm—

But before Ryder could expel the blast, four long claws speared through his chest.

Ryder gasped. His eyes bulged as he released Declan, both his hands now gripping the claws that had pierced through to his back.

Aspen felt the whole world stop. Felt the air knocked out of her lungs as a fractured scream escaped her lips; the sound resembled his name. The water thrashed around her legs as she and Levi reached the other side of the lake. She surged forward as the demon yanked back its claws. Ryder fell to his knees before he collapsed to the ground.

The demon managed to return to Declan's form once more. Blood pooled on the rocks around Ryder as

Aspen rushed to him first; she could hear her own pulse as she knelt beside his body, scooping him into her arms and thudding into a sitting position beneath him. In her periphery, she saw the team surrounding Declan so that neither he nor the demon could escape into the tunnel.

"Please help me! It's inside me!" Declan cried.

River stood dumbstruck, claws extended, hesitating like a fool.

Mackenzie's stance was low, ready for any incoming attacks. "We have to help him before it comes back."

Vox's voice was shaking, pleading. "Let's get him to the plane. Ansel will know how to fix it. We have to help him."

Aspen looked into Ryder's blue eyes, alight like fire for a mere moment as she cradled his head before the light inside them went out. His head lolled heavily in her hands.

She held him close, pressing as much of her body against him as she could. Moonlight flooded through her, starting from her head until it filled her entirely, beaming out in a thousand different directions, like a star that had burst in the night sky. She willed all the light into Ryder, starting with the puncture wounds in his chest, then spreading until the whole cave glowed.

His body awakened against hers. She could feel his muscles shifting and contracting until he had the strength to prop himself up on his own hands, his eyes alight again. He lifted one hand to cradle her face.

Aspen wasn't thinking about anything that had happened on the plane when she buried her cheek against his hand to feel his warmth. She didn't care. He was *alive*. That was all that mattered.

She still had an arm curled around his neck, and he was

so close that his amber-and-cedar scent filled her senses. A small part of her hated that she needed it—needed it like she needed oxygen. She just wanted a minute… One minute of being near him, of feeling how safe his scent made her feel. Her focus was on his mouth. The sensuous curve of his lips.

A rush flowed through her, giving her goose bumps. The sensation woke her from her dreamy state. Her heart stuttered.

What the hell was she thinking?

But just as she tried to convince herself that he was just groggy, still coming to…

His free hand moved to her neck, his calloused hand warm against her skin. His gaze fixed upon her own lips. Her next exhale came out more unsteadily than she would have liked, revealing just how much she yearned for those lips to brush against hers.

They were jolted out of the moment as the team began wrestling with the demon surfacing in Declan again.

Pheromones. It was just the effect of her pheromones. Nothing more. That thought alone snapped her out of it like she'd turned on the cold water in the shower. Vengeance surged through her as Ryder helped her to stand.

She bounded past the team as the demon pierced near Mackenzie's heart, the same way it had got Ryder. River shrieked, grasping its claw and breaking its hand before pulling it out of Mackenzie's chest. Mackenzie fell to her knees, looking down at her chest in shock before falling unconscious onto the ground. Vox rushed to her side, hastily spilling a vial of serum between her unresponsive lips.

Aspen ignited in a nebulous red glow, so bright it encompassed the cave.

"Please help me. Please help me," Declan cried, over and over again.

Aspen pinned him with both hands against the cave wall and looked dead into his sky-blue eyes. "Can you hear me in there, Dec?"

"Aspen, please help him. Please heal him," Vox cried.

"Declan!" Aspen shook his shoulders. Declan's head lolled, his eagle wings now spread wide against the cave wall. *Shit.* One beat of those wings and the whole team was done for. But the fact that the demon hadn't done that yet was proof Declan still had some control.

"Declan, if you can hear me—fight it. You have to fight back."

The demon groaned, accessing the sound from somewhere deep—a sound that could only come from the hellgate.

The light in Declan's eyes went out.

Vox screamed his name. Ryder wrapped both arms around her middle to keep her from running toward them, toward the red storm cloud.

Aspen locked every muscle tight as the demon writhed in her hands. "Look at me. You can do this…" Her voice quaked. "Damn you, Declan, don't make me do this. Fight!"

Declan's Eagle Anima made one last dying call into the ether before something changed within his body.

She could tell, before that moment, that there had been light inside of that man. That he'd been good and pure. But when Aspen beheld the gaze of the thing in her clutches, only a malignant creature remained.

Declan was gone.

Unshed tears brimmed in Aspen's eyes as she turned to look at Ryder, who was cradling Vox to his chest. The order felt like it happened in slow motion: Ryder closed his fist before slicing downward vertically.

Aspen paused to let the order sink in. For every cell to deaden.

Her eyes met Vox's, and she watched as the blood drained from her friend's face. "No… no, please… Aspen…"

Aspen's eyes burned. She turned back to the shell that was Declan, fully possessed by the demon now.

"I'm sorry."

She dropped her hands, but Declan didn't move, as if he were still bound tightly by invisible rope. Aspen raised her hands, and he rose into the air, screaming and kicking. Her crimson cloud grew dense, prickling her skin as it reverberated into his writhing body. Her Anima—the White Wolf—emerged in ether-glow with a mournful howl.

She sent a final wave so powerful it disintegrated the demon, turning it to ashes before her eyes. Declan's lifeless body lay on the rocks, bruised and broken.

When Aspen turned, Mackenzie was healed, but weak, sitting up in River's arms. Thex was being helped up by Levi; he had also thrown back a vial of her healing powers. She didn't know when all of the Animas had appeared, but they stood with starlight coats in the gaps between the team, all staring at her. Vox was still locked into Ryder's chest. She was trying to scream, but all that escaped were weak sobs as her legs gave out in Ryder's grip.

"Nobody touch the body." Aspen's voice was low as she made eye contact with each member of the team, confirming that they understood. "The demon can still come back and take any one of you next."

Vox turned and cried into Ryder's chest. The entire cave resounded with a grief that Aspen knew all too well would never fade.

River wiped the tears from his eyes. "We have to warn the Corps… Every Anima, and our home, is in danger."

Vox squirmed to get free. Ryder reluctantly loosened his grip. She took slow steps toward Declan's unmoving body, unable to see through her sobs. Aspen's arm splayed out, creating a barrier, warning her not to move any closer, but Vox pushed past like she hadn't even seen her. She sank to her knees on the rocky ground and bowed her head with her arms outstretched.

Ryder released a deep sigh. "We have to get Enceladus back. Zalman, you're with me. We have to track that demon down before it gets away."

Mackenzie gaped at Ryder, pointing a shaking finger in Aspen's direction. "She just killed Declan! You have to… You…"

Ryder's eyes were filled with compassion when he crouched down next to her and looked her dead in the eyes. "I have to stop that demon. Before this happens to anybody else."

Mackenzie was panting, so panicked that she just shook her head and buried her head in her hands.

Ryder left the cave in a flash of light, Levi following close behind.

Aspen turned to River. "I'll take care of the body." She nodded toward the rest of the team. "Get them out of here."

"TAKE CARE OF THE BODY?" Vox's voice boomed

so loud that Mackenzie covered her ears. "It's Declan. It's *my* Declan." She continued weeping, her voice becoming muffled and small.

Aspen ground her teeth at River. "Get her out of here, now."

Mackenzie knelt beside Vox, hugging her as she wept, repeating Declan's name, her hands over her mouth. It was Thex who guided them to stand. He cast a helpless look toward Declan's body before ushering them back through the tunnel.

River glanced back at Aspen with a sigh as she stood over the body. He was the last one to disappear behind the ice wall.

Aspen bent down, pulling Declan by his arms closer to the water. With her hands held a few inches above his purple, bruised skin, she began incinerating his body. Her heartbeat had finally slowed.

"I'll suffer the consequences for you," she told Declan as his body atomized. "You would have lived a life of hell, being possessed by that demon. Who knows how long it would have kept you captive inside, subjecting you to only the Virtues know what."

His face dipped below the surface of the water as more of him was swept away by the current.

"You didn't deserve that end, Declan. And Vox... She's going to hate me. But I'll endure it. Because it means you'll be free."

A tear dropped into the water. Because he was dead. Because she'd lose Vox over it. Both...

She sniffed and shook her head, realizing this was the most she'd ever said to Declan. His last remnants disappeared in the dark current, down to the water-fall beneath.

Feeling something hard and smooth, Aspen pulled her hands out of the water. Enclosed in her fist was a golden talon. One of *his* golden talons.

"I'll give this to her for you," she promised.

A deep, earth-rattling *CRACK* echoed around her. Aspen glanced around the cave. Water was dripping through crevices between the rocks, water moving from behind the frozen wall in the entrance. The cave was melting. The once frozen wave where she and Levi had retrieved Enceladus now had a thick fissure running several feet across its surface. What started as a trickle became a thick, continuous stream of water.

"Damn it to hell," she cursed.

Desperate to warn the others, knowing it would take time to get them out, Aspen dashed back down the length of the narrow turquoise wall and into the dark tunnel. She could hear the team up ahead.

"The cave is melting! RUN!"

She saw them hasten their pace, her eyes adjusting to the dark as her boots were washed over with freezing water. She could see the glow of the outside world ahead. Ryder was at the tunnel's entrance, helping to pull them over the threshold.

Aspen heard a loud groan and sloshing water. She was bowled over as the icy wave pulled the earth out from under her and slammed her into the hard walls of the tunnel. Bright pinpricks of light flashed over her vision.

She found the surface and coughed out the water she'd

swallowed, swaying and holding the tunnel wall, knee-deep in water.

Levi climbed out in one swift movement. Another loud rumble echoed around her. Another wave was coming. Ryder ran back into the tunnel; he was coming back for her. But she only had seconds.

"GET OUT!" she screamed. "THERE'S ANOTHER WAVE COMING!"

CHAPTER 23

The cave trembled and groaned as Aspen's legs pumped toward the light-filled opening of the cave, toward Ryder's silhouette. Boulders from the ceiling collapsed, and the light grew smaller and smaller. Thex appeared behind Ryder and yanked him out of the tunnel. He was back seconds later, arms extended toward her. More rumbling behind her told her she was seconds away from being swallowed by ice water.

Her boots slammed against each rock to hoist herself up and up. Her hands smacked into Ryder's and he yanked her hard, thudding her into his chest as the last huge boulder sealed the cave.

She raised her head to meet his solemn gaze. Those ultramarine eyes held the same message as hers. *This was bad.* No, fuck that. This was a nightmare.

Their arms dropped from the hold they had on each other. They turned, both of them looking at the team. Vox was screaming through her teeth, every rasp from her throat a curse to the sky, to the Virtues. River cradled her cheeks and said something low enough that Aspen didn't catch it, before pulling her into a hug. She just cried harder, unable to hold herself up any longer.

Mackenzie wept silent tears, a hand covering her mouth, her eyes darting everywhere. It was as if she couldn't tear her eyes away from Vox, but couldn't bear to watch her either. Levi was standing with his thumb and index fingers squeezing the ridge of his nose, gritting his teeth like he was in agony. Thex sat on a fallen boulder, staring at the ground, his eyes lined with unshed tears.

Aspen looked at Ryder to find him already watching her. Her stone core became molten lava. The rage made her tremble, her hands in tight fists at her sides.

She whispered a promise in a quiet voice, more deadly than a battle cry.

"He's going to pay."

The team had been arguing for over thirty minutes and Aspen had just about had enough. She hadn't approached Vox. Not yet. Vox was sitting next to the fire they'd built— she'd told them she wanted to be alone. Ryder was pressing his fingertips into his forehead. Precious time was being wasted, and Aspen could sense his rising anxiety. The sound of his heartbeat as she stood beside him felt like a lance of steel impaling her. None of the others noticed his heart palpitations, his breathing ragged like he'd run the length of Kore. She couldn't imagine what he was going through. What he was feeling… A marine dead. On *his* team.

She watched his lips begin to quiver—undoubtedly the chill that came to him moments before a panic attack.

"Think of something else other than your breathing," she whispered. He gave her a sidelong glance. "Look at the ground… Think of the ground. The wet soil. The patterns in the glacier over there." She pointed twenty feet away, where the glacier, pale turquoise in color, began its serrated climb up the west face of the mountain.

Ryder's shoulders dropped, his straight, rigid posture returning. His heartbeat slowed to its normal steady rhythm.

He delivered his first order of the next phase of Operation Enceladus, discreetly calling Thex to his side. "Call Gunner. Update our coordinates and let him know there's a marine down."

"What do you want me to say about Declan?"

"KIA," Ryder replied.

Thex nodded and walked out of earshot before pressing the screen on his wristwatch to begin the call. They didn't need Vox overhearing him relaying the news.

Mackenzie's hands were positioned in front of her like two cleavers. "Okay, let's go over this one more time… We have Wolves who can transport us via Phaedra to the next location. Despite the Corps disapproving of this mission, I agree with Ryder. This demon was responsible for Declan's death, and now it has in its possession a key component to Ignatius's plan. I see no other option. We have to go after it."

Levi agreed. "If we don't, the result could be catastrophic."

"If we follow it, it could be even more catastrophic," River rebutted, his voice low, his focus shifting between their tight circle and Vox over near the fire. "Ignatius is sending demons who can possess *us*. What if we lose someone else? I say we abort mission."

Mackenzie baulked, her eyebrows crinkling in deep thought before her eyes widened at Levi. "By the Virtues, what if he *does* take someone else?" she whispered, darting a look in Aspen's direction.

Mackenzie hadn't seen her heal Ryder in the cave and didn't know the vials were made by her. Aspen's healing power reserve felt low—not dangerously so, but making vials for the team this morning and healing Ryder from four wounds that punctured straight through him meant there wasn't much left, so telling them about it now was useless.

Thex joined them again. "We've gotten this far. Besides, Vox was handy enough with those healing vials."

Vox turned at the sound of her name, her cheeks red, but quickly looked back toward the fire. River just stared at the ground. Nobody was willing to divulge the secret about Aspen's healing powers, because they knew what it would mean. An Anima healer was a prized commodity, and the wrong people knowing could put even a skilled marine like Aspen in grave danger. Ryder gave her a long look that told her if they ever made it through this, he wouldn't let that happen.

Mackenzie sighed. "We can't let a demon escape with

Enceladus. Time isn't something we can afford." She walked to the edge of the semicircle they had formed. "If the demon disappeared over the border and Levi got close enough to the portal it opened to escape—"

"Then all we need to do is trace the portal's signature." River smiled grimly, "Lucky we have a tracker."

Ryder approached Levi with a no-nonsense expression. Levi stood still, so still that it was as if he wasn't breathing, glaring at Ryder in that intense way of his. Ryder leaned in, placing his nose on Levi's shoulder. Levi's head tilted up, waiting for him to finish. When Ryder stepped back, River nudged Levi.

"That was pretty intimate. Better not tell Zuri."

Levi cleaved the air with his hand. "I tell Zuri everything."

It must be nice, Aspen thought. Having someone you could tell everything to. Someone to understand you. After her mother's death, she didn't have anyone who knew everything, every side of her. Someone who knew her depths, her secrets, her dreams. Not even Maxen. Maybe that was what Declan had been to Vox… until Aspen took it away from her.

A part of her knew that wasn't entirely true—that the demon had killed the man inside before she'd even considered turning his body to ash. But part of her still felt like it was her fault.

Guilt churned her stomach. She took a sharp breath before putting one step in front of the other until she knelt beside Vox.

The flames crackled and spat inside Vox's violet eyes. Vox didn't turn to her, didn't make any movement that showed she'd registered Aspen was there. Aspen made to reach for her hand in her lap, but thought better of it.

Her voice came out as a rasp. "Vox. I'm so—"

"How do I do it?" Vox's voice was still sweet as bird-song, but with an undertow of anguish, ready to sweep her up. "How do I go on? How do I face Ignatius after he took my person? My Declan…"

Virtues save her. Aspen didn't have an answer. What the hell would she tell her?

Taken. Declan had been stolen from her. And Aspen was going to unleash the monster that she was inside to make sure that Vox never had to.

"I'll kill him, Vox."

Vox settled herself into the promise. She took a steadying breath, as if the words Aspen had spoken were a lullaby. Aspen's focus darted over her face—her pearly skin, her straight brows, her bee-stung lips—before they stared into each other's eyes. Aspen lifted her hands to cradle both sides of Vox's face, feeling her own emotions welling. Tears rolled slowly down Vox's face, wetting Aspen's thumbs as she wiped each one.

"How do I go on to face the demons, to face Ignatius?"

Aspen anchored her there in her gaze. "Become scarier than the thing scaring you."

A rush of breath escaped Vox's lips. She nodded. Like those words were the master key, a flash in her eyes revealed that she suddenly understood every single decision Aspen had made, the driver of every battle plan. Aspen had never said those words out loud before, didn't even know where they came from. But the last puzzle piece became melded with the whole picture of her life.

They stood and walked to Ryder and the rest of the team. Ryder drew a circle with his Phaedra before the scent lingering on the end of his nose could fade. The portal opened, rippling like a pool of water with spectral light arcing through it, swirling before them.

This wasn't over. It was evident on the faces of every marine as they joined hands, ready to travel.

Ignatius had taken one of their own.

And they were going to rain hell.

CHAPTER 24

Ryder took his first step out of the portal, the hair along his muscled arms and the nape of his neck raised. He was always ready for battle. The fabric of the T-shirt beneath his military blouse clung to his skin with clammy sweat as fear raked through him with sharp claws. He wondered why choosing to go after the demon suddenly felt like the wrong decision, but he pushed the clamoring voice down—the one that told him to order everyone to *run*. His hand grazed one of the spots where the demon's claws had pierced through him… What if Thex was next to die? Or Aspen?

"Well, this is convenient." Levi curled his lips in disdain as he scanned the wide, busy street. It was dark; a tall column of buildings on either side stretched out ahead for miles. Music from different venues—some ground level, some rooftop, and some hidden behind large doors in alleyways—mixed together. The team stood on the tram tracks in the middle of the road.

"Where are we?" Thex asked. River shrugged.

"We're in Melbourne."

Vox's voice was nothing but a husk of what it had been only a few hours before. But she continued. Enduring, as Anima marines had been taught to do their whole lives. She pulled out her tablet and followed a sequence, then pressed a button.

"Initializing city mode for each Phaedra. We can now move without being detected by humans."

"Good. Look alive—those demons can't be far," Ryder announced, turning to Levi, who stood beside him. "You'll take the rooftops." Levi nodded.

Ryder called River's and Mackenzie's names next, then went silent. River waited with a quizzical expression before he realized what Ryder was looking at. He turned.

"Cancel that," Ryder announced.

"Oh my god," Thex breathed. "I've never seen—"

An army of demonic creatures filled the main street ahead. They crawled over parked cars and scaled the buildings, creating a tunnel of hellish bodies coming straight for the team. Civilians were screaming and fleeing.

Ignatius walked along the tram tracks. At times he moved like a shadow as he switched between his physical body and an energy-field version of himself. He took each step in a relaxed yet businesslike manner.

Mackenzie gawked. "Is it just me, or is Ignatius really attractive?"

River rolled his eyes, but Levi shrugged in agreement.

"I wouldn't be so quick to give orders," Ignatius warned as he held back the wall of fiends with a wave of his hand. "If you or your team so much as move, I'll ravage this city. Let's see, eight of you…" His voice trailed off as he did a head count. "Oh." His grin was wide, conniving. "And then there were seven. What a shame. Eagle-boy looked like the type who could grow on you."

Vox threw herself forward. The only thing stopping her from attacking was River blocking her with his large frame.

"So, seven of you, and three thousand of us. Hardly seems fair, does it? But you see, this was our home first, before your predecessors cast us out. Now we live in the shadows beneath all of this… banished to the lesser planes."

"I've changed my mind about him being attractive," Levi stated.

"Are you drunk?" Mackenzie asked Ignatius. Ryder could smell the alcohol drifting from his direction.

"I'll admit, humans do have some usefulness—beer, motorbikes… and I quite like art. I marvel at the beauty of what they can create. I myself never really had the time—"

"Do you ever shut up?" Ryder cut him off.

"Forgive me. I tend to babble when I've been at the bar. Drinking away my sorrows, you see." Ignatius stalked closer to Vox. She stiffened in his proximity. "You see, pretty Fox, if they're all drunk…" He swirled his finger around. "It makes it that much easier to slip in unnoticed. Inside their bodies, their minds, and slowly detach them from the souls that they so often forget they have. Just like your winged boyfriend."

He grinned. Vox shoved harder against River's arms, straining to get at Ignatius.

"Something to add to your data." Ignatius paced the space between them. "Eons ago, I made a promise to your Primordials—"

"You knew the Virtues?" River snarled.

"Yes," Ignatius answered with raised brows. "And my promise to them, before they tore my beloved family to pieces, was that neither they, nor the generations of Anima after them, would ever know family." He leaned in and whispered near Ryder's ear, "I see the light of your bonds, like golden cords that tie your souls to each other. Some are as old as time itself." His eyes fixed upon the marking on Ryder's arm. "And some are new. But just know… I will destroy them all. Just like I did with the Fox and the Eagle… Just like Lykaion did mine."

He gave a forced grin as he fumbled for his cigarettes in the breast pocket of his gray suit jacket. Rage spread so thick through the air around him that he shook.

"You took away my happiness. You took away my loved ones. And you still get to have yours? I don't think so. And just so you know—I will be getting them back. They will soon walk this Earth again. I'll take your stamina, your vitality, that damned glow, and I'll fill you with a demon seed. In fact, I'll be doing that to the whole damned human race."

An electric violet beam of power made an explosive sound as it shot toward Ignatius's chest. A second before impact, Ignatius held up Enceladus, and the force of Ryder's power was returned to them as if he'd held up a mirror. Ryder shouted at the team and they dove out of the way just in time.

They slowly curled back to standing positions, glancing at each other, horrified.

"Did you know he could do that?" Thex asked Ryder.

"He can use our powers against us?" Vox gasped.

"Uh… this changes things," River said.

Ignatius stood with his arms open wide. "Is that all?"

Ryder gave the order and the team dispersed in different directions. Their formation produced a wall, a huge hole where Declan should have been hovering overhead. Levi clung with his claws to the second-story ledge of an apartment building, and the other four spread evenly on the ground, poised at the ready. Ignatius tossed Enceladus to a group of three demons behind him and they caught it in their long claws.

"On my mark—don't forget the plan." It occurred to Ryder that those words may be the last his team would ever hear. That thought alone caused him to have an out-of-body experience, like he was watching somebody other than himself charge forward and shoot waves of violet light from their hands.

The demons attacked like a swarm of wasps, crawling over buildings and gliding overhead. River hauled a low-flying demon to the ground. "One down. Two thousand, nine hundred and ninety—"

"Seven to go." Thex flicked his horns up so that the demon clinging to them crashed into another one nearby.

Ryder bounded straight for Enceladus, shooting beams of gamma and fire, scorching the demons in his way until he had the three who held the precious element in his line of vision. His powers blasted through two of them as a swarm of flying demons descended upon him.

Mackenzie took out three by shaking the ground as she landed from a powerful dive. Thex collected a large demon with his antlers, sending it into a restaurant window with one mighty charge. Ryder's chest lightened with relief—but it was only momentary: the army of demons became too many for the three of them to handle as they encircled and attacked from above. They fended the creatures off, but they weren't going to last long in such a suffocating huddle.

They were backed into an alleyway where Thex opened a heavy door and ushered them inside. He'd barely got the door closed when demons began crashing into it. They'd entered a darkened pub fashioned with velvet upholstery and ornate frames and mirrors. The music was still on, but the patrons and staff had evacuated.

"Where are the others?" Mackenzie asked, panic thick in her voice.

Ryder's own voice cracked as he replied, "They're still out there."

Thex looked as though he'd lost hope long ago. "How do we get out of here to get to them… if they're even still alive?"

"Damn it, Thex!" Ryder thundered. He could have launched himself at his friend, but Mackenzie pushed against both of their chests to create distance.

"We don't have time to fight each other."

Ryder pushed his hair back with his hands before rubbing his face. "Let me think this through, let me think this through…"

He half expected some pushback from Thex, but both he and Mackenzie went silent. Ryder leaned his weight up against the door, feeling each impact of the demons crashing into it from the outside. Thex walked behind the bar and turned off the music while Mackenzie peeked behind the thick curtain of a small window. Ryder pressed his spine against the iron door. He hoped that wherever Aspen was, she was plotting to make that one reckless decision… that she had found a way to stop all of those demons. No matter what, she would have to sacrifice to get it done. She saw ways that anyone else would deem unthinkable. That was what they desperately needed right now—a Hell-fire decision.

The heaviness of grief weighed down Ryder's whole being. Declan was dead. He slid down against the door until he reached the floor. The chill reached his legs, his shoulders, his neck, until he was submerged in full teeth-chattering cold panic. His breathing went next, dragging in and out, though he tried his best to steady it. Thex and Mackenzie were keeping a lookout, the war outside too loud for them to notice him.

He heard his own voice in his head, louder than the panic: *You're going to lose more marines.* He wanted to look into Aspen's green eyes and feel his fear melt away. It was her fearlessness and undoubtable capability that he'd held on to, that had been pulling him through. No matter what, she'd get the demon.

His teeth stopped chattering as a wave of calm washed over him. He had to pull this team through, with her as his anchor. He bit down on the inside of his lip, his voice escaping in a rasp.

"We're all going to die here if we don't do this together. Come find me, please."

He released a heavy exhale of sorrow, shaking his head, because the next words were inconceivable.

"Declan's dead. I *need* you."

He propped his forearm up on his knee and stared at the symbols, tracing them with his finger. When he reached the symbol of his power, he felt something inside himself shift.

He felt the Wolf inside him rise.

Eons of raw power rushed through Ryder's veins, like the Virtues had turned on the faucet. His Anima padded a few steps ahead of him down the city street. His Wolf was enormous, with fur of indigo, deep as the night sky above. It emitted a golden aura that slowly writhed like tranquil candlelight. The demons shielded their eyes and parted like the sea as the Animas rose from where they were concealed to join Ryder, Thex, and Mackenzie in walking down the middle of the street with slow, purposeful steps. Vox and River, then Levi. Thank the heavenly Virtues, everyone was alive. Ryder released a breath he wasn't aware he had been holding.

He felt a charge, warm and electric in his chest, when the White Wolf stepped out, surrounded by crimson star-flecked light—Aspen's silhouette following close behind. Her emerald eyes were aglow with lifetimes of stories, her aura as silver as the moon he cried to on his sleepless nights. Their steps to reach the nucleus of the demon army were synchronized and graceful as they held each other's flanks, their power roiling down the path they forged, to where Enceladus was being kept.

Ignatius gave them a long look: first Ryder and his Anima, then the rest of the team. His blood-red irises filled with worry, yet his grin disguised it as pleasure. Ryder threw his arms forward, shooting a steady stream of electric violet power into Enceladus. The power ricocheted, starbursting out in every direction. The entire intersection lit up. The explosion made the world shudder. The power was so potent that it vaporized at least a hundred demons that had surrounded them as they inched closer and closer, trying to get to their light. To swallow it.

More and more demons took their place. Ryder pulled more power from within his reserves—he still had more to give, but enough for this many demons?

Ignatius grinned wide, as if sensing the moment Ryder realized he wasn't going to be able to take on the whole army.

"Thex, how long ago did you call for backup?"

"About ten minutes ago," Thex shouted back over the ear-splitting roar of a demon who attacked the team from behind—the golden aura of his Anima was waning.

"What the hell's taking them so long?" Ryder demanded.

"We can't keep going like this, Captain," Vox called from behind him. "There are just too many demons."

Ignatius chuckled as he stood in the growing darkness beyond the Animas' light. "As entertaining as it is, watching your inevitable demise—you're clearly unprepared for this battle. Does Ansel know you're here?"

Ryder felt the whole team recoil behind him. He held his breath.

"You really should do better background checks on your team." Ignatius's hands clasped behind his back as he walked around the edge of their field of protection.

"What are you talking about?" Mackenzie probed.

Ignatius smiled, more to himself than any of them, the slender muscles shifting in the pale column of his neck. His Adam's apple bobbed like he'd taken a gulp of some phantom substance. *Fear,* Ryder realized. He was drinking their fear.

His voice was like sharp claws stroking down the sides of their light field, looking for an opening. A weakness. "Take Hellfire, for example… Did you ever bother to ask her *how* she killed Hurricane? Or are you too blinded by her hypnotic succubus powers to see her true nature?"

Ryder dropped his guard at the question, flicking his focus back to Aspen. She met his eyes for a mere second before turning away.

"Her powers are nothing like a succubus'," Vox declared.

Thex baulked. "What powers?"

Mackenzie glared at Aspen. "I thought it was advanced combat."

Aspen threw her a begrudging look, one that revealed Mackenzie could only know that information if she'd looked at Aspen's file.

"Nobody knows how it works? Okay, let me educate you on your own powers." Ignatius raised his arms. "I know the truth, if you wish to hear it. I tell you… her killing Hurricane was the most delicious slay I've ever encountered. The highest form of entertainment."

His red eyes danced as he stood before Ryder, who could only meet his gaze with disdain. A cord knotted in his stomach. Ignatius was throwing them off-center. Finding ways to separate them from each other. Trying to make the light field dim enough to push through.

Ignatius inhaled and gulped again, clearly lost in

pleasure at the headiness of their terror. "Or better yet—why believe me? Shouldn't she explain it all?" He looked Ryder dead in the eyes, his voice low. "It is the reason why you haven't bonded in the same pack, isn't it? It's because she knows she's more than capable of doing the same thing to you."

Ryder cut him a look he reserved only for the moment before an attack. But Ignatius picked a speck of lint from his suit jacket, his dress shoes clicking on the asphalt as he walked the circumference of their barrier. Aspen had stepped too far back. Ignatius's hand forcefully turned her jaw to face him; she pushed him into the darkness and retreated into the light.

"Touch me again and I'll—"

"You'll have to save your threats. I'm afraid I won't be the one fighting you after this... You see your team? Look at their faces..."

Ryder watched Aspen's face fall as she looked upon the team, all watching her in anticipation.

"Tell them what we both know to be true," Ignatius boomed.

Aspen trembled, her shoulder blades flexing back slightly. She almost squared them, but it was as if she couldn't muster the posture.

"Nothing but that powerless farm girl underneath it all, aren't you?" Ignatius sneered.

Aspen's eyelids flickered in response. "It had been more than a week since he'd chained me and constantly beat me... On the last night, he knocked me out cold, and when I came to, I—"

She doubled over, cradling her middle.

"Finish it!" Ignatius spat.

Aspen took a shaky breath. "When I came to, I was lying on ice. Maxen had dragged me to an ice lake nearby and he was…"

Mackenzie took a step closer, her eyes wide with terror.

"…drilling a hole in the surface of the lake."

Vox gasped and covered her mouth.

"He pushed me under the ice. The current was so strong. I was trying to find the surface, but everything was so dark. I saw Midnight Wolf above me and I swam to him. I couldn't hold my breath any longer. Where he was, the ice was thin, so I smashed through it. I managed to pull myself up, and I attacked Maxen. I knew there was only one way to get the *Ars Daemonium* and get out alive, so I… I stabbed him."

Ignatius exploded with laughter, a piece of combed-back hair falling over one of his eyes. He clapped his hands together. "Don't stop there. Wait…" He put his hand up to the rest of the team. "There's more!"

"I sliced off his primary flight feathers."

Those words made Vox grow pale.

Ignatius grinned. "And then?"

Aspen swallowed. "I cut along the bone until his whole wingspan was severed off… and then I finished him."

"Now tell them why," Ignatius instructed.

Aspen was staring listlessly as she answered, "I did it for revenge for what he put me through. And because he activated me when I could have lived a normal life."

"You did that to your own kind." Mackenzie's voice broke. "You're a monster."

"Not just your own kind… Your husband," Levi added in disbelief.

Thex was panting. There was terror etched into his large brown eyes. "What's to say that if we were in your way, you wouldn't do the same to us?"

River held his hands up to them all. "Don't you see what he's doing? He's trying to break us apart. And it's working."

"We can't trust her!" Mackenzie growled, her needle fangs bared.

Ryder was silent. He didn't know what to feel first. A heaviness in his chest threatened to force him down to his knees; all he kept seeing was Declan's face. There was nothing but his team holding him back from attacking the Primordial demon in front of him. And the secrets of this woman. When she told her stories, it felt like the hurt was happening to *him*.

He cut her a look. "Well, I guess I know why you didn't want to be partners…"

"Ryder, I didn't want you—"

"To end up like him?" he finished. "You let your vendetta get in the way of honor."

Aspen shut her mouth. The crisp night air left her cheeks kissed with mist.

"We really need to work on that," Ryder said.

Aspen's lips parted. She looked deeper into his eyes, like she was trying to find the lie. "You're not going to turn your back on me?"

A few steps closed the gap between them. "Are you still on our side?"

Her gaze darted to the rest of the team. She answered like he was crazy to assume anything else. "Yes."

Ryder felt Mackenzie's hand on his upper arm. "You're making a big mistake."

He whirled to face her, to the team. "I'm not going to let this demon get what he wants. Are you?"

Mackenzie withdrew, clutching her arm. She seemed hurt by his words.

Hot air rushed out his nose. "Then we fight on the same side."

"But Ry!" Thex protested.

"There are two sides of the war!" Ryder shouted at his team. "*His* and the Anima Corps. Who the hell are we?"

The team buckled under his question, glancing at one another.

"*Who are we?*" Ryder repeated.

"We're First Special Forces," River answered. The team's focus was on him now.

"Us seven are the only operational detachment they can call for this type of threat. I can see what Ignatius is doing, and you're all letting something that happened years ago to a person who—if I can be totally honest—none of you would have questioned her killing, if you knew what he'd done to the Corps." He looked all of them in the eyes. "Hurricane had to be stopped. If there's one thing I understand about Aspen, it's that the story matters. *Her* story matters. I'm grateful that I'm even standing here fighting alongside all of you, and I have her to thank."

When River's gaze fell upon Aspen, she looked as though she could have hugged him. She responded with a tight smile, but it was short-lived as the team turned to her.

"I don't care about your reasons for not trusting me… but that *monster*"—she pointed at Ignatius, throwing

Mackenzie's words back at her—"killed Declan, wants us all dead, and will annihilate all that grows and thrives on this planet if we don't get it together and stop him. I would never let anyone hurt you. I'm loyal to our captain. Nothing can change or come between that." She said the next part begrudgingly. "So if you want me to step aside on this mission—"

"No!" the team said, almost in unison.

"We're the elite," Thex declared. "Let the Virtues reign."

All eyes anchored on Ryder, ready for his order.

"For Declan."

CHAPTER 25

The words caused a chain reaction of power like a wave to ripple through each member of the team, igniting allegiance on the *only* thing binding them—the loss of their comrade. Thex shot forward with his antlers, breaking the field of light surrounding them. The demons came caving in on top of them. It was nothing but writhing bodies of darkness that plunged you into despair as soon as they touched you, before sucking the vital forces out of you.

Ryder dove into the swarm, forging his power into a vicious blade, cleaving through dozens of demons at a time. When he could finally see his surroundings again, Vox was guarding two young teens hiding behind a car and ushering them out of sight. She must have taken her Phaedra off city mode to save them—a risk he was willing to take.

"Where's Ignatius?" Ryder shouted.

Vox started to say that she didn't know, but Ryder heard something that sounded like the wind turbines of a plane. They looked up.

A swirling red smoke storm was levitating Ignatius high above them, with Enceladus floating above him. He was sucking energy into himself like a black hole, and the storm surrounding him grew until it consumed the intersection they were standing in.

Aspen was crouched on the road with a beam of power blasting through her, devouring the life from her. Ryder could only watch on helplessly as she wilted, her power draining, her body becoming a husk.

Ignatius spotted him, his hand flying out to propel power that looked identical to Ryder's own ultraviolet rays. He blasted them with full force straight into Ryder's chest.

Ryder felt nothing—until he began buckling under the pressure. With no pain, it was hard to judge how much he was hurting. He sank to his knees, fatigue washing over him. He clawed at the asphalt, trying to form his power into a barrier, but he was fading. All that surrounded him was a fiery red.

He heard Vox shout his name. She knelt beside him, holding his arm. "He's using your and Aspen's powers against you."

"I can't—" was all he managed to say before his eyes flickered closed. He fought to keep them open. His body was numb. He was fading to nothingness, becoming one with it.

Vox's sweet voice broke through the darkness. "You have to bond together or you're not going to survive this. I may not know much about Wolves, but I know that two lone Wolves are vulnerable on their own. Please, Ryder, get up!"

Ryder managed to get to his feet, staggering over to Aspen. There was a moment of relief as he looked up and realized that Levi had scaled a tall building and attacked Ignatius, stopping the power radiating from Enceladus.

"We don't have much time." His voice sounded like sharp nails had been dragged down his throat. "We're left open here… and I'm not holding back from you anymore."

Aspen held a hand against her forehead. "But what about what happened on the plane… Maxen… My banishment…"

"We find a way. Together."

He took both of her hands in his just as Ansel came wafting through a portal, Gunner at his side.

"I'll take over the frontline," Gunner said. They nodded at each other and the major took off in agile leaps toward the team.

Ansel locked his pearly eyes with Aspen's. "You know what you must do, young Wolf. The question is… are you brave enough to do it?"

Her jaw tightened.

"Defeat is easy." Ansel palmed his staff. The small, solid piece of cryolava, sharpened to a point, was glowing. "Loyalty and courage are harder. Which do you choose?"

Aspen looked back at Ryder. Without a word, her kaleidoscope eyes began to glow. She grasped Ansel's staff and pulled her Phaedra chain over her head.

An earth-shattering blast sent Levi plummeting to the ground. Gunner raced to catch him before he was splattered onto the road.

Aspen hesitated. "Are you sure you want this with me?" she asked Ryder.

He ran his thumb along her jawline, tipping her head

up toward him. "I'm going to follow you anywhere you go, Lovetta, so why the hell not?"

Her smile bared her brilliant white teeth.

Ryder handed her his Phaedra and she threw both tags into the sky, spearing Ansel's staff through both the chains before they could hit the ground. She lifted her tattooed arm and Ryder completed the connection, entwining their fingers together.

"NO!" Ignatius screamed hoarsely, his demonic insides spilling out of his human form. He was bleeding from his eyes, his tongue lashing. "You shouldn't have done that." He convulsed beneath his human mask. "You have no idea of the consequences your bond will have."

An ultraviolet force coursed electricity through Ryder and Aspen's every cell, illuminating them. It grew and orbed around them, lighting up the road, the buildings. Thousands of demons vaporized into nothingness. Ryder's feet left the ground as they were levitated by the strength of their power, becoming a spinning vortex of volatile energy that perforated the seams of dimensions.

It slowed, and they lowered back to the ground, their fingers still enlaced.

Thex ran to them. "Where did he go?"

"He escaped through a portal," Gunner stated in a defeated tone.

Levi and River were clutching their injuries. Aspen walked over to them, placing a hand on each until they regained their strength and their wounds had healed.

"Thanks," River said dreamily.

Thex watched the healing in a frozen stupor. He blinked himself out of it, clearly realizing that the vials that had healed him in the cave had been Aspen's. But alas, he was too angry to care. "What was that?" he snapped at both of them.

There was a quiet pause before Aspen answered, "It's a ritual, bonding Ryder and me in the same pack."

Thex looked expectantly at Ryder. "And you agreed to this?"

Ryder eyed his friend. "Yes."

Thex tossed his head in consternation. Mackenzie stormed away, coming to the same realization about Aspen's healing powers as Thex had.

"If you have something to say, brother, just say it," Ryder demanded.

"Yeah, I do have something to say!" Thex shouted. "With her? Have you lost your mind?"

"She's on our side!" Ryder yelled back. "And she saved your life. You're still standing here because of her."

"She's not on anybody's side!" Thex boomed. Ryder could have sworn he was holding back tears.

Thex stood intimidatingly close. Ryder matched his stance, daring him with nothing but body language. Almost an entire day of battle, and yet their muscles flexed, their chests puffed. Two marines with bodies like weapons, ready to unleash hell.

Thex's antlers were mighty and ready to charge as he leaned in. Ryder gave him a forceful push that sent him stumbling backward. Thex threw him a disbelieving look before he whipped around toward Aspen.

"You bring him down with you and you'll deal with me, Lovetta."

Aspen didn't respond. Thex stormed off down the road

and into an empty shop, where Gunner was holding open a portal. Thex walked through and disappeared.

Aspen looked at Ryder and sighed. Ryder rested his forehead against hers and closed his eyes. He felt her soft skin and breathed in her mesmerizing scent before he leaned back to search her eyes. "I'm putting my trust in you."

She nodded.

"Don't do anything to break *my* loyalty, Aspen." He watched the weight of his words make her silent, her eyes wide. "Because I don't think I could take it if you did." His hands broke away from hers and he went to check on the others.

The team gathered back together to make their way through the portal Gunner had created. Ryder froze at the precipice after Vox went through. Aspen was issuing a standoffish thanks in Gunner's direction. Ryder snatched her hand and pulled her with him through the swirling spectrum.

Their destination was Ansel's office. Ryder could see the other side, as if he were looking through water; all the justices were visible there.

Seconds before they were meant to arrive, he jumped out early, tugging Aspen close to him. They spilled out of the portal that swirled several feet off the ground, landing in a forest with a thud.

CHAPTER 26

Ryder didn't want to move. He grunted. Every muscle ached and the back of his head throbbed where it had flung back as he'd collided with the ground. Aspen's veil of garnet locks fell around him as she braced herself on top of him. He moved his leg down until he could feel every dip and curve of her body against him—if he wasn't so fucking exhausted…

She released a breath and sank into him. He closed his eyes and cradled her head.

"Why did you bring us here?" she asked softly, her ear pressed to his chest.

He caressed her hair lazily with his fingertips. "Didn't you see where they were taking us? All the justices were there. We were walking straight into our dishonorable discharge."

"By *ours*, you mean *yours*… I can't be dishonorably discharged twice."

She rolled off of him, and just in time: he almost didn't roll the other way fast enough before he retched. Aspen rubbed his shoulder until it had all come up.

"Could you have healed me before I threw up?" Ryder asked weakly.

She shook her head. "I can't heal emotions, or any physical reactions they cause."

He'd only asked because he was curious; he knew she was drained, and he would never ask her to heal something so basic anyway. He rolled his eyes at himself, humiliated.

Like she'd heard his thoughts, she huffed, "I'm a medic. You think I care?"

It put him a little more at ease, but not by much. At this point, he was mentally clawing himself through his fatigue as the reality of it all came crashing down on him. The operation had been a disaster. Ignatius had Enceladus.

Fuck… They had made it all too easy for him to steal it. A broken team, their bonds weak with distrust. And Declan…

It was quiet for a while. Even the birds high in the canopy didn't sing—like they'd heard the news; like Kore could sense that he was missing, that his boots had never hit the ground when they'd returned from this mission. An Eagle Anima, fallen. The silence was Kore in mourning.

Ryder buried his head in his hands, elbows propped up on his knees. It was all sinking in as his adrenaline faded. Bile threatened to heave again, burning the back of his throat, which was already sore—from screaming orders or from Ignatius draining his power, he didn't know which.

He reflected on the battle and released a shuddering breath. He could see their broken formation. A huge hole where Declan should have been. He imagined that Declan would have wrapped civilians up in his wings to protect them from harm or fly them to safety. Would have attacked Ignatius long before Levi could have scaled that building. Quicker. They would have been quicker; maybe they would have left with Enceladus and delivered it to the Corps. Then this mission would have been worth it. But now…

When Ryder looked back at Aspen, she was sitting in the same position he was, only her back was straight, her head erect, a vacant expression on her face. Numb, he realized. Ryder got her up and moved them to a patch of trees close by that gave a sparse view of a lake.

"Where are we?" she asked, sitting with her back against a tree.

"About halfway between base and my cabin."

"So why don't we just go to your cabin?"

"Nope. They can find us there." Ryder lowered himself gingerly against the same trunk, every muscle screaming in protest. They sat in silence for a while, staring out at the emerald waters of the lake. He sniffed, bending his knees and propping his arms up on them. "Tell me something you don't want anyone else to know."

Aspen licked her lips. Her focus never left the lake. When she spoke, her words came out in a choked sob. "I'll never get over killing Declan."

Shit.

Shit.

Shit…

And *he* had given her the order.

His head bowed as he watched her sidelong. "You didn't—"

"Oh, but I did." Those words were heavy, thick with sin. She shook her head slowly, staring into the space between them, like the scene was replaying in her mind and she couldn't stop the horror. Her shoulders trembled with repressed tears. "He didn't have a blood debt. He was innocent… and I—"

Her hand clapped over her mouth and she squeezed her eyes shut. A silent cry. But in the ether, Ryder could hear her White Wolf's mournful howl.

She removed her hand to say, "Did you hear his Eagle calling before it died?"

Ryder didn't have words. He hooked an arm around her and tugged her into him. She buried her forehead in his shoulder. He wanted to tell her that she was allowed to cry, or scream; that he wasn't going anywhere. He hoped his body language conveyed the message. But she straightened, swallowed. He watched as her eyes deadened. Somehow she'd taught herself to achieve the opposite of the ether-glow of an Anima's eyes. Like he'd just glimpsed the real Aspen before Hellfire had come up from behind and suffocated her.

She met him with a lifeless, dull stare. But it was too late; he'd witnessed her true self, even if only for a moment.

"It isn't safe to not be her," she said.

He nodded. He understood. He understood too well. He looked deeper into her eyes, to the trapped woman inside. "I'm going to make it safe again, so that you can choose who you want to be. You're not a monster, Aspen."

Her glassy eyes searched his own. Her lips parted, a rush of air escaping.

He hooked her chin with his finger and tilted her face up to his. "Walls down with me. Promise?"

She paused, closed her eyes before opening them again, then finally nodded.

"Tell me that you promise."

"Yes," she breathed. "I promise."

My god, she is gorgeous. Looking at her now, no smirking or glaring… Her features were soft. A warrior with the face of an angel. Those lips. All he had to do was move his thumb higher… to ask. Ask if he could…

This wasn't the time. She'd offered him so much of herself in that promise.

"I should have gotten to Declan before you," he said. "I should have killed that demon."

"No." She shook her head with surety. "You were right to let me see if I could find a way to detach it, to see if he could be healed. Your orders were right. I didn't look back at you because I was waiting for you to give an order… I looked back at you to know for sure that there was no other option. No other way… before I killed him."

He could only sigh. *This fucked-up situation…*

"Let's stop saying 'killed him.' Declan was killed by a demon. We killed the demon."

Aspen pulled back, like she was assessing him. His eyes strained as he blinked back fatigue.

"You don't sleep, do you?"

Ryder's chest caved at the question. "Not a wink."

Aspen nodded. Ryder changed the subject; there was

too much still to go over for them to be worrying about his sleeping habits.

"About Mackenzie—"

She cut him off. "You don't owe me anything, especially not an explanation."

Ryder ground his teeth. "Yeah, well, I'm giving you one anyway, so will you just listen?" She went silent and he continued. "I was pushing her away, Aspen. But you walked in before I had a chance to react."

Aspen leaned the back of her head up against the tree. "I've given you every reason not to trust me. I can't expect—"

"Actually, you've given me plenty of reasons *to* trust you. I've lost count of how many times you've healed me."

Her small hand covered his. He studied the size difference; his were huge in comparison.

"I will never let anything happen to you," she said in a quiet voice.

Ryder nodded. He understood exactly. "And I will never let anything happen to you."

They sat in silence, resting against each other. He yawned. She guided his head down into her lap and he curled up, his eyelids prickling with heat as they threatened to close.

"Sleep," she ordered.

"I can't—" he started to protest.

She shushed him softly and whispered, "I'll guard you."

Ryder was startled awake as a call came through on his

wristwatch. Aspen told him he had been asleep for two hours, which was half a night's rest for an Anima.

He glanced at his watch—Gunner. The major summoned them to General Winters's office immediately. He explained that he'd bought them time by busying the justices with the details regarding Declan's death, Vox's mission data, footage captured by their Phaedras, and interrogation of the team—all of whom had been non-judicially punished for disobeying the general's orders and Corps protocol. They had all been made to clean out some kind of storage barn for the Feast of Foxes celebration in the coming days. This was too light a punishment, considering the circumstances; the major made it clear that General Winters had something to do with their luck.

When they arrived at the general's office, they both stood at attention, and Ryder knocked once. Calais instructed them to enter. They marched in and stopped a few paces before Ansel's desk, where the justices and the general sat in a semicircle.

Justice Silla Borealis was the first to break the silence. "Well, I never thought I'd see your face again, Lovetta."

"I must agree," mused Justice Chaska. "Such strength, to survive the Tundra."

Justice Calais pointed a single finger down onto the wooden lacquer of Ansel's new desk. "How dare you set out on a mission without our consent? A stunt like that should have you dishonorably discharged. What's worse—one of our best marines is dead, and the cryolava that the Primordial demon needs to carry out his heinous plans is now in his possession."

Silla raised his brows and rustled the white feathers

on his folded wings. "Well, if Captain Everett had not succeeded in saving Melbourne, the outcome would have been much worse. I think we can all agree that his methods worked."

Chaska peered at Ryder through her round orange glasses. "I beg you to explain why you kept us in the dark about your mission, and even more so, how Hellfire is standing in front of us, alive and well."

Ryder exchanged a worried glance with Aspen.

"I know exactly what happened! Isn't it obvious?" Calais seethed. "You went after Hellfire, used military equipment to do so—"

"I can explain," Aspen interrupted.

Calais rose slowly from his chair, his eyes filled with fury. "Did I say you had permission to speak?"

"Justice, it is because of Hell—Sergeant Lovetta—that I could lead the team into these missions," Ryder explained. "If it had not been for her intel or her leads, Ignatius would have succeeded in murdering thousands of civilians."

Justice Chaska leaned forward in her seat. "How exactly did you win this battle?"

"Sergeant Lovetta bonded our powers together to generate enough power to overmatch Ignatius. Our team and the city would've been devoured by an army of three thousand demons."

"Did you say three thousand?" Silla linked his fingers together as he leaned forward on the desk.

"Yes, sir. I've never seen anything like it."

"How does this… *Ignatius* have the power to command such legions? And why wasn't he captured?" demanded Chaska.

"With all due respect, Justice," Ryder said, "Sergeant Thomas Thexton called for backup, but none came in time."

Disdain crossed Calais's narrow face. "Captain, if we had *known* about the mission, backup would not have been an issue. Ansel? What do you have to say about all this?"

Ansel rose from his chair, staff in hand. "Witnessing the way the team conducted themselves today, I must say that I have never seen a member of each species of Anima work so diligently together."

Ryder folded his arms, heat prickling off of his shoulders as Calais glowered at Ansel. "Well, since Sergeant Lovetta is no longer part of this Corps, she must leave the grounds imm—"

"I'm afraid I can't allow that, Justice," Ryder interrupted.

Calais's pupils zeroed in as if he had spotted prey. "Come again, Captain?"

"You see, Sergeant Lovetta and I are part of the same pack. Wherever she goes, I go."

His words made Chaska gasp and Silla slump in his chair, rubbing his temples.

A contemptuous grin crossed Calais's face. "Well, then. I have no other choice but to banish you both."

Chaska gasped again. "But Calais—who will lead the Special Forces?"

Ansel fixed Calais with a stone glare. "If you sentence them, you're punishing the whole Corps."

"By weeding out the incompliant?" Justice Calais snapped.

"By going against sacred Anima codes!" Ansel bellowed. Ryder gaped at him, shocked. Everybody did. They had never seen him react this way.

The door to the office opened, drawing their attention. Major Gunner strode to the circle around Ansel's desk, stopping beside Ryder.

"Major, this is a private conversation. I must ask you to leave," Justice Calais demanded.

Silla groaned. "You know what's going on these days? Nobody's listening to orders, nor are they respectful of rank!"

"I cannot stand by and see the lies go on any longer," Gunner informed them.

Chaska leaned forward in her chair. "Whatever are you talking about, Major?"

Gunner released a sharp exhale. "Sergeant Aspen Lovetta saved Sergeant River Borealis the day of Justice Asintmah's death. If she had not taken Asintmah's life, River would be dead right now. This is vital information that was overlooked when she was banished."

Calais's chair dragged against the wooden floor as he stood up, brewing rage making the sides of his mouth twitch. "Are you proclaiming that it is Lovetta's right to decide who should live and who should die?"

"No. What I'm saying is that Sergeant Lovetta saved the son of a justice—and one of the Corps' finest marines. He would have died that day had Asintmah's life not been sacrificed… but he is here to help finish Ignatius."

Justice Chaska shook her head in disapproval. "Nobody has the right to make that decision. Not Hellfire, not *any-body*… even if it was for Sergeant Borealis."

Silla cut Chaska a lethal glare. The tension in the room was building. Aspen's fingers were cold as Ryder interlaced them with his own.

"Yet Anima marine lives are disposable in comparison?" Gunner fired back.

The color drained from each of the Justices' faces. Ryder's heart began racing. Gunner was circling the long-held secret of Justice Bastian Fallow's death involving Asintmah. Was he preparing to tell them that they'd known?

He squeezed Aspen's hand and she squeezed his back—she knew it too. Gunner was bold enough, angry enough, to reveal it, if it meant saving Aspen from the Tundra when he hadn't been able to the first time.

Ryder spoke before Gunner could say anything more. "I think what the major is trying to say is that Lovetta is the reason the Corps even knows about the cryolava, Enceladus, in the first place. And that we've all provided something of value to this Corps."

"You're forgetting, Captain, that you and Lovetta are the reason Ignatius has the cryolava in his possession," Calais replied.

Gunner shook his head in disbelief. "That is not the truth."

Calais's voice boomed through the office, making them flinch. "My sergeant will take responsibility where it is required!"

His sergeant.

His sergeant…

Ryder's entire body went rigid, electricity surrounding his fist, a weapon he was hardly able to contain. She was 'his sergeant' only when it suited him. When he was on the losing end. Calais had revealed so much without realizing. He was an animal backed into a corner.

Aspen tipped her head up and smirked. "I am not your sergeant."

She let go of Ryder's hand and he watched her stride to the desk and lean on it with both hands.

"There is darkness among the Justices, Calais. Just know that I flourish in it."

All the muscles in Calais's face slackened at the gravity of her words. He gritted his teeth.

Ryder scratched the back of his neck. "Look, if we keep operating the way we always have… we are never going to win this war. Sergeant Lovetta has expert knowledge in the elements that we need to take Ignatius down. And the fact of the matter is that they don't exist here on Earth."

The Justices looked back at him skeptically. Silla shook his head and rubbed his hands over his face before addressing Aspen. "What about the years you have been lost at war, Sergeant? Bringing trouble to our Corps… to our people. The time spent running around with Hurricane, killing innocents—"

"But were they innocent?" Gunner challenged. "Have you ever investigated who they were?"

Ryder wanted to hug him there and then. Because that was the thing: they hadn't been innocent people. The story had been spun to serve the justices' agenda. Aspen had been the perfect scapegoat, the mask they hid behind when shit didn't look good on their end.

"Major, she has killed our kind!" Silla exclaimed.

"Yeah, but it's never been without cause," Ryder rebuked. "I'm not defending the poor choices she's made… but in times of war, are we really analyzing whose life was more important than the mission at hand? When Anima marines are already so willing to give their lives for the cause?" He shook his head. "You're all hypocrites."

"Captain!" Chaska breathed.

"I can't believe all of you!" Ryder went on. "As far as I'm concerned, Justice… We're in possession of the *Ars Daemonium because* of Sergeant Lovetta."

Aspen stood close to him, her hand finding his again.

Ansel sighed. "As long as I've known Aspen, she has never wanted to join us. It is my hope that she does, but my heart cannot overlook the disdain that she feels toward us because of the past."

"If you discharge her now, I'm only going to follow her… and you'll lose your captain," Ryder explained resolutely.

"Surely you don't mean that," Silla growled. "Be serious. Don't be stupid!"

Ryder shot him a defiant glare. "I've never been more serious in my life."

"You seem very keen to prove her innocence…" Chaska tilted her head, regarding Ryder with suspicion.

"I am. I'm also willing to lead these marines into battle. To do that, I can't overlook facts."

Silla sighed and slumped in his chair, defeated, before he jerked his wings and straightened. "Where do you propose that she stays, Captain? The whole Corps is against her."

"Minds can be changed, based upon the right evidence," Gunner added.

"I would like Sergeant Lovetta to live with me," Ryder said. "If she'll have me."

He felt her breath hitch as she released his hand.

Ansel leaned toward her. "Is this an arrangement that you are happy with, child?"

Ryder searched her every movement for her answer.

When her intoxicating perfume wafted through the room, the mood changed. Silla was smiling. Chaska sighed dreamily. Gunner had started humming.

Aspen studied Ryder for a long moment before she nodded. "Yes, I'll stay with you."

He took her in his arms. Her hands wrapped around his neck and he lifted her off the ground. He grazed his nose against her neck, smelling the heavenly scent of her hair.

They parted as Ryder realized the room was waiting for them. He walked closer to the desk. "We are not going to win this war if we are not together. And you'll lose the only two Wolves that you have left if you don't do this."

The Justices looked contemplative.

"Very well," Silla answered, clapping both hands in his lap.

Calais lowered himself into a chair, his expression plain. "One foot out of line, one act of war against our people, and the Tundra will be the least of your worries."

"Yes, Justice," Aspen replied.

Calais signaled that the meeting was over with a wave of his hand. Ryder and Aspen saluted and left the office quietly. When they got to the corridor, they chuckled in amazement at what had just transpired.

Ryder noticed River standing at the end of a speed portal. His expression was pained, his mouth a grim line. His gaze darted between them.

"I need you both to come with me."

CHAPTER 27

Aspen and Ryder's moment of exhilaration was temporary. That spark was completely smothered as they traveled swiftly to the labs. Aspen focused on River walking ahead of them so as not to make eye contact with other marines or superiors. Going by the whispers in the long corridors, word had spread that they were back from a mission.

"Hurry up," River threw over his shoulder. Aspen's gaze darted to whatever he'd just looked at that had launched him to move faster than he ever did outside of training or duty.

Nia Colson. A voice recorder gripped in her outstretched hand to capture their words, the way they breathed. Aspen felt Ryder's steps quicken beside her. But it was too late. She'd followed them into the speed portal and quickened her pace to keep up with them.

"Captain Everett, can you comment on Airman Declan McAndor's death? How did he die? Did he sacrifice himself for the rest of the team? As his captain, do you wish it had been you to go in his place?" The voice recorder flailed around Ryder's bowed head as she took two steps to every one of his long strides.

"We're late for a staff briefing. No comment," River growled as he unlocked the lab door with his power signature. Aspen doubted that they were being led to a staff meeting, considering they'd just exited a room full of superiors they alone took orders from. Special Ops missions were highly classified, meaning Nia had to corner them to get any shred of information from the source.

Nia took a step over the threshold, but Ryder turned, his body a wall blocking her from coming in any further. His ultramarine glare was alight, fury burning behind his eyes as he pulled rank. Wordless, and all Wolf.

Nia had the good sense to step back. She swallowed, frozen in place, and he shut the door in her face.

For the briefest moment, Ryder met Aspen's gaze in the darkness of the doorway. The pain behind that look was more than she could bear, but it conveyed something more... the knowledge that whatever they were stepping into was going to be bad. She followed dutifully behind him as he strode into Vox's office.

The scene after the cave had collapsed descended upon them all over again as Aspen surveyed the room. The team was a mess. The only person who wasn't there was Thex. Vox's sobs, guttural and labored, shook the room as she bowed over her knees, clutched in Mackenzie's arms. Mackenzie's focus snapped to them as they entered, her expression begging Ryder to tell her what to do. Vox's cries were on the cusp of screams as she poured out the eternity of pain that Aspen knew could never be emptied. Because once the hole had been put there, nothing could fill it; no one could stitch it back up. The only thing to do now was to find a way to live with it.

Levi closed the few steps to their huddle and crouched there, too, wrapping his arm around Vox's middle. River stood staring at Ryder—waiting for orders, Aspen realized; waiting for him to say *anything*. But Ryder's focus was on Vox. He covered his mouth with his hand, occasionally rubbing at his lips. Aspen could sense those wheels in his head turning… thinking… assessing.

She took slow, quiet strides toward the huddle as Vox's sobs turned into soft whimpers and heavy breaths. Mackenzie and Levi rubbed her back, whispering that it was good to get it all out.

Her lavender eyes, red and swollen, looked up and locked on Aspen, following her down as Aspen crouched before her. Vox's breath was hot on her face as Aspen slipped a hand over her forehead. Her eyes closed, like she could have slept from exhaustion. It wouldn't be long now before she did. And then woke up questioning whether she'd dreamed it all.

"I'm so sorry." God, she wished she was better at this. "We will restrategize. Take down Ignatius. I'll hunt him down again. We'll win this. He won't take anything else— any*one* else from us." Confident words that didn't reach her core. Deep in her bones, she didn't believe it.

"What's the point?" Vox's voice cracked like she hadn't spoken in days, weeks. "He's already taken everything."

Aspen felt a piece of herself, long buried, claw its way up toward oxygen, threatening to grow and consume her. Grief.

"We will make this right," she practically hissed. An oath… A vow.

Vox sniffed, staring at the ground. "You will do no such thing."

She uncurled, standing to her full height. Aspen followed her ascent, touched her wrist. Asking…

"What do you mean?" River came to stand with them, too, seemingly calmed by hearing Vox finally speak. "We can't stop fighting…"

Vox answered by glaring at Aspen, only Aspen, with dead, bruised eyes, like she could see right through her. The air in the room shifted under that look. Like whatever was about to happen, whatever was about to be said, was irrefutable.

In a voice Aspen had never heard her use, never known she could conjure, Vox said, "I never want to see your face again. Never want to hear your voice again."

Aspen could feel the color draining from her face, her stomach twisting.

"Every time I *look* at you, I see you tearing at his wings as he falls through the sky… See your face turn to mine, watch that split-second decision that flashes through your eyes moments before you devour Declan—*my* Declan—in red clouds that he never makes it out of. Him lying on the rocks, dead… with you standing over him."

"Vox… Vox—" Aspen couldn't turn down the panic in her voice. She was about to launch into an explanation when Vox held up her hand, a threatening ripple at her mouth that bared her fangs. Aspen didn't dare speak then.

"The demon may have killed his mind and taken over his body, but all I see… all I will remember forever… is you shutting out his soul from this dimension before I—" She faltered, her voice breaking into a thousand pieces. "I couldn't even say goodbye."

Aspen flinched, a tremor tearing violently through her body until she dropped to her knees. How could she tell her—what words could she use to explain—when all her past actions, all the evidence, always pointed to the fact that she was a killer?

Vox stared into her eyes, and that was worse. Worse to look into her angelic face, always kind, always patient, and see hatred looking back. Hatred for *her*. Aspen cast her eyes down, but Vox turned her chin up with a tough hand, forcing Aspen to look at her as she straightened to her full height again, towering above her.

"You're the monster from my nightmares."

Vox could have kicked her. In this position she would have taken it. But these words had more devastating consequences. They shattered her into pieces she wasn't sure she'd ever find. Lost in the landscape of her internal world. Like the aftermath of a battle that had raged for weeks, all she could feel were raw wounds and death. Vox had carved her up inside without even touching her.

Ryder spoke from somewhere behind her. "You're angry… I understand—"

Vox's voice erupted as she pointed at him. "You will never understand! I always gave her the benefit of the doubt, but she did it anyway! She took Declan's soul"— muffled cries escaped past the hand that flew over her mouth—"seconds, *seconds*, after he died, and took him away… Now I'll never see him again."

The room was silent. Every marine hung their head but Ryder.

His voice was deathly quiet, a mere growl. "It was me. I did it."

"Don't you dare cover for her."

Ryder took a few steps toward them. Looked Vox right in the face, no bullshit. "It was me who gave Aspen the order." He was a Wolf who'd torn out the first chunk of a carcass with his teeth.

Vox shook her head vigorously. "N-No…"

Ryder took another step. The only thing between them now was Aspen on her knees on the floor.

"Ryder, no—" Aspen warned.

"I gave her the signal."

Vox did nothing but whimper as he tore muscle from bone with his words.

"I held you back and made sure she finished him… because the other option was you running to Declan, and the demon taking you or another marine next. And our body count would have been a lot higher… They may have even wiped us all out."

Ryder closed the small gap between himself and Vox. She tried to shove him, but he didn't so much as move.

"You want to hate somebody, Vox? Hate me. I'm the bastard who sent his soul away… but only to protect it from being held prisoner by that demon forever. I protected the one thing that was left of him. I was not going to stand by and watch his soul get taken, too, taken somewhere vicious and hellish. Declan didn't deserve that."

Aspen held her breath, waiting for Vox to run from the room, from the things they had done and would continue to do. Things weren't going to get better, she realized. Not their friendship, not this situation. Ignatius was going to come at them worse than this. And theirs was a broken team. She could see that on every face in this room.

Unbearable cries came from Vox's Anima as tears from a reservoir deep within rolled down her cheeks. She didn't even bother to wipe them away, accepting them, wearing them like a brand. She fell into Ryder's chest, his arms around her in an instant.

The room was frozen like this, minute after unending minute, enduring the strength of Vox's shakes, her cries. It started some of the others crying too, watching their captain console her, watching how he showed up in this moment, rooted as Kore's oaks.

His voice was softer than Aspen had ever heard it when he said, "It was my job to contain it so it didn't get you or one of the others too. It took one of us too many. We will never forget Declan and everything he did for us. He's our hero."

As Ryder moved down the hall, a group of Fox Anima saluted him. He gave them a curt nod and heard them whispering as he passed. He didn't catch what they were saying, and didn't care. He was certain they had picked up on his nervousness. He was on edge, his stomach doing somersaults.

He stopped walking immediately when he felt his

breathing begin to quicken and placed his Phaedra on the door closest to him. *C'mon, let me in.* It denied his access. There were more marines approaching from behind him. He hastened to the next door, his breathing growing louder. He could hear his blood pumping rapidly as he placed the Phaedra on the door. "C'mon!"

The light flashed green. As the door opened, it was as if he'd opened the floodgates to the strength of his panic attack. He leaned against the wall and dragged in air as though his esophagus were the size of a straw. Fear burst through his veins as he clutched his chest. Virtues, was he dying? Ryder lost his grip on the world as the room rocked and spun, bringing him to his knees.

It was then that he felt a warm hand against his back. He jolted in surprise, but Thex's eyes steadied him, a reminder that the ground was beneath his feet.

"You're going to be alright."

Thex bent down to his level and watched as Ryder squeezed the ridge of his nose, feeling his rapid breath against his hand. Thex stayed beside him until his breathing slowed and the room returned to stillness. Exhaustion came over him quickly as he slid to the floor, leaning his head against the wall with his arms balancing on his knees. Thex analyzed him before mirroring his sitting position. They were silent. Ryder was too fatigued to fully feel the regret that was building; he just braced himself for his friend to get mad at him for keeping this a secret.

Finally Thex spoke, low and gentle. "Why didn't you tell me?"

Ryder couldn't muster words, so he just shrugged and gave him a sideways glance.

Thex exhaled through his nose. "Do you remember the fall we went hunting in Sawtooth with my old man?"

That was a trip Ryder would never forget. After it, Thex had changed his name to his grandfather's last name—Thexton. But back then, Ryder had just called Thex's father Mr. Jones. Mr. Jones had a tall and slender build, lacking Thex's muscle mass. He had a neat beard and was balding at the crown of his head. He was the kind of man you would think twice about approaching; his build may not have been intimidating, but he had a mean look in his onyx stare.

He hunted in Sawtooth National Forest every season, but that year he was hellbent on taking his son with him on his first hunting trip. Thex looked ill every day that week at school and asked Ryder numerous times to come on the trip with him. The fourth time he asked, Ryder agreed, and immediately knew he would regret it.

He watched Thex rub the bottom of his lip, a forlorn expression on his face. This was a raw memory surfacing between them, but he figured Thex must have an important point to make.

"He forced me to shoot that deer, and I hesitated and hesitated, and when he…" Thex gritted his teeth. "When he boomed his voice the way he did, and that shot just… fired, I knew two things. One was that the minute we got home, he was going to belt me until I couldn't breathe, and two, that something in me died with that deer."

Ryder exhaled at the heaviness of his friend's pain. He couldn't imagine how it would feel, knowing he'd murdered a creature of his own Anima. Not that they'd known the significance of it at thirteen… They'd been inactivated, and besides, back then, they were told to 'man up'.

He bit the inside of his cheek, remembering the way Mr. Jones had issued a string of vulgar names before slapping his son hard across the face. The slap was as loud as a gunshot ripping across the ranges. Ryder had pulled Mr. Jones up by the neck of his jacket and punched him in the face. Mr. Jones hadn't dreamed of pressing charges, especially since Ryder's father was the most highly sought-after lawyer in Boise.

"I stayed at your place for a few weeks after that happened… I knew I could lean on you."

"I'm always here for you," Ryder assured him.

"But this is my point…You've had all of this going on, and you've been doing it alone. How can I have your back if I have no idea that you're struggling?"

Ryder exhaled heavily. "I guess I just feel like I'm bringing you down with me. And you don't really approve of…"

"Lovetta?" Thex finished. "You're damn right I don't." He sighed. "You think I don't know why you put me with Dec? You don't have to protect me…"

Ryder noted the quaver in Thex's voice at his name. "Fucking hell, Thex, of course I have to protect you. You have two kids!"

"Half the Corps has kids, Ry!"

"*They* fight in platoons! There are only eight of us—" Ryder sighed and pressed his fingertips into his eyelids at his error. How long would he keep thinking there were still eight? "Seven. There are *seven* of us… and half of the team are at each other's throats ninety-five percent of the time."

Thex shifted his feet as he balanced his forearms over

his knees. "I get that you're stressed, but how can I help you? You want me to tell you that being in the same pack with an infamous serial killer is a *good* idea?"

"No, Thex. I need you to trust me. I need you to trust what I'm doing here." Ryder's voice became grave and low. "The Corps can't know our plans. It has to look like we're following protocol."

"And Lovetta?"

"She's on our side… We have too many different agendas at play within the Corps. It's time we made our own."

Thex's brown eyes were wide and fearful, but perhaps it was the fact that Aspen had saved him, healed him in the last mission, that made him finally rest his hand on Ryder's shoulder and speak the exact words Ryder was so desperate to hear.

"I've got your back."

CHAPTER 28

Vox not seeing or speaking to Aspen ever again lasted a whole fourteen hours. Neither Vox nor River left the labs that night; she cried and they talked until they fell asleep close to oh two hundred hours, long after the rest of the team had left. Aspen only left to get them food from DFAC. Vox wouldn't look at her; Aspen only surrendered and left for good when River gave a pointed look toward the door. She'd growled, spun on her heel, and set herself up outside with her back pressed against the lab door.

She succumbed to awkward glances and whispers from passing marines. She was sure news would travel fast that she was alive and back from the Tundra. She scared the hell out of a loitering Nia Colson and her newspaper leeches wanting to question Special Ops, counting down from three before threatening to invert their ribcages. They scampered out of the hall and did not return. Aspen managed three hours of sleep with her arms wrapped around her legs and head tipped back against the door, her dagger locked in her grip.

The next day, the team was made to race past the border of Fox Country without using any advanced speed powers. It was admittedly difficult to remember where to draw the line with that one, but Major Gunner was there to monitor their speeds, while forcing smiles and encouragement when one of them fell behind. It was obvious to Aspen that he was relishing the lives of the ones who had made it out of Operation Enceladus. This was ultimately his team as much as it was Ryder's, if not more so. However, when the rest of the marines were pushing through, their breathing labored, their muscles shaking and burning in protest… She caught the sadness behind those forest-green eyes as they beheld his team, knowing there was one missing.

It took them most of the night to reach the old barn, and once they arrived, they were put to work clearing old snow ploughs, which would need to be taken back up to the Corps before the first snowfall. They slept in sleeping bags inside the barn, and the next day, Michael made Ryder, Thex, and Levi drive the ploughs all the way to base and run back again, warning them that he was keeping track of their time, and if they arrived before nightfall, he would know they had used their powers.

The barn became more charming as Aspen, River, Mackenzie, and Vox restored and cleaned the inside. They arranged benches and tables for the upcoming celebration exactly as Mackenzie envisioned. It was amusing watching River clinging to the facade of the barn to hang string lanterns. River fell off four times because he wasn't allowed to extend his claws.

When Ryder, Thex, and Levi made it back, Aspen and the others were inside their sleeping bags. Michael had already called lights out; Aspen hadn't heard him say those words since cadets. The last thing she saw before she went to sleep was the muted glow of Ryder's eyes in the dark. She longed to reach out her hand to him, knowing he was fighting sleep despite how exhausted he must have been. But Michael, being a Lynx Anima, had excellent night vision, and she didn't want to be the cause of a longer punishment for Ryder.

The next day their order was to paint the barn. By hand.

Aspen grimaced as Michael handed each of them a piece of sandpaper and gave Ryder and River a silicone gun to gap all of the corners. Ryder winked at her before he and Thex disappeared behind the west-facing wall; she and Levi took the east.

River was arguing with Michael about how he'd already hung string lanterns at the front. Michael looked mildly amused. "Well, you'll just have to work around them, or pull them down, paint it, and hang them back up again."

River stormed off to the rear wall, mumbling to himself, with Vox at his heels, taking three steps to each of his strides.

They spent most of the morning sanding the barn's exterior. Levi kept looking Aspen's way with his brow furrowed and his jaw clenched. What was eating him? She didn't dare ask, because Michael watched them like a hawk. *No talking, no fucking around* were his exact words. The only time she looked up from sanding long strokes with the grain of the wood was when Ryder appeared at the corner of their wall, shirtless, holding the caulking gun and squeezing silicone into whatever gaps he could find.

Aspen stilled, holding her breath. Virtues, he was magnificent. His body was sculpted, muscle stacked on top of muscle, honed for military prowess. His corded arms grew taut with every movement, veins protruding like rivers mapping his body. Beautiful. He was so beautiful.

Aspen hadn't realized she was staring, how lost in the sight of him she'd become, until Levi made a sound beside her. He wore a smug expression, brows raised. Aspen's gaze flicked skyward. She huffed as if to say, *What?*

Levi grinned, then tipped his head in Ryder's direction as if to reply, *Nice view.* Aspen shook her head.

When she looked back at Ryder, he was watching her. Heat washed over her under his gaze; it caressed a place deep in her soul. They'd left so much unsaid since they'd become Wolves of the same pack. There was an unexplainable feeling in her chest that threatened to grow, to consume her. It amplified when he looked at her like *that.*

She *cared* about this man… with such ferocity that it scared her. She'd unabashedly let her gaze sweep over him the way he was doing to her. The way *he* was undressing *her* with his eyes. Gazing right through to places inside herself she hadn't known existed, holding up a mirror, revealing her own depths through his eyes.

She felt the gentle, slow sweep of fingertips up the markings on her forearm, even though there were at least ten feet between them. He could hurt her, she realized. Their eyes locked, as if he'd heard her thought, and she raised her defenses so fast that the intensity shifted. He shot her a playful half-smile that threatened to undo her. Like he was above this game.

He wouldn't just hurt her; he would break her. Mind, body, and soul. She reined in any essence of pheromone power. Virtues save her… She'd opened like a goddamned flower.

He doesn't have feelings for you, she reminded herself. *He feels exactly how he's meant to feel around pheromone powers. You don't have feelings for him… You feel this way because he's your pack now.*

Her hand returned to continue with the long sweeps of sandpaper over wood, breaking their connection.

They'd almost finished the second coat of charcoal paint by late afternoon. Now even Levi was painting shirtless, and despite autumn's curling tendrils of chilled air, Aspen had stripped down to her tank top as the sun beat down on them, saturating each leaf in scarlet, auburn, and gold. Aspen snuck a sidelong glance past Levi, making sure Michael was out of earshot. He'd risen from his fold-out chair to check on the others.

When she was sure nobody could be listening in to their conversation, she turned to Levi. He scanned her with that intense glare, walking closer, like he too had been aching to tell her something. A quick head tilt from him told her to go first.

They needed to make this quick if they didn't want to be caught. "You're going to tell me who took your brothers' lives." Levi's eyes grew wide. "If it was in Israel where you were raised, I have contacts there. I trained in Jerusalem."

Levi dropped his paintbrush into the tub. Aspen couldn't tell if he was scowling or trying to hold back emotion.

"Your Krav Maga was too good to have been learned anywhere else. I should have known."

Her hand, slick with paint, clasped around his forearm. "I know you know who did it. Tell me who it is and I will have it done before our next deployment."

Levi grabbed her forcefully by her shoulders, smudging paint there. She wasn't afraid. There was something broken behind those piercing, now glowing amber eyes, something that told her the force was coming from grief. They'd been trained from a young age to think that hell was the worst place in the cosmos. But she and Levi knew otherwise. Hell had nothing on the grief of family stolen too soon.

He pointed toward her jaw, as if it were the very weapon that would make her concede. "You listen to me." He almost broke down in that moment, his lips quivering. "You stay away from my past."

Aspen matched his intensity, her fangs visible as she spoke. "I can do it. Let me handle it." She willed herself to make it sound enticing, to really sell it to him. She'd made her decision in that cave. She'd do it for him.

He pulled her shoulder forward so she had to step closer, bending down so they were staring into each other's eyes. "That's *my* fight. Not yours." He shook his head. "All these idiots talk about how heartless you are, Lovetta, but what they don't know is that you care *too* damn much."

Aspen inhaled. She rested a hand gently on his shoulder. No one had ever said that to her before.

He softened too as he said, "I buried my past a long time ago."

Lies. He's lying.

Her whole body went rigid when she realized he wasn't

going to give her his permission. But he pulled her into a hug, his arms wrapping all the way around her. He rocked her inside his embrace, then whispered into the shell of her ear, "We have more pressing issues right now. Don't you think it's strange that they've removed us from base when things are getting so bad with Ignatius?"

Aspen's body grew even tauter, frozen solid. *Shit!*

"Why are we not strategizing for the next mission?"

Aspen's breath expelled in a shudder as she scanned all the evidence, all the conversations. "We have to complete our punishment…"

"I've seen punishments carried out months later in wartime."

He was right. He was right…

Michael had stood up to the justices after the mission; that was why he was here with them. He wouldn't even have questioned his orders. Ignatius had Enceladus—why was the Corps keeping them away?

Ryder… She had to tell Ryder.

"Don't make it so obvious that you're out for blood right now, Lovetta. We're just two friends hugging."

They parted with tight smiles on their lips.

"Soon you're going to show me your Krav Maga."

Her smile widened.

Levi picked up his paintbrush and pointed it at her. "Next training."

Michael had circled back and plopped into his chair. He didn't tell them to shut up, just gave them a look that said it all. Aspen lifted her paintbrush, pain shooting up her wrists.

All she could think was that she had to get to Ryder.

It was well past nightfall when the team fulfilled their non-judicial punishment. The barn looked like it could have been on the cover of a magazine. The charcoal paint they'd used for the exterior walls threw out a green undertone that incorporated the surrounding forest beautifully. They'd painted the trimmings and windows white, and River had rehung the lanterns, making them more even than the first time.

They were forming a horizontal line in front of the major when Aspen brushed against Ryder as he passed. "We need to talk."

He studied her grave expression before turning to face the major.

None of them were attending the Feast of Foxes, not after they'd lost their airman, so when they were finally dismissed, the major announced that they could explore the surrounding area if they wished, or travel on foot back to base.

Aspen waited behind a thick tree trunk as Ryder finished talking with the major. As his long, casual strides entered the forest, she joined him, and they walked briskly out of earshot, not just of the team and the major, but the other marines arriving for the festivities.

She told Ryder everything Levi had said, studying his features as she did. She waited for shock to fill his eyes, for anger to ripple through him… Something… Anything.

All he said was, "Have you told anyone else?"

She shook her head. It dawned on her then that he had already thought about it. Had already considered why they were carrying out a punishment now rather than during peacetime. This. This was why he was their captain. The man didn't sleep for a reason. He missed nothing.

The world was in jeopardy, and they'd been painting a barn. It made her blood boil.

Ryder fixed his lips into a grim line as they traveled down a grassy sloped hill, stopping when they reached a lake. "I've tried to think of all the reasons the Corps did this. Maybe they found more information and are in the process of carefully narrating what Special Ops are allowed to know…" His jaw set. "Or maybe they're working out how to control what my protocols are, how they want the team to operate."

Aspen nodded. "Well, no one can accuse you of being paranoid… It would make sense to have us all out of the labs. I mean… we're doing our own digging, making our own plans." She sighed bitterly. "After all, we're dealing with demons that can possess. Demons that kill from the inside out. I wonder what they made of Declan's autopsy…"

Ryder hummed in response, but didn't say anything more.

The water moved lazily against the old timber posts of the pier. At the end was a docked rowboat. Aspen leaned against the rails and watched as Ryder put his hands in his camo pockets, looking out at the mountains beyond the lake. The moonlight illuminated his aura, making his hair gleam gold, running along his jawline and contouring his sculpted back. She took a steadying breath. *How could anybody be that inherently good?* She looked out at the lake nervously when he turned to her.

"You're doing that thing where you thousand-yard

stare, only you're doing it *at* me. And something's telling me you're not marveling at my good looks." He leaned on the railing next to her, wearing a grin that reached his eyes.

She looked down at the water, biting her lip. "Always observant, Captain Everett."

"Especially around you." He bent down to pick up a rock, bigger than his palm, from the boardwalk. "How far do you think I can skip it?" he asked, throwing the rock up and catching it. An attempt to lighten their burdens.

Aspen couldn't help but smile. She tilted her head thoughtfully. The lake was wider here, and she pointed past the middle, where a tree had grown in the water. "To the tree."

He pretended to be insulted, then launched the rock across the lake. His strength, coupled with the size of the rock, made sure it skimmed the surface and crossed the entire width. They watched as it disappeared into the forest on the other side.

Aspen exploded into a laugh, becoming self-conscious as he beamed at her, breathing sharply beneath his gaze.

A noise behind them made them turn.

The southern wolf pack had appeared on the hillside. Killa Moon and the omega wolf, Sakari, had partaken in a game. The wolves ran and growled fervently as Sakari pounced on top of Killa Moon. Aspen softened as she watched their hunting game.

She felt Ryder's eyes upon her and looked back at him. It was as though he was going to say something before he changed his mind. Instead, he asked, "What are they doing?"

She hugged her arms, watching Killa Moon tumble over in the grass. "Every so often, even though Killa Moon is the alpha, she has this game that she only plays with

Sakari. For a short while, she plays the omega role and allows him to play the alpha… Like an understanding they have."

Killa Moon shot like a bullet through the tall grass, a gray blur as Sakari bound after her. Ryder chuckled.

"I've always admired her for it," Aspen admitted, slowly grazing her teeth against her lower lip.

"Packs work differently than what most people think," he replied.

Ryder had repeated exactly what beta wolf Nuka had whispered into the ether just moments ago. Aspen's heart leaped inside her chest. "You understand?"

"Not as well as you do."

She could tell he was being modest. They were silent, watching the aurora borealis light up the sky and reach its pillars of light at the top of the mountain, almost as though it were reaching for them. Things were building… Something was off inside the Corps. She could feel it in her bones.

Pulling her from her thoughts, Ryder said, "Something wrong?"

"Hmm?"

"Scenery doesn't get better than this, and you're scowling at the aurora."

She chuckled and shook her head, swishing her garnet locks. Her smile faded. "There are dangerous missions ahead of us."

The weight of the truth was plain on his face. "Yeah… there are."

Aspen shuffled her boot over the lines in the boardwalk. "I don't have your scent… Not all of it, at least. If something happens to you, I won't be able to find you."

"I thought you'd never ask," he replied, his glacier eyes

exploring her. She hoped he couldn't sense the fire kindling in her abdomen.

"I've been putting it off," she admitted.

"You're nervous," he murmured, stepping closer.

"Maybe if we just did it slowly…" She gripped the railing of the pier, feeling like it would be crushed to splinters between her fingers.

The vibration of his voice was heavenly. "That's fine."

Aspen could hear her heartbeat galloping; she knew he could hear it too, and a wave of pheromone power echoed from her, aimed straight for him. He leaned his hands on the rails on either side of her.

"I'm sorry," she breathed.

He took a moment to endure it before he shook his head. "Don't be."

She lifted herself onto the rail, now slightly higher than him. Her spine stiffened and she swallowed against the constriction in her throat. Her hands delicately braced his shoulders. His military blouse was off; she felt the fabric of his olive-drab T-shirt beneath her fingers.

Ryder waited, sensitive to every slight movement she made. She guided him closer until he stood between her legs, her boots hooked to the lower railing of the pier. She slowly lowered her mouth to his neck. Her lips grazed against his throat, tentatively at first, but at the taste of his skin, his scent…

She closed every crevice that was left open between them, pressing the hard wall of his body against her. Her thighs tightened around his hips. His hands slid up over her waist. She felt like she was drowning, like the aurora above them had whirlpooled around them, sinking them further, deeper into a memory. A place where the White Wolf and the Midnight Wolf came home to each other after what felt like an eternity of distance between them.

She didn't want to rush the sequence, for it to be over too soon… but, overcome with insatiable wanting, she had soon retrieved all of it. All of the codes, all of the equations that would inevitably lead her back to him.

Aspen pulled away, feeling unfastened. Unfinished. Ryder pushed her long locks over her shoulder, his warm hand against her neck. What they'd done was irreversible, and for Anima, it meant more than a kiss. But she wanted it anyway. She wanted him to keep holding her, to bind her closer. Wanted to feel his lips against hers.

Her hand traced along his jaw in question, and he pulled her closer until the ache of her chest against his was too much. Ryder's burly arms wrapped around her waist. This man was going to break her.

Aspen's lips grazed against his—

A scream ripped through the night, hastily dividing them. Still gripping each other tightly, their focus cut to where they had heard it.

Aspen slid down from the pier rail. "Did you hear that?" she asked, in case she'd imagined it. "It sounded like Mackenzie."

They bolted from the pier.

River broke through a thicket further down from the lake. He looked as though he was laboring from a deep wound. "Help!" he shouted.

The moment Ryder sprang forward, Aspen matched his velocity. They had never run faster.

CHAPTER 29

Aspen's heart beat wildly in her chest. Her palms were slick with sweat and there was an ache in the back of her throat that had nothing to do with how fast she had run. She dragged her palms down her pant legs as they approached Mackenzie, who was crouched over her knees on the ground.

Aspen froze. "What's wrong with her?"

Ryder walked closer and crouched down on one knee so that he was level with Mackenzie's height.

"I don't know." River's voice shook. "We were walking together. We parted ways. A couple of minutes later I heard her scream, so I sped back, and when I got here she was rolling on the floor, groaning like she was in pain. But it sounded so *wrong*. I scented you, and now here we are."

"You didn't check her?" Ryder questioned, his focus

still on Mackenzie, who was looking down into her lap, her hair falling forward, covering her face.

"I thought she might be injured, and like I said, the sounds she was making sounded so—I don't know—painful. I panicked."

Ryder reached out to her, but Aspen was quick to warn him.

"Ryder, don't touch her."

His hand froze in midair.

Mackenzie's head snapped up. Gone were the whites of her eyes and their bright cognac irises; only an empty blackness akin to the tunnels of the hellgate remained. Inky liquid bled down her cheeks as she bared her needle-like fangs.

"Oh, no," Ryder breathed, pain flickering across his face.

Mackenzie unfurled up to her full height, a demon staring back at them. She pointed a finger at Aspen's chest. "I smell him all over you. You always know how to get exactly what you want, don't you, Aspen?"

"I'm giving you three seconds to leave that body," Aspen spat. "If you don't, I'll do to you what I did to the last demon."

Mackenzie laughed in a way that made the trees' leaves hiss and their boughs groan. As if Kore were telling them to run.

"And what better way to take control of the captain than use your inescapable pheromone powers?"

Aspen sped the few steps to close their distance, but Ryder's arm barricaded her to his side. Mackenzie sidled closer, clicking her tongue in disapproval.

"Are you so confident in your powers that you know

you can have whoever you want? Not even worried that they would stray from you?"

Aspen's energy shifted from annoyance to full realization that a brutal truth was ready to surface. Whatever this demon had found inside Mackenzie... It was about to unleash it upon her now.

She narrowed scrutinizing eyes at Mackenzie and squared her shoulders. "You better choose your next words carefully."

"I don't understand what's going on," River admitted.

"Here's a tip," Aspen advised him. "When you're dealing with a Fox, always read between the lines."

A cracking of leaves underfoot made her turn. Vox was approaching. The wilted expression on her face told Aspen that she'd overheard.

"I didn't know you felt that way about Foxes, Aspen," Vox said, the first words she'd spoken to Aspen in days. "What's happening here? I heard a scream."

"Stay back," River warned. "We have ourselves a demon."

Vox's face paled, tears springing to her eyes easily, like they'd been waiting there for a memory of Declan to surface. It was all happening again. Her chin quivered. "Mackenzie, no..."

But Mackenzie didn't look Vox's way. The demon was solely focused on Aspen. "One thing I always loved about you, Aspen, is that you're so quick. I have to admit, I'm quite annoyed that you never picked up my scent on his clothes... or his skin."

Aspen sped to her in a few steps. She was just out of arm's reach now. She instinctively assumed a fighting stance. Mackenzie did the same, ready to defend herself.

"Wait! Who are we talking about? Ryder?" River asked.

"Not Ryder," Vox whispered. "Hurricane."

"You don't seem the least bit surprised," Mackenzie said, ignoring them. The demon seemed to know that with Mackenzie's reaction time, it had to be on top of its game to watch all of Aspen's movements.

"I was onto you in the cave when you reacted over me killing him," Aspen revealed. A wave of internal numbness washed over her, and the sudden need to see blood—to see Mackenzie hurt—was intoxicating. It spread through her like venom and wouldn't stop raging until she'd seen vengeance. Until the forest was red.

"See what I mean?" Mackenzie cracked a wicked smile. "Faster than a bullet."

The demon tilted Mackenzie's neck as it stared at them all. It was so wrong, so sickening, the way it pulled on her reflexes like strings and picked apart her mind like a disease.

Mackenzie's chest surged forward before she dropped to the ground. The demon fled like smoke thinning into the air. She was panting, looking at them all with confusion furrowing her sculpted brows. "What happened? What am I doing here?"

Aspen approached her, offering an arm to help her off the ground. Mackenzie took it and Aspen hoisted her up, but it was too late. Wrath had poisoned her insides. She felt cold-blooded.

A small smile crossed Mackenzie's lips, but as it did, Aspen pulled her into the sharp point of her dagger. Mackenzie gasped as she pushed against Aspen's shoulders in an effort to put some distance between herself and the blade. But Aspen had locked her in so close that the iron scraped against her neck when she breathed.

Vox shrieked, "Aspen, don't!"

River's hand had almost reached the handle of the dagger when Aspen sent out a shockwave that catapulted him backward. Mackenzie gulped in air as her knees gave way to her fear. Aspen smiled into her shocked face and held her tighter to keep her upright.

"How much blood do you think is enough to pay the debt?"

Mackenzie only answered with loud, rapid breaths.

"Why don't I show you how far I can spread you around?" Aspen's voice was low and deadly. "I'm going to stab you."

Mackenzie began to sob, her eyes pleading. She slipped down further, so Aspen crunched the material of her military blouse until her knuckles were white. The dagger made a small puncture wound on Mackenzie's neck, releasing a tiny bead of blood that ran down to her collarbone.

"Then I'll heal you, before I stab you again."

Mackenzie made an indecipherable sound that almost sounded like *please*. Aspen drove the tip of the dagger in further, until the trickle of blood ran down the front of Mackenzie's chest.

"And I'll just keep healing you… and stabbing you… until you're begging for me to stab you. Do you want to know the sick thing about pheromone powers? I can mess with your pain–pleasure connection to the point where you no longer care about the pain I'm causing you—so long as I heal you at the end."

Aspen's head snapped in the direction of Ryder's approaching scent. She watched him walk around them, Mackenzie pleading to him with gasps and tear-filled eyes.

"This is aiming a little low for Hellfire, don't you think?" His voice was coaxing.

"Stay out of this," she warned him.

His tone remained even. "You don't really want to do this. There's no freedom in revenge."

Aspen froze at his words, her dagger quivering at Mackenzie's neck.

"It only landslides from here… You see that, don't you? You don't have to give all of this up again. Don't let Hurricane win. You're letting him keep a hold on you even after he's dead."

Aspen gave him a blank stare. "She owes a blood debt." In her peripheral vision, she saw Levi land softly from a leap, taking in the situation.

Ryder didn't take his eyes off of her—calm, collected. "Or you could heal that little cut and back away."

"Why would I do that?" Her words came out raspy.

"Because despite how much this situation blows, she's setting you free. Think about it… No more regrets."

Aspen stared hard at Mackenzie sobbing in her grasp. "I can't even tell him how angry I am!" she growled through clenched teeth. "Because he's…"

"I know." Ryder's voice was kind, compassionate. "Aspen, give me the dagger."

"He doesn't get to do this! Not after everything I sacrificed! After all the times I cleaned up his damn messes!" She wiped her brow with her arm.

"I'm sorry," Ryder whispered.

"I was undyingly loyal. And he… and *they*—" A whimper escaped her lips as her eyes met Mackenzie's, wild with fear. She could hear the Wolf—her soul—crying. Howling.

Ryder put his hand on her shoulder, so gentle, so steadying. "You don't want to hurt her… Because you know it will only hurt you."

Aspen breathed a sob, those words hitting her harder than a knock-out punch. She placed both hands over the tiny incision and sent her powers through it, illuminating Mackenzie in silver light. Mackenzie breathed a restful, pleasurable sigh, a tear rolling down her cheek. When she opened her eyes again, she stared at Aspen, dazed.

Aspen held out the dagger to Ryder. She felt his warm hand take it from her grasp. It was like everybody watching had been holding their breath the entire time and could finally breathe again the moment Ryder was in possession of the dagger.

Aspen drew Mackenzie close, her fingers scrunching the fabric of her uniform as she said into the shell of her ear, but loud enough that the others heard it: "It should have been you who died in Declan's place."

She released her grip, sending Mackenzie falling to her knees, then ran through the forest until she couldn't hear their voices anymore.

CHAPTER 30

Aspen waited for two slices of bread to travel around the industrial toaster. Nobody except the team knew about the demon possessing Mackenzie two days ago, and to avoid hysteria in the Corps, nobody was going to tell. At least, that was what River had told her upon arriving, and by the reactions of the other marines, it seemed like word hadn't spread. Instead, she was fighting the awkwardness of marines smiling or sneaking a quick whiff. Nia Colson had printed an article in the *Anima Corps Observer* about Operation Enceladus titled 'Special Ops Save Burn City'. The moment Nia reached DFAC, Aspen overheard Vox informing her that nobody called Melbourne *Burn City*, and educating her on the correct pronunciation: "It's not Mel-burn. Nor is it Mel-born. It's pronounced *Mel-ben*."

With Major Gunner's help, Aspen had been spoken

of highly. She wasn't attracting the attention Ryder would typically receive, but it was undeserved attention all the same. She imagined killing them all with a butter knife as she spread cream cheese over her toast before noticing three marines hovering close by. They were Deer Anima, staring at her as they waited in line for their breakfast.

She clanked her knife onto her plate and snapped, "What are you looking at?"

"Ease up, they're just curious," River said, taking the whole jar of peanut butter and tucking it under his arm.

"I'm going to herd them to their deaths," Aspen replied, loud enough for them to hear. They stood in awkward silence, looking anywhere but at her.

"Before breakfast?" River asked, yawning. "You'd better eat on the go, because we're meeting Vox in the labs."

"When?"

"Now." River shoved the corner of his toast into his mouth and picked up a box filled with breakfast items; she spied some oatmeal-and-raisin cookies inside.

"What's all that for?"

"Everyone," River said through a full mouth.

Aspen scattered wild berries she had picked on her morning run with the wolves on top of her toast before drizzling it with Kore honey. Its sweet pine aroma drifted up to her nose. She had spent the night sleeping near the wolf pack and had almost frozen to death. She'd been inside more than ten minutes now and her bones still hadn't thawed. She hadn't spoken to anyone about what had transpired, and quite honestly, she didn't want to.

They took the speed portal outside DFAC that transported them to Wolf Division. The halls were near silent, as always, a mere ghost of the place's former glory, once teeming with Wolf Anima. The slight thump of River's Phaedra hitting his chest was all Aspen could hear as they briskly walked toward the lab.

He glanced at her sidelong. "You want to talk about it?"

"Nope."

"You don't even know which situation I'm talking about."

"That's because I don't want to talk about any of them, River."

They'd reached the door of the lab, but River was quick to extend a muscular arm to block her from entering, the other still balancing the box, peanut butter wedged under his arm.

He sighed. "Hurricane's a piece of shit."

"Yeah, tell me something I don't know," she ground out.

River studied her expression. Complete emotional detachment. "He never deserved you."

Aspen scoffed. "He was exactly what I deserved. We were perfect for each other, and not in a good way."

"Keep telling yourself that… and isolating yourself from the rest of us. It's really making the rest of the team trust you more."

Her eyes narrowed. "The team, River… or you?"

River clenched his jaw. "Me."

Her shoulders dropped. She softened under his deep brown eyes.

The hand that had been blocking the door now gripped her shoulder. "Promise me you're not going to disappear."

All the grief of the past few days welled in her eyes. Her jaw quivered. It was hard to stay. Hard to work at the relationships she tried to keep at arm's length out of fear for their safety. She nodded vigorously.

River crushed her with one arm into his chest and Aspen bit back tears. She wasn't allowed to cry. Not when Vox's situation was so much worse, and not when so many people were relying on her to help deliver Ignatius's head.

River pulled back to look down at her and angled his head toward the door. "Let's go."

Ryder, Thex, Levi, and Mackenzie were already waiting for them. Aspen took the empty seat next to Ryder at the large oval table the scientists used for meetings.

He leaned in after River dropped the breakfast box in the middle of the table. The sound of his voice took the edge off of Aspen's nerves. "Did you have fun sleeping on the ground?"

She was solemn as she reached for the other piece of toasted sourdough with berries and honey she'd stashed in the box. "I thought you'd be too angry about it to let me inside." A cruel ache subsided within her. She'd missed him, she realized.

Ryder gave her a look that told her she was crazy. "You think I would just put you in the doghouse like the mutt that you are?"

She breathed a laugh through her nose.

Mackenzie appeared beside her chair. "Can we talk?"

For a moment Aspen thought she meant Ryder, then realized it was in fact her who Mackenzie was talking to. Aspen had ignored her from the moment she'd smelled her wine-and-chocolate scent when she walked in.

"I don't have anything to say to you," she said in a scathingly low tone.

"I do." Mackenzie bent down to make eye contact with her. "We should talk about this. We can't go into battle like *this*…"

Aspen sighed and rose from her chair. Mackenzie led her deeper into the lab. They stood in the middle of a U-shaped bench full of containers and trays of empty test tubes.

Aspen folded her arms at her chest. An awkward silence ensued, each waiting for the other to start. While watching Mackenzie search for words, Aspen admitted to herself that she was beautiful. Tanned skin, defined cheekbones, dark brown shoulder-length hair, lips with a natural rosy tint, and eyes that reminded her of gold autumn leaves.

"You wanted me here, now you got me. So talk."

Mackenzie spoke softly. "We shouldn't let this destroy the team. It was… a long time ago."

"I'm not angry."

Mackenzie frowned, giving her a searching look, clearly unwilling to believe her.

"Not anymore," Aspen added. Since her suspicions had been confirmed, her emotions had been difficult to place. Days in the woods with the wolves had given her time to recalibrate.

Mackenzie leaned in with a scrutinizing gaze. "You fell out of love with him."

It wasn't a question. She had been watching Aspen, piecing together this story. Aspen was done caring. Maxen was gone, physically, and now from whatever space he used to occupy in her mind.

"After he kidnapped and tortured Vox almost to her death, I stopped loving him. If that's what it even was to begin with."

Mackenzie's face drained of color, her mouth agape. She took a step back and gripped the bench behind her. "When… How?"

Aspen fixed her with a glare, resolute, unmovable. "I do not speak of it. Neither does Vox."

The horror of the memory flashed in her mind, bringing her back to that dark cell he'd kept her in. The price Vox had paid for her friendship with Aspen. It had taken stealth to keep her fed right under Maxen's nose, and careful planning to help her escape.

Pain cleaved through her so deep that her Anima, the White Wolf, felt it too. She pushed it down, down, down. It dawned on her then that Mackenzie wasn't stupid enough to not believe her. Which meant she knew enough to know that Maxen was capable of such things.

"Please, I want to know—"

"I. Am. Not. Ready," Aspen growled. "I may never be ready. And you will respect that. You will also never mention this to Vox, because if I find out you did…"

"I won't."

Aspen felt a pull to return to the team, to be closer to Vox. Her heart shattered at the thought of their friendship now. Vox was still paying a price for knowing her. Just like they all would. "We don't have to like each other," she told Mackenzie. "Just stay out of my way, and I'll stay out of yours."

Mackenzie looked over her face, her body language, then nodded.

Aspen took a few brisk steps before Mackenzie's words stopped her. "He made you out to be the monster."

She looked back at her over her shoulder, her tone loathing. "I still am."

Mackenzie shrank back slightly, giving Aspen another one of those searching looks that she hated, before Aspen continued back to the table.

She heard the smooth timbre of Ryder's voice as she approached. "Now that they're back, we can start the briefing," he said, sitting with his ankle braced over his knee.

Aspen lowered herself into her seat just as Mackenzie reached hers on the opposite side. Vox had joined the team sometime during Aspen and Mackenzie's conversation. She was wearing her lab coat open, revealing jeans and a blue T-shirt that read *Mermaid Anima*.

She shifted on her feet at the head of the table and opened her tablet. "Yeah, we have loads."

"Actually, before we begin," Ryder interjected. "There's something that's been really fucking with my head… Mackenzie, why wasn't the demon able to fully possess you? What happened should have killed you."

Mackenzie paused before responding. "I hurt myself while we were renovating the barn, so I took one of Aspen's healing vials from the first aid kit. I think because her powers were still in my system, the demon couldn't fully possess me. I could feel it… It's like it created just enough leverage for me to push it out before it took over."

Levi crossed his arms. "How did you hurt yourself?"

"Cut myself with the chisel while we were making new window trimmings."

There was a pause, then Ryder said, "Well, thank the Virtues for that, because it literally saved your life."

Mackenzie looked down into her lap and nodded, her lips pressed together in a thin line.

"Could Aspen make more to protect us all?" Thex asked, his gaze focused on her.

Aspen leaned back in her chair. "While I'd love to have you — well, some of you — attached to my healing powers with a drip, it would kill me. It's not a never-ending reservoir. It does need time to replenish. And I already bottle any excess so that you can use it." She exhaled through her nose. "This might be a good time to remind you all that you can't tell anyone about my healing powers."

"I second that," Ryder added gravely. "If anyone finds out, Aspen becomes a target. So if you want to keep your healing privileges to just us, I strongly suggest you put a lid on it… Got it?"

"Got it," the team said in unison.

"Alright, Vox, let's hear it." Ryder leaned in on his elbows, and so did the rest of the team.

"I assessed Ryder's and Aspen's power that was used on Ignatius, and then I multiplied it a thousandfold, which is what it would be at its full strength. My hypothesis suggests that the amount of power you drew to take him down for only that mere moment…"

Aspen caught the worry in Vox's eyes.

"You can tell us," Ryder reassured her.

Vox exhaled deeply. "Your powers don't draw from Earth at all—not like the rest of ours do."

A cocktail of mixed emotions swished inside Aspen. "It comes from outside of this galaxy."

"Yes, it does," Vox said, then pursed her lips. "I compared it with the signatures from many different stars, planets, and vibrations outside of this galaxy, and I found a match for Aspen's."

Aspen tried to hide her shock, ignoring the team's glances at her.

Ryder's voice sounded close to her ear. "Aspen, that looks like the marking on your arm."

"What is that thing?" River inspected the red flares unfurling from Vox's hologram.

Vox's face was grave. "It's the most violent thing in the universe."

Aspen stared at the identical marking on her arm, dragging in her next breath as if a tight cord were wrapped around her middle. "It's a Magnetar."

Thex locked his hands behind his head and leaned back in his chair. "Oh, we are going to have a fun time explaining this to Gunner and the justices."

Aspen rolled her eyes and huffed. "Like there isn't enough pitted against me already… Now this."

"They don't find out," Ryder ordered. "This doesn't leave this room."

"But Captain, they need to know. We have to prepare," Mackenzie argued.

Ryder didn't falter. "Not until we find out who we can trust with this kind of information. The justices wanted Aspen gone. If they were too ignorant to assess her powers first, then they don't deserve to know."

Aspen didn't realize she was staring at him until he looked back at her. She launched into some knowledge she'd picked up years ago when learning about Magnetars. "Both my powers and Ryder's work as a binary system of electromagnetic energy. When the two powers come together, it's a Magnetar Pulsar that can wipe out the surface of the entire planet… and that's from light-years away."

Levi raised his brows. "We just found out what Ignatius's weapon is."

Thex groaned. "Yeah… It's you two."

Vox tapped her index finger against her tablet. "He's going to try to find a way, bond or no bond, to weaponize you against Earth."

"Based on my calculations…" Mackenzie crossed her legs and leaned on one arm of her chair. "To achieve what Ignatius wants—for Earth's surface to be burned without destroying it—it would require him to have Aspen billions of miles away from Earth."

"Not me?" Ryder questioned.

"If he used your powers alone, with Enceladus magnifying them, you would emit a beam, kind of like a lighthouse, so strong that you'd break Earth's core. Aspen's power can radiate wider, like the symbol on her arm shows—this would help Ignatius achieve that purification he wants."

Aspen watched Ryder's brilliant mind working. He exhaled heavily. "The whole war is a trap, using us as the arsenal."

Thex rubbed his index finger over his bottom lip. "So how does he plan to travel that far into outer space?"

"A Phaedra," Ryder clarified.

"How he got it in the first place remains a mystery, considering there have been no deaths besides Declan at the Corps since before Ignatius arrived in Kore," Levi lamented.

Ryder rubbed his chin. "He could have had it in his possession for years. Levi, we could use your silent paws to get down to the Hall of Honor and check records for all the marines who died without Anima tags in the last five years."

Levi nodded. "On it."

"Had it for years…" Aspen muttered.

"What?" Vox questioned.

"It could be Maxen's Phaedra."

River hunched as he admitted, "That seems likely."

Thex spoke with his hand covering his mouth. "Even dead, he's still a pain in everybody's ass."

Ryder leaned over Vox's tablet. "That still doesn't tell us what direction the attack is going to come from… or the original portal opening for the specific hell dimension."

Vox sighed heavily. "I know… It tells us nothing. We're trying, Ryder, but we are working with time and space measurements here."

Aspen was thoughtful for a moment before she asked, "Vox, do you still have the copies of the *Ars Daemonium* pages?"

"They're right here." Vox took out her clipboard and placed it down facing Aspen. The team was quiet as she read the ancient symbols, her finger touching one.

River leaned in from Ryder's other side. "That looks like a reaper's hook."

"It's the symbol for Saturn," Aspen explained.

"How far away is Saturn?" Thex asked.

They were quiet while Vox searched for the answer, her eyes widening at the result. "About seven hundred and fifty million miles."

Aspen's gaze snapped to Vox, the weight of what this meant dawning on her.

"Aspen…" Vox interrupted her thoughts. Her face lit up, and for a moment she reanimated into her old joyful self. "It makes so much sense—"

"Because it's right next to Saturn's moon, Enceladus," Aspen lamented. "Why didn't I pick up on this before?"

"You're a genius," Ryder overrode her. "Now we can strategize."

Thex still wore a worried expression. "Harvesting hook… Harvesting souls… Anima souls."

"Things were less scary when they didn't make sense," River agreed.

"Good work, team." Levi nodded.

Ryder had that glint in his eye, the one he got when he was anticipating the coming mission. "Thex, get to work on the environment—find anything you can that's going to help us out there. River and Levi, go through the ancient texts and see what you can find on intergalactic warfare—maybe there's been a war of these proportions before that can help us. Vox, pinpoint the exact location with Mackenzie. We can't mess up traveling through the portal when the time comes."

"And me?" Aspen asked him.

"We need to work on your Magnetar power. We could do some training, find out how it works, its limitations…"

Aspen nodded.

"Okay, everybody knows what they have to do?"

The team nodded.

"Ryder, Aspen, I need to speak with you before you leave." Vox whirled on her heel and disappeared into her office.

Aspen locked eyes with Ryder, bracing for the worst.

She rose from her chair, Ryder following behind her, his hand guiding her near the small of her back. Heat hummed through her as she relived the feeling of him pressing his forehead against hers at the end of the mission… Sliding his hand into hers in Ansel's office… The taste of him on her lips when she traced him. She wondered if he somehow knew how she felt about the way he touched her. That it meant everything to her.

She abruptly shunned the thought. *Not a snowball's chance in hell.* He was the Captain of Anima Special Ops; she saw the effect he had on other female marines. Sure, he believed in her capabilities as a marine and as his partner. He was even starting to trust her. But to entertain the idea that he was interested in *her*, a murderer? Laughable.

The cabin sprang to her mind. Ryder had asked her to stay with him in his cabin.

No. Stop it. He'd offered her a place to live because decent Anima didn't let other people live in tents.

A realization rose through her, and by the time she'd fully turned it over in her mind, the door to Vox's office had clicked shut and her heart had broken into a million pieces.

Someone that pure could never belong to *her*.

"What have you got for us?" Ryder asked, leaning against Vox's desk.

Vox picked up her tablet and a hologram appeared in the center of the room. "I've been pulling up the footage from our fight with Ignatius in Melbourne. I found this while assessing both your powers to prepare for the briefing."

Aspen watched a replay of her and Ryder's powers combining during the pack bond, the pair of them levitating inside the gigantic orb of silver and deep violet thunder.

"Yeah, and…" Ryder urged.

"What do you mean, *Yeah, and…*!" Vox scoffed. "Look at the frequency pattern I recorded below!"

Aspen stepped closer. Her hand flew to her mouth, muffling her curse.

"See what I'm talking about now?" Vox replied.

Ryder's brow furrowed. "I don't understand…"

Vox swiped the footage out of the screen and zoomed in on the data. "This is Aspen's power signature, and this is yours." She pointed to the two wavelengths that were side by side on the screen.

Ryder studied them. "They're identical."

Vox nodded. Something about her expression told Aspen that this was what she'd been obsessing over since they got back from their non-judicial punishment. "That's why you could get into Aspen's computer without a Phaedra or a code. It also means you aren't as affected by Aspen's pheromone powers as everyone else."

Ryder chuckled, and Aspen realized it was from nervousness. "So, what does this mean—that we're like…" He sighed. "We're not…"

Aspen's stomach plummeted. "No. We can't be."

"Oh, marshmallow dust! You're not brother and sister!" Vox clarified. "But what it does mean is that your powers are two halves of a whole."

"Lykaion," Ryder breathed.

Aspen glared at both of them. "That's not possible."

"It's the only explanation for both of you having these powers. Lykaion's powers were from outside of this galaxy."

For the first time, Vox met her eyes. Exhaustion was plain on her face.

Aspen's brows knitted together. "How can we both be Lykaion?"

"It makes sense, doesn't it? Lykaion split into two entities because the power of Absolution was so great." Vox walked around the hologram to where Aspen stood and pushed the long sleeve of her coat up to her elbow. "You have a silver tattoo starting on your forearm that finishes on Ryder's forearm. River gave me all the books he could find containing any information about Lykaion, and this is a picture of an old stone carving dating back to the Sumerians."

Vox retrieved a mahogany-covered book with gold stitching, titled *The Early Book of Virtues*, and flipped to a tabbed page. She turned off the hologram and spun the book on the desk to face them.

Aspen stared at the illustration, speechless. Ryder leaned in beside her. The wolf on the pages stared back at them, its long front legs etched with the same symbols on their arms.

Ryder breathed heavily. "Does it say anything about what the markings mean?"

"It says the Lykaion Wolves were bonded by one of the most sacred eternal bonds that an Anima can make." Vox glanced at them, tapping an impatient index finger on her crossed arms.

Ryder straightened at her words, his blue-fire gaze fixed. "The Amaranthine bond."

Vox gaped. "How did you know?"

"I've never heard of it," Aspen murmured.

"Put it down to Wolfish senses. Tell me how we can use this against Ignatius," Ryder pressed.

"Well, here's where it gets delicious... Ignatius was

using your powers against you until you bonded in the same pack. He was relying on you being enemies."

"Which means he's changing his plans as we speak," Ryder pondered, staring at a spot on the ground.

"It's impossible for him to change his plan; he still needs to use the same... ingredients, if you will," Vox clarified.

Aspen sighed, her hair falling over her shoulder as she rolled her neck. She put both her hands on her hips. "He's going to open that demonic realm here on Earth after he wipes Earth's surface."

"Yeah," Ryder agreed. "He's changing his tactics. Bet on the fact that we'll be changing ours." Aspen could tell he wasn't going to rest until he had a solid plan for their next mission.

"Wait." She turned her attention to Vox. "What made you throw yourself into this work so soon? You should be on bereavement leave." It was normal for Animas to assess and test their powers. But *days* after Declan's death?

Vox's lips twitched, her voice laced with pain. "I can't just sit here and do nothing. I need to understand the power that killed my boyfriend." The power... She meant *Aspen's* power. "Ignatius can't get away with this." Vox looked to Ryder, whose sorrow was etched in his expression. "Can I have a moment with Aspen?"

Ryder nodded and left them staring at each other. Vox fidgeted with her fingers in the awkward silence.

"Whatever you have to say, I deserve it, so just go ahead." Aspen stood straight, ready to take her onslaught of words.

Instead, Vox just studied her with curiosity. "Some part of me deep down knows you didn't want to... That you had to dispose of Declan's remains so the demon couldn't jump into someone else's body. But I just can't get that image of you out of my head. You destroying his physical form. That red cloud."

Something inside Aspen withered. "I'm sorry. I'm sorry for everything that I am. You should hate me."

Vox didn't reply to that. She simply asked, her hands clasped in front of her, "Are you leaving?"

"Leaving?"

"Yes. Are you going to disappear? I know this may all seem odd because you haven't had a home for so long."

In that moment, Aspen knew that River and Vox had talked about her. She could do nothing but hold Vox's gaze. She didn't have that answer—so Vox hit her with another question.

"Do you have feelings for Ryder?"

Aspen's voice rose a decibel. "What?"

But Vox kept waiting… For what, Aspen couldn't understand. A confession? Was she serious?

"No…" She shook her head vigorously. "No. It's not like that."

"Then what is it like?"

Aspen wasn't used to this direct no-nonsense approach from Vox. She took a step back to create space between them.

"Because it's okay, you know…" Vox went on. "If you do have feelings for him."

"I don't—"

"Let's be honest. You're not that surprised, nor are you *that* sad, about Maxen's indiscretions. You and I both know that if you were really that mad, you would have stabbed Mackenzie with that dagger. The only reason you didn't was because Ryder's the only one who can convince you otherwise."

Ryder's words replayed in her mind, embedded there: *She's setting you free… No more regrets.*

"Because we're in the same pack," she said.

"So?" Vox shrugged in a way that made it seem like her excuse was invalid, like it was complete and utter bullshit and Vox could see right through it.

Aspen's brows lowered, her tone stern. "You're going to drop this now—"

"Or what?" Vox interjected.

Aspen shut her mouth. Her eyelids fluttered. She reached into the pocket of her camos and took out Declan's talon.

Vox gasped when she realized what Aspen was holding. She covered her face with both her hands, lavender eyes peeking through her fingers as she choked back sobs. Aspen took Vox's hands with as much gentleness as she could muster and cupped them together like she would to hold water. She placed the golden talon, marred with hairline impurities that could only be made by wars bravely fought, in her delicate hands.

Vox's chest caved. Her whole body shook as she tried to contain her cries. She stroked the talon with her fingers, gently, as if Declan could somehow feel it. "Declan…" she sobbed.

Aspen longed to hold her through it, but how could she when she was the reminder of the cause of all of Vox's pain?

"I'm sorry," she said again, before she walked out of the room.

She idled outside the door, listening to Vox's muffled cries. Aspen cradled her head, her fingertips digging deep into her tresses. Vox had just detonated a bomb on her life by telling her that she and Ryder were linked with Lykaion. *The* Lykaion. That Ryder's Anima and hers were bonded, the way souls were when they entwined, so that neither death nor dark forces could separate them. A decision their Animas had made to find each other lifetimes ago, defying natural law and the Virtues' plans.

She was still processing them being in the same pack. How it had altered them and where they now stood. Wolves were sensitive to these kinds of changes. Every advance or decline in a relationship mattered. But feelings for him?

She couldn't. Things would go wrong... He'd die and she'd have to live with it. That... or he would break her.

Because he had the power to hurt her in ways that would disfigure her soul.

And that scared her more than the hellgate ever did.

The next day, Ryder walked the passageways of Arcus Libertatem—the smaller of two buildings shaped like crescent moons that surrounded headquarters—at a brisk pace. He was submitting paperwork to Gunner for new battle strategies to keep up with his team's ever-evolving powers. His mind revisited the other night. Aspen's teeth grazing against his neck. The feeling made his hands charge with power, and he shook them before he could set his report on fire. They had training planned for the afternoon, but… how was he going to train her to control such untamable powers?

Last night they had undergone her first training. It had not gone well. The Magnetar powers vaporized everything in their path, and they'd attempted focusing and bending the emanation, but to no avail.

He reached the main passage of Arcus Libertatem that led to the Gardens of Peace, where he was surprised to find General Winters, sitting on a wooden bench with his hands in his lap. The general had sensed him before he was within eyesight and was already looking at Ryder expectantly when he walked through the glass doors.

"Good morning, Captain Everett."

Ryder saluted. "Morning, General."

The general glanced at the forms in his hand. "Handing those to the major, I presume?"

"Yes, sir. I'd better get going before I miss him." Ryder began walking on before Ansel's voice halted him.

"Why don't you sit down for a while, Captain? There is much to discuss."

Ryder turned back, holding his breath. He walked slowly to the bench and sat. The general looked wistfully into the lush garden of Kore's native trees and flowers. In the middle of the garden, behind the maze of trees, were marines practicing tai chi, others having quiet meetings. Ryder grew skittish when Ansel didn't speak at all. When they did start talking, he was sure everything they said would be overheard.

"Wouldn't your office be a more suitable place to talk, sir?" he asked.

A peaceful smile appeared on the general's thin lips.

He fanned out his gigantic wings and folded them back in again. A metaphysical sphere encircled their proximity.

"We may speak freely." Ansel raised a brow and took the papers from Ryder's hands. "So, what strategies do you have for our world-protecting battle?"

"I don't think you should…" Ryder's sentence trailed off as the general began reading the beginning of the report.

"*Inconclusive training*," he read out loud, referring to last night's attempts.

Ryder evaded eye contact. He was suddenly self-conscious, wondering if Ansel could smell her scent on him.

Ansel sighed. "Never did I think Ignatius could return and cause so much havoc in this world. If anybody can lead us out of this, it's you, Captain."

Ryder shook his head. "I really wish you'd stop saying that."

Ansel tremored with a silent laugh. "Do you not see the togetherness you have created among the team—how you have so quickly earned their trust?"

"If you knew what was really going on, you wouldn't be saying that," Ryder responded bluntly.

"Ahh… you mean the incident between Sergeant Lovetta and Sergeant Bale?"

Ryder gaped at him incredulously. "How did you—"

"I have a knack for smelling wounds. Even ones that have healed over… You develop these senses in war."

The moment Ryder jumped to stand, Ansel's arm pushed him back into his seat.

"Do not worry. Sergeant Lovetta is having her morning hunt with the wolves as we speak."

"She's not in trouble?" Ryder asked, surprised.

"Well, that all depends, Captain… Would you be willing to defend her honor if she was?"

Ryder looked at the general with suspicion. "I don't know what you mean."

Ansel leaned in, his pearl eyes intense. "Would you risk her life if it meant saving the world?"

CHAPTER 31

Ryder clenched his fists until his veins protruded. Prickling heat ignited all over his body as he glowered back at General Winters. "If you're asking me to do what I think you are—"

"What I'm asking," Ansel interjected, "is would you consider destroying the source of the danger before it is used against us?"

Ryder sprang to his feet, this time before Ansel could stop him. The general rose and bent the leaves of a nearby fern with his staff. Another shriveled fern lay behind it; its leaves had turned a bile-colored yellow and were transparent enough to show its skeleton.

"You see, Captain—nature destroys efficiently and indifferently, because it understands a larger concept that humanity cannot comprehend. In her bones and at a cellular level, Sergeant Lovetta understands the cycles of life and death. To us, it appears inhumane, heartless, and lawless—but for the greater good, she understands what it is to restore balance." Ansel placed his hand on Ryder's shoulder with an intense glare. "She would understand your decision more than anybody ever could."

Ryder ripped his shoulder away. If his gamma rays could have flared from his eyes, they would have as they burned at the elder. "I will kill you or anybody else who tries to harm her. And you can consider this my resignation."

Ryder turned on his heel—and froze when he heard the general clapping. He turned, a scowl painted upon his face, confusion mixed with anger.

Ansel laughed light-heartedly. "I am not asking you to terminate Sergeant Lovetta's life."

Through a tight jaw, Ryder replied, "Why don't you tell me what you're getting at?"

"I am wondering, Midnight Wolf, whether you understand what needs to die for something to live. Or better yet… to flourish. A small tip about battling the Primordial…"

Ryder's jaw tightened like an iron clamp.

"Demons don't understand bonds."

Ryder spun to leave again, electric with anger. He hoped nobody would get in his way, because it might be the last thing that sorry soul ever did.

"And Captain…"

Ryder turned once more. "General?"

The general's expression was stern, his owl wings arching higher, making him look taller, broader. Ryder's stomach clenched.

Ansel's next words were a declaration of war. An order meant only for him.

"Clean up this mess."

Aspen was smiling to herself as she walked into the training room in Wolf Division and threw her duffel bag to the floor. With the insight about just how unaffected Ryder was by her pheromone powers, she was less anxious about the Magnetar flares. Using pheromone powers made her squeamish at best, and the fact that the team now knew about them made that feeling even worse. She would take straight-up killing any day. Magnetar powers meant destruction—that sentiment made her comfortable.

Ryder barely acknowledged her as he dropped the last padded mat onto the floor. "Are you ready?"

"Are *you* ready?" Her look was scrutinizing.

"Boots off." He motioned at her shoes before sauntering to the other side of the room.

Aspen ran the tip of her tongue against the underside of her teeth. She paused, staring after him for a moment before she unlaced her boots and pulled them off. She stepped onto the padded floor and waited with her arms folded, suspicion brimming in her mind. Ryder cast his military blouse to the floor, revealing the olive-drab T-shirt beneath, and stood on the other end of the mat, his gaze indifferent.

"Hit me," he ordered.

She refrained from a full scowl. "What?"

"Do you not understand basic instruction, Sergeant? I said, hit me."

Shock froze her solid, her tongue touching the tip of her fang as she studied him. She opened her mouth to speak, then decided against it, shifting beneath his glare.

"Yes, I'm serious," he boomed, answering the question her body language implied.

"Is this about Mackenzie?"

"This is about exactly what it looks like." His arms spread out to draw her attention to the training room. "Getting *this* under control."

Her body stiffened. *Control?* "Getting what under control?" she snapped.

Ryder stalked to the center of the mat where he rephrased the question. "Do you control your powers? Or do they control you?"

She opened her mouth and closed it again.

"Do you know what your record says? It says you're untrainable, dishonorable, can't follow battle strategy or instruction, can't work in a team…"

He drew closer to her with every word. The walls of her stomach became concrete.

"… incapable of eliciting humility or better judgment for the sake of the greater good." He stood intimidatingly close to her now, though she dared not flinch or show her discomfort; years of conditioning wouldn't allow it. "Now I'm about to take you into the biggest battle the Corps has ever prepared for. So answer me…" His voice dropped to a low murmur. "Do you control your powers? Or do they control you?"

Aspen scowled at those glacier-blue eyes, her posture

ramrod straight as she stormed away. She had almost made it to the end of the mat when he said something that made her whip back around to face him.

"That's it, walk away like you always do."

"What is your problem?" she exploded. "I fight—it's wrong. I walk away—it's wrong. What the hell do you want from me, Ryder?"

"I want to know that I can count on you to do the right thing—to stop hiding from everybody trying to get close to you. Especially me." He pointed at his chest as he exhaled sharply. "Your kills have repercussions. Your decisions are paramount. And I want to know that you're watching my six as I lead a whole team into a battle that could kill us all! Whether you like them or not is irrelevant..." Ryder paused, placing his fingertips against his forehead, then taking them down in defeat. "I don't want on-the-surface battle trust. I want you as my ally. I want you close."

The soothing waters of realization washed over her. Her poor, sleepless Ryder, full of worry, the weight of everyone's lives on those strong, capable shoulders, tormenting him without end. His greatest fear forever stitched into his subconscious. Ryder stayed up all night mulling over battle situations that may never happen. He didn't have to tell her; she knew. She knew because she could feel it through their bond. An intuitive sense that was unfolding further the longer she stayed.

Vox had been right. Vox was always right. Her words repeated in Aspen's mind: *I know this may all seem odd because you haven't had a home for so long.* Yes, she felt this about the people, the justices... Heck, the whole Corps. But Ryder... Ryder was different.

From the moment she'd seen their identical vibrations on the hologram, it was as though it had activated secrets that had long been held, locked away somewhere sacred. Maybe that sacred place was her Anima—the White Wolf, though she was too estranged from her soul to acquire such codes embedded with the wisdom of the Virtues and the murmurings of her desires. She didn't deserve them—yet they leaked like luminescent waters at times like these, when she was with him.

"You're not going to lose me," she assured him. She placed her hand against his, connecting their palms, joining their symbols together. They set alight, and she sent a ripple of Magnetar power up his forearm to isolate the last symbol. The symbol of his powers, the perfect mirror of her own. "I control my powers," she explained softly.

Ryder drew in a breath, pressed his lips together, and nodded slowly. Her answer hadn't calmed him. It had somehow made it worse. She saw the way he hunched his broad shoulders in defeat. Aspen's gut plummeted when he avoided eye contact. There was something else… Something she was missing. She read it from his golden aura, the truth descending upon her, making her breath seize in her throat.

"Somebody put a hit on me."

His eyes snapped back to hers, wide and fearful—that was confirmation.

"Mackenzie?" she tested.

His eyes shot to the door as a group of marines passed by outside.

She dropped her voice lower. "Calais?"

He dragged in a ragged breath before he finally spoke. "I think so."

"Who told you?"

"Ansel."

Aspen shook her head. She had felt this coming. Her mind was racing, searching for clues she may have missed, sifting through gut feelings and evidence. "He wanted you to do it."

Ryder shook his head skeptically. "I don't think you're the only one…"

"What do you mean?"

"I think Calais has put a hit on Ansel too."

"What?" Aspen exclaimed.

"I think Ansel's been tipped off. Something about the way he spoke… He started off as if he was the one enforcing the idea to get rid of you, then he changed the story, telling me he wasn't asking me to kill you. I think he was dropping hints."

"Hints about what?"

Ryder spoke like he'd already made up his mind. "That there's corruption in the highest ranks of the Corps."

She didn't doubt his judgment. Didn't question him. "We have to finish this."

Ryder's eyes flashed. "You're not the least bit afraid?"

Aspen huffed dismissively. "Please. Kill me? I'd like to see him try…"

Ryder chuckled before resuming an air of austerity. "Calais isn't coming anywhere near you. I can promise you that much."

Aspen raised her brows. "Is that right?"

"It is," he reassured her with a steadying gaze. "It's Ansel I'm worried about."

Aspen was thoughtful for a moment. She agreed it was Ansel who remained the most unprotected of them all. And if Calais was as corrupt as they thought he was… anything was possible. Anybody could be against each other.

They continued training together, manipulating Aspen's Magnetar powers at different speeds and clashing them with Ryder's powers. The powers went through each other without combining, as they had hoped. They worked on different strengths and practiced focusing the flares onto a more specific target. Ryder taught her to hone the power, to use its energy sequence to forge it into a weapon she alone could wield.

A small smile appeared on her lips. He asked what she was thinking.

"I've always been embarrassed about my powers. The healing and the pheromones. But this…" She sighed. "This is empowering. I've never felt so much force. It's like I'm unlimited…" Despite her elation, the sentiment made her feel timid. "Thank you," she managed.

His smile made her heart quicken. "You're welcome."

Ryder locked up the training room with his power signature while Aspen leaned against the wall, waiting for him. They took a speed portal from Deer Division and followed the lake past the north-east barracks. It was dark out; the snow now reached the bottom of the mountains, making them glisten like enormous silver crystals, while moonbeams illuminated every ripple on the water.

Aspen asked Ryder about the debacle with Thex that had followed the Enceladus mission, which he told her had been smoothed over—at least for now.

"You're asking me about Thex… How are you and Mackenzie?" he said. "I mean, she called you to help her and Vox when we were at training last night. Did you go?"

She shot him a look of disapproval. "I don't need Mackenzie to destroy Ignatius… I can do that myself."

Ryder scratched the back of his head. "You can destroy just fine, but if I can get real honest… Your aim with your Magnetar powers is terrible."

She scowled at him. "Is this my report?"

"Consider it your official review." The hint of a smile formed on his lips, but he resumed his seriousness. "You've become the world's most powerful weapon."

"We," she corrected.

Ryder breathed in sharply and nodded. "*We* have become the world's most powerful weapon. But Ignatius wants to use only your Magnetar powers. You have to choose to fight on the same side, even if we all don't get along."

He could tell she was listening, but her head was turned, looking out at the lake. "You're beginning to sound like Michael," she said.

Ryder shrugged. "Maybe he's right. Look, I know she hurt you. And I know this is going to take time. I'm not asking you to like her. I'm asking you to protect her—to protect all of them."

"Does that include you?"

He sensed the mocking tone in her voice and exhaled. "Just do what you do best so I can pull off these missions."

They reached the crushed-rock path that led to his cabin. Ryder watched the moonlight envelope her silhouette as she gazed at him thoughtfully.

"What's going on in that beautiful head?"

Aspen bit her bottom lip. "Mackenzie's going to tell Calais that I pulled a knife on her the first moment she gets. She still believes he's good. That's a problem."

Ryder shook his head. "Ansel already knows."

"He told you that?"

Ryder nodded. "Besides, she would have said something by now. I don't know… I think you have a lot to learn from each other."

"Me, learn from her?" Aspen walked in front of him on the path. "That's never going to happen."

He threw his hands up in the air with a grin. "Whatever you say."

They approached his A-framed cabin, nestled amid the forest with a timber porch that wrapped all the way around. Aspen froze, her mouth slightly agape, her eyes doe-like with wonder. "Is this…?"

"Yeah," Ryder answered before she could finish, and he took her hand, leading her up the steps.

"Wow… Captaincy sure has its perks."

He placed his fingers over the lock. The sensor read his power signature and unlocked the timber-framed glass door. Ryder kicked off his shoes in the tiny mudroom and placed them underneath two coats that hung from the hooks above. For a mudroom, there was no mud in sight, other than the tiny granules of gravel he'd brought in with him from the path. Aspen unlaced and removed her boots and hung her jacket on a spare hook as Ryder drew the curtains in the dining area to the left. Aspen's gaze danced past the two-seater table to the cozy-looking kitchen. He'd left the window over the sink open a crack, and a leafy vine curled in.

Ryder watched as she walked around slowly, running her fingers against the chocolate leather couch that faced the stone fireplace. He bent down, assembling the logs he had taken from the metal carrier. Aspen approached the wooden cupboard against the wall that held folded checked blankets in autumnal colors. She peered down the small corridor opposite the couch, then moved to the staircase, where she eyed the bookshelf peeking out from the landing. Ryder stood up from the now burning hearth, dusting his hands.

Aspen walked up the steps. A smile lit up her face when she saw that the bookshelf on the landing spread along the wall, revealing a nook with a padded bench seat full of large cushions. She ran her finger over the spines as if she couldn't recall the last time she had been in front of a bookshelf. She had clearly forgotten to conceal her nostalgia; delight softened her face.

Ryder's heart raced as he followed her up the last steps into the loft, to his bedroom. She touched the armchair and the hand-carved wooden chest beside it, then walked across the red tribal rug and sat on the long bench at the end of the bed. Ryder lowered himself into the armchair opposite her, resting his forearms on his knees. She mirrored his body language—she did that when she was calm. Her eyes were warm as they both succumbed to the sensation of finally being alone. Not training. Not on a mission. Hiding from the wars outside.

"I have something to give you," Aspen said, unstrapping the leg pocket of her camos and feeling around until she found something, keeping it hidden in her enclosed fist. Ryder leaned forward as she rotated her palm, revealing what she was holding.

His eyes darted from her open palm to her face. "Is that…?"

"A Phaedra, yes."

Ryder stared at the crystal tag, the golden spiral shining under his bedroom light. Its metal rim was blank. As if she had read his mind, Aspen took his hand. Warmth rose in his abdomen at the gentleness of her touch.

"The Corps can track where we've traveled with our Phaedras. They don't do it unless they have to, but I didn't want to take any chances. The sides of this Phaedra are blank because this is an untraceable dimension portal. This key only goes to one place."

"Where's that?" he asked, dazed by the way her kaleidoscope eyes danced in anticipation.

"Home," she murmured.

Ryder froze. *Home.* Thinking about his mom, dad, and sister made him swallow against the lump that had suddenly formed in his throat.

Aspen's eyes grew wide as she watched his reaction. "I didn't mean to upset you. I just thought you should have a way back that was safe. I know that you wouldn't risk going back at a time like this, but I thought maybe after the war was over…"

Ryder rested his palm on hers to silence her. "I'm not

upset. I just…" He fought for the right words, a buoyant feeling in his chest making the whole room seem brighter. "You did this for me?"

Aspen smiled, rotating their hands until hers were on top. He felt the weight of the Phaedra drop into his palm. "I did."

He didn't know how she'd come into possession of a blank Phaedra, and he didn't care. She knew how much this meant to him and had done it despite the risk of getting caught.

"Thank you." He closed the space between them and embraced her, holding her so tightly he couldn't just hear her heartbeat, he could feel its rhythm pumping against his chest. His lips turned to her ear, and he felt her shiver as he asked, "Do I want to know how much trouble you'd be in for doing something like this?"

She exhaled through her nose. "You don't want to know."

He drew back slightly without completely breaking contact with her and motioned to the room they stood in. "This can be yours."

Aspen shook her head. "No. If you do that I won't stay." He held her gaze, asking her to accept it, but she added, "I mean it."

"Stubborn."

She laughed, a gentle rush of air from her nose. "That's what my father used to say."

He raised a brow and shrugged. "He was right." That made her smile.

She bit her lip. "So where do I sleep?"

CHAPTER 32

Ryder led her downstairs, through to the end of the narrow hallway. He pushed the door open and a cold chill hit their faces as he turned on the light. A double bed was tucked into the corner of the room, its end abutting a wide column of awning windows that looked out to the pine forest. A small side table held an old stained-glass lamp; across from it was a small wood burner.

"It's really small—" Ryder began.

"It's beautiful," Aspen breathed. She glanced at him, then back at the room. *Her* room. "Are you sure this is okay?"

"Are you kidding?" was his only answer. He bit his bottom lip. "Well, uh… I'll start the fire. There's sheets and blankets in the cupboard in the living room. And there's a bathroom next door." He shoved his hands into his pockets and disappeared down the hall.

Aspen smiled at the room and went to work drawing the curtains and making the bed with flannel sheets, a comforter, and two blankets. Ryder returned holding three thick logs and some twigs. She watched him arrange the wood inside the burner and light a small piece of card. He blew gently on the flames until they grew and heated the whole room.

When he rose and turned to her, she was sitting with one leg bent, one leg dangling off the bed. He looked over her and tingles covered her skin. "I have T-shirts… if you need something to borrow."

What little belongings she owned had been sent here by Ansel; the duffel bag lay near the door. She did not own pajamas. It was too cold to wear them in a tent. She always wore her uniform. All she owned were tank tops, undergarments, a hairbrush, and a toothbrush.

"Actually, that would be really nice."

She wasn't sure what to make of the way Ryder looked at the floor, then back at her. His gaze was intense as he bit the inside of his cheek. No, she didn't quite know how to read *that* look. But he soon left the room. She heard the thump of his steps above her, and wasted no time jumping into the shower, reveling in the hot water. She must have stayed there for at least twenty minutes. She wouldn't miss bathing in alpine rivers.

When she returned to her room it was toasty, and a large white T-shirt lay on the bed. She put on boy shorts, a tank top, and Ryder's shirt. It was huge on her, and smelled faintly of his amber-and-cedar scent.

She climbed into bed and listened out for Ryder for a few minutes, hearing nothing, before sleep took her.

The glow of a nearby porch light illuminated two old wooden doors that led underground. They were flung open and smeared with bright, fresh blood. So much blood that the walls deep inside the cellar were painted with it. She descended the steps slowly, her stomach writhing with dread. She didn't want to go down there… but she could hear shuffling.

Someone was still in there.

She tried calling out her brother's name, but she couldn't speak. She pushed for her voice to make the sound.

Giosuè.

Giosuè.

Giosuè.

Nothing came out but a rush of air.

The cellar was bordered with shelves of homemade wine and spirits, with six large wine barrels mounted to the wall at the end. In the middle of the room, she saw him.

She rushed to his side, the ground cold beneath her knees as she lifted the boy of eight years old into her arms. His once tanned skin was pale. His green eyes were open, the story of his last moments alive locked inside them. Horror and pain and helplessness. She sobbed his name, burying her face in his caramel-brown curls.

She was forced to let him go, but her insides screamed for her to never leave his side. Her feet moved against her will, pushing her back outside and into the night air.

She managed to look at him one last time. Her little brother. Alone in the cellar.

No.

No.

No!

She screamed, but only silence prevailed.

She was forced, kicking and flailing, out into the orchard of her childhood home by a force she could not name. In front of her, she felt a presence. But all she could see was blackness. The kind that swallowed you into dimensions you couldn't escape.

Hell.

She could feel hell. Curling around her as the mass in its center took form before her eyes.

Enormous wings spread to their full extension, darker than the sky. Wings of all-consuming obsidian, coming closer and closer, until, through the mist, she could make out the man who towered over her… The planes of his face, his straight nose, his mocking mouth, pieces of his raven hair falling over his brow, and his eyes…

Eyes of orange flame and the deepest teal-blue sea merging together. Promising misery. Black liquid rolled from them like tears. But his hands…

His hands were slick with blood. Giosuè's blood.

He pulled his luscious lips into a wicked slash. She was cemented to the ground, desperate to move. To tear this man apart. But she watched as he turned and walked away, fading into the mist.

The last thing she saw was the white feathers that formed a V between his wings.

A force like rope tied around Aspen's chest made her lurch

into a sitting position. All she could see was a blur of orange. A primal scream ripped from her throat. A scream that the walls absorbed, that the trees outside felt. The familiarity of the room came back to her just before the door burst open. She screamed again; this time it was her brother's name.

Warm hands cupped her face, Ryder's eyes soothing her back into her body. The wood burner spat, the wind shuddered the windowpane, the fleece blanket brushed against her skin. She reached out for his shoulders to prove to herself that he was real, scrunching the fabric of his T-shirt, running her palms over his neck, his jaw.

His voice was rough and soothing at the same time. "It's me."

He pulled her in, and she crawled into his lap, body pressed against his chest. His heartbeat a steady anchor into this world. *This* life. The life that was unfolding further away from the horrors she'd known before, and at the same time catapulting into a series of nightmares she was yet to have. But she wasn't alone. He was here.

"I dreamed…" Her voice cracked. "I dreamed that Maxen was the one who killed Giosuè. And Giosuè…" She whimpered. "Giosuè was alone. He died alone."

She trembled and sobbed, her knuckles turning white as she clutched his T-shirt, his arms wrapped around her until he was all she could feel.

He caressed her hair. "It was just a dream."

Her voice was so small it didn't even sound like hers. "It felt so real."

Ryder held her close until her breathing returned to normal. It reminded her of that time in the empty common room, before Operation Enceladus. It felt like so long ago.

She pulled away from him and tucked her bare legs beneath the blankets. A flicker of pain crossed his features as he let her move away. The space between them was cold. Ryder left only to return with more wood for the fire.

"Did I wake you?" she asked.

He dusted his hands. "No, I was working."

Turning battle strategies over in his head, no doubt.

He ran his fingers through his hair. "Well, uh… Sleep well." He made for the door.

Her mouth suddenly dry, Aspen reached out and touched his hand. He halted.

"Please, don't leave." She hooked her fingers with his and tugged until he stood at the side of her bed.

"Okay," he whispered.

Ryder dragged the chair from beside the wood burner close to the side of the bed. Aspen laid her head down on the pillow, and Ryder leaned his elbows on his knees and linked his fingers with hers, joining both sides of the compass inked on their wrists. A gentle sensation, like fingertips running up her forearm, made her relax.

"I shouldn't be here. The Corps wants me dead. You could be in danger because of me. I don't deserve—"

"It's not about deserving it," he interjected.

"Then tell me what it *is* about."

His voice was hushed, as if he were speaking to his lover in the early hours of the morning. It made her heart skip a beat. "It's about making choices that are true to who we are. You didn't want to kill Mackenzie; that's why you stopped. As much as you think it was me who convinced you not to, it wasn't. You decided against it."

Aspen let out a sharp breath. "Stop making excuses for my actions."

"Are you *that* obsessed with making yourself out to be the bad guy?"

She propped her head up onto her elbow. "Are you that obsessed with finding the good in me?"

"I don't have to search that far." The fire cast a glow onto the side of his face, turning his skin and strands of his hair to molten gold. She wanted to believe him, so badly.

"Michael said we have to battle for the place of alpha."

Ryder raised a brow and chuckled.

"You're laughing? It's usually a fight to the death."

He scoffed. "What does Gunner know about Wolves?"

She shrugged. "I have no interest in being a leader. I don't want to be responsible for anyone's life."

Ryder glanced down at their hands, still joined, and rubbed his thumb against the side of her hand. Their eyes met again, their gazes more intense than before.

"What do you want?" he asked.

Aspen felt an insatiable expansion in her abdomen. "Liberation… To trust myself again… To belong."

His voice was barely a whisper. "I think you and I both know the truth."

"What truth?"

He leaned in closer still, and all she could think was that she only had to move her arm down and press against the mattress a little more, and his lips would be on hers.

"The truth that an alpha comes in pairs…. and that I want you to belong here."

Aspen took a moment to process his words before she rose to her knees on the bed, engulfed by a wave of pleasurable tingles all over her body. She leaned in, hands gripping the sides of his chair, closer and closer, until her lips fused with his.

The beginning was tentative and gentle, each brush of their lips an asking. She drew back slightly, only to find the insatiable hunger of the Wolf staring back at her.

Without hesitation, Ryder closed what little gap lingered between them. His kiss was a refuge from an eternity of living in an unending ice storm. He was the bonfire in the winter, a burning sensation sweeping over her body, stealing her breath and warming her bones. She surrendered, becoming more entwined in his impenetrable lock.

The pressure of his lips against hers deepened as his hands found her waist and pulled her on top of him. She threaded her legs under the armrests and straddled him. He drew her in deeper, claiming her. Every delicious stroke of his tongue was her undoing.

CHAPTER 33

In many ways, Aspen was as sacred and as hidden as Kore. Ryder wanted to feel the shiver of her diamond dust, explore her wild, bathe in all her secret springs. She gasped, sensitive beneath his hands as they roved the outer length of her thighs and braced her hips. She wrapped herself ever tighter around him. Ryder lifted her from the chair and laid her down on the bed, purposefully dropping his weight onto her, pinning her down. Her jasmine scent merged with his own, saturating him in a heady feminine embrace. He also detected the faintest trace of leather and swiped his hand under her pillow, pulling out the dagger hidden there. It made a dull thud as he dropped it to the floor. They never broke the kiss, but she seemed to weaken, soften… tremble, like he'd taken out her last line of defense.

Their lips parted at a sudden sound. Ryder felt her breath on his face as he listened for it again.

The Corps alarm rang loud despite its distance. They held each other's gaze, stunned, before they scrambled off the bed. Aspen pulled on her camos and took off his T-shirt in one swift swipe, covering the tank top beneath with her own olive T-shirt and military blouse.

Ryder's wristwatch started ringing. "Vox?" he answered.

"Ryder, the Corps is under attack!"

"Where are you?"

"I'm hiding in the lab," she whispered. Ryder heard crashing sounds on her end of the line.

"Hold on." He darted out of Aspen's room and raced to his own, changing into his uniform in record time. "Why aren't you evacuating?" he shouted into his watch as Aspen met him at the foot of the stairs, both of them mere flashes of light as they reached the dirt path. There was no reply; all he could decipher was some shifting. "Vox? Are you there?" He drew the watch closer his ear.

A throat-ripping sound pierced through, and he pulled the watch back as Vox's screams rang out.

Aspen almost took off before he caught her arm. "Wait," he warned.

"What are you doing? I have to get her out!"

"No." He shook his head, assessing the exterior of the Corps. "That's what they want…"

A rumbling roar sent them diving into the ferns beside the path as a demon ravaged toward the Corps.

Aspen slowly rose from their hiding spot, her body language telling him she knew he was right. "What do we do?"

"Ignatius has taken down the barrier. Now every

demon can get in. We have to get to the headquarters control room and turn it back on."

She shook her head. "The barrier is made of Kore magic, not controls. There's no such room."

"Yes, there is. It's in Asintmah's office."

Aspen raised a brow. "How do you know all of this?"

He shot her a smirk. "I pay attention. We'll enter from Eagle Division and get to headquarters from there."

She returned a flash of a smile. "Okay, you do that. I'll enter from Wolf Division—it's closer to the labs. I can get Vox out from there."

"No." He stopped her from walking onward.

She glared at him. "Ryder. You have to trust me."

"It's not that. He's here to take our arsenal and use it against us… You realize that's you, right?"

Aspen inhaled sharply.

"If he weaponizes you, we're done for. So you don't play lone Wolf this time…"

"I play the Deer," she finished.

His nod affirmed their plan.

"Great," Aspen grumbled.

They traveled, swift and silent, to the shed entrance of Eagle Division, hiding behind the parked planes and vehicles. Aspen yanked Ryder back down into hiding as one of the crew who took flight inventory stumbled past. As they peeked out from behind the vehicle, they saw onyx blood oozing from her ears and eyes and mouth.

"She's under possession," Ryder whispered.

They'd be caught if they moved now, but lingering gave them the chance to watch the possessed marine looking at her arms and walking around aimlessly, with the occasional sound of the fighting Anima still alive inside, trying to break free.

Aspen hid the hopeless, hollow feeling stabbing her stomach. "We have to keep moving," she told Ryder. "Come on."

They opened the door that led from the hangar to the main corridor.

"We just have to hope we don't come across any Lynxes," Aspen warned as Ryder used the power signature from his fingertips to get through to the speed portal. They zipped through the portal and landed in the first-floor walkway of the executive offices. The corridor was full.

They had appeared directly in front of a dozen demons, landing chest to chest with one whose insides Ryder fried, leaving it sizzling and twitching on the floor. The rest attacked. Aspen leaped on top of the railing and catapulted further down the hallway behind the swarm. The red power blasting from her arms shot into the two demons in front of her. The demons atomized between them, revealing Ryder smiling suggestively at her. She fought a laugh.

"Come on," he said. "It's this way."

It required stealth to enter Asintmah's office. This level was teeming with demons of all kinds; Aspen could hear them. Ryder began sniffing the air, looking for the location of the barrier control. He moved toward a purple drape adorned with gold stars, yanking it back.

A strange feeling hit Aspen's stomach as she peered

around the vacant office. It was as though Asintmah had never left, as though she had just stepped out. The ferns that covered the walls were still verdant and cared for. Smudging leaves and talismans lay ornamentally about, and there was a subtle smell of burnt cedar. Aspen walked to the source, inspecting the freshly burned end of the wood.

"Someone is still lighting this…"

Ryder emerged from behind the drape. "Thex keeps the plants alive, and River lights… whatever that is." He motioned to the piece of wood in her hand.

She looked down at it and dropped it back in the shell it had been burned in.

"Something wrong?" Ryder asked.

"I wish I had made her confess what she found in Bastian Fallow's autopsy before I killed her," Aspen rasped.

He moved behind her, guiding her hair over her shoulder, his arms wrapping around her, locking her to his chest. "I know."

She felt his breath over her neck and the humming inside her bones again. She faced him and laced her fingers behind his neck. "Did you do it?" She flashed a glance toward the draped wall.

"It's done. Barrier is back up, but whatever is already inside has to be driven out."

Aspen sighed, her gaze on the curve of his lips. "Are you ready?"

There was a twinkle in his eyes. "Always."

The scent of three Lynxes made them slide apart. All three were possessed and coming closer.

"Don't you knock?" Ryder asked as the Lynxes appeared.

They threw themselves into the fight.

Between maneuvers, Ryder shouted to her, "Whatever you do, don't kill them."

"Roger that."

They snapped their opponents' necks at the same time, leaving one female Lynx scaling the bookshelf. She leapt for Ryder. Aspen speared her midair and broke the middle of her spine on the landing.

She got up, rolling her neck. "Now what?"

"We find the others."

They were cautious as they moved through the deserted headquarters. Finally, they reached the labs. After a scuffle at the door, where Aspen impaled a possessed private, they scanned the labs, making sure the area was clear. Aspen called Vox's name as they moved further inside, but there was no answer.

Ryder whispered, almost inaudibly, "Stay alert. She could have been possessed too."

Aspen didn't answer him, but walked on, her jaw tightening at the thought. She heard the faintest noise and raised a hand to stop Ryder. They stood frozen until she heard it again.

A heartbeat.

Aspen took calculated steps closer to a desk toward the back wall, and caught Vox's scent. At superspeed, she blew the desk over, crashing it into the wall behind with a loud bang.

Her hands snatched Vox's dainty neck, her eyes alight with fury. "You don't get to take her too," she threatened the smiling demon inside. It curved Vox's mouth into a sadistic grin. Flickers of red and black coursed through her violet eyes. Aspen squeezed Vox's neck tighter.

"Aspen, you're going to kill her," Ryder warned. "Pass her to me. I'll take care of her."

Before she could move, Thex and Mackenzie ran in.

"Oh, thank god," Mackenzie breathed, rushing to Ryder.

"It's bad out there, brother." Thex looked over at Aspen holding Vox. "Is she…?"

"Yeah," Ryder answered.

The demon screeched and Aspen gripped tighter still, burning with rage.

"What are you going to do? Kill your best friend?" Mackenzie exclaimed.

"Why don't you shut your mouth so I can think." Aspen glared at the demon moving through Vox's body. It squirmed and she pinned it against the wall.

She heard Levi's voice. "How do we get it out of her?"

"You can't," Mackenzie stated.

"Mackenzie, the one that possessed you didn't stick," Thex answered. "There has to be a way, otherwise we're going to lose the whole Corps."

Vox's body was twisting in Aspen's grip.

"Fight it," Aspen implored her. "You're going to fight it…"

River's musky scent appeared at her side. "What are we going to do?" he breathed.

General Winters's scent wafted through the room next. Calmly, he pointed his staff at Vox's forehead. She stopped moving, and there was a cracking sound from inside her body.

Mackenzie speed-ran closer to Vox. "What did you do?"

The demon's sinewy cloud of remnants dropped to the floor, and Vox awakened from the possession, her irises now violet once more. Aspen's hands loosened and cast a bright glow, healing the internal damage from the demon.

There was a tug at the general's thin lips. "I took it upon myself to evoke centuries-old magic in fear that something like this would happen again. I've concealed this knowledge in the cryolava of my staff. To make sure that Airman McAndor did not die for nothing."

Vox's embrace took Aspen by surprise. She wrapped her arms around her friend, relieved. When she heard Vox sniffing, she broke away.

"What?"

Vox blushed. "You smell like Ryder. He's all over you."

Aspen gaped at her.

"I smelled it as soon as I walked in," Mackenzie agreed with a half-smile.

Thex was trying to conceal his goofy grin with his hand.

"Like we didn't see that coming," Levi announced.

Aspen rolled her eyes. "Nothing... *happened*. Can we please focus on the war going on outside?"

"Agreed," Ryder added. "We need a plan for how we're going to clear out the Corps and heal everybody affected... now that we know we can."

"*Nothing happened* my ass," Thex probed.

"Up for all the action, aren't you, Captain?" Levi smirked.

Ryder rolled his eyes. "I think the word you're looking for is endurance."

River covered his nose. "Wow... Subtle, Aspen. Seriously, rein it in."

It took a moment for her to realize what he was talking about: her pheromone powers, emanating from her and wafting through the lab.

"The world's biggest distraction," Thex agreed, rubbing his forehead.

Mackenzie was silent, covering her nose, focusing on the ground. Ryder shot a quick, knowing smile in Aspen's direction.

"The world's biggest distraction…" Vox repeated, her voice faraway in contemplation.

The team looked at her, confusion plain on their faces.

"The world's *biggest* distraction!" she repeated, elation bubbling off of her.

Ryder smiled, catching on. "I have a plan."

CHAPTER 34

"Are you crazy? No! She's not doing that," River exclaimed.

"Come on… The demons can't resist her," Levi explained. "It's the fastest way to get them out."

"Stop trying to sell it to me. It's dangerous and stupid." River turned back to Ryder. "Tell me you're joking."

Ryder's voice remained calm. "You're underestimating how powerful she is."

Aspen huffed. "I hate being the active decoy."

Mackenzie drifted nearer to her. "What exactly happens when you're using your pheromone powers? How does it work?"

The room went silent. Aspen shifted on her feet. "Pheromone powers are, put simply, a way of advanced communication. I can convey what I have to say clearly but without words, and I can make chemical changes in the body of the person I'm directing it at. I can make these demons want to attack me."

Mackenzie's hair swished over her shoulders as she looked at the others, then back at Aspen. "Can you make others feel desire?"

Aspen had sensed where this was going the moment Mackenzie asked the question. She balled her fists, cutting her a glassy stare. "Yes."

Mackenzie smirked. "Have you used it on anybody in this room?"

Aspen clenched her jaw. "You mean Ryder… You want to know if I use it on Ryder."

Mackenzie shrugged. "Now that we've got you fessing up… I'm sure Ryder would like to know if he's being deceived or manipulated."

It was quick, but Aspen glimpsed it in her periphery: Ryder's death glare. It cleaved through the argument in an instant. The room fell silent. Not because they were afraid of him, but because they respected him. Because he'd earned it the right way. And when Ryder said enough was enough… they listened. Tension hung in the air until he spoke.

"We have a war to fight. This ends here. Mackenzie?"

"Yes, Captain." She turned to him. "I was only inquiring for the best interest of the team."

"I've never used these powers to manipulate or misguide any one of you," Aspen swore. "But I'm sure you'd have felt it when I wanted you to leave me alone, in the beginning."

Thex nodded. "Okay… but no more hidden powers. Be upfront."

Aspen gave him a terse nod in response.

River slung his arm around her. "Well, we don't want to leave you alone, but we're going to send you outside where all the demons can chase you."

Aspen huffed a laugh.

Vox rubbed at her neck, in the exact place that Aspen had gripped. "Mackenzie should go with you."

Aspen's mouth dropped open. "What?"

"Her Fox leaps can help deter demons that get too close to you on the ground."

"I appreciate the concern, but I don't need her."

At those words, the light left Mackenzie's eyes.

Vox turned her pleading gaze to Aspen. "She is vital to this team, this mission, as are you."

Aspen's patience boiled over. "She doesn't even like you! She doesn't like anybody. Unless they're male… and taken."

Mackenzie fixed her mouth into a grim line and shook her head, an expression that said, *That's what you really think of me.*

Vox flicked her cotton-candy locks over her shoulder. "Mackenzie and I have had our differences, I'll admit, but—"

"It's an order," Ryder interrupted.

Aspen hardened into stone. She would respect Ryder's orders… but Vox?

"Well, since you two are such good friends, I'll leave it to you to find the opening of the hell dimension that's upon us," she said. "In the meantime, I'll just go sacrifice myself for your honor. Maybe they'll give all you heroes a medal in the end."

Aspen walked to the door, ignoring Vox as she called after her.

Ryder stopped her with a tug on her arm. "Be careful."

Aspen shrugged. "You know that's not going to happen."

The team went quiet behind them, watching.

Ryder's strong arms squeezed her into a tight embrace, and she held him the same way. "Out of all my strategies, this one's the biggest gamble."

They broke apart a little so that she could look upon his face. "Bunch of angry demon Anima chasing me? Just another day being me…"

He smiled, but it didn't reach his eyes like it usually did.

She took his hands in hers before she pulled away. "I'll see you outside the barrier."

Aspen snuck around Eagle Division and onto the empty training field. There was an eerie silence surrounding the Corps. No buzzing or clapping of brisk footsteps, no shouting of commands.

She sped to the center of the field, looking at the grandness of the building. She was taking a deep breath in to prepare herself when Mackenzie landed in front of her at super-speed. The ground trembled. Aspen knew it had been a light landing compared to what Mackenzie could do. She supposed that making the demon-possessed Anima fall into the hollows Mackenzie created would give the Corps time to find the lost marines.

She grew tense as Mackenzie gawked at her intently. Aspen shuffled her arms uncomfortably in an attempt to ready herself. "Can you not…"

"What?"

Aspen shot her a glance.

"Am I too close?" Mackenzie asked, taking a step back.

Aspen's shoulders stiffened. "Stop watching me like that. It's weird."

Mackenzie threw her hands up. "Okay."

"Don't stand too close or you'll be caught in the wave."

"Are you afraid I'll kiss you?" Mackenzie teased.

Aspen rolled her eyes. "Just get back."

Mackenzie took another step back, stifling a giggle as Aspen faced the Corps. She steadied herself with her breath and concentrated hard on the shape of the building, covering the whole expanse of it with her mind.

The air in front of her became a translucent mist as the particles bulked together, sending a powerful wave over the Corps.

Mackenzie inched forward, studying the wave projection. "It's working. They're coming…"

Aspen sent another.

"What happens when they're out?" Mackenzie asked as the marines inside the Corps scrambled to the doors.

"We run when I say when," Aspen told her.

"*The* Aspen Lovetta… running?"

"Know when to hold 'em, know when to fold 'em." Aspen pivoted the ball of her foot in the grass.

Mackenzie raised a brow. "Seriously? Kenny Rogers?"

She shrugged. "My dad loved that song… and it's good advice."

Anima marines began pouring out of the door. The Eagles took to the sky, the others leaping and bounding toward Aspen and Mackenzie, causing the ground to tremble.

Mackenzie's eyes grew wide. "Tell me we can run now?"

"Not yet. I'm pretty sure I've had a bad dream about this," Aspen admitted, sending one more wave through them and inside the Corps.

An Eagle shot past them, low overhead, immobilizing them until the feeling came back into their legs.

"Now!" Aspen shouted.

They both bolted, racing through the field and into the forest. Mackenzie was a few paces behind, leaping high into the air and crashing into the earth, creating trenches and hollows for the affected marines to fall into. They were almost at the barrier when Aspen turned to see her lagging further and further behind, exhausted from so many leaps, almost meeting the cusp of the fast-approaching possessed Anima army.

Aspen circled back, yanking Mackenzie's hand as a Bear marine dove and narrowly missed her. She latched Mackenzie onto her own speed time and raced past the barrier.

"We can't outrun them forever," Mackenzie panted.

"No. *You* can't outrun them forever. I, on the other hand, can run circles around them."

"So what do we do?"

"I know a place we can hide."

They ran through rocky terrain, and Aspen slid through a den, yanking Mackenzie in with her. She made quick work of pulling the leaves over the opening. "These will mask our scent."

They hid inside the abandoned den until the sound of trampling footsteps and screeching disappeared.

"I think they're gone," Mackenzie whispered, peeking through the leaves.

She made to climb out, but Aspen pulled her down and pressed a finger against her lips. Mackenzie looked at her with a blank expression.

A Lynx Anima made a soft landing above, just outside the den. Mackenzie crawled back, alarmed. Aspen lunged, pulling the Lynx into the confines of the den. The Anima growled and sliced Aspen's arm with her claws. She recognized this marine; it was one of Levi's friends.

"Ametrine," Mackenzie gasped, as if the woman could understand her.

Aspen broke her neck and slid her further into the den.

She caught the resentful stare Mackenzie was giving her in the dark. Ametrine had apparently been Mackenzie's friend too.

"Next time I'll just let her kill you," Aspen retorted.

Mackenzie shook her head. "I didn't say anything."

"Your judgmental little face says it all."

"Well, your methods are intriguing, to say the least."

They climbed out of the den. "Trust me, princess, there are about half a dozen people I'd rather be saving than you," Aspen replied, pulling the fallen branch back over the den. "And they wouldn't be complaining about my *methods*."

Mackenzie huffed. "What do we do now?"

"We meet the team at the cliffs in Wolf Country."

Aspen's eyes narrowed at Mackenzie's back as she walked away from the den, a stony rigidness setting inside her bones.

"Mackenzie…"

"Hmm?"

"It's this way." Aspen pointed.

It took several hours of running before they reached

the gigantic flat boulders that led to the steep edge, where dark waves crashed against the cliff face below.

"Why aren't they here yet?" Aspen squinted in different directions to sense anyone approaching. There wasn't a sound to be heard but the ocean beneath them.

"Maybe they're flying in?" Mackenzie guessed.

"Who would be flying them when Declan…" She stopped. "Maybe they found Ten?"

As she spoke, Aspen saw a Corps aircraft approaching above the treeline.

"About time," Mackenzie groaned as they watched the people carrier draw closer. They gaped in shock at the sight of an Eagle marine hanging on to the landing skids, trying to get the door open. The helicopter wavered dangerously in the air.

Mackenzie gasped. "Oh my Virtue!"

More Eagles flew to the sides of the helicopter. It was weighed down, jolting as it rotated in the air.

"They're going to bring it down with everyone inside," Aspen exclaimed. "I need to get up there."

"How do you expect to do that?" Mackenzie yelled over the rotor noise. "Hunting down an Eagle to get you up there will take too long."

Aspen thought for a moment. An idea struck. She sent a small red energy explosion upward like a flare.

"What are you doing?" Mackenzie asked.

"If they hover close enough, we can jump on."

Through the pilot screen, she could see Ten, who descended just as Aspen had hoped she would. She waited until the helicopter was about thirty feet above her before she leapt off the ground with arms outstretched to reach the landing slides—

She was pushed mid-jump.

She landed on the edge of the flat boulders of the cliff, swinging out over the waves below. Her knuckles were white, her fingers bleeding as she hung onto the smooth grooves in the rocks for dear life. Her heart hammered in her chest. Mackenzie had almost thrown her over the cliff.

She was about to push herself up when Mackenzie's boot stomped over her fingers. Aspen screamed, desperate to hold on.

Mackenzie bent down to her. "I don't want to do this. But killing you means there's no longer a threat to the world. I'm sorry."

Mackenzie lifted her boot again to stamp down on Aspen's fingers. It was only going to take one more time. She wasn't going to be able to hold on. Aspen struggled, trying to dig her boots into the cliff edge—but Mackenzie abruptly disappeared.

She hoisted herself up, panting on her knees next to the edge. Ryder was pinning Mackenzie down, the ferociousness of Midnight Wolf's jaws inches from her cowering face.

"The hell is wrong with you?" He shoved Mackenzie's clinging grip away, freeing himself from her clutches before running to Aspen. He helped her up and squeezed her against him, as though if he let her go she would fall off the edge again. "Are you okay?"

"Yeah," she breathed.

More possessed Eagle marines were piling onto the helicopter, River and Levi fending them off from the inside. River threw open the door and kicked away the Eagle trying to get in, then threw down a rope.

"Grab on!" he shouted over the noise of the rotors.

Ryder looked over at Mackenzie, who was hunching and clutching her arm. "You first. And this isn't over between you and me."

Mackenzie snatched the billowing rope and began climbing upward in the wind. The helicopter dropped suddenly, but she held on. She was almost at the top when Ryder began climbing up. The whole helicopter shuddered beneath another attack.

Aspen grabbed hold of the rope when Ryder was halfway up. Another Eagle marine slammed into the carrier so hard that it pushed the aircraft out to hover over the dark, devouring ocean. They dangled over monstrous waves that threatened to swallow them whole if they dropped. *Kore is angry,* Aspen thought.

Ryder hoisted himself into a squat on the landing slide and waited for her to climb further up. The wind blew ferociously, throwing her around. She was almost within arm's reach when another Eagle marine swooped. Aspen thrashed as she clung to the rope. Two Eagles hugged onto her legs, but as she tried to kick them off, they bound both her legs with the end of the rope. She growled down at them through gritted teeth.

Out of the corner of her vision, she saw an Eagle marine circling back, ready to swoop again. Ryder was grabbing at the rope, trying to pull her up, when another possessed marine almost pushed him off the helicopter. The carrier felt as if it was going to spin one-eighty. The others were trying to grab the rope as Ryder blasted the Eagle off with his powers. The two marines who clung to Aspen's legs weighed her down, beating their gigantic wings. She was slipping, reaching for Ryder. All she could hear over the helicopter's noise was him screaming her name.

The third swooping marine came into view again. He flew fast toward them, heading straight for Ryder. Ryder was stuck balancing on the bars, his arms wrapped in the rope Aspen was dangling from. The weight of the possessed marines pulled her down further and further, her hands burning from the rope.

She winced up at Ryder. There was no other choice.

Aspen reached behind her and freed her khukuri from its scabbard.

Ryder paused when the realization hit him. "No!" he screamed, over and over again.

Peace filled Aspen as she looked at his face for what could be the last time. Overcome by how handsome he looked when he was worried, by the privilege of knowing him, she smiled, then sliced through the rope in one swing.

She and the Eagles fell until their wings caught the wind, taking her away.

CHAPTER 35

Ryder was so incensed he could barely see. He jumped from the helicopter to the ground before it could land and began calling the wolves to him telepathically. They weren't far off after hearing Aspen's cries for help; he could smell them.

"Ryder, what are you doing?" Mackenzie pulled on his arm.

He whirled around, his eyes alight with blue fire. "Stay the hell away from me before I do something I regret."

"Oh yeah? Like what?" she challenged.

The others had jumped off the helicopter, looking hopeless and despairing.

His fangs were visible as he panted, "Like discharge myself from being your captain!"

It was as though he'd punched the whole team when they were off-guard.

"What?" Thex grasped a firm hold of his shoulder and twisted him so that he was looking into his face. "You can't just leave, Ry… We need you now more than ever!"

"Ryder, think about what you're saying… What about stopping Ignatius?" Vox reasoned, striding over and stopping beside Mackenzie.

Ryder's disdain didn't fade. "Not my problem."

He stormed into the forest, his joints feeling like they were rusted.

"Captain, wait…" River called. "I'll help you! We'll get her back—"

"DON'T YOU GET IT? I don't trust you!" Ryder bellowed, even though, out of the whole team standing here, River didn't deserve it. He was always the one to back Ryder's decisions. "I don't trust *any* of you," Ryder clarified. He glared at Mackenzie. "Especially not you."

"I was only trying to protect the team. I thought if she was out of the picture—"

"What? You thought what? That you'd kill her off and we'd all be better off for it? Kill Ignatius's power source to stop him in his tracks?"

"YES!" Mackenzie yelled. "I did what you couldn't do!"

Ryder took determined strides until he was in front of her. "Have you forgotten that only something as old as Ignatius can kill him? You were going to kill the only person who could stop him—not to mention what it would do to me!"

His hands shook, so he plunged them into his hair, fingers digging into his scalp. Mackenzie was silent.

"And what? What were *we* meant to sit around and do while you and Aspen were off killing Ignatius?" remarked Thex. "Sit around and praise her when it's done like the hero she's not? Or let you take all the glory?"

"No, Thex, you're meant to act as a team and move as a unit," Ryder replied, alarmed by his best friend's response. "All of us have important jobs."

"I agree with Thex. Why do you get all the glory while we do the safe jobs?" Levi added, arms crossed over his chest.

Ryder toned down his anger to a dangerous simmer, holding back from another eruption. "I don't trust you to carry this mission out. You aren't my brothers… or sisters." He watched their faces fall, darting his eyes away from the silent tears rolling down Vox's cheeks. "You're not my family. I'm not your damned captain. And Aspen was right to not want to belong here."

A deadening sorrow swept between them. Ryder felt all their eyes on him as he stalked away into the darkness of the forest, toward the phosphorescent eyes that awaited him.

Aspen blinked her eyes open in the dark. Her hazy vision cleared, and she spotted the silhouette of blue-and-green crystal chimes hanging above her. She knew those chimes.

She bolted upright, only to be soothed by Ignatius, who crouched beside the bed she had been lying on—*her* bed. A wave of panic flooded her. Her bedroom was exactly as she had left it. She sat on her single bed with its rustic ash-wood headboard, adorned with a white comforter and a navy checked blanket draped at the end. Rock band posters hung on the wall next to a timber vanity holding a pair of black satin ballet slippers and a black martial arts belt tied to the post. Everything was covered in a thick film of dust.

Still not believing she was back in her house, she tugged back her pillow, revealing the initials she had etched into her bedhead all those years ago.

Ignatius hushed her. "Easy now, pretty Wolf. I thought you would appreciate the sentiment of being back here after all these years."

"Why the hell would you bring me back here?" She made to stand up, but he held up a finger, warning her.

"How easily undone you are by your past," he crooned, rubbing along his jaw with long, pale fingers as he looked over her. "Come on. Let's take a look around."

His hand covered hers, sending a painful electric shock through her arm. She ripped it away. "No! I'm not leaving this room."

Ignatius came closer, feigned empathy bringing his sculpted lips into a pout, his dark curls touching his shoulders. Aspen buried her head in her hands, but he lifted her chin with the tip of his finger and stroked her face. She suddenly found herself with no energy to fend him off. His presence was somewhat soothing.

Ignatius exhaled deeply. "I don't like doing this to you. It brings me little joy—but it will all be over soon."

"What are you talking about?" Her voice was weak.

He whispered, low and enticing, "I know how to save you."

Her eyes met his, onyx and red. "I cannot be saved."

Ignatius smiled as he took her hand. This time she didn't flinch. He explained in simple words that spoke to the orphan inside—the younger version of herself, still in the fetal position, who would forever occupy this room. *Mum. Dad… Giosuè.* The old wound opened with so much force she felt her stomach would turn inside out.

Then he offered his pomegranate, like Hades to Persephone: "Take away the Anima, and it will be like none of this ever happened. I can take it all away. Isn't that what you want?"

"But if you take away my Anima, I'll die."

"Death isn't so bad," Ignatius whispered.

"I'm not… going to a good place." She stumbled over her words.

Ignatius took her face in his hands, forced her to look back at him. At skin so pale it looked carved from marble. He rubbed a defiant tear from her cheek. "Not if you come with me."

She caved in on herself like a dying star, limp in his grasp.

"There, there…" He sighed. "All you have to do is watch them die again."

Her brow furrowed. What did he mean?

She wasn't sure where the two possessed Eagle Anima had come from, but they stood on either side of her and gripped her arms. She struggled as they pulled her up and dragged her through the doorway to the top of the stairs.

There wasn't a patch of wall that wasn't soaked in blood. Dark arterial blood and grasping hand marks where they'd struggled, held onto the handrail, snapped off fingernails.

Her parents' strewn body parts were visible from the landing.

Aspen unleashed a scream so violent that it awakened every fiber of the house and every demon inside her soul.

The day of her family's death unfolded, and she relived it, over and over again.

Aspen slung over her desk, her hair veiling most of her sight, strands curling over the pages that she scratched the pencil over. She heard dress shoes click over the floorboards, but she didn't look up. She could no longer smell who it was, though she was too busy to care.

"What did you do to her?" Vangelis's voice. It always sounded like he was talking through clenched teeth.

"I'm slowly detaching the Anima using Enceladus," Ignatius replied in his melodically soft tone. "Once the process is done, she should just be a source of power without the White Wolf."

There was a pause before Vangelis spoke again. "She looks like she did… back then."

"Yes. Everything will return to how she looked before she activated. This is what she wants."

Aspen peeked through her locks, watching Vangelis's lips twitch into a satisfied smile. What deal had he made with Ignatius to have his life spared from the world ending?

When Ignatius was called out of the room, her head lolled down as Vangelis began walking toward her. He inhaled sharply. "Aspen?"

She drove the pencil harder into the paper.

"What are you drawing?"

Vangelis picked up one of the other drawings she had laid out, but she snatched it away. "Don't touch the sequence," she warned him.

He stared at her, dumbfounded, as she rearranged the chaotic papers on the desk and bent over to continue drawing. Her mind was an entirely new landscape.

"Aspen, what is he doing to you?" Vangelis picked up a strand of her brown hair, the red fading away at the bottom.

"I *have* to see them dead," she replied bluntly. "It's the only way to get rid of it."

"Get rid of what? The Anima?"

She stared at the drawings as if he weren't there at all. "I have to remember what he looks like," she said to herself.

Vangelis looked at the drawings, all of the same Wolf. "Who is that?"

She didn't answer.

Vangelis bent closer. "Is it Ryder Everett's Wolf?"

"Who?"

Vangelis stared at her with a horrified expression. Something inside her became confused. *Vangelis never cared about you. Why the sudden sympathy?*

His voice cut through her thoughts. "The captain of your team. Is that who you're trying to remember?"

Aspen turned to him for the first time. As if she hadn't heard anything he had said, she asked him, "Have you seen Midnight Wolf? He's looking for me."

She dragged the chair back and walked to her window, Vangelis shadowing her with a saddened look upon his face. "Aspen, Ignatius isn't going to spare me or my family.

We had a bargain, but he lied to me… Aspen, can you hear me?" He shifted behind her, his hands hovering over her shoulders. "You have to fight. You have to win. Please, *please* hear me. I'm sorry for all the pain I've caused you. I would never have done it if they hadn't kidnapped my family. All of this was to free them. My kids… I haven't seen them in years." He choked back tears. "I know that I don't deserve the Corps' help. But think of the billions of other people who do. All the children. My… my children." His voice faded.

"He said he'd find me," Aspen whispered.

Vangelis cast his eyes down to the floor and sighed. "By *him*, you mean Ryder, right? How long have you been waiting for him?"

"I don't know how I got this scar on my arm."

"Aspen? How long?"

She turned to face him. "Since I got here."

"With Ignatius…?"

She looked at him like he was crazy before she clarified, "To Earth."

Vangelis looked like he had been frozen. Aspen turned back to the window, watching the orange sun hide behind the forest.

"As soon as I got to Earth," she mumbled.

The two Eagles entered the room.

"You're going to do it again?" Vangelis exclaimed.

They didn't answer him. Aspen's body dragged as they pulled her away.

"NO, NO! I DON'T WANT TO SEE THEM AGAIN!"

They hauled her past Vangelis, who was covering his mouth, doubled over, choking on his tears as he saw the blood on the landing of the staircase, knowing that the rest of the house looked the same. What she was being made to endure.

"GIOSUÈ, RUN! RUN!" She screamed for him to hide, to escape. The warning she had not been around to give when her precious eight-year-old brother had been murdered by demons.

They took her to the landing and down the stairs. Everything was red. A dirty red, marred with the remnants of demonic attack. She screamed in a way that would frighten even the devil. One continuous, eternal cry as her soul, the White Wolf, was torn from her.

CHAPTER 36

Ryder sped through the abandoned headquarters in search of Ansel. He found Major Gunner standing outside his office, watching security footage on his tablet. Despite the chaos of locating all the marines in the Corps, Gunner asked him where the rest of the team was. Ryder was too disappointed to reply. They had wounded him and deceived him, and he wore his distrust on his face.

Gunner finally dropped his quest to squeeze Ryder for information and instead invited him inside. Ryder put his forehead against his arm as he leaned on the floor-to-ceiling glass wall that overlooked the second story of Lynx Division.

"I can't believe I'm asking, but some of your orders would be helpful about now."

Gunner scoffed, but managed a quick smile. "What do

you want me to say, Captain? There's no protocol for this…
Let's face it, there never was."

"Hell, you're being as cryptic as the old owl." Ryder
sighed deeply before he explained. "Aspen's gone—Ignatius has her. He's infiltrated our marines. He's destroyed
the Corps. He now has the power to wipe our planet
clean and the means of dimensional travel. The team can't
work together…"

The pain in Ryder's heart impaled him. He flicked his
focus back to Gunner, defeated.

"I never should have come here."

Gunner looked determined as he approached. "Hey.
This isn't you talking."

"Oh yeah? Tell me who it is, then." Ryder's breath fogged
up the glass until he couldn't see through it anymore.

Gunner placed his hands on Ryder's shoulders. Ryder
turned to face him. "Where's this all coming from?"

Ryder shook his head slowly and shrugged. "I don't
know."

Gunner scrunched the material of Ryder's uniform in
his fists, but his voice stayed gentle. "Get it together, Captain. You're the only one who can get us out of this."

Ryder sighed and threw his hands up in the air, breaking Gunner's hold on his shoulders. "I don't want to get out
of this. This isn't even my mess. It's not my responsibility."

He wasn't sure how he hadn't sensed Ansel standing
in the room, but the general glided forward, wearing
white robes, the lapels embroidered with silver thread. A
perplexed expression accentuated the crow's feet creases
around his eyes.

Ryder's every cell braced as he reached down into the

pit of his rage and boomed, "Where have you been? The Corps is in disarray! Aspen's been taken. Where the hell are the justices?"

Ansel's brows knitted tighter together. "They are spread out over Kore, tending to the wounded and making sure all the affected marines are safe."

Ryder glared questioningly at the onyx veins under Ansel's skin, traveling up his arms. A trace of scent, as fine as a piece of string, made the hair on his neck stand up. Demon blood.

"Who poisoned you?" Ryder demanded.

Ansel gritted his teeth as he placed a hand over his heart. "Sometimes, when we believe we are acting out of the best interest of the whole, we mistake martyrdom for caring leadership. But martyrdom is no ally, and does not make you a Virtue of any sort."

Ryder's rage dissipated as quickly as it arose. He covered his mouth with his fist. The general was dying. "Did Calais do this to you?" he spat.

Ansel nodded. "He has made deals that we are all paying for."

"He let the demons into the Corps." The truth swayed Ryder off-center. He held onto the window again.

"He has betrayed us all," Ansel panted weakly. Ryder watched the elder's fading aura. The only reason Aspen had survived an ailment like this as long as she had was because of her healing powers.

Gunner pulled a chair closer and Ansel collapsed into it. The major threw a worried glance at Ryder, his jaw taut. "He's not going to last much longer. What are we going to do about the possessed marines? Kill them? How can we kill off all of our people?"

Ansel scrunched up his face as veins like running ink shot out over his skin, slowly turning his russet complexion gray, subjecting him to a slow death. "This has happened before, many lifetimes ago… but the only Wolf we have appears to be uninspired by the fact that everyone will lose their lives."

Ryder gave him a hard stare. "This is not my responsibility. It was yours! You're the general! Now you're dying. The Corps—corrupted. There is nothing more I can do!"

"And YOU are Lykaion!" Ansel boomed. The golden centers of his eyes blazed. "These are *your* people."

"I don't know how to get you out of this," Ryder admitted, voice breaking as he evaded the old man's eyes. "I let Aspen be taken by the underworld. What kind of captain… What kind of Virtue does that?"

Ansel remained hardened, like he was turning to stone as he sat there. "You have fought battles like this before. You have won wars just like this one."

"All of them happened in different lives that I don't remember! The team won't work together. You were wrong, Ansel… We aren't the team that's going to get you through this."

Rage sent heat to his face and neck. Feeling a sudden sensation on his arm, he pulled back the sleeve of his uniform to reveal his golden markings. Further up his arm, where the tattoo ended, a new symbol was being inscribed into his skin before his eyes. Ryder watched it, awestruck.

Gunner looked over his arm. "What's happening?"

"The markings are changing—Aspen…?"

He felt the cloth of Ansel's white robe over his arm. A smile cracked over the general's forlorn expression. "Yes. Your pack reaches to you, Ryder. What are you going to do now?"

The new symbol was the same as Aspen's Magnetar, only now it was changing. Lines etched onto his arm, some taking the shape of ovals, looping over each other to create a new symbol: a beam of power that streamed through the axis of the Magnetar. The lines encompassed and ran through the Magnetar like they were embracing it.

"It's my powers fusing with Aspen's," Ryder murmured in amazement. "My powers can shift the direction of the Magnetar flare."

It dawned on him that he knew exactly what to do. Vox's findings flashed through his mind, parts that had seemed like they had no meaning now clicking into place, so that the secrets of Lykaion created a mural, pieced together by different lifetimes, and all crashing down on him now.

The power of Lykaion was one power source. They both bore the formidable power of a dead star. Their powers had split into two, taking a piece of their power source with them. It was volatile and dangerous unless they fused them together again.

They'd started coming back together when he and Aspen became one pack. But now that she was gone, he could feel the pain in his Anima, at the level of his soul. He knew she could feel it too. But getting there on a lone Wolf mission was going to be risky.

"You understand your path now?" Ansel snapped him out of his revelation.

Ryder looked back at the general and major resolutely. "If I can get to Aspen, I can redirect her Magnetar blast using my powers. All this time I was trying to get her to control the direction. But it's my power that completes the sequence—that can redirect it. If I succeed… the flare will miss Earth."

Worry lines appeared over Gunner's forehead. "How are you going to generate that much energy?"

Ryder forcibly removed the doubt creeping in on what was, once again, an impossible mission. "I've got to try."

He drew the spectral circle with his Phaedra and it illuminated before him. The truth was, he couldn't even sense her. He had been trying to follow a trace of where she could have gone, but it was faint and fading.

He readied himself to take a step, but the sound of his name halted him. It was Vox, along with the whole team, entering Gunner's office.

"We're coming with you," River said.

"We owe you an apology. I… owe you an apology," Mackenzie explained.

Thex strolled up from behind as the team surrounded Ryder. He clapped a hand over Ryder's shoulder. "And so do I."

Ryder was softened by Thex's honest apology; his shoulder loosened under his friend's hand. He looked from Vox's expectant stare to Mackenzie's pleading expression.

His tone was soft as he told her, "Save it for Aspen."

Levi beamed as he saluted. "Ready to deploy for Operation Magnetar, Captain."

The team followed, placing their fingers knife-edge

across their foreheads, so stiff they could have been statues. Ryder beamed like every fiber of his being was shining.

"Alright, Anima Special Operations task force—move out."

They held hands. Thex gave a whoop as the force of the rainbow whirlpool pulled them through to the other side.

When his boots hit the ground, the scent of eucalyptus opened up Ryder's airway. It was nearing nightfall; the sun cast an orange tinge to the pastel blue sky. The trees, a hundred and thirty feet tall, threatened to morph into the horrific shapes that Ryder remembered all too well.

He thought he'd feel different coming back here. He half expected to be breathing through a panic attack as he recalled a man he could barely recognize. He thought about the man he was today—strong and vital—meeting face to face with the one who had lived inside the hellgate all those months ago. Part of him smiled at how miraculous his life had become—but what he wasn't prepared for was how much more in control the man from the hellgate was. He only worried about one life… His own. All his plans worked out the way he'd envisioned them, because he followed his own orders.

Ryder stole a glance at his team around him, and fear ran like a cold clawed hand down the length of his spine.

River grasped the scruff of Levi's uniform to prevent him from falling as he leaned over the gaping dark tunnel in the earth. "Where are we?" Levi asked.

"Welcome to the Australian IO," Ryder announced. "This is where Aspen grew up."

Thex peered cautiously into the hellgate and glanced around at the trees. "The IO is her backyard?"

"Pretty much," Vox replied, her lips pulling into a tight line.

"What makes you think we'll find her here? She's never been back here since…"

River's voice trailed off. Ryder guessed the memory of Aspen activating wasn't a fond one for him.

"Unless Ignatius brought her here," Mackenzie suggested, snapping Ryder out of his thoughts.

"And why would he detour here on the way to outer space?" Thex questioned her, a hint of sarcasm in his tone.

Vox was engrossed in deep thought before she answered. "Because he's conditioning her."

"What?" River took a step closer to her.

Vox shook her head, her gaze refocused back to them. "There's no way she would carry out his plans willingly."

"But she could just heal whatever Ignatius does to her," Levi rebutted.

Vox was slow to answer. "Not if she's no longer an Anima."

Ryder's stomach sank. They all went silent for a moment.

"I read about it in the *Ars Daemonium*… I just didn't think it was relevant to his plan, so I didn't collect it in the data." Vox's expression was forlorn. "I was wrong."

There was another all-consuming silence before Ryder cleared his throat. "We have to move if we're going to find her."

He began trekking in the direction of Livinia's Orchard, leaving the rest of them to catch up to him.

River reached his side, and they walked together for a while before Ryder asked him, "What did you say to her to earn her trust when you found her after her family's murder?"

River swallowed, his eyes darting from the ground back to Ryder. He shrugged. "I recited the words to the 'Hymn of Kore', the one we all learned when we were kids. And this wave of calm came over her. She stopped pushing me away and took my hand, and I led her out of the cellar. I repeated the line 'The bear is your brother, child' a few more times to settle her." River read Ryder's worried frown. "She'll sense it's you through the Amaranthine bond."

Ryder glanced at him sidelong. "That's if it's even still intact."

River placed a hand on his shoulder. "She's not going to forget about you that easily."

CHAPTER 37

The team trekked silently behind Ryder in single file. He became aware of Mackenzie and Vox hovering over the tablet as they walked.

Curiosity got the better of him. "What are they doing?" he questioned River, who trudged behind him. River looked over his shoulder at the pair and shrugged.

Thex was clearly more in the know than River. "Mackenzie's pinpointing the exact location where Aspen needs to be for Ignatius's attack to work."

"How are we all going to get there, is what I want to know," Levi grumbled.

It was getting dark quickly. The trees were becoming sparser; they would be approaching the chestnut tree with the Lovetta family's engraved initials soon.

"I can get us there through a dimension portal," Ryder answered Levi without glancing back.

"Getting there isn't the problem…" Vox shook her pink curls, looking up from the tablet as she took long strides to reach Ryder's side. "It's how we're going to survive with no spacecraft or space equipment in the middle of… well… space."

"So we're just gonna be floating around without a grip, trying to stop Aspen's impending Magnetar blast?" Thex clarified, both index fingers pointing to the ground. "This… *this*… is the plan?"

Every marine looked at Ryder with expressions that told him they were unimpressed. Ryder shrugged. "It's not like I've worked out all the details."

Mackenzie's brow furrowed. "Wait… but your plan suggests that Aspen won't be on our side."

Vox straightened. "Yes, you're right. Ryder, please explain this."

When he stopped walking, the team stopped too, concern on their faces. He took in a breath. "This isn't an easy plan."

Levi scoffed. "Is it ever?"

"Just be honest. We can handle it," River assured him.

Ryder groaned and put his hands on his hips. He didn't know where to look; he decided on the ground. "When we travel through dimensions, we're going to end up in a different time. The further we travel into space, the further back in time we're going to go."

This sparked Vox into regurgitating facts. "That's why most of the stars we see in the night sky are appearing to us as they once were depending on their distance from Earth.

By the time their light is visible to us, we're seeing them the way they were years ago… even a millennia ago, or more."

Mackenzie squinted in displeasure and she asked Vox more than anybody else, "Does that mean we won't know each other?"

"No. We're traveling together, and the rule of dimension traveling is that whoever stays together is unaffected."

"So…" Levi pressed.

Ryder stated the obvious. "It means Aspen won't know who we are. Because she'll most likely already be held at the location."

His comrades' faces become even more grave.

"But if Ignatius is taking her back in time before she knew us," Mackenzie said, "she won't be Hellfire-Aspen, she'll be… Who knew her before her activation?"

Nobody raised their hand.

"We could be dealing with a much easier opponent," Thex suggested hopefully.

But hope diminished as they studied Ryder's solemn expression. "We are dealing with a much worse opponent. We can't rely on Aspen's loyalty to save our lives."

"So no Aspen Lovetta loyalty cards. How do we take her down?" Thex asked.

"*You* don't," Ryder answered.

Thex took a few casual steps to close the gap between them and crossed his arms over his chest. "You can't take this—*her*—on by yourself."

"Everybody has a job to do, and I'll do mine," Ryder said plainly.

Levi tried to intervene. "But Captain—"

Ryder cut him off with a hard stare. "You leave Sergeant

Lovetta to me. If anybody gets in my way, I'll kill you. Fate of the world depends on it. *Our* fate depends on it."

They nodded hesitantly.

"How's that for motivation?" Levi mused as the team followed Ryder the rest of the short distance to the timber gate that bordered the orchard.

They crept along the outskirts of the orange grove, where River mentioned smelling blood. They passed the chestnut tree and approached the farmhouse, careful not to disturb the porch sensor light. Ryder was startled by River almost falling into a hole in the ground. His arm flew out to stop River's fall, but it was Thex who pulled him back.

"Where's your night vision at, man?" Thex whacked him across the arm.

"I was searching the windows on the top floor to see if she's still in there," River whispered.

"What is that?" Mackenzie asked, pointing a shaking finger at the ground ahead.

Freshly spilled blood covered a set of old wooden doors that lay busted open, leading to an underground cellar. The metallic scent wafted through the air.

"This is where Giosuè Lovetta was murdered," Ryder answered solemnly.

"Aspen's brother," Levi confirmed.

Thex's lips grew taut. "Is that what we're going to see inside? The whole murder?"

Vox sighed in a way that sounded like the onset of tears. She tamed her quivering lips, her voice barely a whisper. "This is how he broke her."

Ryder urged them onward despite their sorrowful glances. They lined up on the side of the porch; Ryder was sending them hand signals about when to enter when Thex whispered, "Ry, I don't want to go in there."

Ryder cast him a glare. "Oh, you wanna sit this one out?"

"I don't want to see—"

"None of us wants to see this, but there's no choice. We've gotta stop Ignatius. Pull it together."

"She is the way she is because of this," Levi said from behind Thex. "The least we could do is understand."

With that, Ryder gave the signal. Levi scaled the weatherboards to Aspen's open bedroom window and climbed inside. Thex's antlers protruded and he waited behind the second orange tree from the porch steps.

"Wait, stop—" Vox sniffed the air. "Ryder, I smell fire."

"Me too. It's at the front of the house," Mackenzie confirmed.

A blaze akin to the wrath of hell exploded from inside. The back door was ripped off its hinges, the glass pane smashing over the porch steps as it flew into the first line of trees of the orange grove.

"It's spreading!" River yelled over the roaring flames.

"Levi's inside!" Mackenzie exclaimed.

At that moment, Levi leaped out of Aspen's bedroom window, landing silently on all fours a few paces away from Thex. Aspen, or somebody who resembled her, walked out of the blazing doorway. Her eyes bled onyx ink; her hair, once red as garnet, had turned dark brown. She marched down the stairs and through the corridor of orange trees as if she couldn't sense them at all. Vox called her name, about to go after her, but Mackenzie pulled Vox's arm back without taking her eyes off of the deadened soul that had departed the house.

"Why would you do that to your childhood home?" Vox called after her, distraught.

River came to her side. "That's just it, Vox—she wouldn't…"

Ryder left the team idling by the porch and caught up to Aspen in a few bounds. He tugged at her arm to stop her. She spun around, her face inches away from his as she shrieked, a berserk demon behind the eyes that once adored him. His mouth gaped; the air sucked from his lungs as she sent a pulse through him—so electrifying that each current burned him at his core. It reached so deep that he could feel himself being chemically changed. Molecules shriveling and dissolving in on themselves. The light of his soul being devoured by a demon driven by hunger.

Ryder screamed, experiencing pain for the first time in a long time. Real, mind-shattering pain. He writhed beneath her unending stare, the whites of her eyes now an endless night. She pulled away and continued marching, leaving him clutching his chest on the ground.

He was watching her disappear beyond the orchard when Thex ran to his side to help him up. "What *was* that?"

Ryder clutched the burning flesh of his upper arm where she had touched him, trembling as he got up. He evaded Thex's searching gaze. "I don't know."

"It's not her," Thex attempted to console him. But Ryder stared at the spot in the trees where he'd seen her disappear. He twitched and quivered as if the malignant hand were still touching him, burning him from the inside out.

"That looks bad." Vox clicked her tongue as she inspected the burn. The material of Ryder's military blouse had a hole the size of Aspen's hand. The wound emitted smoke that looked like the ashen clouds from a volcano.

Ryder looked down the length of his arm, his stomach knotting. It looked bad on the outside… but he didn't want to tell them that somehow he could feel the burn spreading inside him, slowly devouring him like a lighter held to a piece of paper.

"It'll be fine." Ryder looked to Levi standing on his other side, holding out a stack of paper.

"Got these from her bedroom," Levi explained. "They're covered in random symbols and numbers."

Ryder squinted as he took the wad of paper into his hands. The team crowded around him, peeking over his shoulders to see them.

"They aren't random numbers!" Mackenzie exclaimed, grabbing a page from Ryder's hand. She laughed loudly. With a cheer like she'd won the lottery, she held it up to show them. "These are coordinates!"

"Let me see that!" Vox snatched the page from her.

"These are all drawings of Animas." River admired the well-sketched Bear.

"She must have drawn them before she was activated," guessed Levi.

Ryder handed Mackenzie the rest of the pages, his broken voice revealing the disarray happening on the inside. "Can you work out where it's happening?"

Mackenzie nodded. "You gotta hand it to her. She comes through when you need her…"

Vox swiped up the holographic screen from the tablet and handed it to River to hold while they entered the coordinates. After Levi and Thex had tamed the fire, they returned to speak about landscape strategy.

"I don't know why you're looking at me like that. My powers only work with nature… That's attached to the Earth," Thex explained in his usual sarcastic tone.

"How do you know if you've never been to outer space?" Levi questioned casually, arms crossed.

"We're going to come out of that dimension portal and fly in opposite directions with nothing to hang onto—this is a landscape strategy nightmare!" Thex exclaimed.

Ryder sighed. "Look, if my strategy is sound—"

"Which it's not," Thex butted in.

Ryder ignored him. "—then your powers should be able to latch on to Earth elements and create some kind of terrain for us to work with."

Thex bent close to his face. "You are crazy!"

"Actually, he isn't," Vox interjected as she, Mackenzie, and River came back to debrief. "Aspen wrote about this in her encrypted files that Ryder found months ago. I kept the file open so I could continue reading. Aspen's projection of Thex's powers is that if he can manipulate the elements on Earth, he should most certainly be able to do that in outer space… and she never stipulated that his powers were only restricted to manipulation of Earth's nature."

Thex looked floored. He made a little sound from his open mouth.

"And I worked out where around Saturn they're located," Mackenzie announced with a proud smile, handing Ryder the rolled-up paper.

"Are we ready?" River asked.

Ryder nodded. "This is what we've trained for."

"And we wouldn't be half ready without you, Captain," Levi said with a firm nod of appreciation.

The team nodded their agreement. River clapped his hands together. Ryder couldn't bring himself to share their encouragement.

"I can't promise we'll live through this," he said, "but I can promise this is what we're meant to be doing."

"Saving a brother," Thex stated.

"Or a sister," Mackenzie added.

Ryder clenched his fists, doubt clinging to him like dead weight. "There's only one way we'll go out."

"And that's together." Vox touched the arm that wasn't burned.

Ryder drew a circle with his Phaedra. The dimension portal opened. There was nothing but the sound of anchoring breaths as they stared into the vortex. It was somehow different this time around: less like water and more like dust and granules of rock.

They took a step toward complete darkness.

CHAPTER 38

Ryder tumbled through space, his vision spinning from eternal night to pale yellow and back again on loop. He fought to keep his eyes open as panic set in. He heard Thex give a prolonged grunt from somewhere near him, right before he crashed into something that knocked him out temporarily.

He felt no pain as his surroundings swirled around him. He held his head until his vision steadied, and found the team strewn across what appeared to be a glass grid-like floor.

Thex lifted his fingertips slowly off the transparent surface. "Dude, I just made a floor!" he yelled at Ryder.

"Could you have made it any more slippery?" complained Levi, hanging on by the ends of his claws before planting his feet on the surface.

Vox and Mackenzie were gaping in awe at what they

saw ahead. Ryder joined them, unable to tear his eyes away. The transparent gridded floor met with a wide, bright ring system that shone in the reflection of the sun. Beyond that…

Saturn.

It was so inconceivably giant that it dominated the sky with swirls of gas in shades of yellow, brown, and red. Ryder could have become lost in the detail of the storms and weather patterns as the gas giant's energy consumed him with its immensity. His focus panned to a large shadow that was cast on part of the planet, and he turned around to see what was casting it.

What he saw startled him; he hadn't expected to see another large object, and so close. A silver-white moon levitated before them. Its surface looked like luminous, pristine ice marred by veins and wavy bands of dark turquoise that made it look like a giant marble.

"Enceladus," Vox breathed.

Another moon hovered not too far away from Enceladus, and many more gleamed like ghosts close by.

"We're beyond the frost line. How are we even alive right now?" River marveled.

"And with no gear," Mackenzie added.

"She was right," Vox stated. "Aspen knew the limits of our powers better than we did. We've completely adapted to this environment."

"And once again, Ry's crazy plan worked." Thex slapped him on the back.

Ryder's orders were blunt, killing the cheerful disposition of his team. "Don't speak too soon and don't forget what we're here to do. We're going to split into teams so that we'll have a better chance at finding Ignatius before the Magnetar blast. Levi, you're with me. Mackenzie, Vox, River, and Thex—you're in charge of finding the opening of the hell dimension and destroying anything that comes out of it. Understood?"

They saluted and the team divided.

Levi followed Ryder toward Saturn's rings. "I can't believe this." He pointed to the wide expanse of the rings.

"Too bad it's going to be a new hellgate in a few minutes," Ryder replied.

They walked on the steady floor Thex had created until they reached the edge that met Saturn's ring system. Shiny rocks whipped around them like cars on a racetrack, some as small as pebbles and others the size of small asteroids. Ryder squinted to the middle of the ring system, where structures were mountain-sized. He then looked out and faced Earth. A beautiful blue star glowing in the sky, with a fainter white star as its partner—the moon.

An overwhelming power swelled in Ryder's core. Something deep inside of him was desperate to save it, that little sapphire he called home. He thought of his family, all their families, and the animals. His Anima, the Midnight Wolf, brushed his coat against Ryder as he padded alongside the Lynx. He looked back at his marines, their auras glowing—they were ready.

"I think that's where we need to go." Levi pointed to the center ring system, where the mountain-sized rocks glided through the belt.

Ryder scrunched up his face in doubt. The gigantic rocks would obstruct the view of Earth. To hit Earth with the Magnetar flare, Ignatius would need a clearer view than where Levi was suggesting.

"Captain, that's the only way you're going to get to the part of Saturn that's facing Earth. You can't travel over those tiny rocks—the rings are affected by both Saturn's magnetosphere and the moons surrounding it," Levi explained.

Ryder dangled his foot into the ring, careful not to let a rock hit his foot. At the speed they were traveling, it would feel like he'd been shot with a bullet. Levi was right; despite their natural powers to generate gravity to adapt to space, it wasn't enough to be able to walk along the rings like they were doing on the gridded floor.

He did a head check in all directions. "I don't see Aspen or Ignatius."

"And now I don't see the others… Are you sure we're in the right place?" Levi questioned. Just as Ryder was about to answer him, he yelled, "Look out!"

Ryder spun around just in time to block the onslaught of an Eagle Anima.

It was one of the two possessed marines that Ignatius had kept from the destruction he'd caused at the Corps. Levi leaped high to drive one of them downward, melding his claws into him to pin him to the transparent floor. The other Eagle extended his wings and beat against Ryder with so much force that they tipped him off balance, his feet lifting off the floor.

He tried to grab onto something as he floated toward the rings. His hands slid over the slippery floor to the edge until he was dangling off the side. His clawed fingers were bone-white as he fought to hang on. A quick look downward caused his heart to race like he'd run from one side of Kore to the other—it was a view that, if he lived, would haunt him for a long time. The underside of Saturn was somehow more petrifying, like he was gazing at the ninety percent of an iceberg that you don't see under the water. And the shadow cast by Enceladus looked closer, like it was going to swallow him whole.

The possessed Eagle Anima raised his boot to stomp on Ryder's fingers. Ryder cried out, but it was too late. He felt the boot crunch down, flattening his fingers—no pain, just wild fear. He grabbed frantically at nothing as Saturn vacuumed him closer.

He must have spun for miles, the ring systems looking like nothing but lines as he flew past them. He lost all hope. If he fell into the enormous gas giant, he'd fall forever, or die from compression—

Ryder collided with something, devastatingly hard. He blacked out, and when he came to, his vision was blurred. A cold, rocky surface pressed against his back. Pain stemming from somewhere deep made him whimper. The burning feeling inside him was spreading. He squeezed underneath the burn wound on the same arm as the Amaranthine bond marking; it felt dead.

His vision cleared. He was lying on a large, shiny rock in the center of Saturn's middle ring system. It had stopped him from falling any further. The object he was traveling on was smaller than the ones beside him that covered some of the view from Saturn. He felt nauseous looking at the raging storms that vortexed aggressively from behind the rocks. He tried to focus instead on the senses that could guide him to Aspen. All he could smell was gases—hydrogen, helium, and a concoction of others.

He doubled back when Aspen jumped down, a rope attaching her to the floating space rock. Her aura was red, like she'd swallowed her own Magnetar flare and it radiated like a fireball around her. Before he could put his hands up to block her, she launched him upward with both hands.

He flew backward until he landed again on another hard surface. The red fireball flew toward him and he blocked her next attack, his powers shooting from his hands. She bowled him over. They toppled. He kicked upward, and Aspen flew off the rock and out of sight.

Ryder shot to his feet and searched the nearby rocks. He couldn't see her anywhere. He whizzed around, dizzying himself as he searched in a frenzy. Had he pushed her into Saturn?

Ryder started as Ignatius appeared, faster than he could snap his fingers. Aspen floated down in her red orb by his side.

"So you've come to save Earth from its inevitable demise," the Primordial said. "Why can't you see that things will be better when the surface has been cleansed? The Animas will be my unstoppable army, the humans' meaningless lives will end, and we can all start again—properly this time, the way it should have always been."

Ryder stood cautiously on the swaying rock so as to not lift off the surface and launch them all into the gas hurricane happening to their right. "It's not all without meaning. It happened the way it did because that was what was meant to be."

Ignatius rolled his eyes and scoffed. "Stop! You sound like Ansel. You cannot possibly understand what is beyond your life right now, Ryder Everett. Everybody dies in the end. It is never a *good* time to end things. It ends when a decision is made to give up the fight. It is time to give up yours."

Ignatius ran his fingers down a lock of Aspen's brunette

hair. She stared ahead with empty eyes, as if she didn't feel it at all.

A dark smirk crossed Ignatius's lips. "She makes a wonderful companion, but I suppose you already knew that. Just another thing I'm taking from you, Captain."

Ryder gawked at Aspen in disbelief. Anger fortified him in that moment, when what he really wanted to do was pass out from the deep pain still eating away at him. Was it the pain, he wondered, or the fact that Aspen was gone?

Ignatius leaned in to speak in her ear. "Make this quick. Fight to the death."

Aspen's black eyes bore no whites. Her soul was vacant; her smile was wicked.

She charged at high speed, rolling the gigantic floating rock off balance. It flipped, sending them catapulting through the rings. Ryder landed on another large rock—Aspen's fingers plunged straight through his skin and into his stomach.

He cried out, feeling all of it.

"I'm going to tear your insides out," she said in a voice that didn't belong to her. It wasn't a threat born of walls built too high, but a cruel promise from the underworld.

Ryder crushed her wrist in his hand. "You've told me worse."

She screamed. He threw her off. Aspen soared back toward him, fighting exactly how she had been ordered to.

"Since when does Aspen Lovetta take orders from anybody?" Ryder furrowed his brow in judgment, blocking her blast with his powers.

"That girl who lived with her family at the orchard? She's dead," Aspen snapped before kicking him back.

Ryder shot a stream of power low and she leaped out of the way. She created a shield with her powers to approach him and resumed close-quarters fighting.

"Death is only temporary," Ryder told her as he blocked her punches.

"Fight back!" she screamed.

"I will not kill the woman I'm bonded with."

Her harsh laugh sent a cold shiver down his spine. "Our bond is broken. That's why you can't feel me anymore."

She wrestled against him until she created enough space to high kick, causing a crimson blast of power as she struck him. Ryder grabbed the fabric of her sleeve. It tore, revealing the glimmering silver markings on her arm. He landed on his knees after the blast of power had dissipated. And as if she'd heard a sound only she could hear, Aspen ceased trying to kill him and flew, as if by jet stream, toward a platform where Ignatius was waiting.

Ignatius must have thought that the blast of power from the high kick had killed Ryder. That… or he no longer saw Ryder as a threat.

Ryder searched for his team. They were far away, but he could see them clearly with Enceladus glowing behind them. A vicious vortex brewed above them—the hellgate was open.

Two sets of wings meant that Ansel had arrived and joined the fight despite his fading state. Ryder watched him lunge as an electric-blue force struck another winged man.

Calais ordered two demons with a pointed finger at Ansel; the team watched on helplessly as they battled against Ignatius's demon legion. A battle Ryder couldn't be a part of.

He said a silent prayer that someone would protect

Ansel, and that, at the very least, they would all live. The world needed Anima. Now more than any other time in history.

Ryder brought his attention back to Aspen and Ignatius, standing on a platform facing Earth. A glittering crimson ball of energy projected from Aspen. He watched it grow to a size unimaginable as he launched himself off of the rock and rode the jet stream from the rings to the platform the way Aspen had done. The fiery red force of her Magnetar powers coned into a thin stream of power. Ryder realized it would take all of her power to push the Magnetar flare millions of miles to Earth, and that Aspen was never meant to make it out of this. Nobody was.

He landed on the platform. Over the Magnetar flare that sounded like a turbine engine, Ignatius shouted, "You're too late! The portal to my dimension is already open."

He pointed to the team, who were fighting near the large portal, demons pouring out, creating a huge tear in the fabric of the universe. Ryder turned back to Ignatius and felt the energy inside him and around him rising. But he faltered, groaning as he endured the deep, soul-level pain. He mustered the strength he had left; it felt like more than his body could handle.

The Magnetar flare was streaming into space. It looked like it had passed Jupiter's orbit and was gaining a steady pace toward Earth. He wasn't sure how long Earth had before it all vanished. Before it would become the underworld, and the human race, the Anima race, the animals and plants, its history, would all be forgotten. But he had to try, until his final breath.

He staggered to Aspen. Before Ignatius could attack him, he took off his Phaedra and drew a circle over Aspen's heart.

Beams of spectral light blinded them. Ignatius stumbled back; Aspen gasped as Ryder escaped through the portal.

This portal didn't feel like a vacuum. He was sucked into an opening that looked like glittering galaxy dust in the shape of a red rose. He walked through the light it emitted, the path he took becoming darker and darker, as if the light were being dimmed. The path led to a green bedroom door with the letter 'A' hanging from it—Aspen's bedroom.

He turned the round handle and entered cautiously; his senses heightened as he looked around. "Aspen?" he called.

There was no answer, but he heard a faint shuffling inside the cupboard. The doors were slatted like old shutters. He paused with his fingers curled around the handles, then threw open the doors.

He had to cover his ears against the penetrating scream.

Beneath the hanging clothes, Aspen threw her arms over her face, her knees to her chest. Her cries were broken, pleading… as if he were going to kill her.

Ryder bent down and tried to gently pry open her tense arms. "I'm not here to hurt you. Look at me," he coaxed. "Look at me."

Her terrified green eyes met his. She was wearing a red flannel jacket and ripped jeans, her face streaming with tears.

"There's a demon! It's in… It's in the house. I can't find my brother."

Every breath in and out was, to Ryder, an indescribable sound. The cries of someone who had just seen their whole family slaughtered. The sound stabbed him all over.

She finally managed to say, "You're one of *them*."

Ryder nodded. "Yes, I am, Miss."

She trembled. "My name is Aspen."

He couldn't help but smile, sadness mixed with warmth for her. "I know." She looked at him curiously. "How old are you, Aspen?"

She swallowed. "Sixteen… but my brother's only eight." Her eyes widened in fear. "I don't know where he is."

Ryder exhaled heavily. "Aspen…"

Before he could continue, lantern light illuminated behind them. Aspen's bedroom warped, like dreams do when they shift. Aspen stood up, mesmerized, like something was calling her. Ryder followed her through her dreamscape.

The scenery transformed into the eucalypt forest on the edge of the orchard. In the shadows, a gigantic wolf with midnight-blue fur emerged, and Aspen walked to the Anima's side. Midnight Wolf enveloped her in its deep indigo glow. She buried her head in his fur and said in a small voice, "I never made it out of here."

Ryder's shoulders dropped. This wasn't a dream she was reliving, but a scar. A scar that was only visible from the inside, one that had shaped who she became and how she chose to live after the grief of losing her family.

Ryder stepped closer. "No, Aspen. You did make it out. A boy named River came for you, and you became best friends."

Aspen spoke into Midnight's fur. "No. I *never* really left." Ryder understood what she meant. "I did terrible things that I can't take back. I became someone I hate."

"Listen to me. I know twenty-three-year-old Aspen Lovetta." Ryder watched Aspen's eyes open wide.

"You do? You know me?"

"I do. And you did find happiness."

She looked up at him as he rested his hands on her shoulders.

"You found a new family at the Anima Corps. You made a new home."

Her eyes narrowed, and for a moment he thought she didn't believe him. She shook her head, then tilted it to the side, peering into his eyes with innocent curiosity. Breathlessly, she whispered, "I recognize those eyes. You're Midnight Wolf."

A small smile crossed Ryder's face, confirming that it was true. He could feel himself slipping away from the dimension where the world was ending. He could feel himself dissolving into diamond dust in the ether.

He took her small hands in his. "Listen to me," he said, his voice hoarse and low. "Meeting you gave me strength and made me fearless in times when I felt anything but that." Ryder squeezed her hands. "I'm not going to make it through the battle that's happening through that portal… but your friends are fighting to save the world. They're going to die too. So you have to make a choice. You can choose to stay here, or you could come back to your family. They're all waiting for you. But only you can make the choice whether you want to be an Anima this time."

Aspen's shoulders slackened in hopelessness as she looked back at the wolf. Her tears reflected the moonlight as they ran down her cheeks. Her breath hitched and she took a step back, forcing Ryder to let go of her hands.

He turned and walked back through the portal, back to Saturn. The last thing he saw was Aspen's eyes of ash before he slid to his knees. The Magnetar that crept through his body, devouring his insides, had burned too much of him.

Ryder dropped sideways, his last breath taken at the feet of the woman he loved.

The White Wolf followed Midnight Wolf through the vortex. Aspen felt a swelling in her heart that kept growing until she could feel all of the limbs of her body again. She pushed out the demon inside with the light of her Anima that brightened the void of the universe like a star.

She looked down at Ryder, who lay at her feet. She swooped down and cradled his head in her arms. Tears ran down her cheeks as she conjured as much healing power as she could and flooded his body with the antidote for the Magnetar. The healing created an orb of light around them. She could see Ignatius in her periphery, on the outside of her shield. But darkness can never enter the light.

She asked the Virtues for more power, and they answered by illuminating the Amaranthine bond marking on her arm. She interlocked her fingers in Ryder's and linked the symbols.

His chest expanded, taking in a healing breath. His aura lit with golden fire; his ultramarine eyes opened.

She pulled him into an embrace. "You did it. You found me."

"Always," he promised, holding her tight.

They rose together and turned their palms to the open hellgate. Red and blue waves joined together, creating a deep shade of purple. The beams collided into the eye of the vortex and they watched it dissolve into Saturn's atmosphere. The light slowed and faded.

They stood holding each other, then turned to Ignatius, who stood with an incredulous expression upon his sharp features.

"NO!" he screamed at the two Wolves. Dark veins covered his face, neck, and body; he was no longer able to sustain his human form.

Aspen's voice was calm. "You cannot hold me prisoner in my pain. You were right about me, Ignatius—I am a destroyer at my core. I thrive in death, and I embrace my darkness."

Ignatius's hands were transforming into long, spindled claws. He gawked at them and gritted his teeth, using what was left of his energy to maintain his appearance. "You will never belong with them. They will cast you out and you'll be sorry. Just like they did to me tens of thousands of years ago. They took my home and banished my family," he sputtered, old blood running down the sides of his mouth.

A portal opened behind them. The team, along with General Winters and Major Gunner, stepped out.

Ryder took Aspen's hand in his. "Darkness cannot survive in the light," he said, and together they built a fortress of light around them.

"And when you embrace your darkness, it will transform," Aspen continued. "On the other side of it, waiting for you, is joy and unbreakable bonds. You only have to be willing to give up everything that's keeping you in the darkness." She pointed the power glowing in her open palm at Ignatius. "I have healed mine."

"And, as you can see," General Winters announced in a buoyant tone, "it is impossible to kill the Anima, because the Anima is eternal. It lives in you."

Ignatius buckled. Blackness began to enshroud him in a thick cloud.

"It's time to send you to your rightful place," Ryder said. As he lifted his palm, parallel to Aspen's, an iridescent light radiated from them, hitting Ignatius in the chest.

He dissolved into fragments that caught a current. They watched as it sailed out into the void of the universe.

The team gathered around the Wolves. Vox and River hugged Aspen in the tightest embrace, followed by Ryder, then Levi and Mackenzie. They formed a huddle, arms around each other.

Ryder broke away as the others rejoiced. He sensed Aspen following him to Justice Calais, who had crawled through the portal on all fours and now lay on the platform. He had been there to ensure that the hellgate opened successfully, and to end Ansel's life.

Calais held the piece of Enceladus to his chest. Ryder saw Ansel watching from his periphery as he glared at Calais, his jaw tight as a vice.

"I wanted to spare the Corps the fate of being destroyed." Calais's voice fractured. "I couldn't bear to see it taken over by the Primordials. The Wolf Anima's power of dimension travel became a prized commodity for anybody trying to destroy us. So I had to destroy all Wolf powers by wiping them out in the War on Wolves. But I see now that this was not the way to stop Ignatius's rise to power. Please don't cast me out. I have been loyal to the Corps for centuries."

Ryder slowly shook his head in disappointment. "As Virtue, I sentence you to a lifetime in the guardhouse outside of the Corps, where you can never poison our home again."

Justice Calais choked on the silent tears that ran into his gray hair.

"I hold you personally responsible for the deaths of thousands of Wolf Anima who perished in the War on Wolves. For the destruction of the Corps; for the wounded and fallen marines of Operation Magnetar. Consider this your dishonorable discharge from the Anima Corps."

Ryder stood up. His hand found Aspen's and he started to guide her away.

"I'll just be a minute," she told him.

Ryder nodded and glared down at Calais once more before walking back to the team.

"He is a merciful and gracious leader." Calais rose gingerly and stretched his wings. He shuddered as he exhaled. "He is the one capable of leading us out of war."

The corner of Aspen's mouth turned up at the truth of his words. "He truly is. I love his humility, the way he makes everybody feel safe in unimaginable danger, the way he makes room for us all to belong… We all have our special place in this team. See, the thing about Ryder is that he's a true hero… He will always make the right decisions. As for me…"

She scrunched the fabric of his uniform with one hand. The other clamped over Calais's mouth, her nails digging into his cheeks, sending a burst of fiery Magnetar power into his esophagus.

"I am not a hero—and I can't trust that you will never be let out in the face of another war."

Calais thrashed, gasping for breath. He was too weak to fight back. Her nails drew beads of blood as she compressed his face tighter.

"This is for slaughtering thousands of Wolf Anima, for Alessio, Livinia, and Giosuè Lovetta, and for assassinating Justice Bastian Fallow."

Calais's chest deflated. He dropped to the floor and froze stiff in the cold atmosphere of Saturn the moment his Anima left his body. His eyes were still open.

Aspen rose and wiped her hands together indifferently. She turned to see Ansel blocking her way. Their eyes met. She threw him a mocking smile before she strode past him without a word and headed to the team, who were joining hands to enter the portal.

Aspen locked her fingers with Ryder's and stepped through.

CHAPTER 39

Five days after their return from Operation Magnetar, Aspen stood at attention in full Corps dress uniform before a stage that had been assembled outside of base for the annual award ceremony. The training field now had a thick blanket of snow that glistened in the soft sunlight that they would soon farewell for months as Kore entered its season of the great white silence.

Hundreds of marines stood in lines, row after row, watching General Winters deliver his speech about Operation Magnetar. Aspen fidgeted with the black bracelet on her wrist that read:

Airman Declan McAndor

Brother and Comrade

'Death is not a foe, but an inevitable adventure.'

A small service had been held for Declan two days after

the mission ended and the justices declared peacetime. It was a good day. All the marines possessed by Ignatius's legion had been healed. Every team member of Special Operations had been awarded a service medal, including Declan, whose medal Vox kept.

Aspen's uniform was not the most decorated out of her peers. She felt awkward marching up onto the stage with everybody else as Justice Borealis, River's father, pinned her new medal to her uniform. He smiled at her and shook her hand. Something glowed inside her. It wasn't power this time; it was pride.

Ansel told them to stay on the stage, as he had some other awards to announce. Aspen smiled at Ryder, who stood next to her. His cheeks flushed as Ansel announced to the Corps that this particular marine had shown courage in the face of unimaginable peril, leading the Special Forces to victory and resulting in the world's survival.

"We are proud to award Captain Ryder Everett with the Star of Courage and the Cross of Valor." Ansel called for him to step forward, and the Corps gave a thunderous applause. Major Gunner pinned both awards to the breast of Ryder's uniform, and all the justices, including Ansel, shook his hand as the applause started again.

Vox and Mackenzie received the Companion of the Order of Kore medal for their outstanding data and analytic support at the highest degree for humanity at large. Together with River, Levi, and Thex, they also received medals of bravery.

Ansel leaned toward the microphone. "In conclusion of our ceremony today, there is one last medal that goes to a marine who has shown outstanding combat skills and excellence in their profession. This award is the first one of its kind."

Ansel turned to Aspen. She looked at Ryder, who confirmed with a glance toward the general that he was in fact calling *her*. Aspen blinked rapidly.

"We are pleased to award Sergeant Aspen Lovetta with the Legion of Bastian Fallow medal."

Aspen stepped forward, and Michael pinned a purple ribbon with a gold wolf's head to her uniform. The applause was too much to bear. She stood back in line with the team, their hands touching her shoulders and back affectionately, before they were dismissed from the stage.

The team celebrated that evening in the cabin Aspen shared with Ryder. River was arguing with voice control to turn the music volume up. NEON's mechanical voice replied that it exceeded comfortable Anima hearing level. Vox was snickering, sitting on the staircase landing with Thex as they manually computed NEON's replies.

Aspen rose, dusting her hands off after starting the fire in the hearth. Thex joined her in watching the others while enjoying the warmth on their backs.

"I owe you an apology," he began.

"For what?" Aspen asked.

He gave her a sideways glance. "You proved me wrong, Lovetta… You saved us all. Of course, you *were* about to kill us all…"

Aspen laughed through her nose. "I can't take the credit. It was all Ryder."

"It was both of you," Thex said adamantly.

She nudged him. "Don't say it too loud. You'll ruin my badass reputation."

He laughed and took a few steps before he turned back. "And Lovetta…"

For the first time, her eyes fully met his.

"We're lucky to have you, marine." He gave her his prankster's grin. She glanced down at her boots before she looked back up, unable to help smiling back.

When it got rowdy inside, with Thex and River coming to blows after Thex worked out who was controlling the NEON's replies, Aspen joined Levi outside. They had enjoyed sitting in silence together a couple of times since they'd arrived back in Kore; it was *their* thing. She loved never having to fill the quiet, and it was never awkward. They listened to the muffled voices coming from inside and enjoyed the view of the snow-covered forest all around them. Their breath formed puffs of steam in the cold.

Levi finally spoke. "You never showed me your Krav Maga."

Aspen chuckled, hugging her arms tighter around her middle. "I showed you a lot more than Krav Maga."

"Oh, it's like that, is it?" Levi grinned.

River opened the door and called them back inside; Mackenzie's attempt at a Black Forest cake was ready. They walked back into the warmth of the cabin.

Aspen leaned against Ryder, and he kissed her on the forehead and smiled. Aspen caressed his jaw. "I wanted to thank you."

"For what?" he murmured.

"This place." She motioned to the cabin. "It's the most at home I've ever been, and that's… It's…"

Ryder understood what she was trying to say without her needing to explain it. His lips pressed against hers, soft and slow. She wanted the others to leave so that she could have him to herself. Her arms wrapped around his neck, pulling him deeper into the kiss. A soft moan escaped his lips that only she could hear.

"Okay, you two!" Vox teased.

"Yeah, can't wait until we're all gone? Geez," Levi joked, his arms over Vox's shoulders.

"Guys…" River bent down and picked something up from the floor near the entrance to the hallway that led to Aspen's room. He raised it between his fingertips.

A long, gleaming, night-black feather.

Levi inspected it. "Is that Declan's?"

Vox approached slowly, and River placed the feather gently in her hand. She turned and looked at the team, confusion set in her brow. "This is too dark to have been Declan's."

Aspen let go of Ryder and went to her.

"Then whose is it?" Mackenzie asked.

Ryder frowned, the lights making strands of his hair burn gold. "It's impossible. Nobody can get in here—the cabin's locked with our powers. It has to be Declan's, from a time he stopped by…"

Aspen's fingers squeezed the tip of the giant feather as she took it from Vox. She ran it under her nose and inhaled.

She didn't get half of the way along before all-consuming fear washed over her. The feather dropped from her fingertips. She let out a gasp.

Ryder's warm hands anchored her, holding her arms. "What is it?" he asked, reading her terrified eyes.

Aspen's breath quivered between her parted lips.

"Hurricane."

AUTHORS NOTE

Never would I have believed that growing up next to an army barracks and falling asleep as a young girl listening to soldiers training and shooting at night would inspire me to write this story, or that the last wolf pack murdered in Yellowstone would fuel this author's despair into these characters. This story will always, first and foremost, be symbolic of my compassion and heartfelt love toward animals, the environment, and humanity.

Despite extensive research from various military companies around the world and discussions with friends in the Australian Defence Force, Special Operation Task Forces and their movements are considered highly classified information. Information that not even a curious and eager writer can obtain. With that said, The Anima Corps does not try to replicate any one military company; instead, it is its own creation. It was a lot of fun to write, and I hope these characters and the story impact you, dear reader, in some magical way.

ACKNOWLEDGMENTS

I would love to extend my deepest gratitude to everyone involved in creating this book, whether they were directly involved in the story or supported me throughout the process.

To my Instagram author community, where would I be without you?! We have good and not-so-good days and are always there for each other on this path. You've been my comrades through it all!

To Danielle, Elisa, Ella, Bonnie, Kristen, Carla, Ryan, Kevin, and Tiffany, who read all or parts of the manuscript, gave feedback, and helped with research beyond the infor-mation I could source myself - thank you for your kind words, honesty, encouragement and excitement about the story. You will always be the first people I welcomed to Kore.

To Jennifer, my soul sister. I am so grateful to have a friendship that transcends time and distance. You have gone above and beyond to help and support me and make this book a reality. I couldn't have done it without you. You are a bright, sparkling star; your voice messages always light up my day.

To Nicole, who helped me realize this story had to be written and helped me build belief in myself to share it with others. This book wouldn't be here without you!

Niki, thank you for helping this story reach as many people as possible with your wicked skills. Without your wisdom, constant encouragement, and support, I don't know where I would be. Love you!

To my family and friends who always asked me how my book was going and endured listening to me talk endlessly about it—it's finally here! Your continued support means everything to me. You all have a special place in my heart.

To my parents, thank you for your ongoing support of my dreams, nurturing my love of reading, and teaching me that I'm capable of anything I put my mind to. You gifted me all my favorite stories, which helped shape the writer I am today. I'm so fortunate to have been given the time and encouragement to immerse myself in all things story-related, from theatre productions to acting classes. I am forever grateful for the both of you. I love you!

To my sister, Danielle, thank you for your unending love and companionship. You light up my life! I appreciate all your encouragement and intuitive hunches about this story. You are forever urging me forward to pursue my dreams.

To my mother and father-in-law, you have always treated me like your own daughter, showering me with love and support and cheering me on during this journey. I love you!

My brilliant editor, Claire, thank you for making this novel everything it is, for challenging me, and for being as excited about all the elements of this story as I am. I always dreamed I'd work on this project with someone who really gets it, and I'm so glad that person was you!

To Rena Violet from Covers By Violet, I'm so grateful to have worked with such a talented designer. Your art completely spellbinds me! Thanks to you, I will never be able to stop staring at this book's beautiful cover!

To my blurb writer, Belinda, I appreciate how you understood the story and boiled down the elements to make a potent, powerful blurb. You did such a beautiful job.

My proofreader, K. Reeves, Fair Crack Of The Whip Editing, you made this book shine! Thank you to the moon and back for your keen eyes and attention to detail.

To the crew at Author Services Australia, I have so much appreciation for your fantastic formatting service. It's been a pleasure working with your team.

Thank you to my cheeky Shiba Inu, Logan, and sweetheart Westie, Skyler, who cuddled me and kept me company during writing sessions for the last eight years while I worked on this project. Your warmth and companionship are what keep me returning to my writing.

My two children, Aston and Scarlett, thank you to the moon and back! If it weren't for your spirit and ability to transform my life into something more beautiful than I could ever imagine for myself, I wouldn't be where I am now. Thank you for filling my days with joy and love.

And finally, but above all, my husband, George. I could write another book just thanking you for all the profound ways that you showed up for me and our family while this story was being written. Firstly, for believing in me. There were a few times I wanted to abandon this work, and your gentle yet no-nonsense way of bringing me back kept me hanging on. Thank you for helping me choreograph combat scenes with your extensive knowledge of martial arts, for looking after the house and the kids while I took time away to write, and so much more. I love you for eternity.

ABOUT THE AUTHOR

N. P. Conti is a fiction author born in Melbourne, Australia. Her debut novel, The Anima Corps, interweaves her passions for fantasy, science fiction, action, adventure, and romance. When she isn't reading or writing about fantasy worlds, she enjoys snowboarding, cooking, and traveling with her family.

For more information about N.P. Conti
stay connected on socials:

Instagram: @n.p.conti
TikTok: @n.p.conti
X: @authornpconti
Website: www.npconti.com